A CRASH OF
SEA & STORM

TAYLOR VANDER LEEST

A CRASH OF SEA AND STORM

First published in the United States in December 2021 by Taylor Vander Leest.

Cover design by Jen Latcham

For Mom and Dad,

Dylan and Mason

CHAPTER ONE

KATLA

The soft skin of my palm gave sharply under the leather hilt, calluses surely forming in the one single motion.

Iron shifted colors in the waning sunlight, adopting trails of red as it tore through hardened scales. Although the creature in peril released a cry upon contact, it merely retreated further when the blade was torn back, now acting on the defensive. My swing had not been strong enough for a killing blow, or even an injury great enough to slow the beast down.

Cursing, I retreated with a now stained sword. The area I had struck was a large joint where the right wing connected to the rest of its body. At least now, I was assured it would not escape me by flight.

Unfortunately, it was by no means rendered helpless by this loss. There was plenty more in my opponent's arsenal, a fact it seemed all too eager to display. A guttural sound emitted low in its throat, a rumbling, my only warning.

I leapt to the right, dodging a stream of flames that had been unleashed from the demon's maw.

Tucking my sword flat against my side, I rolled upon impact with the earth, springing up into a crouch as soon as I could throw myself from the dirt.

The winged basilisk was of a stouter species, but frighteningly light on its large feet. Four legs of deep blue-gray supported the blasted monster's advances. Pale horns of something dirtier than white created a pattern from its back down to its ever-moving tail, and protruded from its skull.

I observed the great muscles pulsing beneath the scales which covered all but the underbelly. Wisps of smoke gathered around the wide nostrils. The ravenous offspring of Loki carried itself as something almost feline, but decorated its body with the skin of a crocodile or slinking lizard.

I was beginning to wish I had chosen a smaller dragon, or at least waited on this one until I held a weapon more suited to long range. Both my spear and bow sat at home, resting on the table where I had left them, completely useless to me now. I hadn't believed I would need them, not intending to take on a dragon of this size in my first official Hunt.

Not to mention, it was likely due only to my use of the sword, the way it flew like an extension of my bones, that I was still alive.

Whatever my prior plans, when I had stumbled upon this fiend in the middle of my attempts to track another, the chance to take down a dragon that was surely much larger than any my opponents had yet found was simply too good to pass up.

A game-winning prize for the girl who came to win.

Standing across from it now, I had to admit I was growing tired. This was proving more challenging than I had first anticipated, but I was surviving all the same.

Blood spilled at a growing rate across the leathery wings, tainting the deep blue membrane with strange patterns of crimson mirrored on the metal of my sword. The large crested head spun to glare in my direction, pupils narrowed to thin slits, making it look all the more hellish as it released its growl of frustration.

Tossing its head like a wild stallion, it stepped closer to me, claws the length of my arm digging into the earth. It twisted as it pulled more of its reptilian body into an approach. Quickly growing angered by my attempts, it was clearly less than enthused by the damage to one of its massive wings.

With ungodly speed the creature struck, closing its jaws around the air where I had just stood, having dived out of the way less gracefully than I would care to admit.

I noticed two things in the creature's move.

The first, and rather difficult to miss, were the teeth which adorned the cobalt dragon's mouth. If they were venomous, I wasn't sure, but they were sharper than the blade I carried.

The second was the imminent conclusion that I needed to end the fight. Despite my small victories, I wasn't much interested in a game of cat and mouse, especially when the roles could easily be reversed.

I began to work towards a new strategy; attacking the opening the creature had revealed in its lunge. The long serpentine neck was still extended, the teeth having violently slammed together.

I took a careful step back, placing myself tantalizingly out of reach. Large eyes narrowed as they took in my new position.

Just as I had hoped, the dragon attempted to pounce in order to catch the prey which had moved just far enough that its neck could not meet it. The devil snarled in what must have been some semblance of aggravation.

Powerful legs bent and pushed, propelling the beast off the ground and out of its crouch, the target obvious.

8

The monster had left the forest floor, jagged claws extended and teeth gleaming in a fiery mouth, outlined by outstretched wings much larger than me.

I was already gone.

I had begun running the moment the dragon tensed its legs in preparation, sprinting in the direction of the scaled beast, not away. Finally, as gravity kicked in and the brute began to descend, promising a gruesome death in the event of my failure, I flew to my knees.

The momentum of my short run allowed me to glide across the damp grass, soaking through the leather fabric. I slid under the lethal incisors, the jaw colliding hard with the ground and likely knocking a few of them loose. I hoped they weren't too damaged.

Too quickly for the demon to draw a claw across my breast, my hand brought up the blade already decorated with blood and buried it in the underside of an exposed neck.

It roared in anguish, but the otherwise powerful sound came out mangled, the helspawn choking on the sword in its throat.

I stayed there, back pressed uncomfortably against my heels as I laid parallel to the serpent's body. My arm remained taunt, sword clenched tightly in my hands. The vast chest that sat in front of me heaved with escaping breaths, and I kept my eyes trained on the pulsing mass of scales.

As another groan fought its way from the belly of the monster, I feared for a moment that I'd failed.

Then, the sound of labored breathing ceased, and the heaving slowed. The animal released its last breath alongside a moan, sounding far more pitiful than when it roared its challenge moments before. The body above shifted, leaning, and the only thing running through my head was how embarrassing this situation would be. To prove the victor over a beast such as this, only to be crushed by its carcass.

With that encouraging thought, I rushed to bring up the hand that had braced my body against the ground and grab the hilt of my blade. With both arms I yanked, trying to free it from the beast's skin.

I grunted with the effort; the retrieval much more difficult than having put it there in the first place.

Finally, the weapon came free in a shower of blood as the body above me swayed dangerously. I scrambled back on my hands, hauling myself out from under the dragon.

To my credit, when the swaying of the beast turned into a full tilt, and the once mighty creature collapsed to the ground, I did not cry out. I simply stared, wide eyes boring into those that were glazed and unseeing, pupils wider in death.

The blood of the demon was something noxious, thicker and darker than the crimson of humans. Where it spilled upon the grass the blades shriveled, curled over themselves and bent to the mercy of the earth. The green patches turned to something dead and dry as the blood seeped further into the dirt.

I was careful not to touch the toxic gore. I'd heard tales that the blood of the creatures was a poison.

For a moment more I looked on in shock, before feeling rushed back strongly, carrying a wave of elation. A hysterical sort of laugh forced its way from my mouth.

"Yes! Odin above, yes!"

I dropped my sword and jumped into the air; fists raised in victory. A smile had broken across my face, only brightened when I focused back on the dragon I had slew.

Gods, it was massive!

It lay dead by no hand but my own. Aside from the dull fire emerging from the scrapes upon my knees and a few cuts, I survived fully intact. This beast must have been larger than any my competitors had yet found.

My heart stopped short in its erratic pounding, hands dropping to my sides in search of the horn tied securely to my belt. My last thought served as a jarring reminder.

This was still a game, and the gods only knew how far along the other players were. I had to be the first to blare my victory.

My lips closed around the horn's carved wood, scratched and worn with age. A bellow filled the air as I raised it to the sky, and pushed through it the force of my breath.

When I finished, there was only the sounds of the forest, the wildlife scared away by the roars of a dragon. It wasn't a struggle to make out the falling footsteps and familiar whooping as soon as they began. I lowered the horn, attaching it to the leather slung around my waist. Hastily, I reattached my sword to the sheath on my hip.

Stepping closer to the dead dragon, I shook my head.

The first person to make it to my small clearing was another member of the Hunt, tripping over roots and dips of the earth in their haste. Calin stopped before me, his halberd clumsily swung over his back, brown hair plastered to his dark forehead with sweat. The long staff which ended in an axe head jostled and swung with his movements.

I noticed dirt and small twigs caught in his hair. My own locks weren't much better, dark curling strands loose and falling into my eyes. I tucked them back into the leather band which held most of it back. There were several rips in his brown tunic, spots of the fabric darker, wet. Drops of whatever had befallen him were splashed across his front. Muck stained his pants.

His form was tall but not lanky, having come into his growth spurt a bit sooner than the rest. He wasn't quite bulky enough for the fact to show plain in his figure, but he could handle himself rather well in friendly combat.

Not that I made a habit of allowing him victories.

His copper skin was littered with small abrasions, one such small graze located just beside the pale scar about two inches long on his right wrist. Had he found a dragon after all?

"Katla! The horn, was it yours? Damn, I was so close!" Calin lamented. "Did you get one? Of course you did, where is it-"

He cut off as his attention fell on the form behind me, mouth agape. I laughed openly at his expression, still elated by my kill.

We had only a single still moment alone before others filled the space all at once, those from the villagers, and other competitors.

Immediately I was surrounded, Calin lost somewhere in the flurry of bodies.

There was cheering, praising, and plenty of ogling the dragon that lay dead a few feet away. My people clapped me on the back with too much force, and yelled louder than my ears found comfortable. The world was blocked out by a thick curtain of congratulatory smiles and bright eyes, of weapons and armor forced into a small space.

I allowed myself to be swept up in the excitement, to be led with the crowd back towards the kingdom.

A group moved towards the fallen beast, intent on bringing it back to our village where its once proud weapons would be made into a possession for the one who slew it. They worked in a hurry, likely hoping to deliver the brute to the blacksmiths of Iona in time to enjoy the coming celebration.

Our throng found its way out of the woods. The noises of festivity plowed on without fail as they did every year, and would likely do long into the night. This time, it was as a result of my own conquest, only a hopeful dream when I had gone to sleep the evening before.

Pale blonde hair flashed in my vision, and soon I found myself with an armful of Eliana. Her bow rested snugly across her back, but her quiver of arrows rattled dangerously over her shoulder.

Her height presented just an inch over mine, and as such, her pale forehead knocked against my own as she plowed into me.

14

She screamed in my ear, pulling back to shake my shoulders.

"No way in Helheim did you win! Where is it, is it big? What kind was it? Fire or acid? Or venom, one of those vermin without wings? You have to let me hold the dagger when you receive it! Oh Leo, I want to see his face! I want to be there when he discovers that you won! He owes me twenty strips of silver." Her voice turned giddy, and I laughed. "Damn you, Kat! I was just about to pounce on one behind the hills!"

We could barely hear each other. Still, that didn't stop her from shouting to explain in full the dragon she had been tracking, how she knew it had been black, based on the scales she'd collected.

She held a few of the gem-like charcoal shards for my view, which I appraised as she continued. Eliana hadn't been able to close in before my horn had interrupted, but she assured me she was close.

I nodded along with her story, the parts I could make out.

I was suddenly grateful I had hurried along and killed the one I'd found when I did. Not that I wouldn't have wanted Eliana to slay one of her own, but it was still a competition. If she claimed that she had been close to catching one, then I had no doubt she had been. If I was any slower, her horn may have ended the game first.

It wasn't long before we reached Estran, the first village.

A CRASH OF SEA AND STORM

We passed the houses resting on the outskirts and left the trees behind. They were wide and close together, made with large beams of wood and stone. A flock of chickens reacted wildly to the approaching mass. A boy and girl, siblings, watched from a high window, their gasps of excitement unheard. Many saw the coming crowd, and doors opened to celebrate the Hunt's end.

It was wild, familiar in its boisterous nature, home.

Our feet met streets of packed dirt and stones. We made it through the first line of extinguished torches and to Iona, my village. I caught a glimpse of the blacksmith's stall, smoke already pouring from the thick stone chimney.

Outside the shop lingered the warriors who had carried my kill from the forest, the dead beast likely around the back. I bit my lip to keep from grinning too widely at the thought of the blade I would be receiving.

We turned the corner, and hurried through town.

Eliana took advantage of the chaotic party of people to snag a pastry from Mr. Damon's half-collapsed market counter as we passed. I scowled at her until she gave me half. Calin maneuvered his way through to us, and stole the other piece out of Eliana's hand.

She smacked at him and I smirked, until she took mine back, and bit into it with triumph.

Finally, the square came into view, the very center of our kingdom. In the middle of the square sat a large fountain, the edges of which were full of people awaiting our arrival. Those who weren't lucky enough to grab a seat along the stone milled about in large clumps. Those who arrived too late filed out into the streets, unable to fit in the square.

In front of us, against the edge of the square, a thin wooden table sat, running the length of several houses. At its middle was the greatest chair. Unlike the other eight seated at the table, all of which were more or less identical, its back was taller. A large piece of oak was carved out of the top to point towards the sky, the wood on either side curving to touch the tip. Six of them were occupied by the King's Council.

Normally, there were only eight, the seventh placed to the right of the king where the heir dined. Tonight, a ninth had been added, a place of honor for the Victor of the Hunt at the high table.

In the ostentatious spot sat King Ivon Evalade, ruler of Lamid. He wasn't too large of a man; it was his face and his actions which told of a quiet strength. He sported a thick black beard, which lay braided down to his front.

A crown was absent from his head, hardly ever worn outside of political gatherings, usually with neighboring kingdoms. He didn't need it, anyway. King Ivon was very well respected in the kingdom. His features were kind, and

17

tonight he sported a rare smile. I was told he was once a very joyous man, before I was born.

His joy had apparently been infectious, prior to the murder of his wife Queen Atarax and their infant child by the Sigurd Clan.

The other two members of the primary royal family were lost during an attack led by the clan chief, Olav Sture. The tragedy had taken its last life under two decades ago, a night still discussed in the quiet after a few too many.

Not to say the king was a brooding sulker now, but he was gentler than most, I supposed. Reserved.

Since he had only ever borne one child, and refused to take another wife, the village was saddled with Leo. Leo Evalade was an interesting heir, to put it in polite understanding. Son of the king's brother, he was unfortunately in line for the throne, something his father was all too proud of. He still had not yet been crowned Prince of Lamid, with the crown and the coronation.

It was both my opinion, as well as many others, that the King was putting it off for as long as he could.

It was fair to say that the kingdom was worried about Leo in any position of authority, especially King of the Isle. Most promised they'd sail off to Medea the day he was crowned. The boy was more obsessed with his title as heir than truly embodying the duties of it.

I hadn't thought the villagers could wrangle a volume any louder, but I had incredibly misjudged their capabilities.

As we stepped foot into the square, and those who had stayed behind realized our entrance, the real racket began. Over half of the gathered crowd already held tankards of mead in their hands, but I paid no mind to it. After all, we took any excuse to celebrate, and the Hunt certainly was one. Eliana stuck by my side, plainly in love with the shouting and passing of ale.

A loud drum echoed through the space, and all shouting ceased immediately.

Everyone present turned towards King Ivon, who had risen from his chair. He thanked everyone for their attention, and then began his speech, the same as last year, and the year before.

Calin listened intently. I at least made an effort to do the same, but then Eliana revealed she had swiped another pastry, and my focus was promptly diverted.

We'd heard it all before.

His speech mostly included a great lot about honor and glory, and a few minutes were devoted to legacy. The vile subject of dragons lingered longer. They were all very kingly words, but nothing new.

Finally his voice began to rise in volume, and we straightened, recognizing the end.

"And this year, I am proud to announce our Victor is Katla Vistel, her beast one for the sagas! Let us celebrate!" He finished his address with a rousing yell, and the crowd yelled with him.

Once again, I found myself smothered in congratulations, all while being pushed eagerly towards the high table.

I was led to an empty seat by the king, and felt immediately nervous as I sat at his left. More tables were placed out, and food began to pile upon them.

There was roasting meat from the butchers and bread from my mother's bakery, vegetables from Ms. Rita's farm and steaming fish caught by Mr. Maurin's crew. The square smelled suddenly of good food and strong mead. When I rose to grab some, I found a plate set before me, already filled, and a mug beside it.

Musicians struck up their instruments by the fountain, drowning out the falling water.

A great deal of those within earshot began to dance merrily to the music, while others helped themselves to what was definitely not their first cup.

I dug eagerly into the food, cringing slightly at the saltiness of the meat. It must have been from Owen's new shop.

He needed business, and was cheaper, but he was clearly still learning.

Glancing up, I realized that King Ivon had turned to regard me.

It was hard to feel anxious around the man once you caught his gaze. His expression was too soft, and the skin around his emerald eyes crinkled with laugh lines when he smiled, though I suspected they were formed long ago.

I had grown up admiring the king, as I was sure others my age did at some point, although I was sure my idolization was born for different reasons. While others wished to be like him due to his power, his status, or his leadership, I respected his resolve.

I knew it was an odd thing for a child to notice in an adult, but I had. Three years prior, my father had been lost to dragons on a Hunt. He left the house on a crisp morning that had been just barely pushing its way through the night, with his sword strapped to his back and a crunching of dusted snow.

They didn't allow me to see the pieces they brought back for my mother. My elder sister had snuck off and found them anyway.

Even now, I know she regrets it.

The king had lost his family too. Yet, he still was able to lead an entire kingdom. To be our king, to command our armada and our men. To fight. Still able to be strong.

He was always particularly gracious to the children. This wasn't to say he wasn't to our elders, but he had always been rather good to me and the others.

So, I had harbored a sense of admiration for him, from thirteen on. His wife and child were taken from him, yet he upheld the responsibility of his island and title, a pillar of solidity and courage. He didn't need to be intimidating and fierce to be a great warrior, but rather respectable and intelligent.

King Ivon was everything I wanted to be; except he might've had a better handle on the calm aspect of it.

"Congratulations on your dragon, Katla. It's a mighty fine beastie." He commended.

"Thank you, Your Majesty."

He shook his head slightly, waving me off.

"No need for any of that. I was told by one of the men on Forebrook's crew that your serpent was quite the haul from the forest to the shop. Your father would be proud."

Somehow, the praise felt more palpable coming from him. Like a warmth which covered and surrounded me. I had ended a child of Hel with nothing more than my hands and my blade.

22

Surely, he would know, wouldn't he, if this was truly worthy of such intense pride?

The festivities continued on as the sky changed colors and the stars emerged. The torches were ignited and flickering flames lit the square, shadows bouncing as their owners danced and drank.

I couldn't bring myself to feel tired, despite the taxing events of the day.

Eliana ran up, bringing with her another cup of ale which she pressed into my hand. She leaned over the table, her upper body inches from my seat. At first, I worried that she might get into trouble, but when the king noticed her, he only seemed amused, the lines around his face deepening.

"Miss Brendean." He greeted her.

"King Ivon." She answered back, spinning on me once his attention was diverted.

With a rolling pair of eyes, she pointed Leo out to me.

The king's nephew was across the square. His one leg was propped upon the fountain as he spoke loudly and with flailing hands to a group of seemingly uninterested girls a few years older than us, and Kari Dahl.

And despite being the only one who was Leo's age, Kari was married.

He was showing around his dagger, spinning it on his finger. The knife itself was the only thing he had to boast of tonight. It was a beautiful iron blade,

23

set in a handle of shining red gemstone, wrapped with intricate and thin wires of gold.

All members of the Evalade Royal Family were given one, as he made sure to remind us all. The moron who had handed him a physical representation of his status should have been shipped off.

According to Eliana, he was wildly exaggerating how close he had been to killing an acid spitter, a highly aggressive species.

He was still proclaiming to any who would listen that he surely would have finished it off, had they not been called away before he could end it.

"I could see it in its eyes." Eliana imitated Leo's lower voice. "The colossal devil was relieved it didn't have to fight me anymore."

I scoffed. Calin walked up to join us, leaning over the table on his elbows once he realized there would be no telling off.

His words mimicked my thoughts.

"Yeah, right. He ran past me screaming when I passed Loufi's River. I hadn't picked up tracks of anything larger than a boar within a mile. A squirrel probably looked at him sideways."

I snorted, and quickly covered it with a cough. Quickly, I looked around, ensuring my mother was nowhere near to have caught it.

My focus turned back to my friends, or more importantly, the state of the clothes Calin still wore. A thin twig was trapped within the short reach of a dark curl.

"And what exactly happened to you?" I gestured vaguely towards his soiled tunic. "Were you drowning in the river, when you saw Leo?"

He glanced down at himself and sighed before allowing us an answer.

"I'd love to tell you I was locked in an epic battle with a serpent, narrowly and heroically managing to get away with my life." He sighed. "I tripped in the forest and fell down the hillside." I tried and failed to contain my snickers, before he added, "Yeah, go ahead. You can laugh. My mother already did."

It was the hint of a smile on his otherwise annoyed face that eased Eliana and I into full blown laughter.

Cheers sounded as the musicians began yet another joyous and upbeat melody. Eliana spun back towards us with an all too familiar glint in her mossy green eyes, one that had both Calin and I inching away.

"Come on." She declared. "This is a celebration, after all. For you. And you haven't properly celebrated until you can't see straight, and Leo Evalade is covered in ale. Sitting at the boring table is done for the night. Let's have some actual fun!"

She seized Calin's arm before he could disappear and escape her. I shook my head, and once I excused myself from the table and made my way around to them, she grabbed my hand as well.

Calin and I shared an amused sigh, and allowed her to drag us into the din.

CHAPTER TWO

AIDAN

I dropped silently to the deck, listening to the wingbeats fading in the distance. Though I was now near the center of the armada, my entrance had gone unnoticed, dark scales blending with the similar sky.

The deck was unsteady on the waves, bobbing on the water as if it alone noticed my presence. Almost immediately I heard a nearing conversation, and dove behind a stack of barrels.

Thin, oval-like shapes piled up in the lidless containers I used to hide myself. One of these strange pieces of cargo fell to the planks, jostled by my body against the curved wood.

A hand dropped to shield the notebook in my belt, hiding the decoration of bright gemstones on its surface from gleaming in the fire's glow. It would have been suspicious to leave it behind, but I couldn't allow it to give me away, either. My fingers brushed the design embroidered on the leather.

The voices reached their loudest as they passed me, and the brief light from their carried torches was enough to illuminate the shape on the ground.

It was a dragon scale, veined patterns running through the hard fragment of lost armor. I studied it in confusion until the people walked away, the sounds of their discussion fading.

Only when they were long gone did I sneak out from the relative safety of my makeshift hiding place.

The moonlight scarcely lit the ship, but it was enough to make out where I needed to go. More than a few times, I was forced to duck out of sight as more Sigurd walked about the vessel, unaware of the new passenger and what they brought.

I came across the large hatch on the floor, breathing a sigh of relief when I found it already open. No time was wasted in disappearing beneath.

It was dim below deck. The walls were lined with torch handles, wrapped in flammable rags, but few were ablaze. I stepped lightly as I climbed down the stairs, immediately spotting what I was looking for.

Backed against the wall, a prison of sorts had been constructed, bars of metal crisscrossing haphazardly from one wall to another. Some were misshapen and lumped, the only reason they weren't torn down being their thickness. The bars bridged the space between the two walls in all directions, some pointing straight while others crossed from the floor to the ceiling and every angle in between.

I supposed the Sigurd couldn't be counted on for anything less than barbaric and strange methods, their odd cells trapping the occupants within three walls of wood and one of iron.

Inside the enclosure, people were forced tightly together. There was no pattern in those who stood behind the bars. Both men and women shuffled uncomfortably, and I spotted a few elders amongst mothers who clutched infants and toddlers to their chests.

I didn't know why they had begun taking people, why Olavi Sture would give his ships such an order.

Until a few months ago I had only ever seen dragons held prisoner. Then, their armadas began a new pattern, travelled with more numbers, and we had found human thralls aboard their boats. The fleets became more of a problem, and I had far less free time. The Sigurd weren't only an issue for the Voluspian Kingdoms, and my family had ample firepower to deal with the rising problems.

They were eager to fight, but they would wait for me.

I neared the cell, sticking to the shadows. Two men stood outside an iron entrance that looked as though it had been forged blindfolded.

My sword crept out from its sheath on my back, and slipped a worn shield onto my arm. There were axes held loosely in their hands, not overly concerning when their backs were to me.

I traveled the distance in three strides, less quietly than I would have liked, but there was no time to turn. I gripped my sword with my right hand as I slammed the hilt into the side of a short man's head, while my left brought my shield around to crash into the other's jaw.

Both were unprepared for the blows, and crumpled to the ground almost instantly. I listened for a moment, but the thumps didn't seem to have alerted anyone above.

I faced those behind the bars.

My skin felt hot as I took in their stares, some gawking. Their eyes seemed to bounce between me and the guards on the floor, until a woman pushed her way to the front. Her hands were holding tightly to a girl's shoulders.

Large strands of the woman's hair fell from what I imagined was once an elegant crown of braids around her head. Like the girl in front of her, her hair was a fiery red, but streaked with gray. The skirt of her gown was torn and hanging limply.

The girl, who seemed to be about my age, sported armor, obviously well made. Tears in the ruined fabric and scuffs on the iron told me her arrival here had not been a pleasant one. Vibrant hair hung in curls, falling down to her waist, joined by thin braids woven throughout. The shade of it matched the freckles which covered her face. A strap of leather circled her chest and back, and I wondered what weapon it once held.

I did my best to ignore them. I would leave as quickly as possible, there was no need for any interaction once the reason I had come was carried out.

The older woman's green eyes followed me, widening in surprise when I brought the shield down on the heavy lock holding the iron restraints together. I stuck my foot out, quickly catching the largest fragments before they could announce their own destruction.

Quickly moving away, I tried to make it to the stairs. A throat cleared, demanding attention, and I froze with my boot on the first step.

Cautiously, I considered the speaker, itching to bolt.

"I am Queen Maria of Briaedor. This is my daughter, Princess Avelyn." She introduced herself. The princess's brown eyes appraised me as her mother introduced her, almost like she was calculating how best to take me in a fight. "Who are you? Did my husband send you?"

We stared at each other, the silence stretching on. My eyes darted towards the hatch, and the queen raised an eyebrow.

Eventually, I shook my head. "I am Aidan. Please stay below."

The two redheads watched on in confusion, waiting for more.

When none came, the princess spun on her heel and began ushering people out of the cell, not sparing me another glance. Looking after her for a moment, her mother quickly followed suit. As the people began to move from their imprisoned area, I departed.

I breathed a relieved sigh once I was out and away from their scrutinizing eyes. Being pinned by the curiosity of humans was certainly not an activity I enjoyed, even those who were weaponless when I was not.

Listening for any Sigurd, I leapt out of the hatch and onto the deck.

With every crack of my boot on a spot of faulty wood, I winced. If I stayed out in the open, I'd be killed before my family arrived.

I scanned for a temporary asylum. A pile of spare rigging dangled from the mast a feet away, and I positioned myself around it. Sheathing my sword to free my hand, I pushed my back up against the thick beam which held the sails.

How long does it take one human to free more bumbling humans from a metal wall?

32

The voice came from nowhere.

No sound was sent into the outside world by the spoken words and yet, I heard them all the same. I responded in the same way.

Your patience is admirable. Do you see me?

See you running about like a flopping fish? Yes. I can also see that you've swam into a net.

I groaned as the meaning of my brother's mirth became apparent.

Two Sigurd came around the side of the ship's cabin, chuckling merrily with sloshing cups of mead in their hands.

The men somehow managed to stand upright, although the weight of all the iron blades stowed in their belts should have dragged them down. I knew that, comparatively, I wasn't too much shorter than most humans. However, even given the shrinking distance between us, I knew they would tower over me.

Their forearms were exposed, as was custom for all in their clan, despite the chill of sea spray out on the ocean. The lack of covering presented in full the tattoos of their right arms. Three thick bands, darker than the waves surrounding us.

There was nowhere to run before they rounded the corner fully, and came face to face with my form pressed against the mast. Golden liquid splashed across the deck as the drinks slipped from their hands. Their voices died.

A certain someone found it all too amusing.

Uproarious laughter of another voice sounded in my mind, delighted with his own personal entertainment, and I resolved to kill my brother when this was all over.

Anything I could have said was lost as their shouts suddenly flew into the night, and the slumbering boat became alive.

I could hear Sigurd coming from all directions. The two who had discovered me first began to draw their axes. I didn't bother with my sword, but I did wish Fafnir would hurry up, instead of simply rolling in his own snickers.

There were more of them now, pounding their way across the ship.

The two began to run, and a large circle of warriors began to close in on the mast. An archer sat in the tower above me, arrow trained down, but unable to reach me through the rigging.

With his diverted focus, it was almost too easy. They weren't even looking in the right direction.

As the circle began to tighten, promising a violent and slow trip to Valhalla complete with war cries and Sigurd swords, the boat gave a mighty lurch.

For an instant, the world's only noise was the shriek of splintering wood.

A roar that shattered the night reverberated through the darkness, and their eyes turned upwards too late.

Fire scattered the dark as the white sail became food for the inferno which sprayed across the cloth. The still burning fabric was torn from the middle outwards as a massive shape shoved its way through, gleaming talons the first to make an appearance. As the figure emerged with a cascade of snarls, the mast groaned once more, before it collapsed under the weight. It fell to the deck just as the form landed hard, throwing its wings out and sending the first Sigurd to the waves.

Screams were cut short, and the archer finally met the floor. The hulking dragon of pure white did not slow in his advance, stalking towards his prey with a graceful and insatiable anger.

Even as they began to back away, he continued forward. Large spines covered his back and protruded from his face, fading into a deep russet brown, torn pieces of sail trailing from the ends.

The next roar revealed teeth which vowed to gift death far sooner than their blades. He snorted haughtily at their retreat, his breath salting the air with the scent of ash.

35

"So dramatic." I announced myself. Fafnir whirled on me, tail crashing into several crates of dragon scales on the way and tossing them across the deck. "Why do they have so many-"

Were you just going to stand there? He exclaimed.

"I knew you were coming!"

He grunted dismissively, raising his head to roar. It was a sound so fierce and loud I would have covered my ears, had I not been straining to remain unimpressed.

Little time passed before the empty black was filled with answering bellows. In what seemed to be the span of a moment, the stars were swarmed with dragons.

Scores of Muspel swooped down, jaws open as they released roaring flames onto the ships. We had unleashed our own contained Ragnarök, at least for the opposing side.

The sail of a Sigurd vessel caught fire, and I watched with satisfaction as the revolting symbol on the fabric burned, the body of a snake curling about a broken arrowhead. The ships would fall soon enough.

Our boat was left untouched, at least from above. Fafnir made quick work of the unwanted passengers. His growl was terrifying to most ears, but I could hear the annoyance in it. Some brave, or much more likely insane Sigurd continued to shout their battle cries. They soon found themselves flying overboard as a result of Fafnir's flinging tail.

A group moved in from the right, and once they were close enough, he extended his wing sharply, knocking the breath from the soldiers.

He roared again; this time gleeful as he cleared another line of aggressors.

His smug shouts echoed through my mind as well, replaying each small victory for me so I was forced to watch it twice. I wasn't sure whether he was speaking to me accidentally, or if he wanted me to hear his self-congratulatory and curse-filled commentary as he sent Sigurd warriors hurtling for the ocean.

Probably the latter.

You saw that, right? Stupid human didn't even have a chance to turn and-

Definitely the latter.

Everything was thrown into a startling brightness, flames rising all at once. Boats burned around us. Cages were broken into with the voice of screeching claws on metal, iron bones torn from devious bodies.

Many dragons were packed together in the cages, their forms given little space to move.

Most had their wings tied down, their maws muzzled. Not for long. The restraints were burned away by the fire of their brethren.

Some cages were much thicker, housing dragons much larger. It was for these doors that could not be ripped free by talons and teeth that the Syre came into play.

The Syre were the next largest in size, behind the fire breathing Muspel, more agile and refined, leaner with smaller wingspans. They seemed to glow the same pale-yellow sort of green as the acid that gathered in the corners of their jaws. The eerie light shone through the grooves in between scales, matching the soft glow of the fish they favored.

They descended from the skies to the ships with growls. Their mouths filled with the bright acid, which they were all too happy to make use of.

The corrosive liquid bubbled and steamed, melting through the locks and burning a considerable hole in the doors as well.

When it ate through the iron, it fell to the floor and began burning through the planks. Thankfully, there were no cages present on our boat, it would be dangerous for the prisoners below.

Dragons flocked towards the sky at an incredible rate as they were freed by their kin. Some headed on to return to their nests and islands, while others stayed behind and joined the attack.

My mind was brushed with frequent musings of excitement and vindictive satisfaction as they passed us, projecting their emotions as they charged the fleet.

Fafnir walked back towards me, looking mighty pleased with himself, his head held ridiculously tall in the air. I surveyed his handiwork.

All the former Sigurd of the ship were either flailing their arms in the surrounding sea, or laid spread-eagled on the deck, unconscious. My brother waited in front of me, preening and expectant.

"Keep your head that high, why don't you? Maybe one of the Kaida will perch upon it." I allowed him, and received a tail whack to the side for my trouble. "Come on. Let's go help the others before your lizard ego smothers us all."

Right. And what did you accomplish, exactly? Besides watching everyone else have fun and nearly being dismembered?

I just met two royalties, which puts me above you.

He lowered to the floor and allowed me to grab onto his wing, hoisting onto his back. I leaned forward into my place on his shoulders, and grabbed hold of his dark horns. White wings rose out to the side, shimmering in strange patterns under the firelight. He pumped them, sudden and sharp, and we were propelled into the air, the boat rocking slightly from the force of our departure.

I hoped everyone was alright below deck, the frequent movement of the boat, along with the sound of dragons, likely wasn't comforting.

Smoke rose towards the sky as ships sank below the black waves and dragons flew into the even darker night. The sea was filled with the splashes of Sigurd who had been forced to abandon ship and were now treading water. Most were left clinging to wreckage as their ships were lost.

Many tried to swim for the boats that had yet to go, but they were always gone before they were reached. I watched an empty iron cage disappear into the inky blackness with triumph, it would be a while before they would recover from this.

Hopefully, that would extend to more time before they were able to capture more dragons, and people. I seemed to be thinking this often lately, but there was always a new fleet before I expected it.

The frequent repopulation of their armada was tiring, but sinking it was thrilling.

I just needed to learn how exactly they continued to replenish their forces, before they became more of a nuisance. Or maybe I was simply giving Olavi Sture too much credit via my paranoia.

Something told me that wasn't the case, either the captive humans or the scales glittering on the deck from overturned barrels.

Finally, there were only two vessels remaining.

The first boat was already devoid of any Sigurd, those who were conscious anyway. It was the ship that still held all the Briaedorian prisoners, and was supposed to remain unsunk. They knew not to attack the ship which briefly carried the scent of us.

However, it was the only boat *meant* to be afforded this luxury.

The other ship lay floating in the water a very short distance from the first, still resting above the waves. I felt Fafnir's confusion mingled with my own, and we sped forward.

I didn't know whether to be awed, amused, or honestly annoyed at the sight that greeted me. Between Fafnir and I, we decided there was room for all three.

A fight was taking place on the boat below us, though not between the dragons and the Sigurd.

Upon closer inspection, I realized that the Princess of Briaedor, Avelyn, had at some point slipped above deck. She then somehow managed to jump ships, and was currently taking on three Sigurd at once.

I introduced my palm to my forehead, and Fafnir groaned.

She was doing rather well, all things considered. I spotted two combatants on the ground, whom I could only assume had been her handiwork.

The royal was fighting with an axe, must have stolen one off of the unconscious from the other boat. Avelyn seemed to be dealing with them just fine, weaving in and out, striking before their own strikes could land. I watched as she swung at a man who jumped away, and unintentionally drove the axe head into the deck. Undeterred, she gripped the handle and pushed off it, using the momentum to kick a woman across the face.

The Sigurd fell unmoving as Avelyn pulled the axe free of the wood and faced the other two warriors, blade arm already swinging. Several Muspel and Syre circled overhead, chirping their bewilderment at me and sharing their thoughts, unsure of whether or not to attack.

It didn't seem as though she would need help at all, before my eyes landed on the tower.

They had to know they were fighting a losing battle, as they were the only boat remaining un-sunk or not soon to be commandeered. That didn't seem to discourage the man in the nest, as his bow was currently aimed for Avelyn, an arrow already nocked and waiting for a shot clear of his fellowmen.

Ah, Hel.

I wasn't sure if the thought was mine or Fafnir's, but I agreed with it all the same. I pulled the strap of my shield off my back.

Fafnir flew for the deck, and as soon as we were twenty feet from the wood I leapt from my seat, Fafnir already streaking for the tower.

I held my arm up as I fell headfirst. Seconds before I would collide with the planks, I brought my shield out in front of me, moving into a roll as soon as it began to touch the ground. The circle of wood took all the impact, and I was already up and running towards where Avelyn was fending off the last man.

"Move!" I tried, but she either didn't hear me or didn't understand why I would give her such a command.

It wasn't as though she could really jump out of the way anyway, I mused, as she blocked a downward striking axe with the handle of her own.

Fafnir was almost to the watchtower now, and I was almost to Avelyn. The marksman decided to take the risk of hitting the warrior still locked in combat with the princess, and let his string slip from his fingers.

Fafnir's snout collided with the perch, but it was too late.

I had reached the fight only a moment earlier, unthinkingly bowling into the man still battling with my shoulder, and sending the assailant sprawling to the ground. My side ached from the force, but I kept running the next few feet. I jumped and raised my arm, landing in front of Avelyn.

43

The arrow buried itself in my shield not an instant later, interrupted on its straight course for her chest.

Avelyn stood frozen as a splash echoed from the ocean, the archer hitting the water. She looked from me to her previous opponent, the latter now sprawled on the ground. Her eyes traveled back to the arrow lodged in my shield.

"Sleipnir's balls." She breathed shakily and with slight exhilaration. "Thanks. That was great."

I stepped back, breathing heavily. I stayed highly aware of the axe she held. She seemed rather unaffected by the exchange.

I glanced at her, expecting a break in the new silence, but I soon realized why I hadn't received one.

She was staring behind me, at where Fafnir was lowering his gargantuan frame to the deck. Her face remained unchanging. A large white head came down to be level with mine, hovering over my shoulder, and his voice filled my mind with a twinge of amused concern.

I think I broke her.

I shoved his head away.

A movement caught my attention, Avelyn bringing her axe up, acting slowly, like she was caught in the gaze of a startled deer.

"Wait!" Was the only thing I managed to say.

"A dragon. Do you have a weapon? Don't move too quickly. Get behind me! Gods, it's huge." She choked out. Like a whip of fantastical realization had struck, she focused intently on me, before lunging back. "Sweet Loki, you jumped off a dragon!"

Her finger pointed accusingly. She began towards me, and I backed away, practically falling over myself. I supposed I should've considered myself lucky she hadn't yet hurled her axe.

Once she seemed to understand how close we were to Fafnir, she stopped abruptly. I took the opportunity to backpedal from the angry girl with the blade.

I came around to his side, and he lowered to the ground again, wordlessly. I climbed onto his back in equal quiet.

Avelyn stood rooted to the spot, her face a mix of confusion and horror as she watched a boy her own age mount a ship-sinking, fire breathing, admittedly rather large dragon. I didn't blame her for her shock, Fafnir was bigger than most.

Her axe hand was hesitating, debating, and I wondered if she was honestly considering attacking Fafnir. That was pretty bold, but I really didn't want him to kill her. We could do without a royal murder on our names.

I heard Avelyn's mother, Queen Maria, calling for her from the other boat, but she did not turn towards the voice. I leaned forward in my place on Fafnir's neck, urging him with my mind. He took to the air once again, Avelyn left stumbling slightly on the tossing deck, her eyes never leaving our shape.

We flew towards the other ship as she took a running leap from one deck to the other. Fafnir and I hovered in the air, the only sound in my ears the thumping of wings as the princess sprinted towards the hatch where her people and her mother were.

I couldn't hear what she was saying, didn't wish to, but a moment later Queen Maria came above, the others following after her.

All reacted at the minimum how Avelyn had.

Others began yelling, mostly insults and curses, screaming. The mothers clutched their children closer, an old man covered his mouth with a hand of wrinkled skin. Briaedorians began reaching for the spots on their backs and hips where their weapons should have been, had they not been stolen from them.

Their cries increased in volume as a few knelt and began to arm themselves with whatever they could find, be it extinguished torches or smoldering remains, and hurled them in our direction.

They weren't strong enough to reach us of course, as high up as we were, but that didn't make it any easier to watch. Some broke from the group towards the motionless Sigurd, for the weapons they had dropped.

Thinking less about how Fafnir had saved them, and more about how they could hurt him.

A few who were close enough to their stationary princess reached for Avelyn's axe. Although she was still staring at me, her analysis had become less horrified, more confused, and she did not let anyone grab the handle from her. Her mother stood at her side, and despite looking as though she had seen us crawl out of Helheim and declare ourselves children of Loki, she still made no move to attack as the others did.

I wondered if Avelyn had told her in their brief conversation that I had managed to save her life a few minutes ago.

I hoped so, if only because the Queen reminded me of my mother. I didn't want to see that look of horror on her face grow any deeper. Even so, she held herself protectively in front of her daughter.

Several Briaedorians ran back towards the group, the still roaring firelight reflecting off the gleaming blades they held. All were taken from the Sigurd that Fafnir had left on the deck.

It was time for us to go, before they tested whether or not they could make the throw. Without a word Fafnir pushed us higher, further from the humans.

At least we saved them. They all escaped, and these ships won't do harm anymore. They can command the vessel and return to their homes. I'm sorry, Aidan.

"Yeah, me too." I whispered, moving my hands down to grip his neck as his wings beat harder. *Let's just go home.*

With another pulse of his wings and a gust of wind, the shouts swept away as we were swallowed by the night sky.

***

It was a loud flight back, Fafnir and I both feeling the mutual tug of thoughts, but sharing nothing more.

Those around us more than made up for our quiet, their joyous and proud musings filling the air, riding the battle high. Some swatted playfully at one another in the air, still wound for a fight. I sighed in defeat, doubting their ability to keep quiet upon our return.

I found it hard to join them in their victorious mood, despite their attempts to pull me in by way of soft nudges and mental calls.

When the island appeared, noticeable due to its massive shadow in the moonlight, I tried in vain to shush them. They would give us all away.

Shh! Keep it down!

A chorus of good-natured groans accompanied my attempts, but they minimally quieted, at least.

We circled the side of the island, most of the group branching off, others following. The air cooled as we fell, pulling up just above the water, the ocean spray like ice on my skin.

It was easy to slip inside the Bay, the stone walls familiar. The ceiling was alive and writhing. I frantically greeted those who crawled above before they could alert her to our presence.

With painstaking caution we set down softly on a floor of rock, Fafnir doing his best to prevent his claws from scraping.

The enclosure was already filled with the slipping of wings on scales, a constant and careful thrum equal to the lapping of waves. The slide of my body down Fafnir's wings should have been undetectable.

My brother laid where he was, assuming a relaxed position, tucking his head down and feigning sleep. Carefully, he opened his wing for me to crawl under. Just a few more steps, and we would have made it.

A dreaded voice, piercing the safety, seemed to be the world's only noise.

"Well, it certainly seems you two have had an eventful evening." I winced, slumping. "Or should I say morning? Imagine my surprise, finding a small flock and one boy missing. I have my guesses, a few hunches, but do you care to explain just where you have been?"

Fafnir and I shared a curse.

CHAPTER THREE

KATLA

To claim my head felt as though I'd lost, and the dragon had consumed me, would be an insult to the ache.

I couldn't quite remember how many cups of mead Eliana had given me, or how many I had stolen from her. At some point in the night, I was rather sure I had been roped into a drinking contest with Leo out of spite over something.

In my defense, from what I could recall of the evening, which wasn't much, I had been crowned champion over the heir.

It was unclear who truly won, however, seeing as I now struggled to orient myself. Opening my eyes, and immediately closing them again as light assaulted my vision, I was just glad to find myself in my own house. I didn't want a repeat of Calin's sixteenth birthday, when I had woken up on Eliana's roof.

It was better than Calin himself, who had found himself butt-naked in an Estran sheep pen a village over.

My mother's snoring reached my ears from downstairs. I sat up slowly in my bed, wondering at the time if she was still asleep. Cautiously, I tried again, my sight blocked by my hand, staving off the light that streamed through my open window.

I pushed myself up and stood, then immediately swayed.

Breathing deeply, and fighting the urge to hunt down Eliana and Leo, I righted myself. Shakily, I walked to the source of the draft lifting the edge of my blanket.

It didn't evade my notice that I had woken on the ground. My limbs struggled to cooperate with each other in a way that didn't involve me splaying across the floor.

The sun was barely peeking over the horizon, but the small amount of light was still murder on my eyes. I pulled the wooden shutters closed, hoping to maintain some heat in my room, but it was likely pointless if it had been open since whenever I stumbled home.

I slumped against the closed window, and contemplated going back to sleep. With a groan, I abandoned the wall and made my way down the stairs, not bothering to move quietly.

If my mother had drank even half as much as she usually did, she certainly wouldn't stir on account of my footsteps.

I drifted closer to the table, plopping myself hard into the nearest chair. Well, I'd made it this far, it couldn't hurt to go back to sleep for a little while.

As I attempted to settle my arms across the wood, rough fabric brushed the back of my hand.

Peering out from behind my elbow, I noticed the small coin pouch. My mother must have left it out for me, which meant I needed to go to the market. She'd been nagging me for two days already.

I sighed into my arm, pushed myself up, and swiped the bag. The table shook as I shoved the chair roughly back into place. There was a dull thump as something fell from the surface, and with another, much louder groan, I knelt down. My wooden horn lay beside the far table leg.

The rush of pleasure was delightfully sobering, and managed to take the edge off of my headache.

Fighting to reign my smile in, I reached for the horn, and carefully set it back on the table. Later today there would be a ceremony, and I would receive my gift.

I already had a knife, but the honor was something to look forward to. Straightening, I held my head a little higher and started for the door.

Once outside I kept my eyes trained on my boots, not quite willing to look anywhere near the rising sun. The pouch of coins jangled on my hip as I walked, light against my side.

I neared the market, where stalls were being set up as more and more people awoke. It was doubtful that anyone in the kingdom wasn't feeling the effects of the night prior but, life must go on. If the village slowed every morning after a party, we'd never get anything done.

I was content to browse through the shops, trying to remember the list my mother had rattled off to me days prior through my mead-addled mind.

We certainly didn't need bread, but maybe I could stop by the bakery before my mother arrived and snag breakfast... How many apples were on the counter last?

I was just handing a few coins to one of the butchers, steering clear of Owen Patrial's shop, when for the second time in as many days, Eliana burst forth into me from nowhere.

I scrambled to catch the basket of food that was slipping from my wrist, and then returned to the trader. I took the wrapped meat he handed me, tossing it into the basket, before I whirled to regard my blonde assailant.

I was expecting to be launched head-first and without warning into a crazy tale of where she had found herself that morning. Soon to be followed by what boys she was sure had been flirting with her last night, even though she undoubtedly couldn't even remember their faces.

Unexpected, was the look she bore.

My mind immediately leapt to the worst conclusions about what she could have gotten herself into, and whether Calin would need to lie for us, before she stopped me.

"I just overheard a Council meeting." Her voice was quite possibly the most serious I had ever heard. Either someone died, or we finally found her mead tolerance.

"A Council meeting." I repeated. "At the break of dawn? What, did they even sleep last night? And what are you doing 'overhearing' a gathering of councilmen anyway?"

She raised an eyebrow at me, her abnormal expression momentarily replaced, as if her early morning snooping was completely normal. Which I supposed for Eliana, it actually was.

"This is something you feel the need to ask?" She threw quick glances around the market, but apparently found nothing worth noting. Her face adopted a more crestfallen look, if such a thing was even possible for Eliana, and something almost...nervous. "They were talking about you."

"Me? What on Midgard for?"

The only thing I could think of was the Hunt. While it forced through me another starburst of pride to think of my victory being mentioned at a Council meeting, I couldn't see why it would be, except in passing conversation.

"At first it was about Leo the Lame and his less than perfect prospects as heir-"

"Nothing new there,"

"Then the Hunt." She continued, and I nodded, still not seeing. "And they talked about some other things, Leo a little more, then...they talked about marriage."

Any feelings of pride were lost to me in that moment. There was nothing but a cold, icy seed of dread that had planted itself in my stomach faster than Thor could light the sky. There was no way.

"Eliana?" I asked, for she didn't seem all too eager to continue.

She looked like she wanted to do the opposite, actually. Like she wanted to erase this conversation and have come to complain to me about something normal. I wanted that more than anything, to go back to a few seconds before, when my fingers didn't feel as though they would break from their grip on the basket. Before Eliana had run up and spoken about marriage as if such a thing were commonplace for an early morning market conversation.

"It was all good! They were talking about your kill, how large the dragon was, wondering if you would elect to mount the horns, for a while." I stared at her with rapt attention, every fiber of my being wanting to reach out and shake her for a faster explanation. "They were bouncing back and forth. Then it came back to Leo again, like it always does."

"I don't understand. Eliana, I need you to spit it out."

"Mr. Maurin mentioned that Leo has been seventeen for a few months and it was 'high time he found a wife'. Lots of agreement, though not from Ivon. Something about reining him in and fixing broken reputations. I think they all believed he would be more responsible, I guess, if he was married to someone. They had been watching during some of our sparring and the competitions that we had, apparently. With the wooden swords and the handle of Calin's halberd? They called you the best fighter of our age."

Moments ago I would have given anything to hear her say that.

Yesterday, the day before, my entire life up to this exact minute I would have jumped to hear it. That the Council and the King of all people believed I was a competent warrior, or that they had taken a notice of me. Why now, did it seem like a bad thing?

Eliana's tone wasn't bitter, and I wish it had been. That would have been logical, normal. For her to be angry with them and their words, even just a small bit.

Not this.

"And what, precisely, does any of that have to do with Leo?"

Say anything else. Tell me my conclusions are false.

"Ivon didn't speak very much. When he did, he said that you could even have wrestled with 'his Atarah." I gasped softly. A warmth bubbled in my chest; it was an honor to be compared to the King's late wife. "He called you something for the village to be proud of in the next generation. I think that's really what got the rest of them on board."

I grabbed her arm, not meaning to be as rough as I was.

"On. Board. With *what*."

She was avoiding my eyes now, repeating what she had heard. "Leo needed somebody by his side, for when he became King. Someone good enough to essentially take his responsibility." I stared at her, praying to every god I could remember in the moment that she would not say what I thought she would. "The Royal Council is arranging a marriage contract between you and Leo. They drafted it before the sun rose."

Just like that, the world was devoid of sound.

The flow of conversation around me as the village came alive and people filled the market, it was all gone. As if someone had climbed into my brain and turned off my hearing.

Eliana was still before me. It looked so strange on her, to be worried. Eliana was never worried. She was always sure. It was why I agreed to half of her crazy plans.

What was happening?

I vaguely registered the slip of twine on the skin of my arm, then the back of my hand, as the basket fell from my grasp. Its contents spilled into the street.

Eliana knelt quickly and began picking it up, but when she stood, she did not hand it back to me. Somewhere in the recesses of my mind I was grateful for it.

"-atla?"

"I have to go."

My first step was unsteady. The second was a sprint.

I pushed my way through the building crowd. Words of congratulations that hadn't reached me last night were thrown my way, I ignored them. I ignored the looks I was given as I shoved through Iona. I crashed into a stumbling couple just leaving their hall, blinking in the light as I had earlier, then jumped up and kept going, not stopping to apologize as they picked themselves off the ground.

I don't know what I thought would await me when I threw my door open so harshly that dust fell from the beams above, but King Ivon sitting in my kitchen didn't make the list.

His black fur cloak fell to the floor from his seat, clasped on by a chest plate, perfectly polished, under which he wore a dark tunic. A large axe sat propped up on the table beside him, and the light that hit it through the open door threw spots of reflection against the far wall.

A rare sight adorned his head, for the king was wearing his crown.

It was a home for the large rubies that glittered at me across the room, for the intricate crisscrossing pattern of diamonds that circled it's base. He looked every bit as regal as a King should, and on any other day I knew I would be both intimidated and awed. The same could not be said about his companion.

Leo Evalade sat smack in the middle of my house, and I was less than enthused.

To his credit, he looked slightly more put together than usual, although I assumed that was his uncle's doing. Even from across the room I caught his smell. Rank, like he had tumbled head-first into a barrel of ale last night.

Maybe he had. I sniffed again. He definitely had.

His brown hair was plastered to his forehead, small beads of water dripping onto his clothes.

My best guess? King Ivon had forced him to hop in a tub and bathe outside of Washday to get rid of his smell, and now we were all acting as if it didn't stink like something died in here. A painful courtesy.

Leo, much like I, was in the same clothes he had worn the day before. That normally wouldn't have been too strange, at least for him. However, I didn't think wearing a shirt bearing the results of our drinking competition was ushering the smell in a pleasant direction.

He looked positively scruffy sitting next to his uncle. A fact I was sure the King was all too aware of, if the annoyance in his eyes as he looked at his nephew was anything to go by.

All heads turned to me as the slamming door rebounded off the wall. I flung out my hand to keep it from catching me on the way back, and it shuddered as it flew to a stop against my fingers. My mother's eyes found mine.

She looked uncomfortable.

"Katla. Come sit down."

Her voice was softer than her normal tone, although she could've been shouting in the suffocating silence of the room. I walked stiffly towards the worn chair next to my mother, unfortunately putting me across from Leo.

For a moment none spoke, the dragging of my chair across the wood floor abrasive in my ears.

Ivon chose to voice his thoughts.

"Katla, I would like to take this opportunity to again acknowledge your victory yesterday." I scoffed at the tabletop. "I have been speaking with the Council this morning, and we all agree that you have risen to the top among your peers. Your fighting skills are admirable, your determination and the way in which you carry yourself respectable. You've presented yourself incredibly, as a staple of this kingdom and its villages."

I finally looked him in the eye, simply staring.

I doubted I could make a king uncomfortable, but it felt good to believe I was doing so.

I hoped against all hope that this was some joke, a stupid, not at all comical joke, the creator of which would find themselves with a fist to the face and a lack of four limbs.

I managed, "Your Majesty."

He didn't correct me on the formalities this time. It was likely hard to do so when you wore the cumulation of royal jewels. It'd be easier to pretend the gold wasn't there if it didn't demand your attention. I swear to Thor, that thing was glittering!

My mother decided to chime in from beside me.

"As you know, Katla, you and Leo are both of age-"

"What a reason to desire a marriage!" I snapped.

Just who could have predicted more silence? To Ivon's credit, he appeared the least shocked, remaining impassive.

I allowed myself two deep breaths, and sat up straighter. Taking a moment to collect myself, I chose my words carefully.

"There has been some discussion this morning-" Ivon tried.

"King Ivon, I assure you what I say is born from the deepest respect, but I don't quite know who any of you think you are to decide my marital life. There has been no prior communication between our two families. My father is not here to speak for me, so I will represent myself. While I appreciate your words and your offer, and I'm sure it is generous, I think it would be best if we ended this now. My answer is no, and it will not change."

You would have thought I had struck my mother across the face, and came back to do it again. There was some relief there too, but mostly simmering disbelief.

Strangely, Ivon didn't seem angry. He nodded slightly, but offered no comment.

Loki must have been blessing me, for it was Leo who decided to break the silence this time.

"Come on, Katla! Think about how great this could be! I'll be King in a few years, a new age for the kingdom." He threw his hands out while I huffed, 'new' was a good word for it. "With you by my side! You're the best fighter in the village, and I'm-"

"Adequacy in combat translates to a resume for royalty, now?"

I couldn't believe I was actually taking part in this conversation. My mother came to Leo's rescue before he could embarrass himself further.

"Katla, you know your father set your bride price before he died. King Ivon and the Council have started a contract." I had about two seconds to start running through my ideas to get out of this room, before my mother said the stupidest thing I had ever heard her say, "I accepted."

It was going to be really hard to find somewhere to live once I murdered the heir to the throne.

Would I have time to make it painful, or would I have to do it quick, before Ivon stopped me? Maybe Eliana had a good hideaway I could borrow.

"What?"

A crash echoed through the room as my chair toppled. I didn't care that the King of the godsdamnned island was sitting before me, or that Leo was watching me with a haughty look in his eyes that I wished to slap out of him. Maybe I would, if I had the chance.

All that mattered was that someone had proposed a marriage contract, Leo of all people, and without even speaking to me my mother accepted. There was that stupid dagger again, flipping in a spun dance around Leo's fingers, flaunting its elegancy.

The crimson and gold twisted in his hand, distracting in its implications and its frequent movement.

"Katla." My mother's voice adopted a colder edge, no doubt already embarrassed by the scene I was making in front of the King.

"Without even asking me? Why was I not told about this before any single choice was made? Because as I stated, the answer is no. I think everyone in this room would do well to abide by it."

I wasn't worried about Leo's reaction; he was more than used to denial from every female in Lamid's four villages. He didn't even seem phased by my outburst, and was instead watching the light catch on his knife.

I glanced towards the king; the kind face saddened. Like he knew exactly who he was trying to tie to me, but was committed to this last-ditch effort, to keeping Leo's eventual reign from going up in flames.

The effort was pitiful. At least allow Leo to attempt a successful rule before you stick him with a wife. Let him flounder a little before he learns how to swim.

"King Ivon is willing to give much more than the price your father set." My mother amended carefully.

"The price was intended to be exchanged once I made the decision on who would be giving it. It's supposed to be a formality, not a business deal. If it was meant as a way to sell me like a trade good, I think he would have asked for a few more sheep. Might have tried for a cow, even."

My mother eyed my snark with warning, jade eyes narrowing, but I couldn't be bothered to heed it. Ivon actually adopted shock, trying to fix what he viewed as a misconception.

"Katla, that is not the intention of the contract in any way. We believe you could be an excellent match for Leo, and there is always an option for...divorce, if you truly..."

Our King was a smart man, but he really should have stopped. My eyes swept the room, trying to remember where in my drunken haze I had left my sword last night. Leo couldn't put on a ring if I cut off his hand.

My lungs worked methodically as I pressed my shaking hands into the worn wood of the table. I had a strong desire to hit someone, and another strong desire for that someone to be Leo.

"Dad wouldn't have agreed to this. I don't care how much they're willing to pay. I don't long to be married, so I will not be. There is no purpose to this meeting outside of that."

We weren't bad off. We carried no need for charity or a sudden, ridiculous sum of money to save us from going hungry in the street. We had more money than most people, with the bakery. Able to live more than just comfortably.

The Vistel family was old, and had roots here almost as deep as the Evalade's. A family of great warriors who all served Lamid well, a history of bravery. It was something people remembered. The Vistel name was an honorable one, brought into the light even further in the wake of my father's death, given ample recognition. In a few more years, it's possible people would have begun to push for Leo and I to court. A daughter of the Vistel's would automatically be in the running, should the heir need to find a wife. Should need ever come to be, I expected to deliver a well-worded refusal.

Never would I have believed that my name and my accomplishments would push me into a union, draw the eyes of the Council for anything other than my use as a warrior. I struggled to find a silver lining, some proof that this wasn't the worst thing that could have come.

I didn't find one.

Leo's hand flipped the dagger, waiting for his uncle.

The King's voice was almost apologetic, when he told me next, "The contract has already been sealed."

And the breath was gone. My mind was paralyzed, firmly guarding itself against the conclusion of the undeniable inevitable that I could not allow myself to process.

They could not have done this.

It was at that moment that I finally felt the pressure behind my eyes, but I would not cry. Not here in front of the King, and especially not before Leo. Not until I had done something about it, until I had shouted at someone, until I had shoved Leo out of my chair and out of my house.

I remained unmoving and silent, the list of things I needed to do steadily growing, and unenacted.

The King excused himself.

He wished a good day to myself and my mother. He dragged Leo out the door. I assumed he was giving her time to explain or trying to save his nephew from a miserable and violent end, as if I wouldn't find him. I hoped they would hear my shouts through the walls as they walked away.

My mother raised her face to mine not a second after the handle stilled.

"You let them do this? You agreed to it? How could you do that? We have to call it off, now. Immediately."

"I didn't have a choice, Katla."

Her voice was even and calm in a way I couldn't fathom. She, like the King, looked sad for me. How dare they act as though they regretted this when they had forced me into it?

"What do you mean? Of course you do! It's a contract, a two-sided deal, you can say no! I am saying no! I don't care that it's sealed. Where is it? I'll burn it, and shove the embers up Leo Evalade's-"

"If it was anyone else, I could've." She jumped in. "And I would've. You're right, your father wouldn't have wanted this for you. And neither do I, really. But the contract was formed and agreed upon by the Council, regarding the heir of the island. It's more than an arranged marriage, it's for a member of the royal family. A decision for the future of Lamid as a whole. My opinion doesn't affect what was decided by the Council. Not even concerning my own daughter."

"And mine? That means nothing to them? How could Ivon allow this?"

"The King didn't decide, as he isn't Leo's father. Mr. Evalade is on the royal council, and has no need for King Ivon's approval to begin a deal, if he can garner enough support. Leo is of age, as are you,"

"Just barely!"

"-and he will be turning eighteen in the coming year. As you can imagine, Leo's father was all too happy to have him married off to the best warrior of his age. The Council voted for you unanimously. I don't believe King Ivon was eager for an arranged marriage, but he agreed with the Council's choice."

"I'm not ready to be married, especially when I have no say in whom it's to. And *especially* not when they are expecting me to wed Leo and not commit an assassination. We'd kill each other within a week, him on my sword, and myself on some account of his stupidity. This won't work in anyone's favor, so it's best to stop it now. They must see that!"

"King Ivon's marriage was arranged. He and the Queen didn't even grow up in the same kingdoms, you know. Kari Dahl married that sweet boy who apprenticed at the mill, and their union was arranged-"

"Kari and Michael were in love! Michael brought her flowers every day, they held hands everywhere they went! They had been courting for over a year before Michael's father asked for a contract! And Michael proposed after!"

"I'm sure Leo will-"

"Oh, a staged proposal, undoubtedly in front of the entire kingdom and the council. How romantic! Will the ring be some gigantic diamond they pulled from the hand of a dead monarch, or do you think he'll have it forged with the finest gold, just for me? Or even better, I'll be the latest to carry an Evalade Family Dagger, showing about a title to bury my misery?"

"Katla, I know you and your friends don't hold Leo in the highest of views." She thought to begin, and a sound halfway between a huff and a snort came out of my mouth. "But he's not that bad. A little rowdy now, but you're both young and-"

"Exactly!"

"And I believe that he can treat you with the respect you deserve. While this would never have been my first choice, I do believe you could...settle him. He comes from an honorable family, his parents are good people, and that shines through somewhere, just as it does for you."

"You're not understanding me. I don't want to be married! It doesn't matter if it's Leo, or anyone else in the village! I won't marry him, and you all are foolish to ever believe I would lie down and go along with this. If they admire my skills so much, maybe they should teach the same to their prized heir, but their mess is not mine to handle."

Life couldn't uproot so drastically in under an hour.

People didn't enter into their kitchens and find they were to be married. They didn't first hear about it in the market.

My mother sounded almost excited, drowning in the status of my apparent promised. I shared none of the same sentiments.

What I felt was nothingness and anger, worming its way into my stomach, unrelenting.

CHAPTER FOUR

AIDAN

Sometimes, the Bond was really, really, inconvenient.

Such instances being now, as I was trying desperately to conceal the half-formed lies in my mind before I had a chance to use them.

Of course, if she really wanted, Ragna would hear them anyway. Fafnir's imagination was utterly non-forthcoming as well, neither of us coming up with a suitable deception fast enough. As if it would have worked. Fafnir's eyes were fixed behind me, his wing still extended outwards.

I had yet to face her. It was safer this way.

"Aidan." Ragna's voice was promising, and it was that which had me spinning around.

Strands of her bright and graying hair fell around her face and away from the usual pile on her head. Her face was pinched in restrained anger, soft wrinkles taunt. Her figure was shrouded in darkness from the cave where she must have emerged, the bear cloak she wore rumpled. A Kaida curled around her shoulders, resting in the stance of her crossed arms. I stood taller than her, but at the very moment I felt as though I was cowering far beneath her gaze.

She radiated displeasure, and I wondered if faking death at sea would have been a smarter option.

I groaned. *We are so certainly grounded.*

If we survive. Fafnir added.

"Night flight." I feigned nonchalance, already doubting its usefulness.

"Really? You boys flew during sunset, and went to sleep hours ago." Ragna didn't wait for me to fumble through a reply. "You took your map."

"Did I? I didn't even notice. We were trying to catch up to this small pack of Amphitrite, actually, and lost track of time-"

"Of all the maps, what exactly made you choose that one, Aidan? The one we had marked Sigurd sightings on, not a day ago?"

A shrug. "I didn't realize I still carried it."

She hummed, walking slowly so that she stood between Fafnir and I. "Is that so?"

I thought it wise not to answer. She tilted her head towards my brother.

What about you, Fafnir? Ragna's words filtered clearly through my ears, and I knew he experienced the same. *What have you been up to?*

And gods, if it wasn't already hard enough to get anything past Ragna. Difficult, but not impossible, were lies through the Bond. However, if she really tried to dig, she would likely have no trouble sifting through our memories. She was far more experienced.

My wings were restless. He fluttered them slightly for emphasis, visibly deflating when she raised an unimpressed eyebrow.

I had to give him credit for trying.

"So, if I were to ask anyone else who returned at the same time this morning, hours before dawn has even broken-"

Fafnir sighed. *We're doomed.*

"-would they tell me you snuck out of the Bay hours ago with that map for a very specific reason? Would they tell me they aided in an attack on Sigurd forces? Or perhaps they only saw you on your night flight, chasing after a school of Amphitrite for a leisurely game."

Fafnir bowed his head, and I crossed my arms.

"If you knew, then why did you ask?"

Almost immediately Fafnir growled. *Idiot! What are you doing?*

75

I'd known getting away with this was a long shot from the start. Yet the very principle of having to sneak around to do this was ridiculous. The stance that clearly implied Ragna was preparing for a scolding was only throwing Syre acid on the flames of my growing ire. If the hole was already dug, might as well see what was on the other side.

Death. Fafnir deadpanned. *Death is on the other side.*

"You two convinced a score of others to leave with you tonight."

"Yes."

"I'm assuming the sneaking off implies you took on the very group of ships I told you to leave well enough alone? The group I meant to deal with myself?" She looked between the two of us with visibly increasing irritation.

Yes.

"There were captured on board, prisoners." I argued.

I saw brown eyes flash in the dull light from above. "You know well that there were more than dragons on those boats, and you know the simple rules we are to live by."

"Why should we choose who is freed? You would have only saved everyone else, left the people there to whatever fate Olavi chose! We saved them all, and sank the fleet. What is so wrong with that?"

"Those people? They are not our people. The dragons are our people. The affairs of men have no place in our responsibilities."

I shook my head. "You're angry with us for helping people? Who was hurt by what we did tonight other than Olavi Sture?"

I felt Fafnir's thoughts nudge against mine, a silent encouragement. Ragna sighed, seeming to take a breath.

"You are a good boy, Aidan. So good, in that you want to help. But it is not our place, and it is simply too dangerous. The risk-"

"What risk?" I demanded, and Ragna abandoned her calm.

"You don't think they will wonder after the boy who saved them? The dragons which swarmed outside but left them untouched? Mystery breeds curiosity, leads to looking further. What will they do with their questions? What will they do when they search for answers? When they find you? This thinking, that those people contain the same goodness, is the risk, is the danger! Men do not think before they act. You, Aidan, will hesitate. They will not. We fight for our own, but we do not lose ourselves for an enemy that would sooner see us on their blade."

"You saved us, why are they any different? They don't deserve the same chance?"

Ragna blanched in surprise, eyes already narrowing.

77

"This is foolish, and reckless." Her tone was sharp, hardened anger underneath. "I refuse to allow this any longer. I forbid it. They do not deserve what you are trying to give them, and you will only be hurt in the end. They will fight their own battles, and us, ours. And ours do not involve citizens of the Isles."

"Then we can call ourselves no better than what you believe of them." I pushed towards Fafnir, not sparing a glance at Ragna behind me. "I'm not going to stop. No prisoner on those ships deserves to be there, dragon or not. It may not be your fight, but Olavi has made it his, and that makes it mine."

I don't think this is going to help our situation. Fafnir tried, but lifted his wings in preparation regardless.

"Aidan." Ragna called, but it sounded more defeated than livid.

We'll be back later. I begrudgingly promised as Fafnir took off.

I didn't turn around as we exited the Bay and flew out into the open air without a destination.

Not even a full minute had passed outside when smooth scales nudged against my head, and then along Fafnir's flank. They were a deep and rich amber brown, familiar and warm. I glared at her before she had the chance to speak, and Fafnir grumbled.

Apology not accepted. I threw out.

Takka laughed, a rumbling chortle. *I didn't reveal your absence, hatchlings. She held suspicions before we spoke.*

I scoffed, resting my head on my hand. *What a conversation that must have been.*

We only worry. Takka assured, gliding gently beside us.

Your worry is unnecessary. Fafnir huffed.

I stood, Fafnir's wing outstretched and strong beside me. In a fluid motion I crossed the white, stepping onto dark scales. I felt a pulse of affection, and guilt gnawed at the idea of being so short with Takka as I crossed her back.

I believe Ragna is afraid. Are you too afraid of them? I questioned, watching as the sun struggled to break through the night.

She shifted, the tip of her wing against Fafnir, my hand on one of her many spines. She was smaller than Fafnir, though many were, but she showed no issues matching his pace in the sky.

I do not hold the same beliefs of the humans as Ragna, though I remain just as wary. Humans are not trusting creatures. She began, and I looked down, but she continued on. *However, neither are we. Yet you have sat upon my scales since you were small, and Ragna has flown with us for most of my lifetime. I believe trust is possible, if we only look past the fear.*

That's what I've been trying to-

But, She sternly interrupted, *that does not mean trust that is blind is our answer. Caution must remain in your actions, however pure.*

"I understand." I allowed, my hand trailing across her back in farewell as I once again made the trek across wings. "You know, I still don't believe you didn't tell. You've always been a snitch."

Takka only laughed, and soon we left her behind.

The ocean, incomprehensibly vast and open, raced beneath us. Rising sunlight painted the world around me in vibrance, dancing through the sky and reflecting across the water as the moon was lost beneath the waves. The morning light revealed our silhouette as we plowed through the skies high above the water, massive wings outstretched, pushing ourselves ever faster.

My muscles relaxed as I leaned forward, thoughts of the Bay and Ragna's scolding to come evaporating. I shouted as we accelerated, the body beneath me shifting as strong beats pounded the wind, lifting us further into the changing world.

I knew we shouldn't have left, and a part of me was angry at myself for leaving Ragna. Just like Takka said, she was only worried, but she was still wrong. She had been fighting the Sigurd for as long as I could remember, not until a few years ago allowing me to join her.

Only recently had they begun capturing humans, and an abundance of dragons higher than any they had before. Neither of us could deduce a reason behind it, one that held firm, anyway. Ragna believed that nothing had changed, that this was simply a clear sign of Olavi Sture's lust for power.

Many years ago, the Sigurd captured people all the time, but were forced to stop when their numbers became too little to sustain their repeated attacks. Despite this, it seemed to me that there had to be more to it.

The place of merchants and sales, Trader's Isle, had become heavy with the Sigurd's presence.

Their boats were almost constantly docked there, no doubt selling the dragons for little more than hides. They must have been auctioning the people as slaves, a practice abandoned in most kingdoms, but Trader's Isle belonged to none of them.

Something was changing, and the Sigurd were growing. What could they possibly need that much money for? That many people, that many dragons? What on Midgard was Olavi trying to pull?

Clearly nothing big enough for the coward to show his face.

A splash pulled my attention, and upon looking for a second more, similar movements followed.

Just around a sea stack which jutted out of the water, the sea twisted with a fluid grace different from waves. I noticed an island to my left, which must have been Vanir. We hadn't traveled too far, but Ragna wouldn't want us to enter the borders of any kingdom.

If I focused hard enough, I could make out which colors were waves and which were Amphitrite. Surely, as long as we went the opposite direction, a little fun wouldn't hurt.

Maybe they'll want to race? I asked Fafnir, who had noticed them as well.

Maybe they'll want to admire my tail, you mean.

I rolled my eyes as Fafnir turned and began to fall in the air, heading towards them. Open as my mind was in preparation to call out to them, I felt the sudden stab of apprehension in the same instantaneous second as my brother.

Our descent twisted to a halt, the lapping of unnatural waves below signaling the retreat of the Amphitrite, fleeing from what assaulted Fafnir's nose. From around the sea stack a boat had emerged, only a few tens of feet from us now.

Aidan!

Already there was frantic shouting from below, and there was no doubt arrows would follow. We were low enough for them to meet their mark.

"Go! Go!"

Hold on! I don't want to have to pull your ass out of the water.

And then we were spinning, the first volley of shafts loud in Fafnir's ears.

I struggled to withdraw from the Bond, the onslaught of his senses coupled with mine slightly disorienting. He righted, wings flinging out to the side to scoop at the air. I was already up, no longer sitting, my legs bent slightly beneath me and a hand on one of his horns. Facing the boat and trusting Fafnir to maneuver us somewhere safe, I took stock of what lay below us.

The ship wasn't too large, and it wasn't long before we were safely out of range. I lowered, trying to make myself smaller on Fafnir's back.

The moment he violently recoiled, his spine raised under me and his wings still, was the very same one in which I smelled it faintly through him. I covered my mouth with my hand as Fafnir shook his head hard.

The scent was heavy, in such atrocious amounts that there was no other explanation.

The body of a dragon lay somewhere below the deck, cold and broken. The invisible trace of blood followed every one of those who manned the vessel.

My hand moved of its own accord, reaching unconsciously for my blade, although there would be no point. There was nothing to be done. They weren't even Sigurd, their sails bare except for the hardly visible insignia, some sort of sword covered in lines.

It was vaguely familiar in my horror and anger.

They were just regular humans from some kingdom. Humans with a body beneath their feet. Fafnir snarled savagely, his wings unfurled and displaying the colossal area of his frame.

Murderers. Fafnir hissed. *They still reek of it.*

As they readied their next arrows, I wished I could return the favor. I sat up, full of hot rage, watching them run about on the deck. Nausea pierced my stomach.

Get us out of here. I ground out, and with a flapping like a whip on the wind, we left the ship behind.

CHAPTER FIVE

KATLA

I had never entertained myself with the idea of being royalty as a child.

We had an heir, and he wasn't all that interesting. Not something to wish for, not a game to play. Now when Leo became the king, I would be crowned alongside him. A sovereign, a monarch.

It was all impossible just the day before, so why was it so crushingly real now? The last place I wanted to be when I tried to unravel the newly stitched seams was once again in the Square, the eyes of the kingdom on me.

Attending a short ceremony to receive my gift, my prize.

King Ivon was before me, Leo somewhere in the throngs. Here I was forced to stand, and give no indication of the fury boiling under my skin. I had to smile. There was no choice but to listen as Ivon spoke.

"It was a fine competition this year, tough to top after the tie of last year's teens! The Hunt is the first step in our children's journey to become warriors, to protect our land, and honor our people! Yesterday, we had our Victor. Katla Vistel felled an admirable beast, and we are all here again to see her through her reception as a true slayer of devils! Now, it was a mighty fine party last night, I'm sure you can all agree! But our Victor is deserving of one more honor! The Smiths finished the work this morning, after a cold bath, of course." There were scattered laughs. "I have the privilege of presenting our Victor with the blade forged from the tooth of her first beast!"

There were cheers on all sides of me.

I saw Calin whooping, and Eliana a little across the way, smiling hesitantly. One of the blacksmiths approached Ivon where he stood in the street, handed him a bundle wrapped in black cloth. He took it, and raised his eyes to me.

He didn't falter as I glared, but he didn't smile, either.

It was my signal to move, and so I walked closer to him until I was mere feet from his outstretched hands. He began again, the same as every year, substituting my name for the previous Victor's.

"Katla Vistel, for your bravery, determination, and skill displayed in the slaying of such a devil, you have brought pride upon yourself, your family, and your people. Lamid thanks you for your acts, and presents you with this gift."

The cloth fell away from the object in his hands.

A stunning blade laid there, not made of iron but of polished white bone. Curved and wicked sharp, cut and perfected, a dragon tooth stretched from the carved handle, wrapped in fine leather. Set in the hilt was a single red gemstone.

Simple and deadly beauty. Formed from my victory, the dragon I had slain. There were more cheers as the blade was revealed, but I simply watched the King.

Was this a joke to them? To hand me a symbol of unbridled pride in this blade, while they plan in secret to give me another which will strip it away? Is this what my honor means to them? They'd already helped themselves to the shreds of my dignity, and now, what, I was supposed to rebuild it? Starting with this dagger, and in their image, their favor.

No.

I would take it back. It was never and would never be theirs. My pride was mine alone, and they would not own it. I would not be tied to this life they chose for me. One way or another, my choices would be mine.

And as such, for only myself did I grasp the perfect handle as the applause rose.

***

Thus far, my aggravation had yielded me no solutions.

Short of murdering Leo, which, however appealing, wouldn't work in the long run, I had no plan. Sitting here with my ire in a quiet room wasn't doing me any good, either. My mother knew the cause of the closed door, and made no attempt to breach it.

I had no wish to travel downstairs and speak to her, but I needed to talk to someone.

I loved Eliana, but I didn't think I could handle her erratic attitude right now, even if it was momentarily watered down by concern. I couldn't go to Calin, he'd likely laugh, then slowly become frantic, and that certainly wouldn't help. I didn't need to entertain the laments of someone telling me how horrid my predicament was.

I opened my window slowly, cringing at the moaning hinges, but no footsteps sounded on the stairs.

I released a breath, looking out into Iona. Soon, I was crouching on the sill, perched on the ledge. I swung my legs over the side, arm muscles straining as I slowly lowered myself as close to the ground as was reachable.

When I could go no further, I pushed off with my hands, falling quickly. I bent my legs and tried to brace myself, but still cried out as I hit the earth, pain jolting through my bones as I lost my balance and fell onto my side.

I slapped a hand over my mouth to muffle the noise, but heard nothing from inside the house which gave any indication that I had been noticed. I stood, ignoring the throbbing in my ankle, and walked as fast as I dared through the streets, trying not to attract too much attention.

The path to the house was familiar, and I saw it soon. The walls were slightly larger, a sheep bleating around the back which spoke that the family inside had a fair bit of wealth.

I knocked loudly, raising my hand to do so again, when the door opened to reveal a young woman holding a restless child.

My sister looked rather similar to me; we were so often told. Her black hair pulled into twin braids at the back of her head that curled at the ends, one of which was currently being pulled on by my niece. The pale blue eyes were a reflection of mine. Her delicate face had hardened slightly with age, but she was beautiful, nevertheless.

It hadn't surprised me in the slightest when Fisk asked her to marry him.

"Kat? What are you doing here?" Her eyes took me in as I stood in the light spilling through the doorway.

"Ingrid." I greeted, trying to peer around, searching for my brother-in-law. "Is Fisk home?"

"No, he-"

"Great." I pushed past her.

I didn't turn around, just stalked over to the blazing hearth that lit the room and soaked in its warmth. Despite the summer season, the nights were cool.

"Katla?" She asked as she shut the door behind her, bouncing Ylva in her arms.

She raised an eyebrow, demanding an explanation. I sat on the edge of her kitchen bar, ignoring the disgruntlement on her face.

"I've been promised to Leo Evalade."

Happiness and annoyance lingered in her features, as if she was relieved to find me finally in a relationship, and peeved I had seemingly neglected to tell her about it. Then, she went abruptly blank, realizing the name attached. I watched on in relief, glad to finally unload.

"What the Hel, Katla? You're engaged to the prince?"

I didn't bother telling her that he wasn't the prince just yet. Nor did I mock her slip of impolite language before her daughter, as I usually would have done. One thing at a time.

"Eliana overheard a Council discussion this morning, eavesdropping, probably hoping to hear about preparations for the next party-"

"We just had a party," Ingrid reminded, as if it held any measure of importance.

"It's Eliana. She's always rearing and ready for the next one by the following morning. That's not the point. When I have spare time from training and chores, I usually spar in the seamstress's lot, with the hill beside it. Do you know what I'm talking about?"

"Yes, I've seen you a few times, you're- get off my table. You're really good."

"Apparently, I've had an audience. Then, I became a Hunt Victor. As far as the Council is concerned, that makes me monarch material, and the best choice to be Leo's...you know."

'Wife' tasted viciously sour in my mind, and I decided to abstain from using it.

Ingrid was quick to jump in with a solution that I had already brought to our mother's attention, to no avail.

"Why don't they send to the other islands? Ask for some princess who isn't the eldest to marry him? Lamid is one of the largest kingdom's in Voluspa, our forests are plentiful and our trade is adequate. Several rulers, and even the lower lords, should be jumping for an allyship. Ivon has kept us rather exclusive, only breaking bread with Briaedor, over the years."

"Mother says they tried. They delivered letters to all the non-hostile islands, especially those we aren't that friendly with, hoping that a marriage would at the very least strengthen relations. They all refused, Hel, Briaedor didn't even respond! Leo's options to marry are confined within the village, and they've decided my life would be a fine one to ruin."

"They chose you." She reiterated slowly, and I responded with a nod. "Wow. That's…"

"Insane? Shocking? Absolutely absurd?"

"Not shocking. I'm not surprised, if they had to choose from our own kingdom, they picked you. You would make a fine wife for any king, Katla, and I believe you could lead."

I watched her face with rising irritation as she appraised me like our mother had. Like she was imagining me standing nobly next to a king.

But Leo was no king.

"I never asked to lead! Please tell me you aren't actually on board with this? I can't marry him, Ingrid! I didn't come here for you to echo Mom, I hoped you could help me!"

The door opened again, and Ingrid's husband made his way into the house. He was a lean man, with close-shaved mousy blond hair, and a thin trail of stubble appearing on his chin. The thin dust of wood shavings was visible from here, settled on his shoulders and wiped on his pants. He was likely returning from the sawmill.

"Hello, Katla." He greeted, turning to kiss Ingrid, and then Ylva on her forehead. He didn't appear too upset at my presence in his home, but mildly curious.

"Fisk."

"Congratulations on your beast, by the way. What brought you here this late?"

He looked to Ingrid as he spoke, inviting an explanation.

"Katla is engaged. To Leo Evalade."

Fisk looked at Ingrid, who shrugged. "You're marrying the King's nephew?"

"Arranged. By the Council. Mother couldn't deny them." I forced out, still glaring at my sister.

93

He nodded along, and I remembered that his father was on the Council. Well, if Ingrid and my mother were useless...

"Because it's a royal marriage regarding the next in line for the throne." He surmised.

"So they say."

Ylva's squirming finally stilled, and Ingrid gestured with her head towards the upper level where her room lay. As she began to take to the stairs, she threw a meaningful look at her husband, and then disappeared.

The resulting silence wasn't necessarily awkward, but I hadn't made much conversation with my brother-in-law without my sister or mother. I wrapped my arms around my middle, looking at the floor, thoughts running aimlessly as I waited for Ingrid to return.

"Katla?"

Fisk pulled the short straw in regards to my patience.

"I don't know what to do. We weren't allowed a say in the contract. My own marriage contract! No say! I don't even know what it entails! And that's just it? I'm going to marry the biggest jerk on the island because a bunch of old men who don't know anything about my life have declared I must?"

I would realize only later than I had insulted his father, but he seemed to brush it off.

"There aren't many ways to get out of a marriage arranged by the Council, not just the royal ones. Before I married Ingrid, had the Council said, for whatever reason, that I was to marry someone else, I would've had to. It wouldn't have mattered if I was already courting her at the time. Seeing as this is a royal matter, your options are extremely limited."

"Thank you so much, Fisk. Welcome to the club of people who have come to the same conclusion."

"Well, you didn't let me finish." He crossed his arms. "Of course there are options."

I perked instantly, but didn't miss the glance he threw towards the stairs.

"Fisk." I said sharply, and sheepishly, he turned to look at me. "What can I do?"

"There are very few ways you can avoid it, and they aren't exactly ideas your sister would allow me to live for suggesting." His eyes darted again to the landing, from which Ingrid still had not returned. "The first would be to exile yourself from the kingdom, freeing you from any binding contracts, but also ensuring that you could never again step foot on the island.

He continued quickly as I sputtered. "If you wished to stay on the island, you could outright refuse to go through with any of it, such as not walking in the wedding ceremony, or even not showing up at all. But it would likely end with you thrown in a cell, no matter how old you are, on grounds of such severe disrespect."

"Do you have any solutions that don't end with me being outcasted or imprisoned?"

Fisk brushed the dust from his tunic nervously. "You could, in theory, earn a Pardon."

"A what?"

"If you were to accomplish something, something grand that would bring honor upon the village, you would be granted a Pardon, amongst the traditional gifts. The Council would have to judge your actions and come to a consensus. Do you remember a few years ago when Jo Felman killed the largest dragon anyone had seen in years? It had killed tens of people, and all we knew was that it was hiding somewhere in the rock. Einar believed he had tracked it to a chain of caves, and so he snuck in and managed to kill the thing, but he lost his arm in the process.

"When he brought its head back to the village we celebrated for days. At the end he was given an additional gift, a Pardon. He was able to allow anyone, himself or another, to be relieved of a judgement brought on them by law. He chose to free his sister, who had been imprisoned for stealing years prior. This contract is imposed on you by the law, so the same should apply. Hypothetically."

"If I accomplished something worthy enough..."

"You could earn a Pardon, and if you told them you wished to use it on yourself to annul your contract, they would have to allow you to do so." He sat down, seeming satisfied in his explanation, before he straightened. "But Katla, you-"

It was really the only option, since I didn't much fancy spending the remainder of my life in prison or banished.

I barely managed a "Thanks Fisk", before the door was open and I was once again racing out into the night, barely bothering to push the door closed behind me.

Surely, King Ivon would still be awake.

He was often one of the last up in the village, ensuring everything was in order. Always scanning the horizon, as if he could make the threats to his people's safety appear so that he could overcome them. I used to wonder when he slept.

It wasn't strange for people to converse casually with the king, very common in fact. I was not one of those people, always too nervous to waltz up to the ruler and hold a conversation.

Those nerves were present now, but dulled.

My course of action was necessary, and thus forth, any other concerns were bound and buried.

I wasn't sure what I would say to him, or how I would even go about it. He would have no reason to take me seriously, a sixteen-year-old girl asking for a hero's problem to solve. If there was something that needed doing, he'd definitely have taken it on himself, or set an accomplished warrior to do it.

I doubted he would be eager to tell me, anyway, if there existed an untaken quest.

It didn't take a genius to guess what I would do with the Pardon I suddenly longed for, less than two days after I had been promised against my will to his nephew.

It wasn't clear how long I ran through the cobblestone streets of Lamid, ignoring the growing ache in my legs as I refused to slow down.

Eventually, I spotted torchlight at the docks. The only people still out conversing at this hour were drunk. Or, they were the King dealing with exactly what I was looking for; a problem.

I found the edge of Estran, the village closest to the water, dirt turning to oak beneath my feet. I clambered my way down the wooden paths built into the ground as silently as I dared. Barely, I could make out a group of five warriors, two men and three women.

Three of them were bearing torches, bows slung over their backs. The other two were conversing with the man I sought. Their hands were flying, gesturing wildly as they explained something I was just fractionally creeping close enough to hear.

"-a big white one! It was just flyin' around out there, didn't even seem to notice us!" One of the men, Rolfe Oswell, shouted.

There was a large shape brought beside the boat which floated behind them, a carcass.

The trip was a success, then? I knew a few of the older group had been invited to a Hunt in Vanir, they had asked Ingrid to come along. Had they only now returned?

At the last moment, I decided not to make myself known, choosing instead to crouch in the darkness. Somewhere in the back of my mind I knew Eliana would be proud. The other man, James Ledon, began speaking over Rolfe.

"It was massive. Wingspan had to be 70 feet, at least!"

I contained a laugh. They were obviously telling of a dragon, but they had to be exaggerating. There was no way they'd spotted a dragon that big on a run of the mill sailing excursion.

I wondered how long Ivon would entertain it.

"We pulled our bows to drag the thing out of the sky, but we heard a voice!" That was Sarah Siv now, astonished resolve splashed across her dark face. She was about my sister's age.

"A voice?" Ivon sighed. It looked as though he was beginning to doubt their story. I was surprised he hadn't sooner.

"At first, we thought the beast had stolen a sailor, maybe to finish them off in its nest or something, you know? But it wasn't carrying anything in its claws." Sarah explained.

James cut in, "We started to think we had imagined it, when we heard it again! It turned to the side and-"

"And there was a person riding it!"

The only response was the gentle rocking of boats tethered to the docks, bouncing on the water.

I gaped at the men, for there was no way their tale was true. The very idea was preposterous, that someone would sink so low as to ride the beasts from Hel's own domain.

One word, impossibly loud against the veil of night and bordering on rage cut through the quiet.

"What?"

All of them took a noticeable step back from the king, and despite my near invisible position, I shrunk back against the planks, eyes wide.

"It's true! We released our arrows of course, but the helspawn avoided them. The person shouted, and the behemoth flew away as we fired a second wave." Sara was quieter this time.

I had never heard the king yell in such a way before, and I didn't know how to feel about it.

On the one hand, it was a perfectly reasonable way to react to being told that there was someone out there *riding* a dragon. It couldn't be possible, so it would be ridiculous to even waste time thinking about it. That had to be why he was angry, because their joke was made in such poor taste.

I watched around a corner as they all began speaking over each other.

"I know what I saw! I'm telling you sir, there was someone on that dragon!" Thora Hawthorne insisted, pressing her torch into another's hand so that she could step closer to the king.

"Whoever it was, they yelled at it once we started shooting. Told the damn thing to go! And it listened to them! Shot straight off, didn't even bother with killing us!"

"Or maybe it was just aware enough to move when arrows tried to bring it to the waves? I told you, I've been telling you all, this whole idea is inane, we don't even know-"

"Oh, shut it. We all heard it, and most all saw it!"

"This is a treachery worthy of the Sigurd, do you think it could be them, Your Majesty?"

"Well, they're the only ones screwed enough in the head to even think of such a thing. Probably get on great with the scaly devils, devouring women and children." James raised, and Thora smacked his arm.

"There was clearly something on its back. Something that spoke well enough for us to hear, and it definitely wasn't trying to help *us* out." Thora implored.

The King waited for them to quiet. "I will call the Councilmen. We will discuss this further. We cannot chance Olavi Sture attempting to meddle where men should never, it would spell nothing good for anyone in Voluspa. A person who consorts with the likes of those beasts is a foe not to be taken lightly." His voice dropped, barely a harsh whisper. "Go to your homes. Tell no one of this, of what you saw, suspect or believe. Return to your families, and think no more on Sture or his doings for tonight. If what you say is true, and there is any chance he is behind this, it will soon be taking up most of our thoughts."

It could not be written off as imagined, for five people stood there perfectly sober, all insisting what they had seen.

It sounded like a story passed between children in the dark. The very notion made my skin feel as though it was squirming on my bones, news that somewhere out there existed a person with power over the demons. Horrifying to think of the destruction that could be caused by someone like that.

A plan made itself known, half-thought out in my mind, but a plan all the same.

I crawled to a jog back the way I had come as noiselessly as I could manage, trying to stay out of the sight of the footsteps that began to follow me unknowingly. I darted off in the opposite direction of the path I knew they would take, towards the castle elevated above, to wake the council members, undoubtedly.

I finally reached my house, sending wordless gratitude to Thor as the door opened without a sound.

There was muted ruffling from inside my mother's room. In the next instant I had thrown myself up the stairs before she could enter the main hall and find me in the doorway.

I stuffed a few stray possessions into a woven bag, a spare outfit, a thicker belt. I stashed my new dagger at my waist, alongside the older one of simple iron. I added the blanket from off my bed, folding it and shoving it in alongside the rest. The basket I used already held the food I had purchased at the market this morning, and I assumed Eliana had placed it here and left it for me while I was gone.

Odin knew I was grateful for it now.

I wondered absently if she had climbed in my window to avoid my mother. I donned the leather armor, clasping it around my chest and on my shoulders, rearranging the fur which covered my back.

My sword still waited in its leather scabbard on my hip. I tore a spare piece of parchment from my unused desk, hastily scribbling a note to my mother. I left it to lay on my now empty bed, a vague apology and empty reassurances.

My movements were hazy, driven by some unbounded need to follow the one thread of possible promise.

The docks were vacant when I came upon them again.

Only the gods and the moon watched on. The latter was enough for me to see my own movements as I untied the rope tethering the boat the hunters had arrived on to a post.

I jumped inside, unraveling the sail. A breeze rushed past me a moment later, forcing the cloth to smooth out into its full shape.

The wind wasn't at an overwhelming strength, but as I began moving away from the port, I knew it would carry me just fast enough. None would catch up, once they realized I was gone.

I turned away from the isle of Lamid to face the open sea, excited and nervous. I did not allow myself to dwell on my own actions, for fear I would lose my resolve, and spin the sails back.

After all, taking down a traitor of humans, a newly declared enemy of Lamid, and a friend of devils seemed a rather decent way to be granted a Pardon to me.

CHAPTER SIX

AIDAN

There shouldn't have been anything unusual about the raid.

Fafnir and I were a speck of white against the clear blue sky. About twenty dragons followed behind us, a spray of color stemming out from the ivory at the flock's head.

Soon enough, Sigurd ships became apparent in the water far beneath.

There were less boats than they had travelled with before. Granted, the fleet was still fairly large, but noticeably smaller than it had been a days prior when we had freed the Briaedorians.

Ragna stood tall and at the ready a few dragons over, riding on the back of a jade scaled female. We hadn't received the wrath of Freyja when we returned home, only more of the same resigned pleading for us to leave well enough alone.

I speculated that the only reason Fafnir and I were allowed to fly with the offensive now, is because there were no human prisoners held in this armada.

As there were none who didn't carry fireproof scales captured, there was no need for a stealthy entrance.

Fafnir angled downward, and I struggled not to whoop at the feeling of my stomach in my throat. I didn't have to turn to know the others were doing the same. By the time the shouts of warriors reached us, we were already upon them.

Fire fell against the wooden ships quicker than their arrows could flee the strung sinew, flickering flames raining from above. Dragons were freed, some leaving and some staying. Men and women were tossed overboard and left floating in the ocean.

Again, there shouldn't have been anything out of the ordinary.

It was routine, the same one we'd followed for six years. Fafnir flew in close to cover a ship's wall with his fiery breath. His wings pulled close to his body as we rolled in the air to avoid a spear that had been thrown, joining four arrows in the quest for one large white dragon. They splashed harmlessly into the water below, but we were already flying upwards again.

I cheered to the sky as we leveled out.

Ragna cut by, pressed against wings and fire. I looked out over the burning ships on the water, white wings lifting in and out of my vision as Fafnir kept us in the air. The attack was already nearly over, only a few dragons hovered over boats, attempting to break out those still trapped.

A small red Muspel floated up beside us on the wind, Ragna smiling from their back.

"Afternoon, Ragna. Seems a fine day to send some Sigurd running scared. If the sails weren't so ugly, I might've thought it was a fishing trip, rather than all Olavi can scrape together."

She laughed lightly as she matched our flight.

"Ah, they were a cowering lot. You'd think they didn't know the sharp end of their swords!" She waved her arm, looking out over the flotsam. "Serves them right. All the dragons they've taken, the eggs they've orphaned, those they've hurt." I nodded quietly as Ragna turned away from the sea to face us, her eyes softened. "You did well today, Aidan. You too, Fafnir. Your mother would be very proud, just as I am."

"Thanks, Ragna."

Even though she was always on our tails about one thing or another, she was still one of the women who raised me, the only human person I still had. Her care was evident, even if her rules were ridiculous and rooted in decades old fear.

Dragons were flocking into the sky, some from home, others newly rescued. Many chirped at us as they flew over our heads, in confusion and gratitude, plentiful excitement. Most began to fly back to the Bay, a few of those recently freed following.

I smiled at a small pack of amber Kaida who swarmed over each other in an elated reunion. They halted their movements when they noticed me watching, growing cautious, smoke leaking from their jaws as they gathered flame.

Hello. I tried, and the reaction was immediate.

Now I was the one being swarmed over, small paws finding purchase on my head and across my shoulders. Trilling filled my ears, their enthusiasm filling my mind with wordless exclamations. My arms moved calmly as I amusedly attempted to remove them. One sat in between Fafnir's eyes, and he growled threateningly, snapping his teeth together with a grating click.

They squeaked in pinched terror, before taking to the air, the rest fleeing after them and away from Fafnir.

Pests. He hissed. *Bloody bunch of nuisances. Which of your strange gods chose to give rats our wings?*

Likely the very same who crafted your stellar personality.

"Come on, then." Ragna chided. "We'd best be getting back. The

109

Mothers would likely enjoy some help in the Roost."

I heard only half her words. There was a small fishing boat in the water a few hundred feet away, a clean sail that definitely didn't belong with the Sigurd fleet.

Fafnir. He shifted, but offered no comment. *That isn't one of Olavi's. Is it the same boat? The ones who…*

He cut me off with a snarl, as if I would have been able to continue, anyway.

Almost bow to bow with the smaller vessel was a Sigurd ship. Anger flooded my veins, the opposite boat from before no doubt still carried the lingering presence of death.

Now, the ship was fraternizing with the Sigurd.

I knew better than to assume myself to be the Voluspian Isles' primary source of gossip, but even then, I had foolishly believed even citizens of the Kingdom's were above associating with Olavi's delegation.

Ragna had not yet realized the subject of our scrutiny, nor was she aware of the previous encounter we shared with it.

"We'll meet you there." I shot for normalcy. "There's still a few more ships on the water, and I've been needing some more books."

Ragna scowled disapprovingly. "Aidan, you have a tremendous accumulation of journals-"

"I read them all." She raised an eyebrow as I shrugged. "Even the volumes on architecture you brought from the wreckage outside the Kingdom of Hestaval. I doubt the Sigurd concern themselves with mathematics, right? Maybe I can find something a bit more interesting in their cabins."

I didn't trust myself to speak through the Bond, for the same reason Fafnir remained silent. Neither of us was prepared to fend off Ragna's searching, if she chose to delve past our words. She was far too adept at reading the truth of your mind.

"Alright, but don't take too long." She warned, and her voice increased in volume as we began to turn. "Aidan! Not too many, unless you plan to clear away those sculptures of dusty leather and parchment you've left lying about!"

We were pulling towards the boat before she was out of sight.

Who would be on board? Fishermen, warriors, merchants? A guard from one of the nearby Kingdoms, attempting to ally with Olavi?

We were a short way west of Briaedor, and it seemed an odd meeting place. I didn't immediately see anyone, but my expectations soon fell flat. Instead of the crew I had expected to be on a boat of its size, I saw a girl. A scream sounded for half of a second, pained.

She was lying on the deck with one arm clutching at her head as she held herself up with a shaking hand. A sword lay a few feet away from her, and she tried to lunge for the weapon before it was cruelly kicked away.

Three Sigurd had come onto the deck, their broad figures crowding around the girl on the ground. We weren't even a quarter of a league away when they finally heard our wingbeats, which had to have been clear for a while now, the morons.

They spun around, and I enjoyed the way the disgusting smirks dropped off their faces. Vibrant red dripped from numerous gashes decorating their faces and arms, the small wounds leaking in such abundance that they nearly covered the tattoos they bore; dense borders encircling their right forearm.

At least the girl gave it to them.

The only one with half a brain and a bit more cowardice in the group decided to jump over the edge right then and there.

The others attempted to draw their weapons, one of the men grabbing the sword which lay next to the girl, struggling to wield two weapons. I doubted he even knew how to use the sword with his left, obvious due to how he fumbled it clumsily in his hand. Fafnir roared, stretching to be directly in their faces. Even I was glad to be on the other side.

Weapons fell in their haste to cover their ears.

I tightened my grip on Fafnir's neck as he shoved his head forward, cutting off his roar and striking one of the men. The water below us was fanning out in ripples, being pushed away by the force of air under Fafnir's wings.

He turned in a half circle, swinging his right wing around to knock the other man from the boat.

The girl still lay in the same spot, no longer upright. She was still on the planks, eyes closed. She couldn't have been one of the boat's original passengers, one who had shot at us.

Fafnir's massive nostrils wrinkled, but reacted with little more. The smell of this girl was less volatile than the other humans had been. Fafnir's senses, and thus my own, were screaming to attack, to defend. Ourselves, each other, the rest of the flock above.

I slid down his wing, hesitating, my eyes locked on the person below. I rolled my shoulders, waiting to feel the familiar weight of the sword on my back before moving again, leaving the asylum of winged membrane.

Tentatively, I set down on a boat of the Voluspian Kingdoms.

Careful! You've gone close enough. There is blood on her skin. Wood whined behind me, Fafnir landing on the large boat beside the one I occupied.

He was rigid, moving when I did, honed on the figure.

Despite the affiliation of this vessel, I felt a thrill run through me, equal parts cautious excitement and adrenaline. A feeling which seemed alive and ravenous in the pit of my stomach, locking my legs and yet itching to flee.

I was on a Kingdom boat.

Which Kingdom did it come from? What was her name? What was she doing here? She was a swordsman, it appeared. Was it customary of all Kingdom citizens to bear swords, or was it a random happenstance? Was there meaning to be found in the braids of her hair, or could it be simple preference? How did-

Aidan! His tail curled nearer, eager to snatch me away. *Get back!*

"She isn't awake. They're harmless like this."

Clearly your knowledge of humans is misguided. You're harmless all the time, not just while you sleep.

Shut up.

I looked back at the girl, lowering instinctively, my hand twitching towards the hilt of my sword. Her raven hair was spiraled in waves beneath her form, two thin pieces pulled away from her face and tied behind her head.

A small white pelt hung around her shoulders, curving down to the small of her back and then up again. She wore a shirt of deep blue covering her shoulders where the fur was settled, and down on to her wrists.

Most of her tunic was covered by her leather cuirass, guarding her front and back. The straps of the soft armor held the white fur in place. Bracers of the same leather were wrapped around her lower arms, beginning a few inches down from her elbows, continuing to her fingers. Brown leggings ended in worn boots of a much darker brown.

I leaned back, unsure.

I say we leave her. Fafnir's voice made me jump.

I almost seconded, but a hundred buried questions had unearthed themselves in light of this new hope.

This was my opportunity, right here. A tangible possibility for answers Takka and Ragna could not give. To know another who was born like me.

Of course, these were not the reasons I gave Fafnir, though I suspected he knew of the true ones, regardless.

"Fafnir, she's hurt."

And how do you find this concerns us? She'll wake eventually, and then she can sail back to wherever she came from.

"And if she weren't to wake? What will you say then? If we left an injured girl on a boat to freeze in the night?"

Good riddance, is actually what I would say. To the letter. The human will be fine.

115

"She was fighting them. That counts for something."

She also reeks of death.

He pushed upon me the smell through his senses, causing my eyes to water.

It was fainter than the previous occupants had been, but nature's warning was there, all the same. My fingers found the worn leather of the simple sword, but did not pull it free.

Knock it off. I hissed, and he conceded.

Righting myself, my gaze landed upward.

One of the massive beams which would usually sit tethered to the sail was hanging loosely, facing away from the remaining wooden supports. The sail was likewise twisted, no longer taunt. I could see a dark pattern on the fabric which faced us, but the sigil was rumpled and turned away.

A tattered mess of slackened ropes hung limply from the displaced beam, once firmly connected to the sail.

"The rigging is ruined." I reasoned, and Fafnir's head swung. "This boat won't be seaworthy, and she's the only one on board. What if she can't mend it? She'll be stranded out here."

There were still plenty of Sigurd in the surrounding water.

As soon as we departed, they would undoubtably swim to the few remaining boats. It didn't seem as though she would wake before they tried to board, and they had been fighting earlier.

Would they try to hurt her when they returned? Surely, her temporary helplessness would not result in their inaction. We couldn't leave a boat out here for them to take, anyway.

It needed to be sunk, rather than allow the chance of the Sigurd pulling together a rowing team.

I'd rather a detailed report of events not make it back to Olavi, although it would likely turn him a shade of red I was disappointed to be missing. Besides, he could figure it out himself, when the armada never made it to wherever on Midgard it was going, on a path to do gods knew what.

I didn't keep the errant thoughts to myself, sharing each notion with Fafnir. Although he was mostly silent, he did not disagree.

The sky was almost entirely devoid of dragons now, but I noticed a small group of Muspel and a few Syre flying overhead. They grumbled questioningly.

Coming, Hatchling? The battle is finished, leave the human ruins and return home! A Muspel shouted down.

Just a second! I called.

They waited above, ready to tear into the fragments of the ship once we

117

left it. Fafnir shifted uneasily, unfurling his wings and drawing them back in. There was disgruntled shouting from the water, curses to the gods and the dragons, me.

I eyed the broken beam again, the ruined sail. The girl was deathly unstirring on the wood.

"What if this is our chance?"

Our chance to what, exactly? Be killed in our sleep by a human? No, thank you.

"No, no listen. If we help her, if we explain what happened, maybe she could help us!"

Fafnir snorted, his voice heavy with sarcasm. *And how do you think she is going to do that?*

"If she knows we saved her, she won't be afraid. Then we can tell her everything! When she goes back to wherever she came from, she can tell them, too. The people won't have to be scared of us anymore. We could work together against Olavi. We just need them to give us a chance. She could be our chance." I exclaimed excitedly.

Fafnir only stared, large eyes half-lidded. *That is the single most inane thing I have ever heard from your mouth. And what about Ragna? If you bring a human into the Bay, we'll be meeting your 'Odin' sooner than*

we planned. Besides, you alone are a human too many.

I shook my head. "It can work! We know it can work, because it worked for me. For Mom." Fafnir stopped at that, some sort of dim realization overtaking his thoughts and leaving me nothing to hear. "And even still, we can't simply leave her here. She'll be stuck in the ocean surrounded by angry Sigurd. We can't allow them this boat, and we aren't going to feed it to the sea with her on it. Come on, Fafnir."

Fafnir exhaled, heavy and slow. Smoke poured from his nostrils as he groaned, and I knew I had won before he even spoke.

When, and I do mean when, he began, *the human tries to kill us all, I* will *let her have you first. And I will laugh with my deepest satisfaction at your idiotic and pointless demise.*

I hoped he could hear the smirk in my voice. *I would never expect anything less, you pretentious scaly kitten.*

I will kill you for her. I will.

Nonetheless, he extended his wing across the two walls as a makeshift bridge. Slowly, I neared the girl on the ground, debating throwing the whole plan into the wind with every step closer.

Steeling myself, I lifted the girl into my arms with an arm under her knees and one behind her back. I stood carefully, the weight foreign in my hold, ebony hair pressed against my chest.

I struggled to step onto Fafnir's wing, and then to maintain my standing position as I crossed with the added load in my arms.

I wonder how nice the quiet will be after this plan ends terribly and you are forcibly removed from life. Fafnir snarked as he took off, but it was the underlying worry in his sass that kept me from snapping back. *Of course, this human will likely get to you even if Ragna fails.*

I had to squeeze my legs almost painfully to keep from falling, my arms full and tipping my body out of balance. He was gifted no answer as we caught up with the others.

They were curious about the new human, to put it mildly.

They flew extremely close, much to Fafnir's chagrin, and I had to listen to his grumblings and complaints. Several of them nudged his wings or bumped him from behind, trying to see the new person. Each of them recoiled as they caught the scent that Fafnir had earlier. I cringed away as well at the knowledge of its presence, even if Fafnir was no longer forcing me to bear the smell.

Dragon blood.

They didn't react violently, though I knew they longed to, trusting me that much. The group branched off as we neared the island which housed the Bay, home.

Fafnir withdrew his wings, making himself more maneuverable.

Sea stacks littered the ocean before the Bay, crumbling monuments draped in moss. The thicker ones fortified the front, thinning the deeper they went, a maze of rock. Plants clung to the sides, some sporting small trees which held to the pillars, roots climbing up and sticking themselves in the stone.

If one looked close enough, the small holes in the stacks deepened into tunnels, Kaida nesting inside.

We ducked under the massive arch which had fallen sideways, wedging itself between the ocean floor and the side of the isle. Fafnir cut low across the water in order to pass through, the chirping of welcoming Amphitrite below his claws.

Darting beneath the fallen stone, we turned our eyes upon what the previous formations of rock all served to hide.

Sea water poured into the space, Amphitrite swimming close to the surface, chattering amongst themselves. Their mental voices grew with the sounds of greeting when they realized our entrance. The water filled only a small portion of the massive cave opening which spanned under the island.

The room was bright despite the lack of sunlight, the source of the glow coming from above. Calor crawled across the ceiling, their ashen bodies shimmering in the light they emanated.

They were about the size of the Kaida, slightly larger in their horns and ridged backs.

In the formed tunnels that lined the walls, several Syre and Muspel laid. Some entered the holes which exited in varying places around the island. A few flocked towards the high ceiling, or outside, but we did not join them.

We headed for our own small cave; a room nestled in the stony wall.

I dismounted much more cautiously than I had ever bothered to before, once Fafnir landed. He eyed me warily as I walked inside, still carrying the strange girl of the Kingdoms.

I looked around, unsure, before I finally headed towards my own bed. A pile of Kaida lay bunched together on its surface.

"Fafnir." I called, gesturing towards them with my leg.

Are you serious?

Of course, forgive me. Fafnir, my dearest brother, would you kindly get off your lizard-

He sulked, and I smirked.

I had expected him to growl, or attempt to wake them. Fafnir had another idea in mind, lowering his snout behind them. In one swift motion, he unceremoniously shoved the living pile to the floor.

All at once they woke, vicious and sleepy. They jumped to their feet, squeaking angrily as they tried to detangle themselves. He watched them for a moment, as deadpan as a dragon could be, before trotting off.

A few of the Kaida rubbed against my legs affectionately as I stepped closer to the bed. I did my best not to trip over them, as I couldn't see my own boots. A particularly playful pair tried to climb up my sides, sniffing curiously at the girl in my arms.

I felt a cool stinging sensation in my left leg, and shook it.

"Hey! No claws! Come on." I laughed. *Get down!*

The offender wasn't rattled by my attempts to remove it, but the talons retracted nonetheless.

One I couldn't see, but could certainly feel, pulled my sword from the sheath, dropping it to the ground when the weight proved too much. It clattered against the stone, the steel bouncing before it stilled.

Bending down, I carefully deposited the girl on the furs.

I let out a breath, the mockery practically tangible from Fafnir lazing on the outcrop. His tail hung over the edge, swaying as he watched the water beneath.

It was too easy to change my stance to one more animalistic, the noise torn from my actions. I stalked out of the room, skating around still disgruntled Kaida and stray books, and leapt upon his neck.

He reared back, making a rather undignified noise he would vehemently deny later.

Aidan! Don't do *that!* He yelled.

Fafnir stood tall, shaking himself and nearly throwing me from my place in the process.

"Hey!"

I rolled down his side, depositing myself in a heap on the ground. I shoved at his wing from my spot, but only succeeded in drawing out a guffaw.

My gaze found the edge of the water opposite us, where firelight flickered on the walls, emerging from a sunken space. Hopefully, Ragna would be preoccupied in the Roost for at least a few more hours.

Fafnir straightened, prodding me with his tail. *What are you going to say when the human wakes?*

*I'm not sure...*I trailed off, moving to stand.

Now wasn't the best time to rethink my plan, but I was quickly realizing this was as far as my rash choice led me.

Well, you might want to figure it out. He tensed, his large head turning. *Invent something eloquent. And also, turn around.*

I spun, and had less than a second to register pale blue eyes before a blade swung for my head.

CHAPTER SEVEN

KATLA

Doubt had begun to creep up in tandem with the sun. What was I thinking? I had stolen a boat!

My mother was going to forgo her sanity, and if I ever managed to make it back, I would be grounded for the rest of my days.

If.

I may not come back. It had been so simple upon conception in my mind. I would find this creature and end it. The Royal Council would be forced to let me out of the contract. I'd be granted a Pardon, and hopefully there would be enough mutual relief going around for my mother to forgive me.

Now, all too late, I was realizing what I had gotten myself into.

I was searching for a person who could control dragons. Someone who used them as boats to chart across the sky where men did not belong. What if they weren't even human? What humane being would align themselves with those beasts?

Paintings of a demon man atop a winged devil filled my brain, and I was becoming increasingly less confident in my own idea.

Now, with nothing around me but vast sea, I was left with the shreds of a plan to follow.

I had scoured the ship for some log of its travels. I'd discovered one in the small cabin, and with it the path of the most recent hunting trip to Vanir. I had a vague idea of how to get to where the boat took its last trip, but I knew I should have taken Calin up on his offerings to teach me sailing.

The first sign I was in over my head appeared in the form of ships.

Just shadows, colorless shapes in the distance. Nearing. I had been so worried about the threats I would encounter when I found the Man of Dragons, there hadn't been room to worry about possible dangers I would find on the open water.

I hadn't been looking ahead, too busy pulling on the ropes and trying to realign the boat correctly, rather sure I was moving too far north. When I finally noticed the ships, they were close, and they had certainly already noticed me.

My movements halted in paralyzing fear as I recognized the insignias on the sails.

A snake caressed the striking tip of an arrow cracked in two on paint and cloth.

It was almost painful when I suddenly regained movement. As if I had been struck by Thor himself, I hurled myself across the deck. I knew it was pointless, the ships were already too close, and could move far faster than I.

And there were so very many of them. A small fleet may as well have been a boasting armada to a recreational hunting boat.

"No, no no no." I whispered as I ran, willing the boat to reverse against the wind that pushed it ever closer to the looming vessels.

The ships plowed forward as I tried in vain to change the direction of my own. I could hear their words now, faint, but growing louder as they drew in.

Gods, how could I have been so stupid?

They were only ten feet away now. The sail would not turn.

My borrowed boat trembled violently as it was slammed against, spinning to the side, and I was thrown into the air. Wood scraped at my skin when I landed. I looked up, pushing my hair out of my face, and saw that one of the largest ships had collided with mine.

The men aboard were laughing rambunctiously, and I caught the distinct scent of alcohol on the sea air as they leaned over the side.

"Sorry about that, miss!" One of them called with false politeness, his large friends laughing loudly behind him as if it was the best thing they'd heard all day.

My right hand lifted at a snail's pace to grip the hilt of my sword. I appraised them, waiting. If I hadn't already guessed at their identities, it was confirmed by their tattoos.

Three thick bands in fading ink wrapped around their meaty arms, the inner elbow, likely having been there since they were very young.

The bands were given to Sigurd clansmen when they took their first life on the battlefield. Here I had believed Eliana was only trying to scare me with her sleepover stories of Sigurd customs.

They were all larger than I, shining halberds strapped to their sides. Pointed spear tips joined with axe heads, nasty pieces of work I didn't particularly look forward to dodging. If only to myself, I thanked Calin for all the times he offered to spar with me, his weapon of choice being the same. There was one with a sword.

I cringed slightly at the sight of hair on all their faces, scraggly and unkept. Their beards were long and tangled, pieces of food visible from even here. One of them scratched at their chin, dislodging crumbs that were swept away by the wind. I was sure hundreds of lice had just lost their lives.

He stepped onto the side and pulled himself up, another copied. The two of them jumped.

I narrowed my eyes as their feet hit my deck. The last man followed their example, boarding behind them a few seconds later. They smiled with false sympathy, smiles that felt for the lost girl on her little boat.

Smiles that did not match the sultry look in their eyes.

I recognized it as a much worse reflection of Leo any time a girl walked by, only he would never dare act on it past some poorly initiated flirting. The Sigurd were practically defined by barbaric tendencies of every sort.

It was well known that they did not have the limitations Leo did when it came to young women. The look in their eyes was a promise, but of my glare, I knew the same. An almost hysterical laughter fought to make its way from my throat.

They would die today.

I tightened my fingers, finally pulling my sword loose and holding the leading edge out before me.

"Oh, come on." The bald one spoke. "This is how you treat those who are trying to help you?"

"Where do you sail from, huh? Don't tell me you're one of those pretty Hestaval girls? Heading for a party, perhaps?" This one's left eyebrow was scared off.

"Oh, Odin, please bless it so! Imagine the things she must have in the cabin! Combs, jewels...could there be regalia? Are you a noble, honey?" A sword sat in the belt of the final Sigurd who had stepped upon the Lamidian ship.

I scoffed, and Eyebrow laughed as he swayed, clearly afflicted by ale. He fought to correct the insinuation of his comrade. "Not that it matters, of course. Status means nothing to me, sweetheart. I'll not turn away even a poor man's daughter."

Their eyes raked over me shamelessly.

My boot shifted backwards, and I lowered, knees bending. I'd have to worry about the others on their ship after, but that problem was for later. This one was standing in front of me in the form of slurred words and uneven smirks.

Would a halberd be more of a menace under a swift hand, or a drunken one?

The muscle of my calf spasmed. I didn't breathe. Whether with intent or not, Baldy placed a foot closer.

Eyebrow barely had time to bring up the handle of his weapon to block a swing which would have cleaved through him.

I withdrew my blade and leapt backwards as if to fade away, but only charged forward again. He was unprepared, and my sword sliced a cut on his arm. I jumped to the side as another's halberd aimed to run me through.

As Eyebrow repositioned himself, the one with the sword took a chance. I deflected his blade with my own, a grating screech defining the contact. I spun as he stepped back, my sword swinging out to the side. Baldy fell gracelessly to the ground in order to avoid it.

I pivoted back, ducking to avoid an axe head swipe whose wielder was still standing. My blade went for his foot. The force of it sent him sprawling to the ground where he landed comically on top of his fellow clansmen, trying to pick himself back up.

Panicked shouts started from the other boats, and smoke was beginning to rise in the distance.

I had little time to wonder at its source, there was still one man standing. Only the swordsman remained, and we launched at each other.

He was more skilled than his friends had been, but I could block his weapon far better than theirs. It soon became obvious who was more skilled with a blade. I was quicker than he, and my iron left several marks upon him, but he always fell away before I could go deeper.

Despite this, there was no question. I would win this.

We were near the mast when he directed his cut upward, a cheap shot for my throat. I bent head over ankles, my body arching as I maneuvered to avoid it.

His sword buried itself in the mast, slicing through the rigging. Creaking filled my ears as a wooden support of the sail came loose. Now only partly tethered to the fabric, it fell vertically, flying towards me as it was pulled by its still attached side.

It was a missed shot; he couldn't even claim he had done it on purpose. Yet he still smiled after, like he had it all planned out.

There wasn't any time to get out of the way entirely, but I jumped anyway. The thick pole met my chest, and I was thrown into the wall of my boat.

Pain exploded in my head, dimming that in my shoulder which took the brunt of my next impact. I saw black at the edges of my vision and tried to blink through it, but the reflexive tears rapidly forming in my eyes made it impossible. The boat was barely rocking on the water, but every shift gave life to throbbing.

I'd had a concussion before, sure.

The first time Eliana convinced me to sneak out and meet up with Gunnar Haldor when we were fourteen.

I tried to jump from my window, something I was now much better at, and my foot slipped as I landed, my head crashing into the earth. The pain had been terrible, but it didn't compare to this.

My skull felt as if it was being rattled from the inside with every shaking breath that exited my lips in a wheeze. The two on the ground had now stood, coming to rest beside their swordsman friend who looked all too pleased with himself.

To the credit of my un-focusing eyes, I couldn't read too much into his expression when the world was so blurry.

I reached for my sword, and bit my lip as it pulled on my bruised chest. They laughed as I struggled for the pommel I could not reach. Baldy came towards me, sunlight reflecting off his pale head. He drew back his foot, and my father's sword was thrown away. He tightened again.

The blow came too quick, and I was too slow, for it to be avoided.

He drove a kick into my middle, flipping me over, and I screamed.

I gasped at the pain, my own breathing laboring harshly in my ears and almost drowning out their chuckling.

The spots in my eyes grew, I was seeing more black than color. I wasn't sure where my sword had gone. Each breath was more painful than the last.

With the fleeing fight in my body I tried to get up, my palm pressed to my temple, for all the good that it did. My last waking thoughts were to Odin, as I prayed he saw my death worthy of Valhalla.

***

An aching throb as I took a breath was my first sensation, but my eyes remained closed.

Only when the twinge continued to grow until it was bordering on pounding did I open them, desperate to find the source of the pain that had seemingly overtaken my body. An unfamiliar ceiling of stone greeted me, laden with grooves and poking edges.

I felt something on my chest, a weight, and looked down.

A small brown reptile with stubby black horns laid inches from my face. Its stomach splayed across my own. A spined tail curled around towards my head, and its own head lay by my feet.

The reptile had wings. The reptile was a dragon.

I steeled myself, and then flung to the side, dislodging us both. Its eyes shot open, the pupils thin slits which slowly began to dilate as it calmed.

I can't say I did the same. I pushed backward in horror, groaning when the pain consequently rose. The dragon jumped and shook itself, and without so much as a backward glance flew towards the light that spilled from an opening.

I was lying on a bed, atop a pile of mismatched furs, looking as though they had come from a variety of different animals. A desk sat to my right, absolutely covered in journals which were open to charcoal covered pages and loose parchment. The sketches were of dragons in flight, so realistic I would have been amazed, had it not been beasts that were depicted.

What appeared to be a table set was stationed in the middle of what I supposed was a room. The wooden table was small and circular, three different chairs around it, one tall and stiff, the other two short and made of different wood. Books littered every available surface, taking refuge in piles on the floor, stacked on and under the chairs.

My breath caught when I realized tiny mouse-sized and winged splashes of color lounged on the volumes.

They dozed on the covers and scrambled up the sides, each book a new foothold for their claws, yet the leather remained unblemished.

A counter of pine and stone was placed against the far wall, looking suspiciously like salvaged bits of a boat. It held jars of varying sizes, and impossibly, several more clumsily stacked books. The small bed was shoved in one corner, a similar one mirroring it on the opposite wall.

A large map, detailing all of Voluspa, hung on the same wall, further down. It was covered in markings, x's and circles. I could see the scribbles of words, but could not make them out.

Bizarrely, I noticed as I turned my head, there was a steering wheel from a ship nailed into a crack in the stone, hanging just above the bed I found myself on. More pages torn from sketchbooks filled the corner.

What on Midgard?

Attempting to take it all in, I deciphered the pounding sensation coming from my head, a dull throb in my chest.

The eyes of the Sigurd men presented themselves before my vision, and my heart fought to sustain the shocks my mind was supplying. There wasn't anyone else in the room.

Something darted in my peripheral, there and then gone.

Throwing one last wary glance towards the small bird-like dragons, I stepped carefully away. There was no use in senselessly attacking now, and I didn't want to bring an entire pack of them on myself.

I brought my gaze from the cave interior to the area it opened up to. I stood slowly, the blinding pain all but forgotten in light of what my eyes fell upon. Taking unsteady steps, I approached the sight which lay before me, uncomprehending.

My mouth hung open, arms limp at my sides.

All directions were enclosed in rock, dotted with green, moss and vines crawling on the walls. Colors, all around, darting in all directions like an airborne frenzy, flying.

Dragons were *everywhere.*

In every crevice, appearing from every tunnel, flocking through the empty air. Many that zipped around were the size of the one that had laid on the bed, not bigger than my own body. Those were the smaller ones, no larger than a common bird, which flew close together, twisting and turning like schools of fish.

Others, well, if I thought my Hunt prize was large.

Winged menaces greater than buildings roamed the space, circling the air. They moved slower, their movements sharper and more defined. The sounds of beating wings filled the area, squawking and muted roars. They were all vibrant colors, in all shades of each, and I noticed a few that were blacker than night.

It was fascinating.

It was terrible.

They looked different, up there. Less horrifying, less blood thirsty than their kind ought to be. They grumbled and chirped at each other as they passed, all living and thriving together in this giant space.

I spotted a figure on the wall, staring at me. The almost glowing nature of its sick green scales told me it possessed the ability to spray acid. It was close enough to do so now.

I watched it with mounting terror, waiting for the moment when it would cry to its kin and alert them to my presence, and then the creatures would deliver onto me my death. However, as I stood there staring at this fiend that stared back at me, the moment did not come. It simply shifted away from me, leaping from the wall to join the masses.

It was beautiful, and it was wrong.

Why had it not killed me the second it noticed me? Why had it not drawn attention to my being here? I woke to a dragon *on* me. Why had that one not killed me, and chose instead to lie and nap like some sort of draconic and demonic house pet? What was going on?

There had to be a hundred dragons out there. I wouldn't last a second, and I would be stupid to try.

Still, I would feel much better with a blade in my hand. There was a sword here, strangely lying only a few feet from the bed, on the floor. The imposing implication of another person here in this space hung over me as I started for it.

I crossed the cave, wincing as my head made its cries known. It wasn't unbearable, as it had been at the start, and I wondered how long I had been asleep.

I grasped the pommel of the sword, the leather unfamiliar and the iron unbalanced to me.

A brute of shining white scales entered my vision as I ventured further from the stone room. Its back was covered in spines that had to be almost as tall as I was, which faded into a russet brown. Its underbelly was a pure white, matching perfectly with its scales. Brown horns jutted outward from its serpentine skull, housing dilated eyes which scrutinized me in something almost akin to shock.

A quiet voice whispered to me, reminding me that this wasn't right. Those evil eyes should hold no emotion.

My headache must have been worse than I thought, or maybe all the rules were broken in this place. Ragnarök caged in stone and housed with monsters.

It stood at what had to be over fifteen feet, and its body was longer than my house. The spiked tail hung over the edge of the stone which jutted out from the rest of the space.

However, it was not the size that drew my attention. Not the undiluted color of its white scales, the only one I had ever seen or heard of with such. It was not the eyes that held more than they should've.

It was the human man who dared sit beside it.

The dragon and I were locked in a silent battle, the third member of our unnatural party oblivious.

I was brimming with disgust. How could someone do such a thing? Ally themselves with the hellhounds that did nothing but kill and dismember? The beings which had taken my father? Whoever would choose to live so lowly did not deserve to be called human, and there was a special place prepared for them in Helheim.

A place I was willing to send them.

I rushed forward, and many things were forgotten. The reason I had come; to do a deed so great I would be freed from a contract I never wanted. The dragon which still stood in all its might beside him. The others which still frolicked through the air. Their likely reaction if I was to succeed. All of them faded away into the background, distant worries of a mind consumed by anger as I took in the unfathomable truth.

This demonic person existed, and he could not be allowed to do so any longer. The Gods of Aesir had permitted this creature to live long enough.

Halfway into my approach, although I had made no sound to alert him, his head twisted around.

I caught his face for a split second before I lunged. He wasn't even a man, he was young. And... normal.

I wasn't sure what I had been expecting, for him to have terrifying slit-pupiled eyes or razor teeth like the beasts he consorted with, but he didn't.

They were very green, a strange thing to notice. His face was tanned, a sign of days spent under the sun. His expression held nothing but surprise, none of the terrible vehemence I had prepared for.

The features were all too human, but it didn't fool me.

Wide, intelligent eyes stared into mine for an infinitesimal moment, and I almost stopped. The connection was severed as iron swung.

To my annoyance, he ducked away from the metal edge with astounding reflexes.

"Woah!" He cried out, his voice as young as he appeared. Low, but not overly deep. Again, I faltered in my step. He sounded so human. Was this his trick? The devil appeared an angel? I looked into his face, and decided that must have been his game. I could not allow myself to be fooled. He jumped away from me as I sprang again, holding his hands out in front of him in a gesture for peace. What was he playing at? "Stop!"

Doubting. I shook my head as if to clear it. I needed to end this quickly, two seconds with him and I was practically floundering. I never lost my edge in a fight. I couldn't afford to before, and I certainly couldn't now. A sword swing away from pride and the restoration of freedom.

"Do not speak to me. Your death will bring honor to my name." I assured, my voice rising as I crept closer to him.

My head protested at the shouting, but I ignored it.

He reached over his shoulder as if to grab his sword, only to grasp air. I saw his eyes narrow as he took in the one I held. I smirked.

He looked frantically from me to the dragon. I allowed myself to glance at it, searching for a threat, but it seemed to be as much at a loss as he was. I might've actually had time to kill the boy before it reacted to save its master. He dodged away from my blade again.

This person was fast, yet he held no weapon, and the dragon didn't seem intent on intervening. It was ridiculous to believe the beast would be protective.

I answered him in the form of a cry as I lunged for him. This time the dragon moved in the corner of my eye.

"No, Fafnir!" The boy shouted.

He had given the dragon a name? And what a name, plucked from the old sagas! Was it meant to be morbidly funny, or simply horrid? Did he know the meaning of it? He truly was insane.

I did wonder briefly why he told it not to stop me. Was the creature actually listening to him? Maybe he thought he could take me himself. No chance.

I thrust my blade again, this time rewarded in the form of a cut on his upper arm, which sliced through the sleeve of his jade tunic. He hissed through his teeth, but did not try to speak again.

It didn't escape my notice that we were nearing the edge.

Even from here, I could see ridges occasionally breaking the water's surface. He seemed aware of it too, as he glanced behind him, but didn't stop backing away from me, and towards it. If anything, he almost seemed to move faster.

He still held his arms out in front of him, but he drew back as I swiped at them.

Then, he stopped moving completely. It was so abrupt that I stopped as well, waiting for his next move with my sword arm still outstretched.

He jumped.

The boy risked a large step back, and without even looking jumped off the edge of the rock.

"No!"

I didn't understand why I shouted. Didn't understand the strange desire not to see the boy I was ready to kill fall to his death, to be eaten by the dragons that surely waited below.

Maybe he really was simply too human. And too not.

I hurried to the edge, leaning as far as I dared, and watched in horror as he fell towards the water. The beast had also come closer, but it showed no desire to catch him. It didn't even act worried.

When he met the water, the dragons would kill him.

Or at least they would have, had he continued to drop.

For the few seconds he fell, air tore and pulled at his clothes, his hair. His face was deadpan, and almost a little smug, looking for all the world as if he was still standing on solid ground.

Almost immediately, a small black dragon shot towards him, grabbing one of his outstretched arms in its deadly talons. The dragon flapped its wings, staying in the same spot as it looked down at the boy. I expected his arm to have been torn to bloody strips of skin, but the talons seemed to have disappeared.

I watched, admittedly baffled.

Even from here I could see it regarding him almost fondly, pupils that should never have been more than slits dilated happily. He appeared to be talking to it, calmly dangling by one arm. It began to fly upwards, but as it rose to slightly above my level it did not set him down. It just hovered there, beating its wings, as he reached up to grab the joint where the membrane met its body.

His forearms flexed as he maneuvered, gripping one of the darkened spines on the creature's back and swinging up. He pulled himself onto a dragon forty feet in the air. I felt myself gawking, and under normal circumstances I would be embarrassed, but I figured I was allotted a little rudeness.

I had just tried to kill him, my reactions to his strangeness weren't going to top that.

For a moment there was nothing.

I took the time to actually observe him, slowly lowering the sword to my side as I continued to take him in. His hair was a light chocolate, streaked with something almost auburn. It was short, but its shape was a little off, as if crudely cut.

His deep green shirt sported a new hole, as the sleeve gave way to a bloodied cut underneath. He wore leather boots the same as mine, but they looked far older, and much more worn.

146

He sat in brown leggings, holding himself in place on the dragon's back. His leather armor was rather simple, and that's what was slightly strange about it. His eyes were vividly green, and they held my own captivatingly. A belt circled his waist, a worn journal identical to the ones I had seen inside was tucked into it.

A circular shield of metal and wood was strapped to his back. I noticed a black scabbard underneath it. That must have been the home of the sword I held.

His face betrayed no anger towards me, and he wasn't calling one of his pets to come end my life. He didn't even seem bothered by the fact that a minute ago I had been trying to end him with his own blade. He only looked curious, almost nervous.

Several dragons that had swooped down when he fell, or jumped from the rock walls, went back to what they had been doing. I was left at a gaping loss, and tried to pull my resolve back together, recovering some of my determination.

"Well? Why are you hiding up there?" I demanded, and he watched me incredulously. "Come down and fight."

He considered me, unblinking. As he hesitated, I wondered if he was going to answer at all.

"I don't want to fight you." He said, before resuming his silence.

Clearly, Dragon Boy wasn't going to be a very plentiful wealth of information.

"It might come as a shock to you, but I wasn't exactly giving you a choice." I mocked, twirling the sword in my hand and groaning internally at the strange weight of it. "Are you going to come down? Hiding behind your demons is a coward's move. Not that I'd expect anyone to have taught you about dignity."

A flicker of disgruntlement crossed his face.

My hand repositioned on the hilt, and the dragon feet away had me itching to try my luck again. If I threw a dagger, would the dragon he sat upon have the mind to intercept it? I had two knives to give, perhaps I could injure the beast with the first throw, kill the boy with the second.

"They aren't demons." He bit out.

"Well, I'd expect a devil's blindness to the nature of his companions."

Instead of the anger I'd been hoping for, he only raised an unamused eyebrow.

"There's one standing two feet from you and, just a heads up, he actually saved your life."

He must have brought me here using his beasts after I lost consciousness.

Did the Sigurd hand me to him willingly? Did they serve him, or was he the thrall? What sort of trade did he make, to bring me here? Was I meant to feed his twisted slaves? There were so many of them, it hardly seemed a worthy plan.

I stepped away slowly as I noticed the large white dragon was indeed close to me. The boy rolled his eyes at the action, and contemplated just how attached I was to my daggers.

If I was going to die anyway, I'd best paint the iron in the boy's unrighteous red while the opportunity stood plain.

"If I come down now, you can't attack us." He declared, and the white dragon made some sort of hacking sound which had the boy sending a glare at it. "I'll only jump again. If you do."

I didn't respond, trying to get my mind to stop spinning.

Nothing made sense, yet again. Why were the serpents acting like this? Was he controlling them? If he was, why hadn't they attacked me when I tried to kill him, or when I angered him? I had concocted an image of what I had prepared to face, and this boy fit into none of it. He seemed quite a normal person, except he also wasn't, in every aspect.

His skin was white and smooth, and only when faced with the jarring reality, did I realize I had expected horns, scales, something. It seemed a sick joke for him to appear so human. The dragon flew lower, and he patted it on the head in a display of odd gratitude.

After, he stepped down onto the rock.

I tried to gauge his mood and guess his actions, but he only looked inquisitive again. Maybe a little frustrated. I supposed that made sense, somewhat. It also made two of us.

"You're the Dragon Rider?" I spit out, for lack of anything else.

He tilted his head with a furrowing brow. Was he truly demented? I'd hardly gotten anything out of him. His attitude was becoming annoying. Finally, as I opened my mouth again, he answered.

"What do you mean 'the Dragon Rider'?"

"Did you think you could traipse around under Loki's devotion forever and remain undiscovered?" I scoffed, but again received no new vexation from him. "Warriors from Lamid saw you on the back of your Helhound days ago, out past Vanir. You left them alive, of course they would spread the news. Try to warn people."

The snowy dragon made a deep noise, dragging it out, like a groan. For a moment the boy closed his eyes in order to let out an exaggerated sigh. I wondered if I should have struck then, but a lack of understanding kept me rooted to the spot until he opened them again.

"Oh, shut it." The boy said, but hilariously, he complained not to me, but to the beast.

"You speak to it like it understands you." I accused.

"He does. And I can understand him, unfortunately."

"Listen, I came here for one thing, Dragon Rider-" The boy huffed loudly, and my voice grew harder at his interruption. I didn't have time for this. "Well if you go by something else, please enlighten me."

"Aidan." He revealed quietly, and I was surprised. I had expected something closer to Jontar. "That's Fafnir." He added, jamming a thumb over his back where the white dragon stood. Seemingly deciding that there was no danger for its human master it laid down, crossing its forepaws. Its eyes didn't leave us however, or more particularly, they didn't leave me. "Yours?"

The boy- Aidan, apparently, looked as though he wanted to jump the overhang again, away from the entire encounter, but not afraid.

I snapped back to the exchange at hand. "My what?"

"Your name."

"Katla. Why am I telling you this?"

"Because that's what you do when you meet someone?" He said it questioningly, but not condescending. Odd.

"You're not going to feed me to your little pet over there?"

For some reason I felt as though I already knew the answer. What I didn't understand was why.

"Who, Fafnir? I wouldn't call him a pet, he's a bit sensitive on that subject. Dragons don't usually want to eat people, actually. No offense to you or anything, but they don't think humans taste all that good."

He spoke about humans as if he wasn't one himself. That made it a bit easier to fall back into the familiar disdain I had mustered up at the existence of his actions.

"Oh, did they tell you that after they took a bite out of someone's leg? What is wrong with you? Why are you only standing there? I tried to kill you."

The dragon grumbled from the side, and I turned to keep both of them in my clear view. The dragon was likely coming back from its strange bout of lethargy, returning to its default state of hellish anger. It would kill me any second, now.

Either way, it seemed more upset about my attempted murder than the boy it was meant for.

"Believe me, I noticed that. You look like you're still thinking about it. But you wouldn't have killed me. You certainly aren't the first to try. Everyone I meet tries to kill me. That, or they just get really, really mad. Which is rather unfair when you think about it, because I've almost always just saved them from the Sigurd." He looked at me pointedly. "Ringing any very recent bells?"

I listened to him ramble almost nervously, wondering if insanity was contagious. If I held my breath, would it stave off what he was clearly putting into the air?

"What are you even saying? Why would you be saving others from your own clan? It seems such treason would result in your head in a basket."

Revulsion twisted his features.

Despite all I told myself, I felt inexplicably guilty for putting it there. Which was simply stupid, so I did my best to ignore it. Maybe if he acted truer to the situation we were in, it would be easier to keep my sword steady. Clearly, being a devotee of Loki, he was a skilled deceiver.

I tried to refocus as he collected his next words. My aim would be true when I needed it to be.

"The Sigurd are no clan of mine."

Liar.

"Then just who are you, *Aidan*? What kingdom does the Dragon Rider serve? Medea? Hestaval? Do your beasts collect gold for them? Are you from a tribe that allows this amount of sheer inhumanity?"

I waved vaguely to the dragons flying above, and the one still watching us, the one he called Fafnir. If he wasn't a part of the Sigurd tribe, why give the dragon such a name? Really, it would be an ingenious way to claim ownership of a devil under their command; branding it with such a title, linked to the ancient stories as it was.

The drumming throb in my bones disagreed with my latest fight, and the continued standing.

"I don't belong to any Kingdom of Voluspa, and I don't have a clan. This is my home. I've lived here my whole life."

I had assumed that whoever had joined with the creatures had chosen to do so, had known exactly what they were doing. Now I held myself before the person I had been searching for, who couldn't be that much older than I, admitting such a tragedy of life.

It made a small bit of sense for him to have been raised with them, maybe taken as a child without understanding the very wrongness of his companions. There was a chance this wasn't his fault.

Surely, he couldn't be saved at this point, but it felt wrong to kill him, even if to rescue him from the misery of his existence. A life led by the claws of Hel.

Yet, how had he learned to speak, albeit hesitant and unforthcoming? Why wasn't he completely feral? There was still the biggest blaring question, why hadn't the dragons harmed him? The beasts treated him like he was one. Any time in the last ten minutes he should have been ripped apart, offering himself up to the helspawns like he was.

He jumped and a dragon saved him.

A completely different serpent than the one he had arrived on allowed him to climb all over it like a child at play, and then sit upon its back while engaging in what was definitely the strangest sort of conversation I'd ever had.

The white one reacted when I spoke about killing Aidan.

It felt *strange* to give a name to the devilish character I had dreamt up in my mind, and compare it to the boy who was nothing like him. They were two separate people, I couldn't combine the two in my thoughts no matter how hard I tried to force them together. The green pushed over the red.

The black one seemed affectionate, the so-called Fafnir; protective and haughty. Their behaviors were different, specific to each. Separate from animalistic instincts, individual in their actions, from their movements, to how they treated *him*.

Their eyes held so much more emotion than I had ever seen, ranging away from what I had assumed was natural. I had always lived watching others take down the beasts, until I finally got the chance to do it myself.

Maybe there was a reason I had only ever seen slits, if an alternative was clearly possible.

Was that why they suddenly carried on like different creatures here? Around the boy who had apparently grown with them?

Only if any of what he said was real, if the truth of these beasts wasn't hidden behind some convoluted falsehood of his design.

His hand twitched, but his arm did not follow, as if he was making an effort not to move. He eyed the sword warily. His sword. My head was thrumming in time with my chest.

"Why are they acting like this?" I asked him, needing to be answered, to be given some explanation, even if it was pulled from childhood stories. "Is it a spell? Are you cursed? What have you done to them?"

He waited for a minute, face pinched in thought, like he was choosing his next words carefully. For the first time since our strange meeting, he actually met my eyes.

"You're not hurting them, attacking them. They're not attacking you. They're cautious, sure, but they don't want to fight with you any more than you want to fight all of them. Like messing with bees, neither of you have to bother each other. If you force yourself to believe they're unholy, you're never going to see anything else. But there is so much more to see." He took a breath, continuing when I didn't stop him. "I'm only asking you to look. You've given me a minute. Give me five more."

There was a finality in his last words.

They were practiced, he delivered them like he was reciting a page, memorized. A cumulation of many thoughts. 'Harmless dragons' seemed to be the general point. It was ludicrous to think it true.

I didn't want it to be, because how could we be so wrong?

It was just the way of the world; the sun rises and someone kills a dragon. Then the sun sets. You celebrate, because it's an accomplishment, a courageous act, a good deed. It was supposed to be right, how could his words make it foul? For the very first time, I felt no pride when I thought of my Hunt.

It was almost like shame, and not even for the dragon! For this boy, for Aidan, and what he would think if he knew I had killed one of the dragons he so readily defended. He probably already assumed-

No. I couldn't let him mess with my head, this was exactly what he wanted! Already forcing me to doubt my proudest moment for him, next I'd be doing it for the beasts themselves. And for what? A ridiculous bee analogy? I needed more than that.

If this is who Loki chose to make such alliances with devils, then gods were a lot less all-knowing than we believed. He failed to spin his tale without the thread falling apart in his hands.

"You're insane." I told him, my voice dripping in false sympathy like I was sorry for his rotten fortune. "And I pray for your sake, that you don't know what you're saying." He only looked crestfallen, unsure once more. Was he lost now that his great spiel had failed? Pity surged among the outrage, for this poor boy who seemed to know no better. He was corrupted by the beasts, too young to have stopped them. It would be better for him, for me to end his life. Odin must have owed him that. I only needed to be a few steps closer, only required a few more seconds. Gripping the stolen sword, I spat my burning question. "Why am I here?"

He began to inch closer to the dragon, visibly uneasy.

He moved in a skittish fashion, one hand out behind him, grasping, in search of the white-scaled reptile. His legs had bent slightly, in an almost defensive position, despite the lack of weapons in his hand. The way in which he shifted; draconic. He stopped only when his fingers brushed the thin wing.

"You were hurt, and your boat was unsalvageable." He sounded defeated.

"And if I knew how to repair it?"

"I didn't, and you were unhelpfully unconscious. There were Sigurd waiting in the water, I chose not to leave you to their lack of mercy."

"Where is my sword?"

He winced. "One of the Sigurd men went overboard with it. I'm sorry."

I knew I would be upset over the loss of my father's blade later, tremendously so, but there simply wasn't room for it now. This boy was filling it, and it was growing tedious.

If he didn't stop contributing to my confusion and my pain, he was going to die slower.

Bitterly, I regretted the chance to end all three of the Sigurd, and felt a hot surge of anger towards poor boat rigging everywhere.

A dragon cut through the air above us and I dropped instinctively, sword already trailing behind the loud rush of air. It was gone already, simply passing us, not attacking. It roared indignantly, and Aidan turned his head after it at the same time as the white Fafnir.

Boy and dragon cocked their heads, as if listening.

Aidan snorted, and I decided that I was indeed going to murder him. Death by one's own sword, how embarrassing for him.

More time was borrowed for myself with another thrown question, pretending I wasn't trying for a real answer.

"I don't understand." I confessed. "They're almost docile."

"Watch this." He advised, and in that second, I almost *laughed.*

He just sounded so absurdly excited. How could such an innocent voice belong to a being of such evil? He practically ran over to the white demon.

Aidan brought his hands up behind one of the large horns. He started...scratching? The dragon raised its head almost immediately, and Aidan put his other hand under its massive jaw to scratch there, too.

A few moments passed, and this strange new view of the world was forced down again in the seconds where nothing happened. Smarter thoughts replaced them as I began to ponder just how hard he was touched in the head.

And then the dragon purred. A dragon. Purred. It sounded like a godsdamn cat. Aidan must have found something in my face to laugh at. Finally, when the dragon had been receiving this treatment for a minute, Aidan suddenly stopped. The white brute let out a noise like a croon and a whine as Aidan took his hands away.

160

The dragon stood, stretching and arching, looking every bit like a cat that slept at Hel's feet.

The two stood there in some sort of silent battle. A minute or two in, Aidan crossed his arms in obvious impatience. It was somewhat relieving, the clear indication of full-blown insanity. These musings dissipated when the dragon made the same groan again, turning.

Turning to lumber towards me.

I scrambled back. My sword flew before I had taken another step.

"What is it doing?" I shouted, and was given only a crooked half smile.

"Just stand still." He instructed, and he sounded so sure, that I did. There was nowhere else to step, anyway.

My heart was screaming in my chest as I stood, unable to run away as the biggest dragon I had ever seen approached me. The sword was heavy in my palm, but could it possibly do anything against this massive demon?

The urge to step back and the inability to move fought within me, the desires increasing in tempo along with my heart. It opened its mouth, rows of teeth mere feet from me.

If I continued to clutch the sword, surely, I would be admitted into Valhalla. Would the pain be too much to bear? Would I drop the blade and damn myself? It ceased in its advance. Aidan's dragon was gazing at me expectantly.

"What is it doing?" I repeated, raising the sword. "What part of my recent demonstration proved to you my unwillingness to use this? Give me straight answers, and for the love of Freyja, get this thing away from me! I'm serious, I'll gouge its eyes out! I'll take pieces of it with me when I go!"

"Try it, and let the Valkyries know how it worked out." And for the very first time, real anger clouded his answer. Maybe I'd get a fight after all. "He's not doing anything to you, you're the one waving a sword around. The only person who's going to be hurt if you attack, is you."

"So the malevolent Dragon Rider finally employs threats?"

"More like friendly warnings. He only means for you to scratch him, like I just did. He's trying to give you a chance. Well, I convinced him to."

"I am not going to touch it! Gods, I knew you were out of your mind, but even you must see. Or are the teeth two feet from my arm invisible to you? But maybe those are harmless too."

The dragon convulsed, its stomach moving with a rumbling that sounded faintly contented. Like some kind of choking laughter.

Maybe it was dying.

Aidan slapped his palm against his forehead, more in response to the obviously sick dragon than myself.

"Oh, would you just do it? The longer you treat him like a big, terrifying beast, the more his pride climbs. I don't need to listen to that. He's not going to bite you, unless you try to stab him."

It doesn't bite. Cute.

And what the Hel did he mean by listening to it?

"Contrary to whatever notion you've dreamed up, I'm treating it as exactly what it is. Maybe if you regarded your actions with the same caution, you could have staved off insanity for longer."

He only sighed, looking faintly disheartened and yet somehow amused.

In our back-and-forth squabbling, the dragon had lost its patience. It shoved its massive head in my direction, and I cried out. The crown of scales was pushed under my left hand.

My fingers sat in between two eyes with pupils larger than them. I froze, holding steady with a blade in my hand, a dragon under the other. My first instinct was to rip myself away and run. Lash out with the iron, though there was nowhere to flee.

I didn't.

Scales were smooth beneath my hands, warm against my touch. Its skin was covered in the hard shards, shining with reflected light from above. As my hand remained stationary, the dragon made a disgruntled sound, and Aidan snickered. I was transfixed by the warm sensation.

I had never touched one of course, that had still been alive.

I could feel the scales shift as it did, move as it breathed. They were glassy, like river stones. The head dwarfed me, and yet the massive eyes simply watched. It was still.

I was touching a dragon and it made no motion to harm me, giving no indication of such an inclination. The sword was a promising comfort, whispering its presence and ability.

Slowly, almost as if it wasn't happening at all, I pushed my hand up, and down.

I didn't know what I was doing.

Dragons were horrible shadows, creatures that would tear your limbs from your body and send you to the realm from which they came. They had killed my *father*.

Was Aidan right?

It was wrong of me to think of that, to even allow those thoughts. Who was I, to think myself so above the rest of society as to even entertain the idea of making a choice on this monumental matter? To pick and choose which morals I would follow? I knew right from wrong, knew what acts would surely offend even the deities, knew what should not be.

Except there I was, petting one that I had just heard purr. Would even this small lapse of judgement cause Odin himself to turn me away from Valhalla? Were the gods watching my betrayal now?

I caught Aidan's smile, a little lopsided and uneven. It was so big, bordering on so much euphoria. And for what?

I knew he was waiting for me to say something, even if I didn't know what I could possibly say. What did you give voice to, when your worldview was dumped on its head? How did you acknowledge the one doing the world turning?

"It's...warm." I managed, trying for some false confidence. "Why exactly is your beast not trying to take my hand off?"

At this he laughed, and my hand moved a little faster. The answering croon made me jump, my hand flitting and ready to pull the rest of me away at a moment's notice.

"Why would he want to?"

I wasn't sure how to answer him, and maybe silence was a stubborn response, but it was supposed to be simple. It was supposed to want to.

That's all they did, and I told him as much.

"Because all dragons do is kill and maim and tarnish what is good. They're more than built for it, and more than often they act on it."

It felt wrong to say now, as my hand still lay upon one's head. I almost thought it released something like a sigh under me, before I reminded myself that dragons could do no such thing and I was being obscene.

"Is that what he's doing?" The joking tone was lost. He was actually asking me, asking me to look, like he said before. "I've never actually gotten this far. Because everyone wants to believe, no matter what they see with their own eyes, that dragons are incapable of being any more than the picture they've created. Then the stories and legends they've grown to fear, only the worst of a whole they've chosen to focus on. Look around you!" I did, at the dragons that lived inside this place in a way our ancestors said they were never meant to. "How can you still say what you are saying? Your eyes tell you it's not true! You can feel the difference, you must."

"The dragons on my island will kill you if they're given a chance. It's the same for every other Kingdom, every village in the Voluspian Isles, and every corner of the world."

"But not this corner? Just how does that fit into your belief, such a large exception? What if there were more exceptions, so many that they weren't quite just exceptions anymore? More like reality."

"They breathe fire! What, are we supposed to wait for an invitation to protect ourselves? A wolf, a bear, Hel, even a boar, will not hesitate to attack you, to fight. It's instinctual for beasts, for predators who are so lethal. Why should they be any different, especially given their attributes? Fire, wings, claws, teeth. Dragons are perfect made killers, likely derived from some twisted god with too much time and a hatred for Midgard. And you're angry that we don't hedge our lives on the fool's bet that they may not be? The evidence is plain in the death they leave behind!"

"Nothing is inherently evil, and it's not our place to decide it is." I snorted loudly, but he continued on. "Dragons are more than simple beasts, more than animals. You just have to give them the opportunity, and the reason to be. They aren't born to hunt you, at least not like this, in the devilish way you see it. They don't live to see you die. They think, and breathe, and act, entirely apart from the downfall of man. There may be a few who are angry enough to want that, but it's not fair to judge the rest on the lives of others."

"What do you mean?" Realizing my hand was still on the devil, I whipped it back, ignoring the annoyed whine.

"I mean, most dragons don't want to seek out and hurt people like that. It's not safe for them, and it's not smart when you've clearly proven you can *kill* them." He said the words like they were dirty, I reasoned to him they were. "No creatures just launch themselves into a fight they may not win, at every available opportunity, across an entire species. Maybe they're a little on edge around people with weapons, because humans have made entertainment out of hunting them down. That's your sport, isn't it? A tournament that ends only in blood? But no, of course it's the dragons who are sick."

The very game he spoke of, I had already won. The prize for doing such sat in my belt at this moment.

But I wasn't an imbecile. While clever, his speech would not be bought so easily.

"You're trying to tell me that dragons don't want to harm people. When did you last associate with a wingless being? Do you believe us this stupid?"

He was growing more animated, less reserved, the longer I poked holes. His hands began to move with his shaking head, all signs of his previous unease drifting away. His eyes stayed firmly in contact with my own now, a smile pulling on his lips, like he was drawing happiness from my interest.

"I'm not saying that, because they can't all fall under my claims, just the same as they can't fall under yours. Every dragon is different, in the same way people are. Some really don't like humans, even if you leave them well enough alone, believe me." He shuddered. Could it be that all dragons didn't serve him? "They would much sooner kill you than let you have a shot. Or they would simply kill you for the Hel of it. But you could pass a murderer every day on the street and never know. That doesn't mean the rest of the village wants to gut you."

"Just a majority of the village, then?"

His smile hitched upward.

"Most of them aren't like that. Although, they all have some wariness for people, especially Sigurd, and in a battle, they may not bother with differentiating."

Oh joy, there were evil dragons and good dragons existing in his sense of the universe.

Because that made a world of sense.

"This is demented." I exclaimed, nearing the breaking point and giving him no time to answer. "So you ride dragons? They allow you? Do you do this all the time? You fly around in the sky, despite the two legs and lack of wings which are generally nature's sign of saying you should do otherwise?"

He nodded eagerly, choosing to ignore some parts.

"I mainly ride Fafnir, but I've definitely been on every Muspel and Syre in here, save some of the younger ones." My brain was far too burnt out to ask what the Hel that meant. "They don't mind me. It's similar to how they let the hatchings fly on their backs when they're too young to do it themselves."

"Hatchings?"

"Baby dragons." He alluded, talking at a pace almost unintelligible. "They're almost always flying outside, but we all go together later on. We always fly out when the sun sets, when its safer, and I go with all of them. I could show you-"

"Where are we, exactly?"

"The Bay. The cave is under the island, which is mostly hollow. It's hidden enough so that when a human or two finds the isle, we can stay safe inside. Olavi's never found us, or any Sigurd." He explained with a hint of smugness, and I re-evaluated our surroundings.

I put a stop to that quickly when I noticed the glowing dragons on the ceiling. Knowing the limits of your own mind was a good skill, and if I pushed it further, I would be experiencing a mental break.

The aching in my skull continued to grow. I figured that I shouldn't have fought with a probable concussion, or ribs that wouldn't allow themselves to be forgotten.

I pulled at the string of the leather bracer on my wrist, trying to make my thoughts coherent.

A dragon riding boy. Passive dragons. Absolutely mad! Next, he would be telling me he could talk to them.

I glanced back at the white dragon, thinking of its name. It was a rather well-known story in the realm of the gods, after all.

Sigurd, the legendary hero. Fafnir, the evil dragon which he slew. Maybe Aidan was bold for such a name, if the roles were truly so reversed.

"Oh, Loki shit."

I was honestly surprised to hear him curse.

In the same instant, 'Fafnir' lowered his head to the floor in clear dismay. Was the beast hurt? Aidan was no better, his hand on the back of his neck, staring fixatedly at the ground.

"Aidan, you didn't tell me we had company."

CHAPTER EIGHT

AIDAN

I was dead. This was a terrible idea, and I was dead. I could see the girl's, Katla's, eyes widen as they took in my imminent death behind me. I whirled. Ragna was stepping down from the back of a red Muspel, eerily calm.

Listen to me first. "Ragna." *It's not as bad as it looks.*

You brought a human here. "Aidan." *Why? Why would you do this? How could you condemn us like this?*

I have it under control. "This is Katla." *Let me explain.*

Ragna walked past me, her brown eyes holding mine before passing on just as quickly. She stopped before Katla, who I now noticed was slowly releasing the sword she must have brandished. She glanced at me before focusing on Ragna, all the while looking suitably shocked at the appearance of another person.

Justifiably so, Ragna was terrifying. Katla straightened, keeping the sword in clear view.

"Katla Vistel." She announced, her voice much firmer than mine had been.

Ragna hummed. "Ragna Malarch. It is a joy to meet you, dear. How did you come to find yourself in our home?" *She holds your sword, there is blood on its tip. Your arm.*

It's nothing. "Katla was hurt in the Sigurd raid, her boat was attacked on the far side of the fleet. The sail was ruined."

So you brought her here? Aidan.

She was injured.

"Apparently the Sigurd fight dirty, who would have guessed?" Katla intoned, oblivious to the conversation Ragna and I passed through the Bond. Ragna hummed in agreement. "I woke up in your...home. There was a dragon on my chest."

"Yes, they do tend to seek the warmer places for their naps." Ragna said.

"It didn't rip my throat out."

Ragna laughed quietly. *You fought her?*

'Fought' is a loose term. I was prepared for the possibility.

You were not. Fafnir broke in.

Okay, maybe not in the exact moment, but I knew that any human finding themselves here would likely have a more...violent, reaction.

The cut on your arm. Did she harm either of you further? Ragna asked, concern coloring her voice.

She allowed me to touch her, but I kept my distance beyond it. They haven't done more than trade words like hatchlings. Fafnir explained, and I decided not to snap at him in hopes of prolonging Ragna's temporary lack of shouting.

"And how are you doing, Katla?" Ragna asked.

I was surprised how gracefully she fell into conversation with another person. I wished I could do the same, with the same ease.

"With the head, or with the cave full of dragons that are behaving uncharacteristically like dragons?"

"Either, I suppose." Ragna smiled.

Katla's light eyes roamed over the whole of the Bay, making frequent but fleeting stops on me.

"I don't know yet."

Ragna nodded in understanding. "Would you be alright with some time to yourself, Katla? If Aidan and I went for a quick flight."

Oh, gods.

I always knew you'd get us killed. Fafnir exhaled in dismay.

Ragna turned away without another word, climbing onto the female Muspel she had arrived with. Fafnir unfolded his wings as I slowly mounted as well. Ragna had already taken off for the entrance. Katla was staring in disbelief, her features overwhelmed, but she no longer looked horrified, or nauseated. Almost imperceptibly, I watched her shake her head.

"I'll be back." *I hope.*

I wondered if the statement would help as I intended, or only increase her dread.

"Whatever you say, Dragon Boy." Her voice was so quiet I wondered if I heard it through Fafnir's ears, or mine.

Then we were flying, back through the fallen arch and worn sea stacks. Once we were out, it was up, flying towards those who flocked about, but stopping short of them. It was risky to argue my piece before Ragna could speak.

The sail of her boat was destroyed. "She was unconscious." *There were still Sigurd in the water.* "Someone might have tried to sink her boat if we left her. She carries the scent of blood, no one would have known she wasn't Sigurd." *But we couldn't just leave her there.*

175

For good measure, I pressed into her mind my own memory of the scene. Men leering, a tattered sail, swords and cuts, the girl. Just as I was getting to our involvement, Ragna cut through the picture.

"Aidan." Surprisingly, she sounded not upset, but weary. "You should not have brought her here."

I sighed heavily. "I know, I knew you wouldn't approve, but-"

"And yet, you did it anyway. What will you do when we return? When she demands to be taken home, or attacks you, again. We will have to leave immediately, before she tells her people, and they come for us. It could take months for us to find a new home, who knows how far we will now have to travel-"

"No, no! We can't go! We don't have to leave. I don't think that she will. Not if I talk to her for a while longer. We have no boat, and she's injured. She won't be able to return anywhere for some time, anyway. We have time!"

Ragna narrowed her eyes. "You intend for a citizen of the Voluspian Kingdoms to reside with us. One you have already identified as a *killer*. You think you can make her see as we do. Have you not heard your own words? Blood. Blood is what she carries."

I clenched my fists. "We have to take a step somewhere. If we refuse to give chances, how can we expect our own?"

"I forbid it-

"She lowered her sword."

"Aidan. This is dangerous, what you are trying to do. It is reckless. Both us and the Kingdoms are fine as we are. We don't need to mess with the way of things. Fear that inborn is unshakeable, their stories are so deeply inlaid that one boy will not pull them from their roots. I believe that you-"

"We can't keep hiding!" I shouted. "I know you're afraid. Of people, what they're capable of. What they would do if they knew about me, about you. I know that you would be perfectly happy, just us and the dragons, for the rest of your life! But Olavi is planning something, as much as you want to believe he isn't. I just, I can feel it. I know this. There're crates full of dragon scales, and I don't know why! Neither do you! He's taking more dragons, he's capturing people, he's building his wealth, increasing his armada! This is different, you can't deny that. Something has changed. And we're going to need help."

And Ragna's head was already shaking. "You think that girl could be our help? That you could change her mind to change theirs?"

"I think it's a start, far more than anything else we've got!"

"You're giving too much thought to the intelligence of Sture. They've hit a lucky patch, likely plundered from Hestaval or Baldur, some richer kingdom, and are reaping the rewards now. Their resources will fall again once the fools have expended them-"

"They are building warships! And not just a single one to head off a small armada! I've seen a fleet with five of them-"

Aidan! Fafnir cried.

"And where exactly did you see this mammoth fleet? I certainly don't recall happening across it, which means you never should have engaged-"

"Ragna! You took a risk on my mother. On me. Let me have my chance to take one. I'm already halfway there."

Ragna said nothing, breathing deeply and watching others fly above us. Privately, I voiced my concerns to Fafnir.

Was that terrible?

No. You are right. She knows it too, even if she doesn't believe there's a problem to be fearful of.

I know this likely isn't your favorite thing. Having a human here. Smelling her. I'm sorry.

Don't be, Aidan. I'm not fond of prancing with the humans, but you were a part of their people first, even if you are ours now. You can tell Ragna you mean only to erase the human's fear of you, or about gaining aid in our battles, but we both know those are secondary reasons.

I sighed, worrying irrationally that Ragna would hear our words as Fafnir revealed the truth, the need I didn't share. *Is it selfish of me?*

Wishing to know the people from which you came? It felt traitorous as he spoke it, as he voiced the secret wondering. *No, not at all. If this helps you do that, then you deserve it. You deserve to know them. Who they were, and who they are now.*

Ragna was still silent, looking away, so I allowed myself to smile slightly at my brother's understanding. I placed my hand on his scales.

Thanks, Fafnir. But you're always my family first.

Of course. He snorted, making it clear there was no alternative.

Ragna inhaled, drawn out of her temporary thought.

"You really believe you can do this?"

Oh my gods. Fafnir and I shared disbelief. *No way.*

"I do, and I will."

Okay, now you're pushing it. Fafnir chastised.

"Well, then." Her voice hardened. "I cannot promise that she will lead to more, or that you will be able to change her mind. And the very first second she becomes a threat in our home, we shall leave. But she is here now, and I suppose there is little more to be done about it than for you to have your chance."

***

The day passed without any more interaction between myself and the human girl Katla.

Fafnir and I spent most of it flying. Periodically, we would go slowly past the entrance to the cave that served as Ragna and I's room, but were never able to spot her outside. I knew none of the dragons would bother her, and it seemed only right to let her have some time to herself, especially if she was hurt.

Sure. Fafnir would cut in when I said this, or some equally unhelpful variation. *Keep telling yourself that, and we'll all pretend you're not scared of the human you brought here.*

Ragna slept in the Roost, as she had been doing often to help the mothers, and I joined her, sleeping under Fafnir's wing.

Morning came, and I woke to a tent of silver membrane above my head. I braced myself as it pulled away, knowing I could put this aside no longer. Ragna was already up and about, helping the mothers.

She greeted me as we left, but otherwise stayed. When we exited the Roost and took to the new day's air, I immediately noticed Katla. She was sitting on the edge of the stone, legs hanging over the open space.

Those around her, a few Kaida and a Muspel, gave her a wide berth, but were still in close enough proximity to set off human warriors. And though Fafnir's eyes showed me the glint of light on the sword she held beside her, she did not scramble away from them, or act to fight.

So she was brave, then? Brave or stubborn, which sometimes went hand in hand.

She saw us, and hesitantly, as if she wasn't sure of the action herself, raised two fingers. I cheered to myself and Fafnir, who groaned. My hand raised in response so fast it was probably embarrassing, but what did I know?

We landed a short distance behind her, and she turned to follow us with her eyes. She watched as I dismounted, looking a little uncomfortable as I jumped off, but nowhere near as appalled as yesterday. She did not reach for the sword, but I saw her hand shift towards it.

So did Fafnir.

If she tries to kill you, you are on your own.

I knew he didn't mean it; he'd be studying her every move. My heart pounded irrationally. I rode dragons and battled barbarians, but this had to be the most terrifying thing I had ever done. I fought hard to keep Fafnir from hearing that one.

"Hello." I said, as I sat down on the ledge, mirroring her position and leaving a few feet between us. Relief flooded through me when she did not shift away. What were you meant to say to humans beyond that? Where were you to even start? What about her did I know? "You were injured yesterday. Are you...better now?"

"Still a headache, but it hurts less." She answered eventually, like she had to drag the words from her mind.

Again, I felt relieved. Both that she apparently wasn't against speaking to me, and that her pain was less.

"I'm glad. I was hoping we could just talk-"

"I don't know you." She interrupted, but she didn't seem mad. More like, just as confused as I was. "Your words tempt me to kill you."

"I'd rather you didn't. And I don't know you, but I want to."

"And why is that?" She hummed. "It seems contradicting that you are still alive, if this is how you handle those who wish to end you."

"You're here. I don't know any other...humans, aside from Ragna. I'd like to."

Apparently, she decided I spoke the truth, but her hand did not drift from my sword.

"You would like to know me?" I could hear the almost laugh.

182

"Yes."

"You need to know nothing, other than my purpose here, no matter how unintentional, is to run you through. I may not understand your serpents, but my goal has not changed."

"Except it has. You're not trying to kill me now."

Oh, goad her into it. It's a mystery how I believed that reading all those pages would increase your intelligence. Fafnir drawled.

"And in light of that very easily changed fact, you would see me do what? Have a picnic of a conversation? You aren't comical, so how about you reveal where you hide the stolen souls, or better yet, simply announce your demonic status, and we can be done with this."

"I have no idea what you're talking about." I glared. "So you think I'm a devil. Point made. You said you didn't understand the dragons. What do you want to understand?"

"Oh, I don't know, what's your favorite color? What do you think I want to-"?

"Red." I smirked. "What is yours?"

"It's white, Lokison. Are we finished?"

"I thought we were having a picnic of a conversation."

"Your mind games are weak."

"I think you're the only one playing a game."

"Okay, fine!" Her eyes were livid, her tone sharp. "Everything I learn here is another line they'll add to the speech made once I return home, and you have been felled. Although, I'll admit, I'm leaning towards you actually being human. I believe it is only your morals which are evil and corrupt. So, how old is the human body your devil soul wears?"

"My corrupt morals and I are sixteen last winter."

"Aren't you just witty. Me too. Only, in the spring."

"It's my turn then. Where are you from?"

"Village of Iona, Kingdom of Lamid." She said, and I recognized the island from maps. "How about we take a faithful jump to the matters of importance? How did you get here?"

"You mean to the Bay." I clarified "My mother brought me here. With Ragna's help."

"Your mother?"

"We were taken by the Sigurd when I was a baby. Back when taking human slaves was more common for them." She straightened as I spoke, her face softening as she contemplated, and didn't focus on upholding her ire. "A dragon was on the ship with us, but my mother set her free. She was trying to use her as a distraction, a loose dragon on the ship. She wanted to take one of their weapons, but she couldn't fight well with me. Ragna saved us, with a dragon, mind. Eventually Takka, the dragon my mother freed, became my mother's Companion."

Katla rolled her shoulders. "Companion? What is that?"

I glanced at Fafnir, cautious to share. He read the tone of my thoughts.

You won't offend me by revealing this. Try not to scare the human off with your apparent manners.

I concentrated, trying to give an accurate explanation. "A Companion is the one to which you built your Bond. The Bond is...special. All the dragons can communicate with each other through the impression of thoughts, feelings and memories. They have their own connection, as a whole entity and to the individual kin.

"To be Bonded is to be let inside that connection, a human to a dragon. To share with them in the same way, and by doing so, become open to other dragons as well, and others who are Bonded. It's more than a friendship, and it transcends beyond a simple trust. It's a gradual, building thing, for both."

I felt Fafnir's affection as I finished, though he tried to hide it.

Love you, too, you massive sack of ungrateful scales. I cheeked, and he huffed.

"And are you?" Katla was staring into my eyes so intensely it was

185

as though I could feel her gaze, part wonder and disbelief. "Bonded?"

"I'm Bonded to Fafnir. We are each other's Companion. I can communicate with him. Ragna as well, her Bond is still intact. Everyone else, too." I gestured to the Bay and everyone who lazed about. "And any more I come across."

"The dragons. You can talk to them? Hear them?" She gaped, but didn't seem ready to push me off the small cliff quite yet.

I struggled to find the right words. "Yes, but it's more than speaking, if that makes sense. Sometimes it's just a feeling. Or a memory, it could be an image or a still moment, seen and shared. Senses, too. When I can't hear a sound, I can through Fafnir. I could see from afar what dragon eyes can pick up on. Occasionally helpful, unless Fafnir's trying to make me smell through heightened senses something unpleasant." A choked sort of laugh escaped Katla's mouth. "Makes it really difficult to sneak out, though. Harder to get a lie past Takka, Ragna, and it was really difficult to get through my mother. Those more experienced in the Bond can push through your mental defenses if they really try."

"You. Can talk. To dragons." Katla repeated. "I don't think there's going to be any use trying to wrap my head around anything you say." She admitted, and I shrugged. "You keep saying Ragna, but also your mother. Ragna isn't-"

I smiled as I shook my head. "She's like one, but she isn't my mother. Ragna lived with wings before we did, and once she saved my mother and I, we lived with her."

"Is she here too? How many of you are there?"

"It's only Ragna and I." I corrected, swallowing. "Ragna had been fighting Sigurd for years with the help of dragons. As soon as I could be left alone, my mother joined her. Olavi Sture killed her in battle."

Katla looked at me with unpredicted sincerity. "That is a gracious and honorable death, against the Sigurd, and in combat. I'm sure Odin was lucky to have her in Valhalla."

"Thank you." Even if she likely doubted my mother's sanity.

A few minutes passed in silence, but it wasn't uncomfortable as it had been at the start.

"So, there's your mother, and Ragna. What about the father of the wingless serpent?"

And wasn't that just the question we'd all like an answer to. Fafnir's sympathy coated my nerves. I fought to maintain an indifferent tone about the subject as I responded.

"I never knew him. Mom got upset when I asked about him. She never told me anything, never told Ragna, never shared with Takka, and eventually...I stopped asking. I think she still loved him, though, even though he must have been a dragon killer. She was one too once, after all. Even Ragna may have been, a long time ago." I blew through my lips, trying to pretend the question hadn't kept me awake at night for years. "I've got Ragna and Fafnir, and everyone here. My family is good." I shook lightly, turning the topic away from myself. "What about your family?"

"Well, if we're sharing lineage stories on a flat rock, I live with my mother, she's a baker. The house always smells like bread. I have a sister, Ingrid, she's six years older than me and has her own family now. I have a niece, Ylva, she's three." She smiled, before her tone became wistful. "My father died three years ago. He was killed by a dragon on a Hunt."

She ended her words with a glance towards Fafnir that I wasn't even sure she meant.

"I'm sorry."

"A dragon killed him, but another saved you." I opened my mouth, but she didn't stop. "He likely charged in, sword at the ready and unthinkingly brave. He gave it one Hel of a fight, though. Always did. He was stubborn like that, passed it on to me."

I pretended to study her for a minute. "No, I don't see it."

She laughed, the second time I had made her do so, now.

"Believe me, it's there. He was one of the best fighters in the village, he's the one who taught me how to be a warrior. He trained me every day."

"He sounds great."

"And yours sounds like a great mom."

I smirked, hope making my chest warm. "Even with the dragon riding?"

"You have so many things to explain." She warned. "And I still know you're crazy, don't think I'll forget, but yeah. Maybe so."

Again, she smiled. I decided I liked it when she did.

CHAPTER NINE

KATLA

We developed a routine over the next few days as my headache lessened and the throbbing in my chest evaporated.

Aidan would return from a flight with Fafnir when the sun did. I was always awake before he arrived, either having been woken naturally, or rudely awakened by a dragon that tried to turn me into a pillow. It hadn't gone over well the first time, and I was two seconds away from killing the creature when I stopped myself, Aidan's face prominent before my mind as I dropped his sword.

I was surprised, and a little flattered that he seemed to trust me enough to leave his sword with me. I supposed it was only right that I not use it to kill one of his...glorified lizards. Family? That terminology was still foggy.

I could no longer coax hate into my words when I spoke to him.

We would talk when he arrived, usually over a breakfast of fish that Fafnir had caught.

We talked about anything, everything. Our queries seemed to go together, each venturing for the truth of what they did not know. I asked him about the dragons and he asked me about my village.

What I gave him seemed inconsequential, descriptions of the homes and markets.

The existence of dances and parties amazed him, of friendly duels and stories around a fire. I struggled not to laugh at his lack of worldly knowledge on the daily.

"You really didn't know that people keep chickens?"

"I've read about it, but I didn't know it was real! Why would you want to keep one of those feathered things, anyway? They're louder than the Kaida, and they take forever to catch. They don't even taste that good."

I no longer startled when Fafnir approached me.

Yesterday, he laid his head in my lap. Aidan's frantic glances between his head and my face proved he expected me to have a less than content reaction. It was partially his expression that convinced me against it, and partially that I found I didn't want to.

I had still frozen, my muscles locking, two daggers digging into my back, the space between my hand and a sword an almost physical feel. I restrained myself, fought instinct. Aidan looked like he was about to lose his jaw, it dropped so low.

It wasn't so bad.

There was no revulsion at the feel of warm scales on my legs, albeit a little foreign. There existed no desire to shove away his head as there had been when I first touched him.

I simply began to stroke a patch of scales above his crown, and continued answering Aidan's question about jobs in my kingdom. The action sent shocks of unease and the need to yank away up through my fingers, but I plowed through.

Fighting nature, that's what we were doing here. The look on Aidan's face, relief and happiness mixed with a sort of awe, made it entirely worth it.

Talking with Aidan wasn't uncomfortable, and the silences that stretched when one of us was searching for a good question weren't awkward.

He was always astounded by my mundane, and I think it was similar for me, though I doubted how his draconic life could be comparable to my boring.

I hardly ever saw Ragna, whom I began to think of as something like a grandmother to him. I decided she was a woman of few words, or possibly that was only to me.

Aidan said she was spending most of her time somewhere he called the Roost, and I only spotted her on occasion with a short greeting.

Other dragons began to approach me when we sat at the rocky edge. Aidan claimed they were becoming used to me. That despite the fact that they could smell blood on me, which made me feel inexplicably dirty, they trusted him. Since he seemed to be okay with the new human girl, and I hadn't tried to kill any of them...again, they were working towards accepting me.

Days ago I would have been horrified, maybe even revolted by this knowledge.

Now, I wasn't sure how I felt, but it wasn't strictly negative.

I was learning a lot of things about the serpents from him, such as new names I refused to admit were sticking in my brain.

"Amphitrite? What are those?" I had asked, interrupting a story of flying close to the water on Fafnir.

"Oh, that's what I call the sea dragons. The ones that live mainly in the water. Some of them have wings, but they're much more aquatic than, say, Fafnir. Fafnir can't swim too deep, and he can't hold his breath underwater for much longer than half an hour. The water dragons are more like fish, their scales lay differently, they have gills, and can stay under for hours. They blend into the water much better. They're smaller than the fire breathing dragons, and spit water instead of flame, but they're just as lethal in the ocean as Fafnir is in the air."

"Why did you name them Amphitrite?"

"I found it in a book I stole from a Sigurd ship. I think it's Greek, a sea deity. It seemed to fit."

I nodded in understanding. "Clever. We don't see many ocean dragons in the waters around Lamid. Do you have names for all of them?"

He scratched the crook of his arm. "Yes?"

"Oh, now you have to tell."

His nose scrunched in discomfort. "The fire-breathers are Muspel."

I coughed a laugh into my hand. "Like Muspelheim, right? Realm of fire, fire breathers. Okay, I got it. What else?"

"Acid spitters; Syre. It just means acid."

"Find that one in a book, too, Dragon Boy?" I bit my lip, and he glared. "Any more?"

He looked away, focusing on a 'Syre' a rock away. "Those on the ceiling, the ones who glow, those are Calor." He pointed upwards, and I looked at the light emanating from their storm-cloud gray bodies. "We call the tiny ones Kaida. It's meant to depict their size. Fafnir's idea, he thinks everyone little. Sometimes Pests, because most of the time they're a lot of brats. There are others, but the Muspel, Amphitrite, Calor, Kaida, and Syre are the only species which live here with us."

I couldn't stay here; I would have to go back eventually.

At the same time, how could I just leave? With what I now knew, how could I return? Each of Aidan's words, intended or not, pierced a crack through our actions, my actions. Making our weapons from their bones, and using them to kill more.

I had torn my dagger from my belt the very moment those thoughts had come into my mind. A tooth of the dragon I had slain. Ceremonial, and a gift.

I threw it off the side of our cliff, watching with satisfaction as it grew smaller before falling below the water, lost. One more knife resided in my belt, simple and standard.

I had forced it into his hands.

"I can't take that." His eyes lingered after the lost dagger. "That was dragon-"

"Yes. I have your sword, the least I can do is give you my knife, so take it."

He slipped the leather handle of my iron dagger into his belt, and said nothing else.

I told him about Eliana.

He had been so genuinely interested in my friends that I ended up going on about her for hours. He simply let me keep talking about every little thing, every small adventure or funny detail I suddenly remembered. It was easy to talk to him. He listened with such rapt attention, following every word, that I went on to tell him about Calin as well.

He enjoyed my personal feelings towards Leo Evalade, the words I conjured to convey them.

I left out the engagement.

It didn't exist here. In that way, I was successful. Besides, we filled the space with words easily.

"Have you ever been to the mainland? Outside the Isles?"

"Gods, no. It would be weeks of sailing, and I've never fancied myself a pirate. The only people with any real need to go are merchants, collectors, or the incredibly wealthy. And anything they've found, you can barter for on Trader's Isle." I watched him over my shoulder as he teetered back and forth, an unnecessarily tall column of books in his hands. "Wait, have you been? To the mainland?"

He smiled faintly behind the volumes. "Once, I think I saw it on the horizon. It was the furthest Fafnir and I ever flew. We spotted it there, through the rolling storm and the fog; a massive stretch of land. The shore must have stretched for miles and miles, endlessly on."

I rolled my eyes. "There is no land that large."

"Ragna claims to have been, in her youth. The dragons are different up there, but I've never met any of them. Takka swears she has, a time or two." He said. "One day, I'll go."

"If the idea of oxen frightens you, I'm not sure you could handle the mainland."

"Oh, please. It's not the oxen, it's the idea that you've strapped deep blades to cows and let them roam free!"

"To plow fields! It speeds along the harvest in Atori."

"It sounds as though it speeds along *death*."

My fingers found a fallen book, launching it at him without mercy. A chorus of reptilian chuckles from all corners of the Bay accompanied me as the carefully constructed tower of novels tumbled to the floor.

The Dragon Boy regarded me with a look of utmost betrayal, and my laughter didn't stop for a long time.

***

The first rays were beginning to light the inside of the Bay. The few dragons that had stayed inside were beginning to stretch from the holes they slept in.

I myself had woken for the first time without any pounding in my head, and no dragons on my chest, or in my boot. I was in a rather good mood. Now, if Aidan would only hurry his hide.

A flash of silvery scales exited the large hole opposite me I had come to recognize as the Roost. The dragon I had become familiar with carried a certain chestnut-haired boy in tow. He waved as they approached, and I did the same, though I raised an eyebrow as they landed.

"You certainly milked your time this morning." I called as Fafnir touched down.

"Fafnir and I have an idea. I- I have an idea."

He hadn't dismounted. Aidan just continued to sit there, grinning his growingly familiar lopsided smile like an idiot.

"Do you now?"

"How's your head?" He asked me, in lieu of a response.

"It's fine, actually." I told him, confused. "Why?"

"Well, I only assumed that you most likely shouldn't fly with a head injury."

"I'm sorry?"

He couldn't be serious.

"I want you to fly with me. With us." He quickly amended.

He was serious. Oh, I knew I should have killed him when it was easy, now he was going to go and make it difficult.

"You want me to go up there?" I demanded, gesturing upwards.

"Are you going to be angry if I say yes?"

"Did you fall into the ocean and hit your head on a very hard rock?"

Fafnir snorted.

"One flight?"

"No, absolutely not. No way."

"You've already flown."

"It doesn't count if I was unconscious!" I nearly shrieked at him.

I couldn't lie and say I hadn't thought about it. After all, there weren't any stairs out of here. Aidan did it every day, but could I? No, I didn't think so.

"Come on, Katla. Don't you trust me?"

The words were spoken carelessly, I didn't think he understood what he was asking. I had been ready to kill him, or drag him back to my people. That had been a week ago, a week since being here with him.

There was still a lingering possibility that he was just an incredibly skilled liar, one I wasn't quite ready to dispel. It was a cautious trust, if it even existed at all. And cautious trust did not involve almost certain death.

"Certainly not, when you're asking this." I retorted. "And that doesn't mean I trust myself a thousand feet above the ground. Are you Bonded with gravity as well?"

"I'll be with you the whole time, I promise! Plus, there's lots of places to hold onto a dragon."

Fafnir's neck drooped. Aidan stretched out his arm, holding his hand out to me.

"Do I have to?"

"No." His face started to drop; green eyes so determined that I felt my resolve crumble before he even spoke. "No, no. I just thought-"

Damn him.

"Oh, shut up! I'll get on the Loki-sired beast." I started to step forward, before I glared. "If I start to fall, I will grab you, and take you down with me, Dragon Boy. Either I survive this glimpse of Hel, or neither of us do."

Exhaling quickly I shook myself, instant anxiety seizing my heart.

I reached up to grasp his hand. He pulled me up, arm flexing as he brought my weight up and behind him. My breathing quickened impossibly as

I settled into place, spread legged behind him.

I was sitting on a dragon. I could feel the body shift with every breath taken and released through mammoth lungs. My seat was alive. About to fly.

I tried to put some distance between Aidan and I, but that only lasted a second. Fafnir raised his wings and I launched myself forward.

"Oh gods, what am I doing? This is mad! People aren't meant to fly!"

He turned his head to look at me, and I felt my heart calm a little, then quicken.

"I, personally, believe you'll enjoy it. After a while,"

Fafnir raised his wings to the fullest and stepped closer to the edge, and I realized the ground had become immensely further away.

The waves swayed beneath us as the dragon moved. An Amphitrite popped a serpentine head above the surface to peer at us.

"Wait, what do you mean 'after a while'?"

Faster than I could even comprehend we were airborne, the safety of the earth; lost. Then I was wrapping my arms so tightly around Aidan's chest he wheezed abruptly, an action I felt rather than heard over my own screaming in my ears. He deserved it for doing this to me. Would Fafnir catch him if I shoved him off?

The stone walls rushed around us as the entrance that led outward grew larger, closer. My legs burned from how firmly they braced, fighting desperately to stay on.

We hadn't even gone the most despicable direction yet. Up.

"Oh my Gods! Sweet mother of Odin!" I was yelling in Aidan's ear, but judging by the shaking of his shoulders, he didn't seem to mind.

I squeezed my eyes shut, blocking the rushing world from my view as my hold on Aidan became a vice.

I could feel the air moving around us, Fafnir's scales beneath me, leather armor under my fist. It was unclear how long we climbed, if it was hours or seconds.

The world and, consequently I, moved in strange directions. There was nothing but the cry of wind in my ears, Aidan's breathing form. Also fear. There was a lot of that going around, too.

The gale began to die down, I could feel us leveling off, becoming horizontal as people should be. The air whipped about, and wingbeats that must have belonged to Fafnir finally became audible among it. Aidan adjusted in my grip, as much as he could, at least.

He must have glanced at me behind him, because soon the dark was filled with his breathy laugh.

"Katla, open your eyes."

I imagined how I must look, but I didn't really care. This was turning out to be the single worst mistake of my entire life. Worse than when I spent an entire night being hit on by Leo's friend from Atori, and enduring Eliana's delight at the occurrence.

"The only reason you are still alive is because I don't know how to get this thing down on my own! How high are we?" My voice sounded high and strangled, like I was being choked as I refused. He snickered again.

"The sun is still rising. I don't think you want to miss it."

There was no way in any season on Midgard.

I waited, but he didn't attempt to incite my opening of them again. Finally, against all of my better judgement, my curiosity got the best of me. I cracked open one eye, then the other, and was met with the leather of Aidan's back, my head still buried in his armor. This was safe, and yet still I pushed on.

Slowly, incredibly slowly, I raised my head.

I had often imagined what Valhalla held, for people to wish for it so. I listened to the stories, the tales that described Odin's kingdom. Nothing, *nothing*, that I had ever imagined of the heavens could come anywhere close to what lay before me.

The sky was painted a million shades, pinks that faded into oranges, purples into blues, an ever-changing mirage of colors never seen. The morning sunlight pouring over a crystal ocean that crested hundreds of feet below. Stars shone, pale and barely visible in the lightening day, but so very there.

Dragons of every shape and kind flew with the grace of Valkyries, the vibrant color of every one matched somewhere in the changing sky. We flew among them, the vivid sight interrupted by a wing of clear silver shining in the emerging light. Magnificent beasts dove into the rocking waves below us to catch a morning meal, emerging trailed by water droplets that sparked like millions of diamonds. The water clung to their scales, allowing them almost to glow as the sun lit the earth.

My eyes could not be torn from it.

I felt free when I trained with my sword. When there was no one around, no one to watch and no one to expect. Just me, and the sword my father gave me, practicing an art he taught me as the world faded into the background for a while.

I thought I had known freedom, but how could I have, if I had never known this?

Looking upon it I knew, my father would never begrudge me this. With wide eyes I found Aidan, saw him facing me with an expression that was all too knowing. Had these been the sights he grew with?

Any harbored feelings of fear, of anger, of loss dropped away in that moment as I looked at him, his form outlined against the ever-moving morning. This was the life he led, and he had shown me it.

"It's beautiful." I whispered. "Thank you."

He smiled widely, and seemed to understand.

We flew, sometimes met by another dragon who chirped at us in greeting. My eyes could not be full of the sight they beheld. Aidan sat straighter, head cocking as if he had an idea.

I had little time to ponder this however, as I had just realized the position we were in, my arms still wrapped around him, pressing our bodies together. I could feel his legs on mine, not an inch between his back and my chest. My face burned, and I shifted backwards slightly, loosening my hold on him, but not daring to let go.

It may have been pretty, but I had by no means forgotten that we were hundreds of feet in the air.

Then Aidan brought his legs up in front of him and leaned forward as if he was going to rise. I gasped a little as my hold fell away, but as he began to stand, he turned around to face me, grabbing my hands in his. He wasn't going to let me fall.

I was a bit more concerned with *him* falling.

What was he doing? He stood fully before me. He balanced easily on the mere three-foot-wide scales of a dragon's neck, leaning easily against the russet horns. One slip and he was gone, yet he had never seemed more eased. If Fafnir turned his head too quickly-

He tugged my hand lightly. "It's even better from up here."

He wanted me to *stand* with him.

"I should, in good conscience, maim you for the very suggestion." My voice once again returned to embarrassingly high. "Isn't that dangerous?"

"Katla, I've been walking on dragons since I could walk."

"Good for you! I've been standing on solid ground without wings and a mind of its own as Odin intended. Unlike you, I am also plagued by a horrible self-preservation instinct you seem to be lacking. It has the unfortunate side effect of keeping me alive."

"Nothing will happen. If one of us were to fall, someone would catch us..."

It sounded like he wanted to add a 'probably', but refrained for my sake. I wasn't sure whether to be grateful for that or not.

I wasn't much comfortable with the idea of falling off for any period of time, even if I eventually was caught.

Aidan didn't seem to mind, as he stepped over my leg and made his way to Fafnir's back where his spines lay, one hand still holding mine. I understood that his words were meant to be comforting, but I doubted I'd have the same grace on the top of a dragon that he would.

I sat there, glancing between the sea and Aidan's hand, biting my lip.

"You trust me, right?" He asked, and I realized that his isolation had made him so incredibly naive.

That he would so readily hope for trust, in the differences that surrounded us. That he didn't see why what he clearly wanted just wasn't possible. To trust him was to be a traitor to all I had ever known. But yet, I grabbed his other hand, with a promise not to look down.

As he began to pull me up, I brought one damningly shaking leg beneath me, and then the other. Soon I was crouching on the neck of a dragon, finding myself in the same position from when I first heard of his existence.

I didn't look at the heavenly sky as I rose. I didn't look at the dragons, seeming to fly more ethereally than ever before.

I just looked at him, my gaze not once leaving his face as I carefully pushed up.

I wobbled a bit a second later and exhaled sharply, sure I was about to topple over. Aidan was there, his hand suddenly on my waist, steadying. His brief touch was like a jolting burn, and I felt myself lean into it slightly. For balance.

"Is this okay?" He asked me, and I nodded quickly. "You don't need to sit?"

He was giving me an out, I knew, but I could do this. I wanted to see what he wished I could.

I walked closer to him, and he released my waist to hold one of Fafnir's spines behind him to strengthen his own balance, though I doubted *he* needed it.

He nodded as I put one trembling boot in front of the other, crossing the milky scales to him. Fafnir let out a rumbling laugh beneath us, his frame shaking slightly, but Aidan kept us straight. Once I came to rest a few inches away from him, he guided my hand to one of Fafnir's spines, wrapping it around scales. The spine was harder than the rest of Fafnir, and I clutched it with all the strength I dared, bringing my other hand to join it.

Aidan held on to nothing, and I worried for him despite the fact that he looked completely natural, tied to nothing in the open air.

He studied me anxiously, as if at any second, I would crumble and demand we return to the ground. I wouldn't dare, even if I wasn't enjoying this as much as I was. I had a feeling he'd been waiting for this for a while, I wouldn't ruin it for him.

I hoped.

He seemed to notice I had not yet looked, so he pointed outwards towards the sky. The smile that grew on his face was so excited by the very prospect that I couldn't deny him.

I hadn't thought what I was seeing could grow in its allure, but it seemed Aidan was right once again.

It wasn't the sight that had changed, any more than the colors beginning to turn 1 to a blue in the sky. I wasn't hidden, using Fafnir's neck and Aidan to keep me grounded. I held tall on the back of a beast, the breeze pushing my hair behind me, only my two hands grounding me. I could see so much more, neither Aidan's back nor Fafnir's head blocking my view of the world before me, incomprehensibly grand.

The freedom was almost palpable, as if I was stuck mesmerizingly in the definition of the word.

Hesitantly, I withdrew my right hand from Fafnir's spine, so only my left was attached. My fingers trailed through the passing wind, and looking out I prayed my father was able to see even a fraction of this in his death. The sun moved steadily, every fixture and fragment of the world above and below me twisting as it climbed. For a moment, all was almost painfully still.

Then Aidan began walking backwards.

Fafnir beat his wings, keeping them outwards and allowing us to glide, and as they stuck out Aidan stepped onto one. He continued trekking back, held in the sky only by the thin membrane of a wing. In shock I watched him, and he kept smirking back at me, until finally he was feet away from the tip of Fafnir's wing.

Without a moment's glance for the ground beneath him he took another step.

"What was it you were saying about a self-preservation instinct?"

His feet hit nothing and he dropped like a stone.

"Aidan!" I yelled, gripping the spine with both hands now.

I readied for Fafnir to dart after him, securing myself. Except, Fafnir wasn't flying, wasn't chasing after him. What was he doing?

I heard Aidan whoop from below.

What the Hel?

A small Muspel dragon the color of autumn leaves rose up beside us, and I caught sight of chocolate hair and tanned skin on its back.

And Aidan was laughing at me, the Loki-strung Odin-damned fool he was. I glared, my cheeks flushed with embarrassment and frustration as he made fun of my worry. A chartreuse Syre, emitting its strange light, flew up beside the Muspel, and Aidan crossed from one dragon to another, walking across their wings with grace. The amber left as the green took its place, and Aidan drifted closer to us, his cheeks red with the sting of the wind, and smile wide.

"Would you like to try?"

"Oh, no! You complete idiot! You are not talking me into that one, that was suicidal! That's it, you are officially out of your mind entirely. What if they hadn't caught you?"

He jumped the distance from the Syre to Fafnir, landing in front of me.

"So... you like it?"

The smile was gone from his face, and I missed it. He sounded apprehensive, but how could he possibly be? How could he even entertain the idea that this was anything less than amazing?

"I... I can't believe you see this every day. It's incredible." I told him honestly, and his face lit up, looking at the sky.

I wondered if it ever lost its beauty for him, or if he still saw it the way

I did now.

"Would you come again?"

I understood what he was asking, and if he thought I would ever go back to a life without this he was as crazy as those stunts he kept pulling. I told him that exactly. He laughed, and it dripped with relief. I turned my face once again, gazing upon sights I never dreamed I would see, finding a new one every second.

CHAPTER TEN

AIDAN

Yesterday had to have been the greatest day of my entire life. The greatest flight, the greatest-

Would you quit? Fafnir grumbled, shifting as he tried to fall back into sleep.

Even Fafnir's sour attitude couldn't dampen my mood.

I had flown with Katla. Better even, she seemed to like it, love it. He shoved at me with one of his forelegs. I tumbled out from under his wing, only to be met with the sight of Katla watching from my bed. She smirked, and I blushed as I tried to right myself. I got up to push at Fafnir's head.

Get up, you lazy beast.

He huffed. *Says the one who snores.*

If I haven't heard my own, it is only because yours have deafened me.

What? I don't snore.

"There's something I want to show you." I admitted to Katla, and she raised a brow in interest.

I jumped onto Fafnir's neck, laughing as he groaned. Katla was walking over slowly, and I held my hand out to her. Fafnir's scales were still pressed into the floor, close to the ground, but she took my hand anyway. She settled into place behind me, hands firm on my shoulders. Fafnir was still moping about, groaning about being woken.

"Fafnir?" Katla called down, and he was suddenly up and about.

"Oh, really?" I demanded, and she laughed, as did he. "Never thought I'd see you eating out of a Voluspian villager's hand, Fafnir."

It's no fault of mine that your mate is far more polite. He continued before I could object. *And just where are we going?*

If you don't want to go, I'll ask one of the Amphitrite to take us across. And then, quieter. *The Roost.*

He bristled. *You want to put the human who still smells faintly of blood in front of them? They hardly let* me *roam there.*

It'll be alright. I tried to assure both of us, pushing aside my concerns on the probable reactions of the mothers.

He crept out of the cave, intentionally knocking aside a meticulously stacked bundle of my books with his tail as he went. The resulting crash dispelled several sleeping Kaida.

You're an ass. I informed him, and he laughed.

He took flight gently, forward rather than up, leaving the small waves only feet below. I heard Katla gasp as she took in all the Amphitrite. Fafnir landed lightly in the tunnel entrance. Already I could feel the heat from inside.

Fafnir dove into the water after we dismounted, chasing fish for the mothers. His draconic chortle arose moments later, along with splashing, and I knew he had once again succeeded in frightened the Amphitrite.

Katla removed her white pelt, also noticing the warmth of the fires not twenty feet ahead. She laid it on a rock beside a lump of brown, Ragna's discarded bear fur. She gestured to lead the way, and I started on, the heat rising with every step.

Aidan, is that you? Ragna called.

Good morning, Ragna. I greeted, my voice light. *I've brought Katla.*

Ragna's aversion to Katla's presence had lessened greatly with the knowledge that our flight had been successful. Though she tried to hide it, I knew she was worried yesterday when I told her of my plan to fly with Katla. Likely due to fear that she would murder me in the air, but I liked to hope it was because I would be disappointed by a negative outcome.

Undoubtably, Ragna would have loved Katla to have hated it and fled.

215

Katla stilled as the Roost came into view. The entrance was near enough to dimly light the space, revealing the ground which was dense with holes. She took a hesitant step forward, towards one of the holes in front of us.

There was only one egg, the outside covered in hard stones of pale blue, some fading to white.

She knelt by the dugout cavity, eyes trailing over the other holes in the cave. Some were tended by Muspel mothers, some not. Ragna stood across the deep cavern, her face lit by fire and passing Calor who were drawn to the heat.

"Hello, Katla." Ragna managed, and Katla waved from her spot on the ground.

"The Roost is where they lay their eggs?" She surmised, and I nodded. "There's an egg here, but no dragon. Where is the mother?"

"She's gone." I told her solemnly, and her inky waves whipped around as looked at me. "The Sigurd have been capturing more dragons. Sometimes, it's only a boat from one of the Kingdoms that pulls them down. They don't come back." She regarded me in horror, then the five holes which were devoid of their parent. "That's why Ragna stays here so often this time of year. To aid the eggs. The mothers usually don't leave the cave at this stage, so their mates bring them food, too. If it's their mates that don't return, Ragna and I bring fish to them. We manage."

216

Katla studied the various eggs. She reached out to touch the singular ice blue egg whose mother had never come home.

"There's only Muspel mothers here. What about the Amphitrite and the Syre? Or the Kaida? The Calor? Where do they keep their eggs?"

A grin split my face. "You're using their names."

"It's easier than descriptions."

I opened my mouth for an 'I told you so', prepared for both of the humans in the cave.

Aidan, be polite. Ragna chided, and Katla's voice stopped me from arguing.

"I'm going to stop doing it now. Answer the question."

I waved her off. "The Amphitrite have laid their eggs, a few weeks ago at the start of the summer, since the ocean is warmer. You just can't see them, and they take longer to develop. Amphitrite lay their eggs underwater, and the Syre attach theirs to the Bay walls. The ones who don't live here, I've seen eggs from on the side of cliffs and in crevices. They tend to thrive in the cold more than anything else, and they won't lay their eggs until winter. Calor actually carry their eggs on their back until they hatch, and they won't have theirs until the warm months begin to end. Kaida lay their eggs in nests, like birds."

217

"You're kidding?"

"Nope. They build them with things they find, but it's less sticks and more shiny rocks, stolen scales, things that will preserve warmth or reflect sunlight. Or, they just steal a nest from an actual bird."

She laughed, somewhat disbelieving in the influx of information. Flames erupted around us as the mothers breathed heat onto their eggs. Katla jumped abruptly, gaping at the eggs in utter shock. She made to run towards the closest mother who was caring for her eggs, though what she would have done when she got there, I wasn't sure. I doubted she knew either.

I reached out and grabbed her hand, pulling her back. Fire coursed through the space, and the temperature rose to roasting.

"What are they doing?" She nearly yelled, unexpected concern in her tone.

"It's okay! The eggs have to be kept hot, so the mothers breathe fire on them all day. If they don't, the eggs won't hatch, and the hatchlings inside will die."

"Oh." She calmed, inspecting again the eggs which were being licked by fire. "Sorry."

"I should have told you they were going to do that. Join me?" I asked, and her brow furrowed. "You told me about washing in rivers, and bakery

218

errands. I think my chores are a bit more interesting."

"Ah, I see. This entire ordeal was only but a scheme for my labor."

"It took you this long to uncover my grand plan?" Fafnir waltzed in, his mouth full of fish which poked out comically, silver tails squirming. He trotted over to Katla, his new annoying habit. Always bringing *her* the fish, even if she didn't know what to do with them. "Let's see if you can really convince a dragon to eat out of your hand."

Her eyes widened, and she appraised the fish with a new uncertainty.

I snatched a few of the slippery creatures and moved to one of the mothers, whose scales were a dark almost green. I held the fish out to her, and she sniffed it before opening her jaws.

Tossing it into the air, she lunged for it, and it disappeared down her throat.

Thank you. She hummed.

I turned back to Katla, who still appeared incredibly nervous. She was carrying a decent number of fish in her arms, having gathered them, but didn't seem sure of her actions.

"As long as you don't try to steal an egg, or throw a blade, it'll be easy." I assured, pushing lightly on her back and leading her to a large mother who's scales shared the color of tree trunks.

She eyed us nervously, not having seen Katla before. She growled, but it wasn't threatening, more confused.

It's okay. I promised soothingly, before Fafnir's laughing voice entered my mind in response to her growl.

Ha! That isn't why she's confused. She wants to know why she hasn't met the human hatchling's mate yet.

I hurled my general ire at his mind, but his mirth only grew. I knew Ragna was watching from the other side of the cave, where she was patting the scales of a red mother, ready to step in. Ready to recognize my failings and end my attempts.

"This is Katla." I introduced. *She's been staying with us, and she is a* friend. *I brought her to meet you all.*

I felt the exchange as she processed my words, my tone.

Okay. Her simple murmur of general assent passed through me, and I waited for her reaction. Sure enough, she leaned forward and recoiled as she smelt blood upon Katla's hand. She shifted closer, trying to protect me, and stay away from Katla. Her voice shouted. *Murderer. Children. Blood killer-*

Katla looked hurt and tensed her legs as if to bolt, while the mother covered her eggs with a protective wing, snarling at her.

"Hey, hey." I approached, my hands held out, and she relaxed as she caught my familiar scent which pushed over Katla's, slit-pupils widening minimally. *It's okay. Nobody is going to get hurt. Not me, not you, not them. She has fish, and they are all she brings for you. Can you let her give them?*

She turned her head to consider Katla, sniffing the air again. She pulled back, revealing sharp teeth that had Katla paling beside me, but did not snarl again.

Aidan! That is enough! You are only antagonizing her- Ragna tried, but the mother only cautioned.

Careful, Hatchling.

I beckoned Katla closer, taking one of the fish from her arms. I presented it to the mahogany mother, throwing it when she opened her mouth.

"Alright, now it's your turn." I motioned for her to raise a hand.

She laid the pile of fish on the ground so that she could extend an arm, but when she straightened, she made no move to do so.

"Aidan, I'm really not sure-"

"Trust me." I implored, and she stiffened.

Katla breathed deeply. She raised a hand, gripping the wet scales of a fish so tightly I feared it would shoot from her hands. The mother studied her, and a few moments passed where nothing happened. I worried that Katla would quit, that she would drop her arm and declare it pointless, but she did not. She held still, her hand outstretched, and she waited.

We stood there for a long and drawn out while, draconic eyes judging Katla as her arm surely began to ache.

Then the mother opened her mouth. A smile broke across Katla's face, and she eagerly threw the fish which was snagged from its arc. Katla laughed exuberantly.

What a ridiculous human you have chosen, Hatchling. The mother sighed, but her tone was slightly fond, if a little wary still. I smiled at her sheepishly.

Then, all on her own, Katla stepped forward and placed her hand on the mother's head, who leaned into the touch. It was incredible, to finally be able to share all of this with her, and so I smiled because she was happy. She was here with me, another person to fly with, someone to show my life to, and I was unbelievably glad it was her.

"Are you seeing this?" She exclaimed, her elation no doubt having to do with being accepted despite the scent that marred her to them.

I chuckled, when suddenly she took her hand from the mother and launched at me. Her arms wrapped around my back, and slowly, I found my own mirroring the action. Her cheek rested against my chest, and the spot where her skin met mine reacted strangely to the touch.

Was I growing ill?

We stayed that way for a moment, before she quickly pulled away. I found myself missing the contact, and noticed a reddish tinge to her skin as she turned her head from me. We stood there, me looking at her as she looked at the floor.

My back was to Ragna, but I saw Katla's eyes drift to her, and quickly drop. Finally, after an extended period of the first silence that had been slightly uncomfortable since we met, I spoke up.

"I suppose we should feed the others, Fafnir can heat the eggs with Ragna-"

"Right, of course."

Fafnir's laugh drowned out the mother's in my mind, and I instructed both of them to grow up.

Well done, Aidan. Ragna faintly praised.

I crouched quickly to reclaim more fish, but Katla would not glance at me. We stayed there as the room began to darken, the small bit of sun from outside fading. We had already fed every Muspel in the room at least once, but Katla kept going.

The mothers certainly weren't complaining, nor did they cease their senseless teasing of me.

They began to refer to Katla and I's friendship as Fafnir did, because they were all an insufferable lot of gossips.

Katla had gone off on her own a while ago. She was now sitting cross-legged on the ground, stroking the head of the first mother she had fed, who had laid her head in Katla's lap.

The smell was losing some of its power as a deterrent, clearly. Her hand would leap to her hip, and her shoulders would tense when one of them moved outside of her expectations.

Even then, she forced herself to remain still, to study and realize the lack of malicious intent. This was a moment that was hers alone, I could see that.

I sat further away, perched upon a rock, a leather notebook of my mother's open to a parchment page on my leg.

The half-finished drawing in charcoal displayed the scene as Katla pet the head of a dragon. The eggs and mother had taken shape before me, and I was currently sketching another strand of a dark braid and loose curls.

"What are you drawing?" Katla's soft voice sounded through the cave, and I jerked, narrowly avoiding streaking black across the paper.

"Just the eggs! I like to document- it's nothing!" I called back, and she nodded understandingly, pushing a curl behind her ear. She returned her focus to the mother who had whined when her spoiling had been interrupted.

I let out a breath. It wasn't a lie, really.

There *was* a dragon in the drawing.

I usually only drew them, the evidence in the notebooks and pages that covered the cave. However, sometimes my subjects varied, when there was something I wanted to remember, an image that I wanted to look back on.

The thought of her looking at what I had placed on the page now had blood rushing to my skin. I was glad I already had pointed my head down, lest she ask me about it and demand to see what had me red.

The similarity of the drawing in my lap to one years prior was most certainly not lost on me, nor was its position further in the book.

Hesitantly, I flipped the pages back, thumbing slowly for the picture despite knowing its place by heart. Only a few pages into the journal, on the first of the papers where her drawings ended and mine began, was where my memory laid.

In ashy sketch marks the face of my mother was formed, outlined against our cave home. Kaida curled on her head, rested on her shoulders among strands of long hair I remembered brown. Her face was content, eyes gazing down at the pack of Kaida that pushed to fit inside her lap.

It was easy to see the memory in color while I gazed into the dark lines across yellow parchment.

Katla stood up and began walking over, eyes alight when she noticed something different depicted on the paper. As she crept closer, she nudged me with a silent question.

"It's an older one. I like to keep important things in here, the best things. So I can make her book last. This is the first time I drew my mom."

"Aidan, this is amazing. I didn't know you could draw people." She knelt closer to the book. "Your mother was beautiful. She looks just like you."

"Except for the eyes. Her's were brown, like Ragna's, but lighter. She said the eyes were all my father."

Katla smiled. I forced my hand to close the notebook, bringing the cover back down to meet the paper. The leather moved easily, and once closed revealed the array of gems that fell in a line down the center in varying colors, to the left of the pressed pattern.

"Oh!" She said, inspecting the leather closely. "Those stones."

I turned the book over in my hands, now in her clear view, and missed how she suddenly regarded the cover with more avid attention.

"It was a gift, I think. I don't use it all that often. I don't want to run out of pages, so-"

"What is that? Beside the stones?" She interrupted, and I raised my head.

"What?"

Her finger pointed to the design etched to the right of them. It was familiar to me, a downward pointing sword with vines wrapping around its sides like a caduceus. Nine small roses in total climbed up and down them. The vines ended in golden badges, or shields, maybe, at the top. The looping lines formed the outline of Huginn inside the left circle, the outline of Muninn in the right. Odin's two ravens.

It had been there when my mother gave it to me. It was nice to look at, I supposed, but Katla seemed to see value beyond that.

"That's Lamid's insignia." Katla explained, perplexed.

In my peripheral I saw Ragna bristle, her head whip around to us.

I laughed. "What? No, I don't-"

"It's plastered over every sail, every banner. My mother has even burned it into bread. I know the mark of my own Kingdom, and that is it."

My gaze flickered from the book to her. I had never figured the small design to have meaning. Fafnir raised his head from where he was breathing fire onto a small clutch of eggs.

A memory pushed through from his mind to mine, a draconic view of a white sail, much clearer in his sight than it had been through mine. For a fleeting second, I observed the boat which had tried to shoot us down, bearing a crest identical to the one stitched into the leather in my hands.

The same boat, its sail twisted and torn away when we found Katla, the mark hidden and maimed.

I glanced over at Ragna, surprised to find her absolutely still, not even looking at me. Her eyes were trained on the book in my hands, blown wide. She must have been shocked as well. Katla looked up at me with a dazed expression that was slowly morphing into a slight smirk.

"That's doesn't- it was a gift, she always told me. Someone from Lamid could have…" They were fleeting excuses, ones I wanted her to deny.

Tell me that it is true. That I have something to *know*.

"One wouldn't carry a borrowed insignia, nor one they held no allegiance to. If this was your mothers then… you are from Lamid."

Fafnir came to sit behind me, saying nothing, but present. Katla did not leave again to be with the mothers, but instead stayed at the bottom of the rock I had sat upon. I was silent while I struggled to fit this new piece into the identity of myself I had built.

A piece that was solid, real.

***

I woke one morning before Katla, and as we had begun the last few days, Fafnir and I flew down to the Roost alone.

We had been checking the eggs more often, knowing the time should have been fast approaching. I had been feeding the tawny mother Katla had become fond of, when both our heads snapped towards the same sound a few feet away.

Ragna gasped in joyful surprise, which was nice to hear.

She had been in a sterner mood of sorts since the day Katla and I discovered where I had once lived.

The room was as silent as it could possibly be, all inside listening for the same noise to come again. A crack.

CHAPTER ELEVEN

KATLA

Someone was shouting. I moaned as I rolled, trying to slip again into sleep. The calls continued, rising in volume until I was able to make some of it out.

"-atla!"

I raised my head off the furs, the gray hide of a wolf tickling my face as the voice came again.

Aidan.

I jumped up, realizing Fafnir and his rider were absent from the room. I heard wingbeats approaching as a wild strand of my bedhead fell before my face. I pushed it behind my ear, trying my best to smooth my hair frantically as Aidan drew closer, still yelling my name.

I had just finished tying my hair behind me with a piece of cloth when Aidan landed, a huge smile on his face. I drifted towards the entrance, confused as he hit the ground already running.

"Something in this cave had better be miraculously on fire-"

"They're hatching!" He exclaimed, and the moment stretched before what he was saying registered in my less than half awakened brain.

'They're hatching'? What is he- Oh. Oh! The eggs!

"The eggs are hatching? In the Roost? Right now?"

"Yes, come on!"

In a display of boldness unusual for his reserved nature, he grabbed one of my hands and tugged me after him as he dashed again towards Fafnir. I felt the electricity of excitement run through our clasped hands. He placed his foot on Fafnir's wing joint, hoisting himself up and pulling me along effortlessly.

I found myself scrambling for purchase as he lifted me beside him without slowing, and I laughed. As Fafnir approached the edge and prepared to leap, I wrapped my arms around him once again. I had stopped needing the tether a while ago, but I still gripped his chest.

Accidents were entirely capable of creating themselves.

Fafnir jumped and we were weightless, my stomach in my throat. We appeared at the Roost's tunnel within seconds.

231

Apparently, Fafnir was excited as well, judged both by how fast we arrived, and that he didn't even stop to let us hop down before running into the Roost.

We jolted from side to side as he tore through the entrance, his four-legged footfalls miniature explosions on the rock. Less walking, I optimistically supposed. I wanted to get there quickly too.

As we neared, I could hear sounds, sharp and loud, echoing through the walls towards us. Like tens of people all continuously snapping sticks. I looked to Aidan, and he must have felt my confusion, because he turned to me with a smile that lit up his eyes.

"They're breaking out of their eggs." He was practically shaking, and I patted his arm in a mock attempt to calm him. "I think they're early this year! It wasn't until almost a week later the last summer, the first may have triggered the rest, but it could also have been-"

I ducked under one of his wildly moving hands. We reached the nests, and I took in the scene as Aidan slid from Fafnir.

The mothers were upright, wings spread circularly out before them as if to shelter the source of the loud cracking. Pieces of the eggs chipped away before my eyes, falling to the dirt below them.

Occasionally one of them shook.

It was such a vivid sign of life I nearly threw myself from Fafnir to get a closer look. Aidan stretched his hand up. I took hold of it, warmth spreading through me as he helped me down, clearly struggling not to appear impatient.

I noticed Ragna in another corner of the Roost. There was a small smile on her weathered face, wrinkles more defined, but softer when her expression was content.

She had seemingly escaped the odd mood that had hovered around her for the last few days. Since her reaction to the discovery of Aidan's homeland. I wondered...

"What do we do?" I asked him, tearing my eyes away.

"Nothing. We can only wait. And watch!"

Fafnir arranged his limbs down beside us, and Aidan pulled me by our still interlocked hands to sit against his warm scales.

Time passed, however much I didn't track, as we watched and the noises grew louder. Fafnir, Aidan, and one of the mothers whose scales were a deep red all startled at the same time, reacting to a sound my ears couldn't hear.

Aidan turned to stare towards the eggs that lay before the scarlet mother.

A much more audible crack echoed above the same quieter sounds, and I leaned forward.

An egg covered in fiery shards, smooth and shimmering from the fire it had endured, lay in the middle of the hole, surrounded by three others of the same shade. It shook, once and then again, before it toppled over onto the ground.

Cracks spread across the surface of the side upturned, fast and sudden like stepping upon thin ice.

All at once a shard of blood red flung off, sticking in the soft earth gouged out by the talons of a mother. A second passed, and a head emerged, greater than the size of my own. The figure fell clumsily as it was freed from the egg.

It matched its mother in coloration, darker patches that must have been from its sire decorating the scales. Thin wings of vivid red shook as new eyes opened with black pupils.

How could anyone have ever taken this away? How could I have done so? Aidan had his own words, that day I threw my dagger to the deep water. His own blameless reassurances. No matter what he said, I would remember. I would remember the breath that had left the chest of the same creature whose eyes I now watched see the world for the first time. The celebration that had followed, the joy I had felt, I would not allow myself to forget.

Maybe I wouldn't mourn a beast I hadn't known, but I would not forget them. I owed them this much, of that, I was sure.

A symphony of small eruptions filled the room, as if brought about by the first.

All over the room, mothers watched as their young broke their way free. Each hatchling was different, unique in their own right as their scales, horns, tails, and wings, everything varied. Even from their own siblings they were different.

As the nests that had no mothers to watch over them began to awaken, Aidan rushed over. He navigated through the eggs as they opened for their inhabitants, stroking each one lightly as they emerged. His face was adoring, positively enraptured. They would not wake to be alone in the world simply because their mothers were gone. Aidan was the first sensation for every one.

Ragna did not do the same.

She gave her attention only to Aidan as he rushed about the Roost, seeming as though he had entirely forgotten both of us. Her eyes were alight with a sort of fierce affection as they tracked him about the room. Ragna may not have been his parent, but she watched him with a maternal fondness, displaying a usually well-hidden gentleness. What else did she hide?

My own focus fell back to the subject of hers.

He looked at me and smiled widely, holding up a vivid bronze hatchling in his arms. He laughed as it caught him in the chest with its already large wings. I felt an answering smile appear on my face without asking it to, as if tied to his own.

I, too, soon forgot our surroundings, and the presence of Ragna. The questions she invoked.

Chirps began to take over the cavern as the babies gained more liveliness. Some of them fought to stand, flapping their new wings and attempting to come closer to their siblings and mothers, or in some cases, Aidan.

I watched him, and the thought struck me that even when I thought it was over, that there was nothing left he could give to me, he gave me this. He continued to give me these things, these sights and these experiences, moments that I never could have reached, never could have dreamed of. I supposed my reasoning was a bit more broad than simple gratitude for a single act.

He let me into this life that he lived, allowed me to become a part of it in every aspect. He let me fly with him through a world I had only imagined the holiest departed to enjoy. He was patient with me, those first few days, when I was still uncomfortable with the creatures that were his family. Aidan was the boy who despite it all continued to save people regardless of their treatment of him. He seemed to want nothing more than someone to share it all with, someone who could change their minds to change a Kingdom. I believed it was more than that, at this point. More than showing his life to another person, it had to be, with the way his face lit up when there was something new I could experience.

I had to believe it was important, because he was showing it to *me*.

He had been raised on the sights I couldn't believe my eyes were capable of grasping. He knew what he was giving to me, and he was glad for it. These thoughts echoed through my soul as life sprang up around me, and I knew I would be forever thankful for Aidan.

Thankful for that day at the docks when I had first been told of him, unknowing of what he truly was. Such a terribly far cry from the demonic creature I had first set out to find, he truly had the loveliest heart I had ever encountered. Whether he knew it or not, I would never stop thanking Odin for that day. I couldn't imagine my life without this, without him and the things he had so simply given me.

I glanced at the cave around me, spotting him. He was struggling not to tumble over, a hatchling had made its home on his head it seemed, although its body was already far bigger than where it tried to lay. He was tipping this way and that, trying desperately to stay vertical and keep from crushing it. The hatchling was oblivious to the danger of its swaying nest, stretching its legs contentedly. Its tail wrapped over his face.

I laughed outright at the sight, and Aidan turned to me, giving me a mock pout that looked out of place with his flailing arms. A mother of deep gray, almost black, shook with chortles, not caring to save Aidan from her offspring.

Though the sounds of cracking had faded from the air, I heard a shuffling to my right.

I finally stood from my place against Fafnir's scales. He seemed grateful for it as he immediately started to stick his nose into the groups of newly hatched dragons, much to the disgruntlement of the mothers who growled at him. A small crater still held the pale blue egg I had seen first, days before, unhatched. That statement wouldn't remain true for much longer.

I watched it shake again.

I crept closer, kneeling beside the trench. I felt Aidan's eyes on me. Despite the grin he gave, he did not come to join me. He was letting me have this, letting me experience this for myself without him there. I didn't know whether to be awed, or to call him over, wanting him to be a part of it, even if he believed I should see it without his guiding hand. I didn't need him to help me through it, but I still wanted him there.

The egg was too impatient to allow me time to decide.

It chose that moment to shake, a large spiderweb of broken shards appearing in the left side. An instant, and then a chunk of scaled shell disappeared from the rest. A hatchling stumbled into the world, scales shining the color of pale blue ice.

Small white horns adorned her head, rising inward, a fashion Aidan had pointed out to me, telling me she was a female. Inward for females, outward for males. Her underbelly was pure white, and I was shocked at the difference in color for a moment.

Most of the dragons I had seen had undersides only slightly lighter than the shade of their scales. Fafnir was an exception to this of course, his scales being unable to get any lighter. This hatchling must have been as well.

She blinked up at me, her own body roughly the size of mine. Freyja, baby dragons were big. I had guessed at that, given the size of the eggs and the towering adults. Still, seeing a newborn creature already almost longer than you were tall was shocking, to say the least.

Her own size didn't hinder her as she began to trot forward on shaking legs in my direction. I moved to be lower to the ground, pulling my legs under me and crossing them. Although I was unsure of her intent, I felt no fear while she drew near to me.

When had that instinct been changed?

There was no time lost to pondering this however, as a claw landed on my leg. It didn't hurt as she used her talons to climb her way into my lap, nor would I have noticed if it had. I stared in wonder as she stretched her large body across my legs, uncaring of the fact that more of her was off of me than on.

Absentmindedly, as the warmth of her scales began to seep through to my skin, I began to stroke the small spines on her back. They faded to the same white of her underbelly at the tips, similar to how Fafnir's fell to a deep brown.

I raised my head, searching for him, needing him to see what I saw. I needed him to know.

I had been wrong before I met him.

I found him quickly, standing by the maroon mother once again as she nuzzled her young, but he was not watching them. He was watching me, once again with a look in his eyes that was far too aware, and I saw his shoulders raise as he breathed a quiet laugh.

I gestured dramatically with my head and arms towards the hatchling in my lap, and his laughter increased so that I could hear it from across the cave.

This was the display of life that I had witnessed, a product of which now lay in my lap. It was beautiful. It was *natural,* not evil or demonic as I watched mothers nurture their children affectionately, and it was good. I made a decision then and there that I wanted this. I wanted to protect this, as Aidan did. I wanted this with him, because what was what I had been shown without him there?

Only one question remained; how much convincing would it take?

***

We had retired to Aidan's cave, our legs dangling over the edge.

The waves pushed gently at the rock stories down. A smooth head broke the surface, scales looking as though they were morphed from the water itself. The color was a mixture of seaweed and the same vivid blue as a large expanse of sea.

Its shape was much leaner than that of the Muspel dragons who flew through the air, and even the Syre. It was more streamlined, the ridges which adorned its shape less spiked, translucent webs stretching between them.

As it pulled more of its body from the small ripples, I noticed wings folded to its sides. These wings were paper thin, almost more like fins than anything, and even from here I doubted their ability to pull the dragon high above the strong winds. Its legs were much thinner, webbing between its claws.

Those talons stuck suddenly to the base of the outcrop we sat upon, and I hurriedly pulled my legs back over the side.

The Amphitrite began to pull itself vertically along the rock, scaling the wall of stone.

Behind it, several more broke the water, their scales managing to display some cumulation of natural ocean, grays and blues. They chattered excitedly as Aidan leaned over the edge to be closer, and I scooted backwards. I tossed a glance to Ragna, who only rolled her eyes in amusement.

I tried my luck, peeking over the edge. The Amphitrite was almost to us now, having dug its claws into the small cliff. I threw myself back, content to reside at least ten feet away.

I knew better at this point than to push Aidan to move away as well.

No dragon here would harm him, this much had been made clear. Still, my comfort as a sea serpent pulled its way towards me from a miniature precipice was nowhere near his own. Now unable to see the dragon, I took in Aidan's face, instead. It scrunched in thought, and I wondered if he was talking to it. He suddenly risked a double take of the Amphitrite waiting in the water, before looking sharply towards the sounds I could hear growing louder, talons on stone. His emerald eyes narrowed.

"No-"

Whatever he meant to say passed no further, because in that instant, a webbed tail shot from the edge.

The blue limb ended in a large fin, rather than the spikes that adorned the land flyers. Water flung through the air as it raced towards the boy waiting foolishly on the bluff, wrapping firmly around his waist.

In the infinitesimal moment that passed, I had time to register the look of bored resignation that crossed his features before the serpentine tail wrenched him from the edge.

Instincts took hold. "Aidan!"

There was a hand on my shoulder. Ragna smiled lightly, gestured forward. I needed no further prompting, and scrambled for the end of the overhang.

The water was still writhing with Amphitrite, their warbles now a cascade of draconic laughter. There was one particularly large section of bubbles, and I contemplated jumping in after him.

Suddenly, Aidan cut through the glassy surface, sputtering and throwing water from his hair. This elicited another round of chuckles from the watching Amphitrite, and a sigh of relief that almost stole the breath from my breast.

"Very funny." Aidan managed as the perpetrator surfaced beside him, nudging him with its head.

Aidan made the move that would be his downfall, attempting to splash the Amphitrite nearest to him.

Within seconds the mood in the water changed from amusement, to downright playfulness. Those closest to him beat their tails and wings against the water, trying all manner of things to bring about a spray of seawater in his face. Aidan cried out loudly in amusement and ire with his arms over his head, trying in vain to shield himself.

His chestnut hair, which was usually unruly and faintly curled, was now plastered to his forehead. The clothes he wore hung soaked to his skin.

Aidan attempted to seek shelter on the back of a passing Amphitrite, climbing up their wing, but was promptly flung into the air by the head of another. He let out an exaggerated groan as he fell back below the waves.

I smiled, and was content to spend the rest of my time watching this, watching him. But the nagging of my thoughts would not be ignored any longer, and an opportunity had just arisen.

Sighing, I turned away from the rock.

Ragna had busied herself in their small cave home, trying in vain to rearrange Aidan's monstrous collection of books. The faint noises of Aidan and the Amphitrite accompanied me as I walked further inside, steeling myself.

I had been waiting for a chance to speak with the woman, alone, since Aidan first showed me the cover of that journal.

Hesitantly, I sat myself on the edge of Aidan's bed. I wondered at how to start with the off-putting elder without Aidan as a buffer. My eyes fell on the wheel of a ship that lay tethered to the wall, hung above his bed. Ragna had noticed, seen me looking.

"Now that one was torn from the very first Sigurd ship he and Fafnir sank, all on their own. He was so proud." She smiled. "He was ten, then."

I raised an eyebrow. "Sinking the Sigurd fleets? He was doing that when he was ten years old?"

It wasn't as bad as it could have been, seeing as he had the dragons to back him, and supposedly Ragna. Even still, I hadn't been in a real battle until twelve, and only then because I had taken off with my father's sword during an attempted pillaging by the Sigurd.

My mother hadn't condoned it until fourteen.

"That was the year his mother died." Ragna said quietly, resuming the shuffling of books, her back to me. "Oh, he was angry for the longest time. At her, at me, at Sture. Of course, I understood. She was like my daughter." Her hands did not halt in their movement, though her voice was strained. "And Olavi Sture pulled her from the sky with his arrows and his men. It was hard for both of us. It seemed only right to let Aidan join in the fight, now that Sture had taken his mother. The thought of waiting came later. I was angry as well."

I could do this carefully, I was sure. Nonchalant. "Did she have a surname?"

Aidan was preoccupied. Even Fafnir paid us no attention, busy chortling at Aidan from the overhang.

"Nice to know Odin saddled me with a brother-" He shouted, his voice suddenly garbled, like someone whose mouth had been met with water. "-who holds a faltering sense of loyalty!"

It was only the two of us.

"Not any she attached meaning to, dear. Whatever her true, she did not carry it with her to this place."

"Oh. I only wondered after Aidan's own second name. He would have inherited it from his father."

Ragna's grip on a leather-bound volume slipped fractionally. "Aidan's father. I believe she loved him; she only loved the freedom more. And Aidan, more than anything. She was Bonded with Takka as well, and loved her dearly."

It was an excellent deflection. However, I came for answers, and she knew hers were not the kind I sought.

"Do you know who he is?"

The piles before her were rearranged, stacked nicely.

"No." Her tone was slow, measured. There was no indication of falsehood. Yet her hands still moved upon the books she had long since finished with. "She kept her family before to herself."

"Really? I don't mean to be rude, I'm only curious." I started.

"Of course."

"And you never asked?"

"It was as unimportant then as it remains now." The message was clear, but pitifully easy to pretend remained unreceived.

"It's so strange to think they must have originated from Lamid. The insignia of the kingdom lying in Aidan's journal. He tells me it was actually his mother's." I intoned, watching as her shoulders tensed, only minimally. She was very good at hiding it, I would not have noticed, had I not been looking. I had not missed Ragna's reaction, my first day in the Roost. Our discovery of Aidan's ties to Lamid. I waited, now, for the same reaction, as I delivered my next prepared line, praying Aidan had seen the information inconsequential, and thus not shared. "It's clear he longs to know as well. I'll have to ask around when I return home."

Ragna's hands ceased, and it took too many seconds for her to respond, to realize.

"What?"

"Aidan, didn't tell you?" I asked innocently. "I'm from Iona. The capital village of Lamid's dominion." I paused under the guise of shifting one of the furs that covered the bed, allowing time for it to sink in. "Surely, I could help when I return. To find any signs of Aidan's heritage."

"You are from Lamid?"

Finally, Ragna spun, tone nothing but conversational and her composure regained. I hummed in affirmation.

"There's nothing to worry about, though." I cheerfully assured her, winking. "I'll be careful not to mention dragons."

Her brown eyes were wide, and I blinked curiously at her.

She made to speak, but a voice from outside beat her to it. Ragna's head whipped to the sound so quickly that the gray blonde braid that had been done down to her shoulders smacked into the skin of her neck.

Her entire form had frozen. What was she so afraid he would hear?

Much slower, and after scrutinizing the alarm that had flashed upon her face, I also turned. Aidan was flopping to the stone, a Syre who must have taken pity on him flying in the opposite direction. Fafnir snorted.

He was entirely sodden, and as he started forward, Ragna called out.

"No, no. You stay out there, young man!" Her voice was high, even as she tried to feign normalcy and comment on the water dripping from his clothing.

Aidan was drenched, his shirt stuck to his chest. For a moment, the sight of unexpected muscle through the fabric almost cleared my mind. He turned to glare at the Amphitrite almost certainly still watching behind him. The picture solidified another decision in my mind.

Ah, to Hel with it.

Before I could regret my newfound choice, I voiced it.

"The next time you go on a Sigurd raid." I began, declaring decidedly to Aidan. My questioning was done for now, so my thoughts strayed from Ragna. Pushed aside to contemplate later, but certainly not absolved. "I will be going with you."

***

Simply stating that Aidan had been against it would be a painful understatement. The boy was incessantly stubborn.

It didn't help that the Roost served as the perfect distraction, during what would grow to be a week as he continued to vehemently deny the very idea. Brimming with newly hatched dragons as it was, I supposed there could have been worse ways to spend the time.

The newborns grew shockingly fast, far surpassing my own size within that first week. When I questioned their growth, he informed me that they would soon become almost entirely independent from their mothers.

Whenever the chance presented itself, I would ask him again.

Despite the ever-consistent denial, I knew I was wearing him down. It was easier however, now that it was two against one.

Ragna shared none of Aidan's worries.

"Flying for *fun* is not the same as fighting an armada from dragonback."

"I'm an entirely capable warrior, Aidan. In the end, I am still a human against warriors of ships, either backed by wings and fire, or not. I'm sure I can handle it."

"Katla, you could be killed. There is a multitude of things to be wary of! Arrows, for one."

"Then it must be a great relief that you and Fafnir will be the one's flying, not me. And I should think that I am competent enough to hold on tight when necessary, don't you?"

"That is not what I-"

"A warrior on the ground sure would be helpful when it comes time to

250

release those caged in Sigurd metal, Aidan." Ragna would chime in, much to his chagrin.

The woman had become incredibly more welcoming in the last week since our conversation. As if pleasantries and arguing my side could dissuade my questions and halt my suspicions. In part however, it seemed as though she truly was becoming more used to my presence in the Bay.

We all were.

I tried to keep the thought of returning to Lamid from my mind, knowing the decisions that must be made. No, not now.

Besides, it was a victimless crime, apart from the Sigurd. It would be doing everyone in Voluspa some good to set out and sink a few ships. I knew he was slowly considering it, but I was worried he was far too focused on my last run-in with the Sigurd. Which I had assured him over, multiple times, because what had happened was completely accidental and that two-bit sword stealer couldn't do it again if he tried.

I would have won that fight, Hel, I was winning it, before Loki decided to hand out favors to the wrong team.

I was more than ready to make a destructive impact on one of their armadas. The Sigurd were enemies to essentially everybody, and that was the way they liked it.

They had no allies, not that any would agree to a treaty with them, anyway. Except possibly Medea, or Hestaval, if it served to grow their wealth, but everyone had to have a limit, and I hoped the Sigurd would remain their's. To align yourself with the Sigurd would certainly not send a positive message to any other kingdoms, who would likely rescind any alliance they held with the traitorous countries.

No one associated with them, and for good reason.

As we left the Roost for the night, I marched up to him, prepared to dole out the new points I had come up with. Aidan had been doing some thinking of his own.

"Aidan-" I started, but was immediately cut off as he took a deep breath, green eyes glowing like the acid of the Syre who spat it.

"Fine. You can come." He sighed, and a vicious smugness enveloped me. "But there are going to be some bits you have to follow me on."

I cocked a hip, resting my hand. "Tell me what I need to know, Dragon Boy."

And tell he did.

"It shouldn't be hard to get into the thick of it. The initial arrows pass quickly once we're able to reach the towers. It's the archers on the deck who usually serve to be more of a problem. More than likely, it will be easy enough, and with any luck, we won't ever have to leave Fafnir. Most of the dragons are kept in cages above deck. Muspel and Syre most commonly. If a ship holds too many warriors for safe landing, we'll come in to help on the ground. Once we can clear a path, we open the cages. They're usually angry enough to do the work for us. The fleet Ragna found is small. As long as we keep our wits about us, it should be relatively smooth sailing."

"You don't have to worry about me. Last I checked, I know the right way to swing a sword. Besides, it's not like I'll be steering, right?"

He didn't answer. He was distracted, looking back into the Roost. Ragna was still inside, helping to clean the scales of the motherless hatchlings.

He grabbed my hand suddenly, his fingers curling around mine. He pulled us around to the outside of the tunnel, a wall of rock at our back.

"Aidan, what-"

"Listen." He took a deep breath, his voice low. For one idiotic moment, I stilled at our sudden secretive proximity. "When we take the fleet, Ragna is not going to come."

"Why not?"

"Because I'm not going to tell her we're going."

Flaring suspicion. "I'm going to assume you don't need to hear me ask the same question twice over."

Again his eyes shifted, this time towards Fafnir, who was positioned discreetly in the tunnel opening. His massive body faced the water, yet his head was inclined towards the Roost.

He was acting as the guard dog.

"Ragna discovered the ships, a few days past. She didn't tell me about the armada she found." He nodded towards a small black Muspel in a hole a few feet away, scales turning white at her spines. The very same who had grabbed him the day we met. "I asked around. A few scratches isn't much in exchange for being flown to where Ragna found boats on the water."

"Why wouldn't she tell you about a Sigurd fleet? Don't you attack them together?"

"We do, when one of us isn't trying to keep the other from something." In that very moment, I toyed with the idea of spilling my beliefs then and there. Of revealing my conversation with her, and what I made of it. "Ragna often forgets to inform me of Sigurd raids when there are human captives involved. Not every one of Olavi's fleets carries human prisoners, but when they do... Ragna is of the opinion that we should leave well enough alone. That I should. She doesn't want me involved, and that includes freeing humans during raids. She'll go on her own."

I felt sick. "The boats with the prisoners? She sinks them, too?"

"Gods, no!" He exclaimed. "But she doesn't free them, either. She's content to let that one ship pass, as long as there are no dragons on board."

My left hand curled into a fist, and my right attempted to do the same, before I realized it was still interlocked with his. I didn't bring myself to drop it despite the words I prepared to throw.

"She would leave them to the Sigurd? To be forced into a life as nothing more than thralls? Auctioned off at Trader's Isle?" The day Aidan had found me, three men dropping into my boat one by one. "Or worse? How could anyone leave anyone to that fate when they have more than the means to stop it?"

Aidan's eyes flashed, and all my plans of telling him what I suspected were lost, at least for the moment.

He clearly held none of the same doubts. The same questions.

"Don't think of her that way."

"What other way is there to think of it? Why would she do this? Go through all that effort to hide an armada from you so that you would not help?"

"Ragna's Companion was killed by a group of warriors in what you call a 'Hunt'." Aidan said angrily. "They were Bonded. Like Fafnir and I, my mother and Takka. They got caught in a storm, crashed onto an island. His wing was broken, he couldn't fly. Ragna thought that if she went alone, she

255

could venture into the nearest village and find help, supplies. She was on her way back when she realized what was happening. She couldn't make it in time to stop them, but she was close enough to hear him as he died. So no, she's not exactly...comfortable, with the idea of me around the citizens of Voluspian Kingdoms."

My initial ire was already fading, but not faster than my lips.

"Right. Us dirty kingdom-goers are nothing more than conniving murderers, right?"

"What? No-"

"I know." I sighed. "She's afraid for you, but I don't understand. Surely, she can free the people herself, if she won't allow you to do it?"

"I think she's afraid for her, too. She doesn't want the Kingdoms to know about us. 'Dragon Riders'. Although clearly-" He gestured to me with his free hand. "I haven't exactly lived up to her expectations in that aspect, either."

"Fafnir is a little conspicuous." I conceded.

"She doesn't know. That the Kingdom's know of me, I mean. I didn't tell her of the boat from your homeland that tried to shoot us down. If she knew, she would definitely make us go. Abandon the entire archipelago, more than likely. My mother lived here, in Voluspa, and now that I know she was from Lamid- we can't leave."

I had been so worried about when I would be forced to depart, I'd never entertained the possibility of *him* leaving.

"You don't have to convince me." I said fiercely. "What's our plan?"

"Now that the eggs have hatched, Ragna should be down there all day, all night. She plans to leave tomorrow evening."

"And we leave…"

"Tomorrow morning. The ships should be mostly sunken by the time she arrives to do what has already been done." He smiled, but then sighed. "Odin willing, she won't think of us when she can't find the armada again."

"Something tells me you don't exactly believe that."

"Not in the slightest bit, no. Chances are, she'll catch a victory story from someone or another after we're done. They're a prideful lot." He gestured around. "But I'm still going to do it. You in?"

"Now here I was thinking you were a smart one, Dragon Boy. What kind of a question is that?"

***

I did not cry out when a hand on my shoulder woke me.

A Calor scrambled up the far wall, illuminating Aidan's face. Silently, I left the warm comfort of the furs, and grabbed the sword that sat against one of the unused chairs. Aidan danced around the books on the floor with practiced ease, and I followed after him, much slower to prevent knocking aside a heap.

There was no way he had read all of these stolen books.

Even so, I supposed it could get a bit boring, when only one other voice could talk back to you out loud.

Fafnir was already waiting for us by the cave's edge. He remained stiff and tall as Aidan tried to climb on, only lowering his neck to allow me easier passage once Aidan had already fought to mount him.

I bit my lip to hide my smirk, moving to follow Aidan onto Fafnir's back. Aidan reached for me. Fafnir's head was at my knees, hoisting my body up would be no difficult feat. There were plenty of places to grab hold, and so I chose his waiting hand. He helped me gently up, into place behind him.

We began to rise, and my hands found purchase around his middle.

The path out of the Bay, though secretive, was plainly beautiful. Fafnir's wing dipped into the water, a cool spray wetting my shirt. An arch of stone, one support crumbled and eroded, fell over the mouth of the Bay.

Once we passed under, we were thrown into the world of structures which rose from the ocean. Sea stacks, dense with greenery, shrouded the path in protection. Leaves from a hanging tree were dispelled by Fafnir as he cut by, and I laughed quietly as one caught Aidan's face.

There were passing chirps from Kaida, gone before I could see them. The shores of the island stretched out on either side, a protective barrier of sand and earth, of large cliff walls obscuring what hid within the mess of rock.

I watched as the head of a Syre poked out of a cavity high in the bluff.

We left the path of sea, ivory scales joining the ocean of color that already darted about in the early morning. High in the air, the island which housed the Bay was little more than a shape below us. Fafnir roared, a great and terrible sound.

Draconic eyes found us, must have heard Aidan's words in their minds, Fafnir's call in their ears.

Both turned back to look at me. Fafnir was practically preening. Aidan displayed sheepish excitement. I shook my head.

"Lead the way, boys."

CHAPTER TWELVE

AIDAN

The large ship which was our destination had realized our approach, its occupants readying themselves.

I released my grip on Fafnir, instead reaching to hold Katla's arms wrapped around me. I wasn't a second too late, as at that moment the first archers fired. Fafnir was forced to roll in the air, changing directions abruptly. Katla stifled a scream behind me, and tightened her grip almost painfully.

I acted as an anchor to keep the less experienced rider among us safely stationary on Fafnir's back. Feathered projectiles raced past us, splitting the air.

Brace. Fafnir warned.

His claws tore wood from the deck as his body slammed into the closest boat. I loosened, as to move with the impact of his body, rather than be shaken by it.

My hold on Katla remained, so that she too would flow with the motion.

The marksmen were never given the chance to fire upon us again. Those from the Bay had been close behind. Sigurd archers were being thrown from their stations; flesh met painfully with the brunt of scales.

I jumped down quickly, only one hand against another's connecting Katla and I now. We were running once we hit the ground.

Fafnir trailed behind us, knocking away anyone who came close as we headed for the hatch. I got there first, pushing it open and letting it crash loudly to the floor. Katla ran down the steps, and I followed.

As the sky awakened with the rush of dragons, wood cut off our view of the harbingers of acid and fire.

The cell stood out; bars the same mess of iron I had come to expect. Unsurprisingly, the noise from above already had the guards on edge. Hats off to them, they weren't as clueless as they appeared.

No matter, the stealth approach was abandoned when we decided to attack during the daytime.

Katla charged them immediately, drawing my sword from its place on her hip. The guards, two men and a woman who wielded a spear, all bearing chests of steel, plating at their elbows and knees. They drew their own weapons in a disorganized fashion. Katla took quick advantage of their shock, leaping at the first one.

She knocked the first man's axe from his hand before he could move to strike her, and raised a foot to kick him in the chest before his shield could protect it. It fell from his hands, and Katla immediately raised her sword to deflect another attack.

I ducked to avoid a dislodged axe.

As I straightened, I found that two of the guards were already sprawled on the floor. One was still standing, her back to me as she fought Katla. I moved forward to help, but Katla didn't need it.

Dodging a rogue swipe of her opponent's spear, she brought the pommel of the sword up. The woman toppled to the floor as the hilt collided with her chin. Katla twirled the blade, an impossibly wide smile on her face, and I was glad for more than one reason to have brought her along.

She dropped into an overdramatic bow, and I waved her off.

Katla hefted an axe from the fallen Sigurd, turning it on its flat side. She swung the hard metal against the lock, dropping it to the floor with a metallic clang.

Those behind watched her movements.

She turned to find me, confusion crossing her features when she noticed me waiting by the stairs.

A dark-skinned man made his way to the front, pushing gently but urgently through the throngs of people crowded at the door. He was tall and lean, laden in rich blue armor patterned with gold, stripped of weapons. Katla stood taller, eyeing him for a moment before lowering her head towards him respectfully.

I surveyed the exchange, uncomprehending, but also unwilling to move closer.

"King Asmund." She acknowledged. "Of Atori."

He appraised her for a moment. When he found me, I let my eyes fall on Katla's face, keeping them decidedly in place there. He spoke with a deep and commanding voice as I waited for her.

"Thank you, for freeing us." Shouting was unmistakable from the deck, the air tinged with roars. "What is happening above? Has a Kingdom sought to seize the armada? Unadine? Vanir?"

I could feel stares, saw Katla glance at me for an answer. I only glanced at the hatch, watching as a Syre scaled a mast through the rectangular window.

"A dragon attack, Your Majesty." Katla said. "You must all stay below deck, it isn't safe, yet."

"Surely you are not going out there?"

They would have no weapons, right? There was nothing to worry for, yet I couldn't help my anxiety.

"Katla." I murmured.

She blinked at me. "Stay here, please."

Kneeling, she grabbed a displaced sword, handing it to me as she neared. I ignored the look she threw me, charging up the stairs. Unsurprisingly, the deck was empty of any conscious warriors. Fafnir stalked over with a feline gait, head in the air as it always was, the proud brute.

Katla took in the space.

"Good job, Fafnir!" She praised, patting him on the side as we approached.

He crooned in delight, pushing his head into her chest. I took her hand as I passed, pulling her gently away, much to his annoyance.

At least your mate knows how to show a little appreciation.

I glared at him as I stepped up, although his words did not stop me from extending a hand to Katla.

Fafnir took off, and we were given an aerial view of the battle. Wood and sails caught fire before our eyes as dragons swooped low, many landing on the vessels. It was almost comical to watch as they towered over the boats, one roar sending the 'brave' Sigurd running like scared children.

Doors were torn off cages, the dragons inside released. We soon caught sight of a ship that had far too many Sigurd on its surface for a safe landing. They couldn't approach without being fired upon, to land would mean leaving their wings vulnerable.

There were six cages, Muspel and Syre tied down to the iron that encased them. Fafnir angled towards it, and instead of trying to approach from above like the others, he flew low to the water.

I leapt from his back the distance from the waves to the side of the boat, pushing myself up on my arms and over the side. None of the Sigurd had noticed my entrance, too preoccupied with the threat from above. Katla surveyed my entry in surprise.

I leaned over the side, reaching down to her.

Katla began to stand, carefully on Fafnir's neck. She wobbled a bit at first as Fafnir shifted, still beating his wings as softly as he could. She crouched before jumping, aiming less for the boat and more for my hand.

I caught her, and she was suspended for a moment before I pulled back so her feet landed against the wooden side, held upright by me. I hoisted, and her other hand found purchase on the rim.

She climbed silently over the edge.

I angled my head towards the Sigurd who still had not noticed the ship's newest occupants. Katla drew my sword in response, a dangerous look flitting through her eyes.

I drew my own stolen weapon, hefting a shield dropped by a warrior on my left arm. Katla stormed forward first, and I followed after her. We were finally noticed, a small man turning just to be knocked backward by Katla's sword against his chest plate.

I jumped into the battle, immediately finding myself in combat against a woman with a blade. The Sigurd on the ship were sidetracked by the newcomers, and their distracted states cost them.

Dragons crept onto the deck from above, a large sapphire Muspel taking down the archer in the mast.

I ducked under the woman's sword, shoving her hand with my shield and forcing the weapon from her grip. She didn't even glance at it as it fell, instantly grabbing a dagger from her belt. I raised the circle of wood and iron as she slashed, but she changed direction and aimed for my sword arm. I bit back a curse as a cut opened, but didn't focus on it. She thrust the blade towards me again, leaning too far forward, putting all her weight into the strike.

I raised the shield slower this time, so that once she had committed to a

Spot, she wouldn't have time to change it. The blade bounced harmlessly off my shield, and the woman shifted to follow her motion. I took the opportunity to swing my blade at her ankle.

She fell to the floor, already unbalanced, and I ran past her.

Not two seconds after I began to move, I was tackled from behind, slamming into the deck.

I cried out as my arm was crushed, still holding the shield, and a heavy body lay on top of me. I felt my belt give; my mother's book gone from my side. Panic flashed. A shadow flung over me, my vision limited to the boards an inch before my face. The weight lessened slightly, and I took the small amount of space I was given to maneuver.

My elbow flew, catching the chin of my assailant.

His head snapped back, but this only lasted only a moment, before he swung his axe for my skull. I lurched to the side as the iron head broke through the floorboards where I had just laid.

He moved to tear the axe from its spot, but I grabbed hold of it with one arm, bringing a leg up with all the force I could manage in my current position. I slammed my knee into his chest, and with the armor I likely managed to do more damage to myself than to him.

Still, I succeeded in loosening his hold, which meant success despite the ache that now sprung up in my bones.

I took advantage of the extra space, bringing both legs above me and kicking outward, hitting the man square in the stomach. I forced myself over with the momentum, rolling onto my heels. He fell back, his hand losing its grip on the axe I still held, one tattooed arm flailing. I lurched to my feet, taking his axe with me.

I stared him in the eyes as he tried to stand, and without looking I threw his axe over the side of the ship, grinning cheekily.

He stared after it, and I dashed off again. A Syre approached him a second later, scales glowing even in the daylight, and he soon followed the axe.

The deck was some manner of calm chaos, one happening always replacing another. At least in this, it was organized.

A lean man raced towards me, his double-edged sword gleaming.

His size meant more maneuverability than his much larger comrades, but it certainly didn't mean his intelligence was any greater. Three dark lines wrapped around his exposed right arm.

He lunged at me, and my muscles protested violently as I pulled my blade to meet his own. His first strike collided with the iron so vigorously, that the resulting vibrations trembled down into my hands and up my arms. My grip was almost lost as the ripples of force rattled my teeth.

I allowed him to move me, each step he took to force me back leading him unknowingly closer to the open hatch in the ships center. I parried a swing for my legs, shoving him and moving faster towards the hole in the deck behind me, anxious to end the combat.

He smiled, misinterpreting my movements as retreat.

"Even if I don't end you today, Chief Olavi will have your head." He assured as our swords glanced.

Anger forced my tongue, though I normally refrained from speaking. "And just where is the great chief? Hiding behind an armada?"

"Our Chief is no coward!" He snarled, his strikes becoming sloppier in the face of this apparent dishonor.

"And yet I haven't seen his unfortunate hide in years. Seems he can't do better than people like you as a shield."

He slammed his sword against mine with a yell, and I analyzed his strikes quickly. The insults to his clan had brought more chaos to his swings.

It wasn't hard to anger him, insulting Olavi was a cherished pastime.

There was too much strength into his blows, jumping more than he stepped. His stance was uneven, attempting to use more brute force than skill to force me backwards. A tactic better served for his heavier friends than himself.

Unbeknownst to him, of course, this was exactly what I wanted.

I stayed just out of his reach, forcing him to jump further and further each time, trying to get his blade to my open chest. Finally, as he was growing increasingly more irritated, we neared the open hatch.

I lowered my sword slightly. It would be a clear opportunity, and from the widening of his eyes he saw it. He was just too clueless to realize the mistake he was making. He lurched, extending himself far too much. In the seconds as the iron tooth of his sword fell to me, I shifted.

"Your Chief will fare no better than you." I promised.

His confusion came too late.

I jumped aside, and he careened past me, unable to stop himself as he fell down the hatch. He landed on one of the bottom stairs below, rolling the rest of the way to the floor with a painful and drawn-out groan.

A symphony of mutilated wood echoed across our small stretch of ocean, the crackling of fire. Shouts echoed from all directions, most faint, sent nowhere in particular.

Murderers!

Look at them run-

-reeks of the burning liquid they horde?

They carry scales of kin on their boats? From where have they been stolen?

Your blades burn no slower than you!

In one instant my mind cleared, the voices quiet. My vision tunneled, fingers on the hilt loosened.

Katla was whirling in an arc, my sword outstretched in her hand and a shield in her other. Strands of dark hair flew behind her, catching in the sunlight as she spun, falling loose from the crown of braids which encircled her temple.

Eyes lighter than the sky above seemed to flare across the deck, lighting with a victorious smile as a Sigurd lost their weapon to her own.

She spun on her heel, raising her opposite leg high in the air to kick an approaching woman in the gut. Katla advanced as she stumbled back, thrusting her blade down the handle of the spear her opponent held, the edge slipping against the woman's hand. Their weapons now parallel, Katla twisted her wrist, forcing the spear out of her challenger's grasp.

She faded back just in time for an amber wing to hurl the woman a good distance away, not bothering to rise from her heap on the floor.

Katla wasted no time, rushing into battle once more. She was swung at by a man with a terrible mustache and an overly large halberd. Katla rolled under his blade.

As the man swung again, she blocked it with both her sword and shield, ripping the two apart and sending the man flailing. She thrust the borrowed shield towards the man's head as he fought to regain his balance, countering the hastily swung tip with her own blow. He fell to the floor, and she rolled her shoulders, tightening one of her leather bracers.

At that moment, she noticed me.

The might of her counter pushed the man backward into a crate, which opened, spilling mixed dragon scales all over the deck.

Had I been focusing on it; I would have wondered once again at the strange appearance.

However, my mind was entirely occupied. Her smirk was deadly.

She raised a hand to wave avidly, and I laughed. She gracefully collapsed back into the battle. Her blade met her foe's, a picture of gleaming steel, shining eyes, and ebony hair.

Did Valkyries look different to each? I pitied those who would not see the same.

She disappeared around a mast, and sound returned viciously. I shook my head, scolding myself for losing focus, before leaping back into the fight myself.

Although she was not in front of me, Katla still whirled with an outstretched sword in my vision.

Alright. I no longer care if Ragna kills us both. This is the greatest day of my entire life. Fafnir guffawed uproariously. *Oh, I am never forgetting this.*

Godsdamned Bond. I hadn't realized I had let my attention slip so far as to project whatever entered my mind.

Once the ship had been rid of all the Sigurd, Katla and I made for the cages. The six that sat on the deck were being attacked brutally as Muspel tried to break in.

The ear-splitting screeches that followed the disfigurement of steel were grating, but satisfying.

Those trapped whined between closed jaws from inside, struggling in vain to free themselves from the restraints. I swallowed hard, and saw the corner of Katla's eye land on me.

I noticed my mother's notebook had found a home in her belt, she must have snatched it from the deck. Thank the gods.

Five of the cages had been broken open, dragons from outside now crawling in to tear the ropes from the trapped. I headed for the last cage, the door considerably thicker to contain the larger russet Muspel inside, horns rising straight out in a male indication.

I tried to calm him as I approached the cage.

I'm going to help. I swore.

But there was no response.

My brows drew together, and I pushed further, searching for his mind, for the feeling of him through the Bond. There was nothing but empty space, even as I delved deeper.

Spreading myself, I could feel the others around me, Fafnir at my back. I could feel the draconic minds on this boat, all but the one before me. I reached, grasped for the space where a voice should have been, but there was nothing to grab.

As if the Muspel before me had no thoughts, no words to hear. As if, through the eyes of the Bond, there was no one trapped there at all.

In my distraction, a Syre crept beside me, nudging me out of the way so they could reach the cage. I registered their movements dumbfoundedly, still scoping the desolate space and eliciting no reaction. Blank pupils regarded me.

The lock melted in a heap of metal, the acidic scent burning my nostrils. It had to be uncomfortable for the trapped Muspel, Fafnir was always complaining of the scents brought by Syre. Yet, he did not twitch, or react at all.

I tried again.

It's alright. You can come out. I may as well have been speaking to the iron walls. I could feel that my voice was unreceived, the words bouncing off nothing. *Come out.*

There, a jolt.

Finally, he began to leave the restrictive enclosure, movements controlled and even, strange. Usually, they were elated to leave the cages, acting jubilant and slightly wild.

Instead, it was with slow and measured steps that the Muspel exited the bars.

Okay. Good. You can go, now. Wherever you want. They will not bother you, anymore. I promised, but there was no further movement. *Go.*

He took to the air, leaving me behind, staring after the Muspel with an unreachable mind and un-answering voice.

The rest followed him, no more to be done. All around us they rose to the sky, heading back in the direction we came from, towards home. Ours was again the last of the two ships that had not sunk, though it was getting there.

The entire mast pitched over behind us with a deafening crash, and both Katla and I jumped with twin startled cries.

"Hey. Are you okay?" Katla asked.

"What?" I blinked. "Oh. Yes, yes I'm fine. That was just...I don't know. Odd."

She walked closer, entering my full view.

"So, Dragon Boy." She began, resting my sword on her shoulder. "How'd I do? Meet your standards?"

"You were incredible! I've never seen anyone fight like that! What do you even need me for-"

As your brother, and one forced to endure your later embarrassment, I'd advise that you shut it, while you can.

I clamped my mouth shut.

"Thanks." She smiled. "Not too bad yourself. Though, I did see you almost get crushed like a bug by Ten Ton over there."

I coughed. "There were a few dull moments."

Of course, she couldn't have seen me trick the man into the hatch, or toss a stolen axe to the sea. My failures in the battle, though, those she recalled perfectly.

Lovely.

She snickered, patting my shoulder.

We both listened as wingbeats drew near, Fafnir returning to the deck beside us. His eyes narrowed immediately, leaning forward to sniff at the blood from the cut on my arm.

He raised his head to be level with mine, worry in his eyes.

I'm fine, Fafnir. Nothing but a scratch.

Katla abandoned my side, seemingly on a whim, spinning for Fafnir. I watched in bemusement as she climbed on via Fafnir's wing, swinging her leg over his neck. She faced me, looking mighty proud, and held her hand down for me.

I stared at it, smaller than mine, clearly searching for my own.

"Come on, then. If the Helfire of Ragna is to rain down upon us, I'd prefer we got it out of the way before dinner."

I scoffed, somewhat disbelievingly. Her hand still laid out for me.

She gave a triumphant smirk when my fingers slid into hers, pulling me up behind her.

Fafnir rose into the air as the deck became level with the water, milky wings spreading to both our sides. Despite certainly not needing the balance or the tether, I hesitantly wrapped my arms lightly around Katla's waist as we climbed.

For lack of anywhere else to set them.

Cringing slightly, though I barely allowed my skin to touch her, I feared she would shove me off Fafnir. I heard her breath catch, and I worried for a terrible second that I had done something I shouldn't have. However, she didn't move away, or try to remove my arms from around her lower half. Quite the opposite, actually. She leaned back minimally into my chest, and I thought I saw a small smile.

The ship disappeared below us, and as the sounds of battle faded, people began to emerge from below deck on the only remaining boat. The prisoners from Atori.

I nudged Fafnir softly. I was used to the reactions our presence would elicit, but Katla was not. She was in a visibly good mood, as she should have been, she had truly been fantastic today.

I wasn't willing to effectively ruin her elation by sticking around so we could be called traitors to humanity.

We trailed behind the masses as we advanced towards the Bay. Sitting in front of me seemed to add to Katla's merriment as we travelled. I waited for an indication that she no longer wanted me to rest so close, but one never came.

She had begun recounting her fight with the spear carrying woman, unaware of the fact that I had seen it, rather than just locked eyes with her across the deck. I listened intently, reimagining the scene in my mind with her commentary flowing in the background.

I kept my mind firmly in my own head, not willing to endure Fafnir's opinion.

I found another section of my thoughts delving onto a deeper path as I listened to the dark-haired girl in the sky.

I hadn't known what was to come that day in the Bay, when she had lowered her weapon. Katla arrived, and everything became more. If she were to leave, and someone else came to fill the hole that she had left, I knew it wouldn't be the same.

I didn't know what would happen when she realized she must return home, if she would desire to. It was unclear what I would do when the time came.

I think I would follow her, if she would let me, to wherever she wanted to go.

279

Katla had now asked about my endeavors during the battle, and it was with a smirk that I regaled her with the Sigurd man's tumble down the hatch. She laughed loudly as I re-enacted it for her, and I could see no higher reason to say anything.

She didn't allow me to gain too big of a head. "Still doesn't outweigh being tackled, though."

The Bay appeared on the horizon as the sun had not yet begun to dim. We watched contentedly as the ocean rushed by, bringing the island closer, our inevitable descent. I searched for a way to prolong this, her back against me.

"In the interest of avoiding general Helfire," I suggested. "Take a lap around the island?"

Really?

"As long as you step before Ragna first." She teased.

And so Fafnir flew lower, skirting across the ocean and yet passing the sea stacks indicating the Bay's shrouded entrance. We pulled above a cliff face, Katla leaning to see into a tunnel from which a Syre looked. The tips of trees soon swayed beneath us, Kaida rushing to the top to chirp greetings, hidden in the foliage. She hummed in amusement.

Fafnir twisted, and our world was briefly upside down. Her hands dug into my arms, but she only laughed loudly as we righted.

Wings beat and carried us higher, the island spread before us. Just ahead now, a brush of color pressed against the grass. Katla's head turned towards it, her mouth open to ask.

"What is that?"

The flowers which sprawled densely in every direction lay waiting, a circular garden of vibrance. Though human eyes could not see it from this distance, I knew the location of the rock contained within, the knife.

"The Kaida's primary nesting spot. They like to burrow among the flowers. It was my mother's favorite place on the whole island." I smiled. "There was no body to honor when she died, so this is what I chose. A stone sits in the center, along with her favorite weapon."

"Her favorite weapon?"

"Something she carried with her from...wherever we came from. She never actually fought with it. Didn't want to lose it." I blew out a breath. "This seemed the closest way to give it to her."

Katla shifted. "You really don't know anything about your lives before? Before Ragna found you?"

I contained a wince. "No. My mother never told me anything before I was old enough to really understand what I needed to ask. That some things needed an answer. Then she was gone, and since she kept it from Ragna and Takka too... she took all my answers with her."

"Ragna." Katla said. "You don't think that she could be lying-"

I shook my head so hard my neck cracked. "Ragna wouldn't do that. She knows better than anyone how much I...wanted to know."

"But are you sure-"

"Yes."

The wind pushed past for a handful of minutes as Fafnir circled the field, flying back towards the Bay.

"It's beautiful." Katla voiced.

I only nodded.

Little attention was paid to the sea stacks as we entered. My thoughts were somewhere far away. Greetings erupted from every corner of the Bay.

Hatchling!

Small human, you must take the air with us-

You missed a race!

My eyes caught on Ragna, waving us frantically on from the entrance to the Roost. Inwardly, I grieved for the free time I would no longer have once she questioned our whereabouts.

Rough estimate? I questioned Fafnir hopelessly.

Not good. She may go for months, this time.

Still, we angled for her as she beckoned us down.

Wait- Aidan!

I soon saw what he did. The mothers were all crammed into the entrance, several large hatchlings on their backs. They hadn't left in a month. I gasped. Katla seemed to only now notice Ragna, practically knocking me down in her haste to sit straight once again.

That, I would ponder later.

"Look!" I pointed. "It's time! The mothers are going to teach them how to fly!"

One moment I was staring at the braids that wrapped about her head, and the next, ice eyes were vividly connected to mine.

"Aidan, can we go with them?"

I think my heart seized.

She looked back as the mothers began to jump from the ledge, their offspring clinging to their backs. Fafnir flew downwards and landed in the

283

opening.

"Right on time, you two!" Ragna called.

The excitement of the hatchlings was infectious. I felt the realization and elation in their consciousness as they reached out to me.

Hello to you, too! I laughed. *Oh, are you all ready? The sky is so wonderful outside the Roost! And of course, I'll show you the spot down past the ravine where all the best fish swim, though we may need to wait on teaching you to hunt a boar until your wings grow stronger, but that's alright, we can still-*

Ragna was helping those without mothers find a Muspel to take them. As they were herded towards the larger dragons, they latched on quickly and instinctively.

Only one hatchling remained, the female with pale blue scales that Katla had become fond of.

Come over here, Little One. I called, and she chirped excitedly, her light wings flapping.

She scuttled over to Fafnir, and I fought a grin when Katla gasped as she realized who would be accompanying us. Fafnir laid on the ground so that she could climb onto his back. The mothers were already taking flight. Ragna stepped lightly from the tunnel's entrance, falling for no more than a second before she was scooped up to follow them.

Hurry, Aidan. You don't want to miss their first try! She reminded in her wake.

We exited the Bay only a few minutes after we had entered, Fafnir steering us towards where the others had gone.

The mothers and their hatchlings stood upon a grassy cliff not far from the Bay. Katla craned quickly over the side to get a better look, beginning to slip slightly from Fafnir's neck.

I snaked an arm around her waist before she could tip over, as she was dangerously close to doing so.

She leaned into the touch to move out further, but did not otherwise object. Fafnir landed softly on the grass, and Katla jumped. I chuckled at her enthusiasm as I did the same, and Fafnir let out a draconic snicker.

Katla's favored hatchling landed clumsily in the green beside me, already standing taller than myself. Taking in her size, I hoped none of the hatchlings would attempt to bring me on their flights, they could surely hold me.

The thought gave me an explosive and unrelenting idea, one I would have to ask Katla about.

She trotted towards the cliff's edge where the others waited, now with the addition of Katla. Ragna sat down beside Fafnir, content to see from afar.

I raced right up against the cliff as the mothers leapt, circling above us as they watched their young.

The hatchlings were quick to follow, up and running right off the edge. Katla tensed as they fell, but I nodded at her reassuringly.

The mothers followed their respective hatchlings as they dropped, ready to catch them should they fail. Fafnir did the same with those whose parent was not here to teach them. He may have acted indifferent, but we both knew he was a massive softie when it came to hatchlings.

Before they reached the ground, a clutch of them began fighting to flap their wings as their mothers had, the others following when a pattern was noticed.

Moving their wings more eagerly, the hatchlings began to gain altitude, albeit sloppily. Their flight was crooked, some falling several feet before they were able to rise again. They were learning.

Unsurprisingly, I noticed Katla tracking the progress of the ice blue hatchling through the air. We stayed there on the cliff side, legs hanging over the edge much as they did when we talked inside the Bay.

Outside of Ragna's view, I tied a strip of fabric over the slice on my shoulder. It seemed our forbidden excursion had gone undiscovered, for now, and Ragna wouldn't ask me the details of a missing fleet, lest she admit she knew of one. The gods must have been smiling.

Ragna had retired for the day, but not before I spoke to her.

I'm going to ask her. I think she will.

This is the point of no turning back, Aidan. The girl must one day return to the lands from whence she came. Do not make it more difficult for yourself by pulling her deeper. Her world is not yours.

Or was it just that Ragna did not want it to be?

It could be.

As the sunlight began to fall, and the flying of the hatchlings progressed greatly, I readied myself. Her gaze was again turned upon her hatchling, who was now flying in perfect circles a few feet above us.

"So." I began, gesturing towards her circle obsessed hatchling. "Does the esteemed warrior care to learn how to fly?"

CHAPTER THIRTEEN

KATLA

Bluebell.

That's what I had chosen to name her, the ice pale hatchling.

Though her scales were also a shade of blue, it was not for them that she was named. Her name was in honor of another blue armored beast, the one whom I had slain. Her scales were a reminder, a ringing from the past.

When Aidan asked his question, there had been little hesitation in my acceptance. The sights from our first flight still spun before my mind, and I couldn't imagine the sensation from atop my own dragon. Not

to mention, I had taken quite the liking to Bluebell.

Still, I had been hesitant at first to fly on a dragon that was just learning to fly itself. However, Aidan assured that over the years he would fly with the hatchlings, if they would let him.

He had demonstrated by calling over a hatching whose scales shimmered like fire, the first to hatch in the Roost.

After over-exaggerating his movements and settling himself onto the nestling in a sequence that appeared quite simple, the hatchling flew excitedly with him, if not a bit wild.

A day later, trying to follow his instruction, I would revoke my previous thoughts. It was not easy, and I blamed him for making it seem as such.

We stood on one of the many golden beaches, Aidan uncomfortable with my first flight being from a clifftop. As was I, but it was nice that he had the foresight to worry.

It was calm today, and he said that would make for a lesser burden on her wings. The sky was overcast, covered in a layer of gray clouds I would soon be much closer to. Bluebell was running around me eagerly, darting occasionally to Aidan and Fafnir. I put my hands out in front of her, and she stopped to sniff me. Her head flew around as she tried to surpass my hands and reach my face, likely to lick it again.

How to begin?

"She doesn't slow for a minute." I said frustratedly, and in truth. After leaving the Roost for the first time, Bluebell was a never smoldering fire of energy. "How am I meant to ever get onto her back? Let alone not be thrown into the cliffs once I manage?"

"It's not a matter of asking me what to do. It's one of asking *her*." Aidan explained, walking closer. "She's excited, but there's calm in the sky, especially for hatchlings. You want to fly, don't you, Bluebell?" Aidan's voice grew sweet for her. "She won't throw you anywhere, nor will she be as wild, once she's up there. There's not much room to run about in the Roost, she's just enjoying the ground. She'll cherish the sky more. Everything is about trust, almost more in yourself. Let Bluebell know what you want to do. She'll slow for you, but must be aware of what is going to happen. She's never had anyone on her back before."

"Bluebell." I tried slowly. "Hi, hi girl. You're just a bundle of speed today, aren't you? Yes, yes, hi-" I dodged her tongue. "You flew so brilliantly yesterday. I would like to fly with you, if you would allow me. We can take it slow together, yeah?"

She no longer fought to reach my face.

While she bounced on her hind legs, she did not dart through the sand. Her wide pupils watched me.

"She isn't fond of the ideas surrounding 'taking it slow'". Aidan laughed. I knew she couldn't understand all of my words, and that the majority of my meaning was likely translated through Aidan, or Fafnir. Even then, I smiled at the clear reception of my statements to her, to hear she had taken them in. "But she will allow you to fly with her."

"She said that?"

"In a much different, less vocal way. Mainly there was a lot of shouting, a desire to fly. The prospect has made her very eager."

"Eager. That isn't a terrifying addition to her mood at all. Hey, girl." I started. "I'm going to climb onto your back, now, is that alright?"

A wet lick upon my face from a forked tongue was my response, and I took it as a good one. I resisted the urge to wipe the dragon spit away in what Aidan would have called paranoia. A slight fear of somehow upsetting the winged creature I was about to put my life into the talons of.

I circled around to her right wing, my feet dragging in the sand. Cautiously, I placed one foot on her wing joint, another on her neck. So far so good.

I began to pull myself up, as I had become used to doing on Fafnir, just on a much smaller scale.

However, just as I began to stand so that I could move to a sitting position, Bluebell lurched forward. Apparently, she had spotted a fish in the water.

Fun for her, not so much for me, left to fall to the beach as my scaly earth disappeared.

Aidan jumped forward, catching me in his arms before I could crash into the sand. He seemed to be fighting his mirth.

He didn't appear bothered by our proximity, the intense feel of his arm under my knees and around my back, but I was increasingly aware of the press of my skin to his.

"Thanks." I fought a blush as he set me upright. Due to the embarrassment of having fallen.

My glare fell short once a small number of his chuckles escaped.

After several more unsuccessful attempts, I finally managed to collapse completely onto Bluebell's back. I scrambled into a seated position, sitting where her shoulders met her neck, leaning against one of the frost tipped spines.

She chirped happily, and I was relieved that she didn't plan on tossing me from her back like a wild stallion.

Bluebell seemed to have taken a liking to me too, and for that I smiled. She ran around in a quick jagged circle, looking back at me in every step she took, as if showing me she could do so. I latched onto her horns in a death grip to keep from being tossed.

She bounded around like an excited puppy until Aidan stepped in front of her, trying to calm her while he spoke to me.

"That was good! She let you on fast." He shrugged, and I resisted the urge to roll my eyes.

"The red hatchling yesterday let onto their back immediately."

"True, but I also smell-," There was an almost unnoticeable pause where he changed his wording, "I'm a dragon to them. Just, you know, smaller and with better hair. A tad more fragile."

Poor wording aside, I appreciated that he remembered my aversion to the fact. Even if it was undoubtedly hard to forget me throwing my dagger off a cliff.

"What now?"

"Well, first I would say you ought to hold onto something." He said, and I hurried to oblige, retaking hold of the white horns. Bluebell seemed to take my reattachment as a sign to go crazy again, but Aidan shushed her and she slowed. He climbed onto Fafnir, who had walked over to us. Aidan was considerably higher up than I was, Fafnir being much taller than Bluebell, but soon it wouldn't matter. "Balance is the only thing you need to prepare yourself for. Everything else just…comes."

Leaning down to pat her neck, I spoke. "Alright Bluebell, let's see how we fare off the ground, shall we? Slowly?"

She rumbled softly beneath me; her individual sound much lighter than Fafnir's. Her pale wings began to beat at my sides. I felt my nerves rise with them, as terrified as I had been on my first fight with Aidan.

There was no one else flying the dragon this time. No one but me. My breathing quickened as Bluebell took a step and we began to move steadily upwards, the sand falling away from her claws.

"Hey." I heard Aidan to my left, and turned to see him on Fafnir. He was there. "You got this, I know you do. Plus, Fafnir and I won't let you fall. I don't think Bluebell will, either."

It was his words that calmed my breathing, slowed my heart as emerald became my focal point. As gravity became meaningless, his eyes became my new tether to the earth. If nothing else, their pull was enough to keep me flying.

I took another deep breath, and we rose. Just as on my first flight I banned myself from looking down. Instead, I looked at Bluebell, or Aidan.

I tried to steer her towards Fafnir at our left, at the same time she tried to veer right. Had it not been for my grip on her horns I would have been dislodged from her back. I gasped sharply, but didn't turn to see the unspoken concern etched on Aidan's face.

We would not be going back down, I could do this. Swallowing, I tried again, putting more emphasis on my shifting weight to the left.

Bluebell chirped below me, and began to turn left as well.

"That's it! You're doing great, work with each other. Anticipate each other's moves, feel the way she shifts before she turns and follow through. Like how your hand turns to swing your sword, the end follows the start, you only have to learn it." Aidan encouraged.

I pulled back lightly on Bluebell's horns, trying to get her higher. I whooped when she did so, Aidan's laugh echoing behind us. I wobbled a bit as she leveled out, but managed to stay on.

The sky surrounding the island was filled with dragons milling about, and I angled her horns towards them. Bluebell got the message, flapping her small wings towards the much larger dragons.

I smirked as I heard Aidan call indignantly. "Hey, wait for us!"

We were noticed immediately, and dragons flew over to roar greetings in our direction.

I noticed Fafnir's signature white scales below us, and knew Aidan was ready if anything went wrong, but he wasn't going to intervene. He was letting me learn what to do on my own, figure out what worked between the two of us uniquely.

He hadn't given me many instructions on how to direct Bluebell once we were in the air, other than the most basic.

I realized we were meant to put it together ourselves, Bluebell and I. I was already noticing how she moved her head in reference to her destination, how she repositioned beneath me when she readied to turn.

She would learn what I wanted, but it would go both ways.

Flying with Aidan had been my first taste of the sky, a glimpse of the world that lay above. It was one he had lived in his whole life, and one I was beginning to live in myself.

This was freedom, untainted and uncontained. There was no one else up here. It was Bluebell and I working together to soar through Thor's realm with the creatures who were born to reach it. I was bound to her and to nothing, scaled wings pushing us through the air. She was beginning her own understanding, and I was too.

I leaned slightly to the right, and Bluebell reacted.

I felt her move, angling to the left before she did so, and I did as well. It was almost natural to fall into rhythm with her movements, cutting through the air around us with ease.

We stumbled occasionally, Bluebell becoming used to flight and to having a rider, but I fell victim to no worry.

Maybe it was because I still knew Aidan was there, maybe because I was trusting in Bluebell. I decided it was both, and searched for the first. I found Aidan below me, and what I found there made me bite my lip to hold back a smile, a sight I was glad he wasn't close enough to see.

He was sitting sideways, both legs hanging off the side of Fafnir's neck. Aidan flew about twenty feet below me, staring up at my flight with pure awe and adoration. My lip stung with the force of my teeth, and I waved him up.

Fafnir noticed my signaling, though his human brother didn't seem to, and turned his wings upwards. Aidan was still smiling as Fafnir matched the pace of Bluebell, the two dragons rumbling softly at each other.

"Do I deserve an expert opinion from the resident Dragon Boy?"

"You're doing amazing, Katla! I'm serious, you're a natural! I can't even tell that it's your first flight. Do you have some other dragon riding friends giving you lessons I don't know about?"

"One's enough for me, thank you *very* much." I snorted as he stuck his tongue out at me, turning his childish display of annoyance on Fafnir when he chortled. "I could get used to this."

And I meant more than Bluebell, more than Fafnir.

I meant more than days under a never-ending sky from the back of a dragon. More than the ever-changing view, the new cycles of life I got to witness. I meant all of it, with him, and none of it without.

"Yeah." He began, and there was a new sort of something in the open air when stormy eyes met sea green. "I could, too."

***

Night had fallen some hours ago, and I rested inside the Bay with Bluebell.

We had returned here after our flight, when Aidan had finally dragged me from the sky so we could eat. When I asked if Bluebell could stay with us, since she had no mother down at the Roost, he agreed instantly.

Fafnir and Aidan had taken off a while ago on a solo flight, their first one in a few weeks. Aidan asked me if I was alright with being alone, and at that point, I had all but shoved him out of the cave. I had Bluebell, not to mention the fact that I was perfectly capable of surviving a night without their snoring. Aidan and Fafnir's flights had been something they had always done together.

Although Aidan tried to hide it, Fafnir not as much, I could tell they both missed them.

Despite the advancing hour, I still did not sleep, lingering excitement from the day keeping me up.

I was sitting on the edge of the stone outcrop in the dim light from the moon outside. One of Aidan's books sat loosely in my hand, pages splayed open to a chart of the stars. I didn't understand the mathematics of it, but the constellations were captivating enough.

Bluebell was flying near the water, trying to snag fish as they jumped above the small waves. I watched her in amusement, laughing as she was caught in the face by a squirming tail instead of doing the catching. It was rather silent inside the Bay, most of the flying about outside. Bluebell chirped at the Bay's entrance, and I looked after her focus.

Curiosity turned to confusion as I gained sight of white scales entering the hole.

"Aidan?"

"Katla!" Was the answering shout, but he didn't sound worried. Or afraid. Or hurt. That was good.

Fafnir landed beside me, looking rather excited for a dragon. Aidan was practically being tossed around from his spot-on Fafnir's neck, but he didn't seem to notice.

"You have to come see this!" He exclaimed, startling some lounging dragons from a tunnel a few feet below.

"But- your flight with Fafnir, I don't want to interrupt-"

"We both want you to come."

Given Fafnir's approving rumble, I couldn't help but agree.

I hurried over, taking Aidan's hand and allowing him to pull me up. I was excited, for whatever it was he wanted to show me, and because I had yet to fly during the night.

I wrapped my hands around his waist as Fafnir took off, waved to Bluebell, and within seconds we were out of the cave. I shivered slightly in the night air, thankful for the white pelt that hung around my shoulders and the warmth of Aidan's back against my chest.

Warmth running under Fafnir's scales heated the air around us.

Flying in the dark was so entirely different than during the day that my breath was stolen before I had a chance to comprehend. We sailed over the ocean, and as the minutes ticked by, I held down the urge to ask Aidan where we were going.

An island appeared on the waves, too large to be home to a simple clan, or a patch of shore. There were lights visible. This was a Voluspian Kingdom, people clearly lived there, so what were we doing?

"Aidan, there are people-"

"They won't see us."

I frowned slightly, but listened regardless. We rose higher as we came upon the island, likely to stay out of sight. Fafnir had crossed over the beaches then, and was still climbing.

Then, Aidan pointed to the pitch sky above us, and simply said; "Look."

I followed his hand, but didn't see anything out of the ordinary. Feeling as though I was missing something rather obvious, I asked;

"The stars?"

He shook his head gently. "Look closer."

I squinted, not understanding, but still willing to do as he asked. Eventually, I noticed something peculiar about a specific patch of stars. The small flames were moving.

"What?" I asked, lost as to how the stars could possibly be doing so. "What is that?"

"Not stars, *dragons*."

The lights were twinkling, and as we approached them and they us, I soon began to make out serpentine shapes. The dragons were very small, familiar. Calor, Aidan had named them.

They flew in a mass around us, flickering like fireflies, light the same shade as the moon spreading from the middle of their stomachs and moving across their gray scales. It was stunning, as they circled us, shining as imitation stars against the pitch-black sky. Moonlight fell down, illuminating the shimmering ivory of Fafnir's scales.

It was incredible, but not all that Aidan had to show me.

I began to hear noises as we came over the center of the island, the dragons still swarming around us. I gasped as I recognized the sounds as music coming from the middle of a small village.

We rose above the lit square, not too high to be seen on a normal night, but I knew no one from any village would be paying attention during a party. The town below was awash with orange light from their torches. People danced and drank to the lively music.

I didn't register Aidan standing, simply leaning closer to capture the wondrous view. It was amazing to see from this angle the parties I had so regularly attended. Even though I did not know these people, I had so easily been one of them, not that long ago.

I wondered what I was now.

The music below changed, the musicians striking up their instruments once more. The song was upbeat but slow, and I smiled as the lovely song reached my ears. We didn't play many songs like it back on Lamid, the music fit more for the drinking competitions, to weave around the victorious shouts of celebration.

I was content to listen, to enjoy the song while it lasted, certain this was why Aidan had brought me. I turned to look around, wanting to share this with him. It seemed he had the same idea, but as usual held a surprise so unexpected and wonderful.

Aidan waited on Fafnir's wing.

I stood slowly from my place on a scaled neck, squinting in confusion. The music swelled beneath us, wind raising it perfectly to our ears. As I stepped slowly towards him, careful to keep a hand on Fafnir's spines, he lowered himself lightly into what was almost a *bow*, unpracticed as it was.

Then, he extended a hand towards me, and my eyes flicked from him to the people dancing below.

Oh.

This was what he wanted to show me? In order to reach his hand, I would have to let go of Fafnir's spine completely. There would be nothing holding us here.

A small smile found its way to his face. "Do you trust me?"

The question just seemed to keep popping up, always with the same answer. I gave it to him this time.

"Of course."

I let go.

Stepping forward, I stole his hand in mine.

He pulled me out further onto the silver wing. My heart was pounding, not because of the height, nor the potential danger. A grin revealed itself on my lips.

The music continued, and Aidan carefully put his right hand on my side, unsure. The contact burned, although not unpleasantly. I contained a laugh, grabbing his fingers and moving them down to my waist. I took the other, guiding it to the same spot on my right. He smiled gratefully.

I placed my own hands on his shoulders. He rolled them, shifting a little closer, an eyebrow raised, clearly rather lost. His hands were stiff, not a single touch fluid, rigid. I giggled, nodding in assurance at the dragon riding boy's attempts.

The music suddenly rose from below us, and at once we began moving. It was light, joyous and happy, slow.

The townsfolk spun around their musicians, though none below could have predicted the dance they were missing in the sky.

The flickering dragons swirled around us in our very own sea of stars, enraptured by the people below them. Moonlight scattered and reflected brilliantly across the pure scales of the dragon whose wings we moved upon.

Aidan held me gently, and we fell into step with the rhythm.

"And just where did you learn to dance?"

"I watched for a while. Before I came back." He admitted sheepishly.

"Oh, I see. That's why we've been doing the same two moves over and over, then?" I asked teasingly. He blushed and ducked his head, and mine tipped back as I laughed. He looked disappointed as he resurfaced, glancing uncertainly at the smooth movements of those below. "I'm messing with you."

I wasn't. But that was perfectly alright with me.

The music reached a crescendo, and I let go of Aidan's shoulder.

"Are you ready?" I encouraged, smirking at the expression which proclaimed he was not.

I nudged his hand until it dropped from my skin, taking it in my free one and stepping back. The movement of ducking under his outstretched arm was so endearingly awkward that I nearly did it again in the same motion.

The people cheered at something below, unaware of what they contributed to.

I had danced at celebrations before, for the fun of it. Usually with Eliana or Calin, Ingrid. This was different, its purpose more than simple fun when our touches burned.

I knew this, and I couldn't bring myself to mind.

I tugged his arm lightly, he pulled in response, and I swung back into him. His nervous smile turned proud, and again I lost control of a laugh.

We spun together as we crossed a dragon's wing. The music wrapped around us, and with him so close the night air wasn't so frigid.

There was no village below us, only the sweet melody that lifted on night air. There were no dragons around us, only shimmering spots of silver in my vision. There was only him, only Aidan, auburn hair and emerald eyes, the leather padding of soft armor under my fingers.

He spun me again, and when I was brought back to him I reached up, placing my arms around his neck. He hesitated for only a moment, before wrapping his arms around my waist, drawing me closer. We were stepping backwards, and although I couldn't see where we were going, I knew he could, and that was enough.

He stumbled, knocking against me.

We righted and continued, until we went opposite directions, our hands breaking apart.

He looked at me, embarrassed, trying again. He tugged too early, and my shoulder jostled him.

Apologetic, he stepped back, leaving an almost physical emptiness against me.

"Sorry. Maybe this wasn't such a good idea." His hands were lowering.

He was going to end this, whatever this was.

I reached for him as calmly as I could manage, gently bringing him into my movements. Measured steps.

"Don't think. Feel."

My hand slid into his, soft and firm.

"I won't do it right." He implored.

"There is no 'right'." I promised. "There's only you and me, right here, right now. There is only your hands, and mine. There's no one but us, so who is going to tell you what's wrong? Feel me." My hand drew his higher, his body closer. "Feel how I move? Feel the music. You only have to feel, and follow me. That's as right as it gets."

And then it was moving in time, in step, practically seamless.

Each of my shifts followed his, each beat of the music matching us. His touch was warm against the air, against me. Calor light spilled across his eyes, brilliant green against the darkness. A few times he dropped his gaze, but I waited, and it always found mine again.

"This is... something." He whispered.

"Dancing?"

"Feeling."

We danced in a comfortable lapse of words for only a few minutes, music pressing between us, Aidan's expression growing more and more distant each time I spun back to face him. Eventually he had slowed his moves so thoroughly that my attempt to continue pulled him forward, but he didn't seem to notice.

I halted in my turn, contenting myself to sway in his hold as I attempted to draw him back from his thoughts. I was enjoying this, wasn't he?

"Aidan?"

"I don't want you to leave."

And we stepped again, slightly out of rhythm. Somewhere on the horizon there was Ingrid, Ylva, Eliana and Calin. My mother. Lamid.

Somewhere so unreachable was the life I had left behind; one I would have to return to.

Not now.

"I'm not leaving."

He seemed quite suddenly to come back to himself, eyes locking onto mine with such intensity that I slowed my movements. Hesitantly, in our crawling sway, his hand rose. We turned to one side, and when I came back to him, his palm fit gently around my cheek. Painfully cautious.

I stepped a little nearer then. Swaying.

"How do you know when you're in love with someone?"

There was an embarrassingly long stretch of time in which I tried to fit meaning into his words, to understand what he had so earnestly asked.

Aidan breathed deeply, and I watched as he swallowed. His mouth opened, moving without spoken words as he searched for the right ones. Eyes dropped to the scales beneath us for a moment, and then snapped back up to me with fragile determination.

"I believe that I am in love with you."

It was so quiet and unsure, the voice in which he spoke to me.

And it was really so sudden, so unexpected, that I couldn't convince myself to give a response, if I had even thought of one to begin with. I was blank, moving aimlessly under his hand.

Almost immediately he glanced over my shoulder, refusing to meet my stare as his words tumbled out, each stammered explanation chased by another one, just as hastily released.

"Sorry. I- I don't know...I don't know how to do *this*. How can I even- only- I want to dance with you. This. This, right now, is what I want. I want to fly with you. I want you to see all the ways the sky can change from above, and I really, really want to be there when you do. I want to hear more about Ylva learning to walk or your crazy schemes with Eliana, because you're telling me about them, and I want to listen to you for hours. I want to give you things, and show you things, and tell you things. I can't stop thinking about you, Katla, every moment you're with me and every second you're not. And I don't think I'll be able to stay behind if you go."

His hands remained silk on mine, tension in his arms as they moved us unthinkingly. "I don't really know what that means, but I believe I am in love with you. I want that to be what this is." My expression must have been so terribly devoid of anything but shock, because I watched sudden worry crash over his features. "I don't know what you're meant to do, or if there's a way about it? If you tell me, I can-"

"No." I interrupted him, realizing the turn of his words and managing to choke out some sort of answer, albeit far too little compared to what he was giving me. "There's no way."

A simple, "Okay,"

I was aware of the music under us, the wind that sent shivers racing along my skin. The warm spots where Aidan touched me in the dark sky.

There was a certain excitement in the late hour that fed upon my tired body and served only to elate my senses further. The air smelled golden, like spilling ale and the falling ash of torchlight.

So slowly did I spin under his hand, caught in a dazed mind still uncomprehending. How did I feel? What was this, what we were doing, what we had been? I faced him again, bringing my focus slowly to his eyes.

"Katla."

A pause. We didn't move. My earth was in his hold.

Gently, I felt a slight tug as a breeze pushed a fallen curl behind me. His other hand joined its partner, impossibly soft against my skin, my cheek. His face was inches from mine.

I breathed. "Some feeling."

And then Aidan whispered, so careful and still.

"Is it wrong that this is the most fearsome thing I have ever done, but I want it to stretch on?"

And for the love of all the gods who may have been, that was my final pull back to reality. Back to the stunning clarity of what he had said, what he was now saying. To me, in this simple moment that we held above the world.

It was of no sense but my own that I leaned in and gave us both an answer.

CHAPTER FOURTEEN

AIDAN

Light.

Pure and relentless light, assaulting me blissfully wherever it found purchase.

I was blind to the world; my eyes had closed upon her form. Yet, I could see her so clearly, feel her perfectly against me. My hands had found their way to her face, cupping the sides of it, though I couldn't recall telling them to do so.

I felt her fingers wrap around the back of my neck, and suddenly she was closer to me, if such a thing were possible. Her lips were soft on mine, unbelievably soft, more so than I had allowed myself to imagine.

It was slow and deep, such a strange sensation, so foreign and new.

This was my answer to the agonizing questions.

Though I doubted I could give her anything close to what she was giving me as I fumbled my way through this, I couldn't imagine a greater euphoria.

Although it felt all too immediate, we pulled away slowly. Her eyes searched mine, moving slightly in the shifting light. I wondered what she was searching for, and if I was meant to find answers in my captivation of her. She smiled then, and I did the same.

It hadn't been anything more than interest when we first came upon the island where the people danced.

The sky was alight with shimmering Calor, though the people below couldn't have known it. I was caught by a curious realization when I discovered I wanted her there. It was just a passing thought which continued to build, and despite my attempts, refused to be hidden from Fafnir.

I didn't want to abandon our original flight, to turn back. However, Fafnir wouldn't have it, utterly gleeful at my rising idea, his laugh reverberating in my mind as he tried to force out his encouragement. This was all far too entertaining for him.

I was forced to endure his horrible jokes, and thank every power higher than myself that Katla couldn't hear him.

Alright, alright. We already have enough little hatchlings running about, thank you.

Fafnir's voice echoed through my mind with the latest wisecrack, and I couldn't bring myself to be annoyed with him.

I only half-heartedly listened to what he was saying, anyway. I hardly heard the music. To be truly honest, there was really only one thing I was focusing on, and she was standing in front of me.

Strands of dark curls fell into her face, and ice eyes sparked in the moonlight. It was enchanting, and I couldn't look away, nor did I want to.

I spun her again, the laugh she produced at the action was sweeter music than the sound from below could ever hope to imitate. The song had changed at this point, and we simply changed with it, neither of us stopping or slowing.

Calor flew around us, chirping to Fafnir in quiet delight. He didn't reciprocate their excitement, growling quietly whenever they neared.

I was lucky they had come out tonight, usually sticking to their caves and the protective dark for their beacon-like communications. The night sky lay above us, moonshine wafting down. It was beautiful, but none such as the raven-haired girl I held.

I wasn't sure what she thought as we danced on a dragon's wing, if her feelings mirrored my own.

My thoughts were filled with the memory of that first flight with her, which had felt like my first in a long time. She had been struck by the perfectly lovely sight, as I was by her now. I wanted nothing more than to share with her a world so beautiful.

To share it with *her*, because it couldn't just be *someone* anymore.

It was only her, and I think it had been for a long while. It could be only her, and I believed it was the same for Katla, too, the moment she put down my sword and truly listened.

I wasn't sure what led me to this, to such an open action, although she didn't deny it. What had lent me the courage to jump on the smoldering spark of this insane notion of confession. To attempt this dance, my every hopeless action surely contradictory to human precedents.

I was a fumbling mess, but she did not cast aside my efforts. Efforts to fly, as the humans did. My own drive for these words and these movements was a jumbled cumulation of instances and feelings.

I had sat and talked with her for hours, leaning over a stony ledge as we learned about each other. Quiet smiles as she played with baby dragons in the home I had always known. The light in her eyes when I was able to show her something new. The way I was struck silent when I watched her in battle, a valkyrie among men. A soft kindness as she opened herself to the creatures she had always feared, an underlying bravery to have done so.

315

She was the girl who decided to defend those she had been taught to hate, who showed more compassion than I could have imagined. I couldn't believe it was simply because she was the girl I found on that boat, but because she was the girl who stayed.

My hands found her as she came back to me. I continued to dance on wings of moonlight with the only girl I would ever truly see.

***

It had been late when we returned to the Bay, and Katla was still sleeping. The sun had not yet risen, and I was feeling rather tired myself, but I had something to do this morning.

I strapped two pouches to my leather belt, feeling their weights burden me to either side. Hopefully, Ragna would never realize I had left for anything more than a simple flight.

And then there was Takka.

She laid in the opening of our cave home, watching me with dilated eyes. Her concern made the air thick, but I had already done my convincing. Regardless, I did my best to assuage her worry, if only so that her nervously flicking tail would not wake Katla.

I'll return in a handful of hours. There is nothing to be worried about-

She huffed. *You smell richly of your own fear, Her's of Mine. You enjoy the idea no more than I.*

Takka. I sighed. *It's not as if I will be parading Fafnir about. Human senses cannot trace the scent of dragons. I can handle it.*

You've never attempted anything of the sort! She retorted, not angry, but firm.

I restrained my mental tone from giving insight into my annoyance, knowing that if I lost this foothold I had managed, Takka would have no qualms informing Ragna. Or sitting on me. Struggling against a smirk, I attempted a new tactic.

So you don't approve, then? Subtly, as nothing more than an undercurrent of thought, I recalled the other human in the room.

Her eyes narrowed, but her voice softened. *Your reasoning for this undertaking may be the only aspect of it which I approve of.*

Thank you, Takka. I smiled. *And, I have been near humans before.*

A draconic scoff bounced quietly off the rock walls.

The much larger of the pouches held dragon teeth I had collected, the best I could find, and my favorites of the collection.

In the other pouch lay dragon scales. Scales of brilliant colors, from only the rarest of dragons I had encountered. There was a scale that shone gold, one that was composed only of the most vibrant blues seen only in Amphitrite. Scales I had found with the most stunning patterns, gems in their own right.

There were several of Fafnir's own inside as well, being the only one of a few dragons I had met of pure white. I had managed to procure one of Bluebell's, one she was all too happy to relinquish once I had explained its intended purpose.

She had grown exceedingly enamored with Katla. There was a drawing as well, sketched over and over, finally copied onto a page tucked in my belt.

I was slightly nervous, as Takka had accurately deduced. I had never been to a market before.

It hadn't been intentional to clue in Takka. However, in my excitement at her return from hunting on isles outside our waters, I had let my defenses slip. My foremost thoughts of anticipation had become visible, my idea.

If Ragna knew of my plans, she would take violent pleasure in my death, likely after smothering me in a hug. Takka stood, sauntering out of the cave.

I will be flying over this isle you venture to. The very instant one of them bares their wrath at you, I will snatch you from the ground and burn those left in our wake.

I love you, too, Takka. I promised with a grin.

She passed my brother and departed.

318

Fafnir was already standing by the edge, waiting for me, grouchy and tired. I walked to him as quietly as I could, trying not to disturb Katla. Thinking of her brought back our dance the previous night, and for a moment I could still hear the music spinning.

I patted Fafnir lightly on the side, both in thanks and apology for getting so little sleep to lug me around.

Alright, Fafnir. I began. *Let's see if we've gotten any better at sneaking out of here.*

He greeted me by pushing his large head into my chest, and I scratched his scales for a moment. Fafnir, too, was very excited about how the night had gone. He had insisted for the majority of our flight home that he enjoyed it more than we did.

This was followed by a few choice comments about Katla and I that had me poking him in the small spots between scales when Katla wasn't looking.

In an instant I was sitting, and he took off gently. Despite us both wishing to fly with Katla, there was no denying that we missed our flights together, alone. Missed the death taunting tricks that we couldn't do with her, and the high speeds she would disapprove of. Last night had been our first in a while, the idea of which had gone out the window when we happened upon the village party in Vanir.

319

While the idea had originally been mine, I was hesitant to go through with it, knowing that I was stopping our flight. Fafnir had no such reservations, turning and heading for the Bay, deaf to all I said, entirely ready for me to finally do something a bit 'bolder' with Katla.

His words.

Everything had really come together when we noticed the Calor. I immediately knew I had to show them to her, even if I couldn't work up the nerve to go through with...the rest.

She had looked entranced by the dragons who shone like stars, so much livelier against the night than the dark of the Bay cave. It was a look that I felt mirrored on my own face as I watched her.

So now I left the Bay, resting loose on Fafnir's neck. I held a small map in my hands, a copy of the large one which took up a wall of our cave lodgings.

Trader's Isle was our destination, north of the Isle of the Bay. Anything you needed to purchase, anything you were looking to find, could be found on Trader's Isle.

That is, if the words overheard from Sigurd lips could be trusted.

I believed it was where they took all the people they captured, to be sold as thralls, slaves. Why they needed the money, and so much of it, I had yet to piece together. There was no pattern to their plans, no system to who they attacked, or the size of their fleets.

The fact that Olavi's motives were becoming increasingly difficult to decipher did not bode well.

It certainly hadn't escaped my notice that the Sigurd frequented the island. That was why we had left so early, so that Fafnir would not be noticed upon arrival.

I vowed to myself that I would do my best to free any captives I saw. I knew slavery was common on Trader's Isle, it had to be, if they were to host the auctions. However, even if I wasn't all that well-versed in the laws, I knew most of the kingdoms did not partake in slavery of any form. It would do only good to set those people free.

Some of them were children, and the Sigurd certainly didn't care about that fact for any moral reason. Nor did anyone who came to the Isle to participate in the auctions.

It took quite some time for the island to appear on the horizon, nothing too special about its shape. Still, I was incredibly on edge. Even in the Sigurd raids I had never been around as many people as were sure to flood the markets.

Already, I could make out tens of ships at the docks, none quite the same. Thankfully, none of them sported the dark wood and serpentine insignias associated with the Sigurd. I intensely doubted my chances attempting to free prisoners from a group of them without any dragons, but I'd likely try anyway.

There was an idea Ragna would scold me for.

We flew high, almost to the bottom cloud level to avoid being seen from below. The sun was still down, but it soon would climb. We were being overly cautious, though neither of us would admit it. Fafnir landed on the opposite shore from the ships. The area was thick with foliage, the paths overgrown and sand bare. There would be no people around here.

Here goes nothing. Stay hidden, okay? I told Fafnir, readying myself for a walk through the forest.

Be careful. He nearly snarled.

I gasped. "My own brother. You think so little of me?"

Fafnir grumbled. *Less, even.*

He knew I received the warning, and he, mine. I turned and began my trek through the thick woods, heading in the direction of the buildings visible from the air. I reached the market not long after the sun had peaked above the ocean, a little more than tired from my trip. Not for the first time, I envied the wings of my family. It was easy to forget my annoyance when I finally dragged my eyes from the dirt beneath my boots.

I nearly sprinted back the way I had come, but the urge, the need to devour more of what I saw, was stronger than the desire to run.

The strange area was bursting with people, despite what I believed to be an early hour. Crates, wheelbarrows, spare wood and small tables converged into stalls, unique to each corner of the market. Canopies of bright fabric stretched over them, held in place by the thinnest string, or the thickest coils of rope.

And each of them sported something new!

Furs spilled over the side of one such table, so much neater and cleaner sewn than the ones which adorned my bed that I forced back a wince. The light caught on a particularly white fur, larger than the one which usually sat on Katla's shoulders. It was clear the light fibers were not from near the Voluspian Isles, and I wondered which animal had produced such a pure coat. Perhaps Katla's had been an exotic gift.

There was another setup, composed of crates stacked in some crude semi-circle, overflowing with apples. A sign leant haphazardly against a box, the harsh handwriting describing the apples as the best in all of Voluspa, brought straight from Atori. Another stall across the street boasted the very same.

A young woman with skin the same honey chocolate as the sweets Ragna had once brought was glaring from behind her stand at the opposing fruits. Her hands worked in a flurry, attempting to spruce up her own arrangement of produce, clearly hoping a superior display would lure would-be apple purchasers into her folds.

A harried looking old woman flitted about, no clear stall in sight, nearly drowning in the violent vibrance of the plants which surrounded her.

Flowers spilled from pots, vines littered the cobblestone street they traveled into, and a package of seeds opened at her feet. A bushy bunch of wild brown hair chased after her as she weaved between the leaves, drawing several eyes as she ran about her apparent garden.

A weathered arm lashed out, seizing an unfortunate man and drawing him towards what appeared to be an old keg, emptied of liquid and filled with roses. She twittered endlessly on, either uncaring or unaware of the obvious disgruntlement of the man at her side.

I nearly leapt out of my skin when a violent force swept into me from behind, shoving me forward.

A hand fought to find my sword as I turned, full of regret and volatile turmoil in this gathering place of humans.

A mop of bright blonde hair pushed past my elbow, not at all deterred by the very solid obstacle it had collided with. The small girl was spurred on ever faster, short legs pumping in pursuit of several chickens. Her cries were part annoyance and part glee as she ducked through the legs of various Voluspians, chasing alabaster tail feathers just beyond her reach.

Unbidden, a startled laugh escaped me, my stomach burning with swallowed terror.

A soft sound of contentment floated from my lips as a scent graced my nose, warm despite its distance. Arms which were tanned and brown carried a tray of pastries which were immediately noticed. The man smiled jovially as his load gained the attention of a crowd, all flocking towards the wonderful smell.

In a trance, I almost followed them, before a woman laden with daggers cut past me, and I flung back. But she did not turn towards me, did not see with inhuman eyes the invisible truth, that I was separate from them, and fling her blades into my heart. Did not regard me at all.

And I could breathe easier for it.

Noise erupted all around, an endless and tumultuous falling and rising of whispers and shouts. The faces which surrounded me were so intensely and individually unique that I was taken aback. Not only in their shapes and colors, but in the expressions they bore. Not the stern face of Ragna, the murderous curling lips of the Sigurd, or the soft smile I remembered of my mother.

Different, even, from Katla's determined eyes.

Even though the hustle and bustle of a hundred moving bodies was close knit, tight and squeezed, the people were unbothered.

They moved in tandem with the swelling crowd as if it meant nothing, naturally. Was I capable of the same? It seemed even they had their own secluded world, tucked against and tied to the earth. Though the sky was unbounded and vast, not burdened by gravity and space, the land had its own rules.

A ripple of faint amusement passed over me, like the last ring of water disturbed by a small pebble, fanning out into nothingness. Somewhere in the clouds, almost out of reach, Takka watched on. She was held back by the cover of the sky, and Fafnir by the shade of the forest. I was the only one of us who could step now into the light which poured onto the street of dirt and stone.

My hands shook with something excited and nervous as I did.

Burlap ghosting over my hand was enough of a reminder to pull me back into my original purpose. Not stopping to think, I dropped myself into the masses.

My eyes tried to stay down, to avoid any contact with the strangers around me, but I had not yet had my fill of awe.

I fell quickly into the crowd, the voices louder yet, but I found the thrum of words familiar. There was nothing foreign about a constant flow of voiced thoughts, so they were rather easy to ignore. I tried to keep my movements from identifying me as some sort of outsider, but still jumped back when a person strayed too close.

While I walked, I searched. This island was not restricted only to furs and foods. My pupils filled with hanging steel and swinging iron, deadly sharp blades and curved handles. Critically, I scrutinized these stalls which carted weapons of average magnificence, casual travelers lined up beside them.

Simplicity was easily obtained, taken with almost no effort from a Sigurd ship, if I truly wanted. It was not what I had come for.

The sun had fully cleared the water when I finally located a shop. It was clearly far more permanent than the temporary stalls I had seen. Stakes were driven deep into the earth, supporting a roof of pine. A chimney loosed plumes of smoke into the air, the roaring furnace it sat above releasing a wave of heat out into the alley.

Not only a stall, but a forge.

The weapons it held were pristine, dangling from various racks and littering a large wooden counter. There was no one waiting in a line, only the occasional onlooker gazing at the shop before checking their pouches and hurrying off.

A man stood inside, banging a hammer on a twisted sword which glowed red in the embers. His beard ran down to his stomach in a thick braid, black hair cut short to his head. He was rather large, but not threatening.

I was struck with a sudden recognition.

Was he possibly a Sigurd clansman? It faded when he turned and his face was revealed, dark brown eyes finding me. His arm was pale, but bare of thick bands. Not Sigurd.

I proceeded towards the worktable, confronting the fact that I possessed not the slightest sense as to what I was doing. I'd never bought anything in my life, much less ordered anything. I'd never had need to. At the very least, I didn't have to worry about striking up a conversation.

"What do you want, kid?" The smith asked, his voice low and gruff. It was not unkind, just annoyed.

I cleared my throat. "I'd like to have a sword made. The finest you could forge."

"You and everyone else on this rock. I've got requests and repairs out the back door. Get lost, boy, you couldn't afford it."

"This is Trader's Isle, isn't it? I can trade."

The man raised an eyebrow at that. My fingers fumbled at my hip. I started first by withdrawing the sketch from my belt, unfolding it to reveal the hilt of a sword.

The pommel was sure something to look at, if I did say so myself. Or at least, it would be.

The golden metal was adorned with polished gems, and if you peered close enough, you could see that they were dragon scales. The man lumbered closer, holding the drawing up to his eye. The look he gave implied he wasn't taking it at all seriously, humoring me with his next question.

"You're going to provide the stones yourself, I assume?"

"Yes, actually." I ignored his surprise, pulling the smaller of the two pouches free. I let it open to reveal the polished scales inside. He took in the contents with shock, glancing from me to the scales. I knew he was trying to compare them to any other he had seen before, and was unable to do so. They were unique, patterns and colors I doubted others had seen. "The parchment has all of the places labeled with what scales to use, and where."

The man didn't even seem shocked that I wished to use scales as gemstones, they were certainly beautiful enough to rival any stones I could have chosen. I recalled the dragons from which they had come, they had been beautiful and amazing, most allowing me one of their scales. Others, I had simply found, washed up in the sand or in the nest of a Kaida.

I hadn't had a real purpose for them, and although I treasured them, wanted to use them for this. Had they not been worthy of taking the place of precious stones, I would have purchased gems instead. Surely there was a merchant here who dabbled in them.

"How did you come to have these?" He asked, still enraptured by the bag I had sat on his counter.

The prepared lie tasted bitter, even if I knew it wasn't true. "Victory spoils."

Gods, please don't let Takka be listening.

"You?" The laugh was mocking.

I didn't have a more believable excuse as to how I came to possess them, and the lie would explain the next bag as well. I ignored him, drawing two scales from the woven pouch. Pure white and pale blue. Fafnir's and Bluebell's.

"These two go here." I told the smith, pointing at the sketch. At the top of the hilt I had drawn two scales, entwined with each other. The skeptical man seemed to have overcome his initial doubt.

"A trade, you said? What exactly are you proposing?"

Taking a breath, I gave up the much larger sack, allowing the man to open it for himself. Even more than he had when I presented the scales, the man gaped with widened eyes at the dragon teeth and claws.

I allowed myself to feel inward pride, they were the finest I had collected. Extremely sharp, and much larger than an average dragon's. I was likely the only person, besides my mother or Ragna, who had ever been able to explore dwellings of dragons big enough to lose them.

It was hard to see them go, but I knew it was well worth it.

The man was still looking in the bag, and he brought one of the teeth outside the reaches of the shadowed roof, taking in its condition. He picked through all of them carefully, silent, and I began to wonder if he would say anything at all. Had I misjudged human transactions so incredibly?

"Will that be enough?"

I had been sure when I selected the teeth and claws that it would be, but the man wasn't responding. He startled, as if he had forgotten I was there. Then he drew back with the sack of teeth, as if he was worried I would suddenly snatch it away and take my business elsewhere. That had to be a good sign, right?

"Sure kid, sure. Absolutely." He let out a breathy chuckle, pulling the paper closer to him. "What was your name, again?"

"Aidan." I said slowly, contemplating his sudden change of heart while he pulled a list of names from a shelf. Instead of starting at the bottom, he added my name to the very top of the list.

"Well, Aidan, I'm Hagen. You've managed yourself a deal, congratulations. Now, explain this hilt to me. What exactly am I meant to do with these damned things?"

I smiled in victory, and was all too happy to detail the design I had spent nights on. It was easy to ramble on about the complicated metalwork I envisioned, even if my words slowed when I remembered the listening party was not Ragna. Or Katla.

We spoke about the blade, the weight and length it should be. The man had raised an eyebrow when it became clear the sword was not for someone of my stature, but didn't ask. Hagen was almost overly polite, despite having already declared a deal.

As I left the stall, I mused over the value of those teeth. Hagen immediately took them out for inspection again upon my departure.

The sun was high in the sky, and I made my way back to the forest's edge. It was odd, how the sounds of this strange new world faded into silence as the whispers of the forest overtook them. Driven either by lingering nerves, or knowing the humans were at my back, I strode quickly through the undergrowth.

A rough and dripping tongue was my greeting when I met the beach. Fafnir had retreated from his hiding place in the thick trees, lowering his neck while laughing at me. I sputtered, wiping the unexpected dragon saliva from my face.

It's a shame. I prayed to your gods that the humans would take you back.

"Yeah, yeah. You're hilarious." *Let's go!*

Someone's in a hurry to see his mate!

I sputtered again for a different reason, receiving another rumbling snicker for my troubles.

CHAPTER FIFTEEN

AIDAN

There shouldn't have been anything unusual about the raid.

No human captives, and thus forth, Ragna allowed us to handle the small fleet on our own. She had said nothing about my absence the day Fafnir and I flew to Trader's Isle. I suspected she knew my flight path had not been one approved by her standards, but had yet to mention it.

I wasn't sure if I would rather she believed I had been scouting for more of Olavi's armadas, or if she knew the truth. That I had not only been on a human held island, but ventured into the depths of it.

No, believing her own conclusion was far safer for all involved.

"Aidan!" Katla gripped my arm, and I was pulled back into my focus.

What in the- Fafnir cursed colorfully as he spun.

I found myself surprised by vibrant green which graced the top of my vision as our world twisted. Not the tanned brown and white of feathered

334

arrows chasing us, but a nearly glowing liquid. Not a human projectile, but a draconic one.

"Hey!" I shouted as we returned to normal alignment. *Who just shot at us?*

Someone with a grudge? We hadn't recently bested any Syre in races, or playful hunting for Kaida.

Even if we had, most were responsible enough not to launch the burning dredges of their stomach towards us during a battle. Was it simply a missed shot? Who was soon to be teased relentlessly for their aim?

Fafnir snarled, whipping his head and surveying the water. *I don't know, but whoever is down there had better watch where they're hurling their reeking-*

"You okay?" I asked, looking over my shoulder.

Katla smiled, taking a breath. "Of course. It'll take a few more loops to throw me."

"Careful," I advised, "Fafnir just might challenge that."

Other than the misfire which served only to put Fafnir in a foul mood, the fight was predictable.

Those captured were set loose, the Sigurd ships sunk. A few hurled arrows and passing curses on our lives and future children. The last painted arrowhead wrapped in a snake's hold disappeared with the top of a sail, and Fafnir turned for the Bay. All in a day's work, and quite honestly, my thoughts were wandering down the path of boar for lunch.

At first, the flight back was normal, too.

Katla sat in front of me, and my attention deviated to the shifts of her, rather than the ocean beneath us. In hindsight, I supposed we were flying rather low.

I was listening to Katla animatedly recount a particular move she had pulled against a man she was rather sure had been drunk at the time. Neither of us was paying attention to the water. Thank the gods for Fafnir.

A straggler? Can we- hey!

His voice in my head was the only warning I received, and the only one I needed. I tightened my legs so that we wouldn't fall, and pulled Katla even further into me, so that we were completely pressed together.

I had my arms wrapped around her now, and strangely enough, it didn't seem as though she was going to question it.

I shoved that aside to analyze later, for not a second later we were upside down. Fafnir had tucked his wings close to his body and rolled upwards, narrowly avoiding an arrow which cut through the space that his chest had previously occupied. To Katla's credit, she did not cry out, and instead tightened her own grip on my arms, trying to keep me in place as much as I was to her.

Fafnir righted, and both Katla and I leaned over his neck to survey the sea.

There was a fishing boat in the water, shouted orders audible from its deck. The rest of the dragons from the Bay were higher up, and those who had realized what happened were circling above, ready to help if it seemed we were in danger.

I raised a hand and threw my thoughts out to them, we were startled but not distressed, and they followed the others.

The people onboard were running about, scrambling and uncoordinated. I was about to tell Fafnir to get us out of there before they could fire again. Katla stopped me.

"Wait, Aidan! Wait! Look at that sail!"

She was pointing, her voice laced with equal parts excitement and unease. I followed her hand to the sail of the ship, the symbol on its surface. It was the same one she had recognized on the cover of my mother's notebook, vines twisting over that falling sword.

The boat was from Lamid, Katla's home. Maybe once mine.

A hostile boat was, regardless of origin, a hostile boat, in my opinion as well as Fafnir's. Ultimately, however, I wasn't going to make the decision for her. We hadn't spoken much about the future, if Katla would return home. As much as it would hurt, if she asked me to set her down on the ship below so she could go, I'd do it.

Maybe I'd even find a way to go with her, if those Lamidians didn't kill us first.

"What should we do?" I asked despite my dread at her possible answer, and she turned to me.

She had a strange look on her face, as if surprised by the query. There was a softness to her that made me hopeful, her eyes almost grateful for the question. Yet, now that I had asked, she seemed unsure. Something like reluctant determination settled deep into her features.

"I think we should just head...wait a second." Katla cut off, suddenly scrutinizing the ship with fiercer attention. She let out a strangled sort of laugh at what she was seeing, though what that was, I had no idea. Her voice was shaky. "I don't believe it. Aidan, let's go lower."

She can't be serious! After...everything? Fafnir cried.

I took a deep breath, trying to force down the rising dread before it could choke me. Katla was about to leave. This didn't have to be the end. I had wandered the streets of Trader's Isle, hadn't I? Pathetically, and with the grace of an awe-struck child, yes, but I had done it. I wasn't sure how I would do *this*, manage to be with the dragons and go where Katla would go. But I could do it, somehow.

"Fafnir, land on the deck, please."

Are you sure?

No. "Yes." *Just do it, please.*

Katla didn't react to the one-sided conversation, one-sided on her end, at least. She must have been used to it then, listening to words I shared with someone she couldn't hear.

Warily, Fafnir began to drop, angling for the boat. Apparently, those below had tried to nock another arrow, because Fafnir let out a warning roar. I still expected them to fire, but no arrows came screaming for us.

Who was down there?

Fafnir landed, intentionally or not, with jarring force. Clearly, the Lamidian vessel couldn't hold Fafnir all that comfortably. His legs were forced close together, the majority of his back end trailing into the ocean below. I felt the confusion of some Amphitrite at the sudden disturbance, invisible deep in the water.

My dread at what I believed to be future happenings was so strong that

I did not see the mistake in dismounting.

Locks of pale blonde hair were immediately discernible, and I heard a feminine battle cry. An instinct built from years of being almost killed by those who shouted as they charged had me ducking before the blade was fully swung. An axe ghosted over my head, and I followed it to a girl.

Green eyes were glaring into mine, blade outstretched. She swung again, and I was grateful I had decided to keep one of the Sigurd shields I had stolen. It danced out in front of me just before her blade took one of my arms.

Lamidians and their penchant for decapitation!

"Stop!" Katla cried out, and the girl in front of me stopped.

More than stopped, she completely froze up at the sound of Katla's voice. She turned slowly, axe whirling to face the noise. What she found was Katla, jumping down from Fafnir's neck.

"Katla?" The blonde girl whispered, her eyes frantically flipping between Katla, Fafnir, and myself.

I noticed two other teens behind the blonde girl, both boys, who were staring at me in a mixture of shock and horror.

"What are you all doing here?" Katla angrily demanded, coming to stand by my side.

340

"What are we doing? What are *you* doing? Katla, oh my gods! You've been missing for almost two months! And *that* is a dragon!" The sand-haired girl was on the verge of shouting now, switching between tearful glances at Katla and hateful ones towards me faster than I could have thought possible.

"What the Hel is going on, Katla? Because it looks like you flew down here with him, on a dragon." The dark-skinned boy spoke up from behind the girl, giving me the same glances. He clenched a halberd.

I felt Katla's hand tighten around my own. She was there, it was fine. Nothing that hadn't happened before. She would speak to them. My sight lingered on their weapons.

Gods, and I'd thought I had done so well on Trader's Isle.

"That's because I did. That's Fafnir, he's Aidan's brother, and he isn't going to hurt any of us." Katla spoke far too smoothly.

She obviously knew these people, and they hadn't tried to draw any more weapons on us. Yet. There was another boy with hair so darkly brown it was almost black, and instead of appraising Fafnir, he was inspecting my hand and Katla's, interlinked. I suppose he also looked at Fafnir a lot. I chanced a step closer to her.

"His *brother*? Katla, that's crazy!" The green-eyed girl was yelling, stepping apprehensively away from Fafnir, who huffed. He, too, was growing

341

tired of this reaction. "Get away from that beast! Do you have a sword? Move slowly- come on! That thing will tear us apart!"

"Then why hasn't he?"

I regarded Katla in substantial awe.

If I had approached this group alone, it would have never been possible, but they knew Katla. Already I could see them considering her words.

Horrifying expressions were beginning to morph into suspicion as they took in Fafnir, who was doing his best to act in a non-threatening manner. It really wasn't working, given the way he moved each second they did. Always keeping me directly within his reach, angling himself in terms of their position, and mine.

The boy with the long halberd finally tore his gaze from Fafnir, but his eyes were not aimless, latching immediately onto His eyebrows almost disappeared into his hair.

"Katla," He began slowly, "Where have you been? You entirely disappeared overnight. You stole a hunting boat! There is a dragon. Behind you. Who are you with? Is he keeping you-"

"I've been with Aidan," Katla interrupted firmly, as if that summed everything up. I supposed, in a 'completely skirting over a lot of things' way, it did. "And I've been with dragons." The reaction wasn't staggered, the three new teenagers gasped in shock all at once. "We don't have to be afraid of them. Not the ones at the Bay, at least. I've seen more than proof of that. I've *flown*, Calin. What I've seen, I can't even describe to you, and it's incredible. But I can try, to explain and to tell you, if you'll let me."

I wondered if the sort of smile which would overtake my entire face would be inappropriate.

The dark halberd boy, Calin, let out a breath, but stopped gaping. It could have been the honesty in her voice, or the dragon who was fighting to appear docile. Either way, Calin slowly loosened his grip on the handle he held. Not dropped, but not poised to kill.

The dark-haired boy hesitated before letting his axe down, but his eyes remained cold. The girl slung a wooden bow over her shoulder. It was likely the source of the arrow which had nearly made itself at home in Fafnir's underbelly. The axe she had carried clattered to the ground, having slipped carelessly from her fingers.

It was apparently borrowed. The other boy grabbed it, another axe in his left hand. He must have been dual-wielding. It would have been impressive, if he didn't look as though he wanted to bury his twin axes in my chest.

The first to move was the blonde girl, who was throwing whatever caution that she was conflicted with to the winds. She rushed forward, enveloping Katla in a tight hug. I stepped back, releasing Katla's hand so she could embrace someone who was very clearly a friend. After a few moments the two girls moved apart. Katla suddenly gestured to me, and I fumbled slightly, highly uncomfortable with the idea of being the new center of attention.

"This is Aidan, everyone. Aidan, this is Eliana, Calin... and Leo."

Something about how she said the last name was not extremely unkind, but there was an obvious distaste there. It was clear that the first two were friends of Katla, but I wasn't sure about 'Leo'.

Eliana shook her head, her voice disbelieving. "So this is the Dragon Rider. We've heard a lot about you back on Lamid, obviously." I wasn't so sure how I felt about that, probably negatively. "Katla. Care to explain how you came into the company of the man who rides Hel's beasts? Please tell me this is all a part of your glorious quest to bring him to Lamid for a trial?"

I saw Katla bristle a bit at the words, which I found ironic, since not all that long ago they had essentially been her own. And, a trial? How had I wronged them, exactly?

Of course Katla wasn't going to bring me back to her homeland. At least, not with all the fanfare that would likely follow announcing me as the 'Dragon Rider'.

Why would she want to?

Despite this, her tone was sharp and defensive.

"How do you know about that?"

"Your brother-in-law looked so guilty, I thought he was going to lose his breakfast when I said hello to your sister. Fisk spewed it all before I could even threaten to tell Ingrid he knew something." She swallowed, hard. "Is it going to leave, or is it only picking the easiest meal?"

No, of course not. I prefer my humans from the colder regions of your Isles. Fafnir growled.

"Well, I suppose if he is, I might as well make it easier for him." And then Katla strode straight for Fafnir, not so much as turning when her friends called for her to return.

"Katla!" Calin cried.

"Stop! What are you doing?" Leo.

"Move! I can't shoot without hitting you!" Eliana, who had brought her bow back to her hands.

Did they not realize how we arrived here? Katla climbed onto Fafnir's wing, patting him gently while dropping herself into place on his neck. Fafnir and I were victim to mutual confusion.

"You once said he'll catch me?"

I blinked at her, a sea of black waves falling over her shoulders, mimicking those which rocked the boat. It was sort of hard to breathe, like the time I had fallen into the frigid waters of the north, and gotten sick.

I somehow strung together a response which wasn't a verbal echo of the admiration coursing through me.

"Well, he does favor you more than me."

"No different from Bluebell. Just much larger. Much, much larger." Fafnir heard her whisper, and the sound filtered secondhand through my ears. "Fafnir? Could you, please? Slowly! Hatchling pace?"

The three Lamidians behind me practically choked as Fafnir took off. He was being gentle, mindful of Katla on his back and her nervousness, but they didn't know that. Honestly, it was quite comical.

Eliana was obviously torn between grabbing an arrow, and what could have been shocked pride. The eyes of Calin and Leo widened to a size that must have been painful when Katla's elated whoop wafted down. Eventually, they realized that I had been left behind. Shock mixed with expectation, waiting for me to voice something. Anything.

Oh, Odin.

"Hi." I tried, but it was so quiet I may as well have said nothing.

Not to say my attempt went unnoticed. Eliana smirked, and I knew too little to judge whether it was mocking or humored. I would take mocking over a raised axe, any day for the rest of my life. Curiosity began creeping over Calin's face. The terror behind Leo's glare was going, the contempt not absolved, but the revulsion fading.

What would we do now? There were people here for her. Clearly there were those who were searching. Word would spread, others would come. These three would surely relay their knowledge of the 'Dragon Rider'. Not the knowledge Katla had, of flying and hatchlings and Olavi's armadas, but of a potential threat.

Ragna would seize the opportunity, demand Katla return home to her people. Katla would leave, and Ragna could never allow us to stay within the Voluspian Archipelago.

But Ragna wasn't the only one who could hide things.

CHAPTER SIXTEEN

KATLA

We were cutting through the water much faster than a boat should have been capable.

Responsibility for that fell to a long rope tethering a sparkling white dragon to the mast. Aidan sat on Fafnir, while I stood on the deck below, facing my friends. Well, two of them. I had an inkling of why Leo was here, and I wasn't all that thrilled about it. I wondered if we were close enough to Lamid-friendly waters that someone would pick him up if I threw him out of the ship. Or maybe an Amphitrite would eat him.

Calin leaned forward, shaking his head under the overwhelming onslaught of information.

"You're telling us that for the last month and a half, you've been living in a cave full of dragons? Underneath an island on the very outskirts of Voluspa?"

We were finally around to this part of the conversation. I was glad that the topic of 'the dragons don't originate from Hel' was over, *mostly*. Leo was still unconvinced, but Eliana and Calin weren't dense. After all, how often did a dragon pull your ship around? The wariness had yet to be left behind, however.

I understood. I hadn't fully abandoned the idea of treating Aidan to the end of my sword until at least the second day.

Maybe the third.

"Yes. Rescuing captives, both human and dragon, from the Sigurd. They have an annoying habit of breeding armadas."

Leo was doing a rather good impression of a fish brought out of the water, trying to inhale. Especially since I had an increasing desire to feed him to Fafnir.

"I thought the Dragon Rider... Aidan, was with the Sigurd?" Eliana asked, and I quickly shook my head. I prayed there weren't too many of those rumors floating across the Square, but what other logical conclusion was there to jump to?

"No, absolutely not. Not at all. Aidan and his mother were taken by the Sigurd when he was young." I was glad Aidan wasn't there to see it, he wouldn't have wanted to be looked at with pity, like they were doing at his back. "His mother died fighting them. He took her place, battling the Sigurd and freeing those they've taken since then."

I hoped Fafnir couldn't hear me, but he almost certainly could. I hoped he didn't relay my words to Aidan, then.

"Dragons, I can understand. The Sigurd are proficient trappers, everyone knows half of the hides in any market on this side of the archipelago are brought from their ships. But ransacking a kingdomside just to get away with a boat full of people?" Calin waved his hand. "Why would they do that?"

"Aidan doesn't know, and I have no idea where to even begin guessing. They need the money and the extra hands for something, but they haven't acted yet. If anything, their fleets are getting smaller."

"A draconic force the equivalent of a naval fleet ravaging the skies and descending with helfire from above in an organized pack." Leo shook his head. "My uncle would soil his-"

Eliana groaned in disgust. We had decided on going to the Bay, although what we would do after that was still unclear. The situation had become incredibly more complicated. There must have been people out looking for me, but I doubted anyone was searching far enough to find the Bay. Or searching the skies. Then again...

"Why are you out this far, anyway? We're almost to Atori, for Valhalla's sake. You must've been sailing for days."

Eliana looked quite proud of herself. "No one was turning up anything, so we decided to look for ourselves. Calin can sail better than a quarter of the fishermen, we were out of Lamidian waters within an hour. Took a page out of your book, borrowed a boat. Nice, by the way." She threw another glance at Fafnir, and seemed to be focusing much more on the boy sitting there than the dragon. "Seems you've learned something after all."

I glared at her, wishing she was close enough for a shove to appear accidental. The boys, thankfully, took her comment at surface value. I understood Eliana was teasing, but based on her lingering looks, we needed to have a 'hands-off' conversation. As in, no scaring my...friend away with insistent flirting.

However, this posed its own problem. Obviously, if the stolen ship was any indication, they weren't supposed to be out here.

We couldn't simply stay away from Lamid. Not anymore. A missing teen is one thing, four is another. Especially if one of them is the only heir to the throne and a member of the royal family. Yes, we were in trouble. They were certain to come looking, likely with more manpower and no limits. Why they had allowed Leo to come with them, I couldn't fathom.

It was doubtful that they all had become best friends after I left.

Leo's eyes flitted between Fafnir, the sky, and myself. He twirled his family dagger in his hands, the sun catching on the crimson handle, the gold wire. Finally, it seemed he couldn't wait any longer.

"Katla, do you- do you ride the beasts? Like horses? You rode the white one earlier, but I mean…before that-"

"If a horse was big enough to eat all the other horses, then yes. Not just any dragons, though. I've ridden Fafnir, and another. Her name is Bluebell, and Aidan has never flown with her before. Only me."

There was pride in my voice when I spoke of her. Already, I missed flying with her. We hadn't done so since yesterday. Hopefully, we would be at Aidan's Bay soon, but Fafnir flew considerably slower when he was lugging the weight of a ship and its occupants.

"You have a dragon?" Eliana spit out. "Damn, Kat. This is a messed-up basket of berries you've picked."

I didn't have a chance to refute. Leo turned, looking me full in the eyes for the first time since we arrived on the boat. Oh, curse of *Loki*.

"You have to go back to Lamid with me."

"Excuse me? Like Hel I-"

"We have a contract-"

Eliana rolled her eyes, my confirmation. Yes, this is why he had come. Why she had let him tag along was a reason I didn't care to understand, but at least she didn't seem pleased.

"Are you serious? Or only mentally lacking? I need to shake the hand of whoever finally knocked loose what remained of your brain while I was gone, I always hoped I'd have the pleasure."

"The contract has already been signed Katla, my uncle paid your bride price." His voice was infuriatingly condescending, like he was informing a child they had to give up a new toy. "Uncle Ivon was worried when you disappeared, and the Council was livid. My father suggested being married as soon as you return. The Council backed it. It should have happened already."

I hadn't thought much about the contract, it hadn't been an issue out here. Out of sight, out of mind, I supposed. But being married whenever I returned? That in itself seemed punishment enough for stealing a boat and disappearing for near two months. There would certainly be repercussions for that stunt, and I wasn't even sure what laws I was breaking by running from the contract in the first place. Surely nothing good would come of that.

Piles and piles of consequences, all starting to converge. What if they found out about Bluebell?

About Aidan?

A quiet voice spoke up then, and my blood froze in my veins, thoughts careening to a stop as panic set in. It paused my mind, extracted my breath.

"You're engaged?"

I hadn't realized Aidan was on deck.

He was slowly stepping down from the side of the boat. He must have only just jumped, probably come to try and join the conversation, even though it would have made him uncomfortable. He looked resigned, and his widened eyes found me in something that could only be hurt.

I heard an intensely satisfying smack behind me, and a yelp, that indicated Eliana was giving Leo the justice I was too stunned to enact.

Aidan was already moving back the way he came, returning to Fafnir. His draconic brother was too high to be reached from the deck, and his neck too far away. That didn't seem like a problem for Aidan, who was eyeing Fafnir's hanging tail like he was going to leap to it.

I was already racing forward, towards the opposite side of the boat where Aidan perched with perfect balance on the wall. He was tensing his legs, aiming for one of the small spines on Fafnir's tail.

I grabbed one of his loosely hanging hands, and without another thought I pulled. He stumbled heavily as I turned him around, spilling off the side of the boat entirely.

I winced as he fell, hurrying to help him back up. Aidan exhaled softly as he stood, but otherwise did nothing. No anger. Not mad when he should have been, when I didn't tell him.

I should have told him.

"Aidan! I'm-"

"It's fine, Katla, you don't have to explain anything to me." His voice missed the levity it was aiming for.

"Hey, listen. It was arranged, I didn't have a choice. That's why I left in the first place!"

"You left to kill me. That's what she said." He stepped back. "I didn't find you on that boat, you found me. You were searching for the 'Dragon Rider', and for what? What value have they given to my death?" I thought his eyes would drop, thought he would become nervous or gentle when in the face of eyes which weren't draconic. He didn't. "Were you just waiting for me to fly you back to Lamid? For me to be away from the others, to give you a clear shot without the entirety of the Bay descending-"

"No! Aidan, what- how could you-"

"This is everything she promised would happen." He wasn't even looking at me as he said it, his eyes unfocused.

"Ragna? She's not- Aidan, you don't really believe that. You can't believe that."

All those hours we spent sitting on the stone edge, talking. Simply existing within the confines of the Roost, the other-worldly simplicity. Our dance. That perfect, wondrous dance that was so much more, and gods, I wanted that. I wanted whatever that was, whatever it had been. And here I was, teetering on the edge of screwing it all up.

Now he would see truth in Ragna's warnings.

"But after everything? You were engaged, every second of it. When the newborns hatched, every time we fought the Sigurd."

"Aidan-"

"All of that, and you're going to be married-"

"I'm *not*-"

"Why did you kiss me?" His voice dropped to the point that even I could barely hear him in the close space between us. "Why did you...you *let* me- I don't understand. Even if you still want to kill me. Surely you could have stabbed me just the same if you hadn't- if you hadn't danced with me or...Everything I told you, I thought that you-"

The rest of his words were cut off as my hand harshly tore his face down to my height.

In the same second, I used the leverage to pull myself into him, craning up as he angled down. I kissed him deeply, weaving my free hand into his hair and drawing him in with the other. His lips were cold with wind and tasted like the salty air, somehow soft despite the frigid currents of sky he swam through each day.

After a moment's hesitation he reacted, his arm around my waist. When I fell away, it was only into the crease of his arm, no further.

"Are you going to close your mouth and listen to me now, or do we need to do that again?" I asked, my peace made with the second option. He said nothing, slightly dazed. "I am the only person on this godsdamned boat with the power to say so, so I will say so. I will not be married. As far as the two of us are concerned, I am not engaged, nor have I ever been."

I heard an indignant scoff behind me, along with a much louder meeting of palm and skin than before. Thank the gods for Eliana. It should have occurred to me that they were listening, that they were *watching*, but the reality was lost. Still, I lowered my voice until only he could possibly understand.

"I'm sorry. I should have told you, I know that, but Aidan, I kissed you that night because I wanted to. Because of what you said, and the truth that was in it for both of us. I meant it, like I mean this one, and will mean whatever else."

"Oh." He breathed, nodding more to himself than to me.

"I'm sorry for not telling you. It wasn't something I meant to hide." I smiled. "I have nothing to hide from you."

Aidan blinked; eyes slightly unfocused. "Okay."

His back was to his brother, but my sight was painfully clear as Fafnir craned around his massive head, an interconnected mass of white scales and brown horns. The beastly head contained gigantic pupils which were filled with so much mirth I felt my cheeks burn nearly instantly.

Fafnir had no eyebrows to raise, no lips to smirk with, but damn, if he didn't convey the expression regardless. A serpentine head tilted, a rumbling sound of amusement escaping.

Aidan began to turn, forehead creased in intrigue for what lay behind, and I quickly dragged him away from the water.

Calin had paid his attention elsewhere, obviously trying to be polite, whereas Leo was studying the exchange as if his eyeballs were on fire. Eliana was watching shamelessly.

"Oh my gods," She mouthed aggressively when Aidan was preoccupied with noticing Leo. A few other choice words followed.

I flipped my free hand, motioning for her to cut it out. She donned an innocent expression, but her eyes were glowing with delight. I sat on a crate, bringing Aidan down alongside me.

Leo was directly across from my newfound position, how convenient.

"I suppose the most pressing issue should be cleared first, and I can't quite stand it anymore. Leo, kindly shut the Loki-forsaken Hel up."

"You can't ignore the contract, Katla. That's illegal," He stated stubbornly.

"I was well aware of that the night I borrowed a boat from the Lamidian harbor and fled the island. I haven't exactly been upholding the law for a while, Leo. Seems a little pointless to start now. Especially to marry you. I had enough reasons not to do so already, but I thought Aidan and I did quite well demonstrating my newest one."

I heard the poor Dragon Boy in question choke a little beside me.

Eliana erupted into full out laughter. Calin tried to turn his snort into a cough, and failed miserably. Leo sat and sulked, but nothing more was expected of him, really. Sure, had Leo actually been in love with me, or anything close to it, I would never have joked about it or rejected him as harshly.

But he wasn't, and so I had no qualms about it.

I didn't belong to him, no matter what he would quote from the idiotic contract the council had written. There was likely plenty King Ivon redacted, and Leo's father must've had a real great time writing it. I was a pretty face and a capable fighter; a woman his family's title had handed him. There was no affection and no feelings attached.

Neither of us was ready to be married, regardless.

"Ten gold pieces." Eliana finally managed in Leo's direction. "That was the deal."

"I hope none of you are opposed to camping out on the shore?" Aidan asked, his voice slightly shaky. It was the first he had spoken to them.

"We aren't going to the Bay?" I questioned.

"Well... there's just so many of us. I doubt we'd all fit. And the others may be anxious around so many newcomers."

"Will Ragna-"

"I'll tell her later." Aidan said quickly. "Oh. We're almost there, Fafnir can see the island."

The three before us squinted at him, before looking past us in the direction Fafnir was flying. There was in fact an island on the horizon, large cliffs jutting up in its outline. The dragons weren't visible from here, too high and too far away, but I knew they were flocking around the open peak. I wondered how many even now were hidden in the clouds.

"What?" Eliana raised.

Aidan had known we were coming up on the Bay without even turning to see, his back to Fafnir. His brother must've told him. That had been Hel for me to wrap my mind around, but I admitted it was funny to be on this side.

"Oh, right." Aidan said as he realized. "I can hear Fafnir in my mind."

I snickered at the change in their faces, readying myself for another long explanation. For now though, I'd simply enjoy Leo sputtering about 'demon magic', and Aidan's hand still in mine.

CHAPTER SEVENTEEN

AIDAN

Fafnir yanked the boat onto the shore, and I jumped over the side hurriedly to untie the rope from around his middle.

"Thanks, Fafnir." I told him, patting his head as I passed.

It was worth it and more to see that. Fafnir hadn't stopped laughing since Katla and I... well he wouldn't shut up. *And I'm not so sure that this is going to keep us hidden from Ragna for long. Someone is bound to notice, and if one of the Pests see, you know they won't keep it to themselves.*

"The insane boy gets a kiss, but I haven't seen you in two months, and I've spent several terrible days on a boat with Leo Evalade. Where's my hug for making me think you were dead?"

I turned around in time to hear Eliana laugh, and receive a tight hug from Katla. She turned and hugged Calin too, who looked surprised, but

362

reciprocated it. Katla noticed.

"Really, Calin? You didn't miss me?"

"I'm a little busy being mad at you right now, both for scaring the Helheim out of me and apparently risking your life by flying a dragon. Repeatedly. But, maybe I missed you a little, somewhere in there. I bought myself a spot on this crazy boat trip. I hope you realize we're all going to sit behind bars for the rest of our lives."

"Missed you too."

Katla's friends hesitantly began leaving the boat. Well, two of them. Eliana leapt right off the side into the sand, staring up at those flying above. Katla came down after her, walking over to thank Fafnir for speeding the voyage along.

"I can't wrap my head around it. There's a creature like those that's yours?" Eliana's tone was doubtful, and Katla found me, still beside Fafnir.

"Aidan?" She asked hopefully.

Fafnir? Are you up for another trip?

Well, I can't be the reason your mate turns tail and flees, can I?

I grit my teeth. "He would be happy to." *Run yourself into the cliffside, why don't you?*

We should ask these humans if they are all as sensitive as you, soft scales.

The last Amphitrite race we lost was because of you.

Oh, it was not-

"Come on boy, let's go find Bluebell!" Katla unknowingly stopped him.

I shielded my eyes as his wings beat against the sand, sending the small grains flying in all directions. We watched them fly away, soon disappearing around the side of the island. Eliana was considering me again, but she was also tossing her gaze after the path Katla had taken.

She appeared so smug, I worried that she planned to resume her attempt to lob off my head now that both Katla and Fafnir had left. It was really rather awkward now that Katla was gone, her friends simply regarding me.

It seemed Leo, for whatever reason, was trying his best to seem uninterested by the island, and consequently, by me. He wasn't succeeding, of course, clearly spooked by those from the Bay who spun in the air above.

Clearly irked by me.

I kept my focus on the ocean, trying to ignore their scrutinizing presence. I guessed I couldn't blame them, I landed on their boat with a dragon not two hours ago. Still, it was uncomfortable.

Finally, two shapes approached.

Fafnir was followed by a much smaller Muspel of pale blue, and I could only just barely make out the rider on her back. Katla had returned with Bluebell. The Lamidian party had differing reactions from my own relief, immediately and instinctually reaching for their blades and bows once they noticed the second dragon.

There wasn't time for them to contemplate pulling their weapons free. Fafnir landed beside me first, Katla and Bluebell following seconds after.

I knew immediately that this would be good, if Eliana's sudden enamored expression meant anything. Bluebell was only a few weeks old, large enough to tote around a human passenger, but dwarfed by Fafnir. It was hard to imagine a devilish murderer when looking at a hatchling.

If babies had been the answer the whole time, I was going to be seriously annoyed with the gods. I doubted it was that easy.

Katla let herself fall to the ground from Bluebell's back, landing with a slight stumble. Eliana immediately began taking steps closer, stopping a short distance away. Bluebell was nuzzling Katla affectionately with her head, and Katla was petting her scales absentmindedly.

"Calin, Eliana, Leo...this is Bluebell." She said cheerily, but there was worry in her voice that was strikingly like my own whenever I showed her something.

They took in Katla, and the dragon standing beside her.

"This is incredible." Calin stated as Bluebell nudged her friend.

There was nothing dangerous or terrifying about her actions, only affection for Katla. Eliana looked as if she wanted to come closer, but didn't bring herself to do it. She seemed conflicted. Already they were being far more accepting than Katla had been at the start.

There was no resentment in their eyes. Although the constant stares were awkward, I would rather they were curious than horrified. Katla noticed Eliana's reluctant behavior as well, for she raised her head and spoke again.

"Do you want to pet her?" She offered, and I almost snorted.

I remembered the last time the two of us had been together, and one of us had more or less asked that question. Katla threw me a mischievous glance, remembering it too.

Eliana was still doubtful, before she saw Bluebell pushing her head under Katla's arm in search of a scratch.

"At least going by the teeth of the Dragon Rider's acolyte is a sweet way to die." Eliana convinced herself. "Just don't tear the bow from my back when you kill me, beastie. I'd like to see Valhalla."

And then Eliana was in front of Bluebell, a ball of nervous anticipation and warring instincts. She raised her hand, but that was where her plan ended.

Luckily for her, it was all the invitation Bluebell needed, shoving her head under Eliana's fingers as soon as she seemed willing. Eliana froze.

"Oh my gods." I heard Eliana whisper, and she carefully brought her other hand up as well, placing it on Bluebell's scales. With a peek at Katla, she began to stroke the scales as her friend had done. "Okay, this is awesome. Calin! Get your ass over here and pet Katla's dragon!"

I wondered at his reaction, but it seemed as soon as he was sure Eliana wasn't about to lose a hand, he was quick to follow.

He rushed over, Eliana stepping to the side, making room for him. He began to scratch Bluebell, both he and Eliana jumping when she began to purr loudly. Someone was loving all the attention, and I heard Fafnir huff behind me. Rolling my eyes, I reached over and began scratching behind his umber horns.

Katla was beaming at her friends who had wide smiles of their own as they fawned over Bluebell. I'd never thought there would be anyone but Katla to accept us, but there I was.

"She's beautiful. More like a scaly mare than a dragon." Eliana laughed. "She doesn't look like much of a killer."

"Looks can be deceiving. I've watched her tear into a man and devour him in three seconds."

I felt my jaw drop, and wasn't alone. Bluebell squawked indignantly, and Eliana ripped her hand away so quickly I thought she was going to hit herself in the face.

"What?" She screeched.

"I'm kidding."

Eliana sighed in relief. "Well Odin damnit, that's disappointing. I was going to volunteer Leo-"

"Hey!"

"Well, she still can," Katla offered helpfully.

"*Hey!*"

"She's yours?"

Katla nodded proudly. "She hatched just a few weeks ago. Already outflying half the flock, aren't you, Bluebell?"

"Gods above, Katla. I cannot believe you stole a boat, ran away, lived in a cave, and then found a Loki-damned dragon on top of it. Not to mention fighting Sigurd all the time! This is not the sort of thing you do without me!"

"I wasn't running away. You're just jealous you wouldn't have thought of this one." Katla cheeked.

"I find it safer to slightly bend the laws, not blow them to Niflheim. Like nabbing one of Mr. Felman's sheep and hiding it in the Healer's Hall, rather than riding devils among men. No offense, Aidan."

I raised a hand in acknowledgement as Katla argued.

"There's no law against riding a dragon."

"Not explicitly, but the very notion has the whole kingdom in a frenzy. I heard they're trying to close down all the forges in the Elysian village."

"What? There are more blacksmiths living in Elysia than even Iona. Why would they close them down?"

"The smiths are still working, but under Ivon's orders. They aren't taking requests from the villagers any longer. Seems even the king is susceptible to rumors. He's trying to better outfit the military's armory." She shrugged at me. "The idea of your existence has caught a lot of important people with their trousers down."

I would never be able to hide it from Ragna. The second she was close enough to hear me through the Bond, my defenses would give like a worn dam.

Katla looked unnerved, smoothing the scales on Bluebell's crown. Eliana and Calin peered at her actions interestedly.

I searched for the third member of their group. Leo was still standing by the boat, not having been called over. He was watching the other's enviously, his face almost longing. Granted, he still fought to appear as though he was above going over and joining them, but it seemed that was on purpose.

It wasn't real.

I understood the other's distaste for the boy, after all, he didn't present himself to be that easy to get along with. I hadn't made peace with the idea that he was Katla's promised, one-sided as it seemed.

Regardless, loneliness wasn't deserved.

Oh, no. I don't like that look, *and I don't like that* boy. *Quit that, let Grumpy over there sulk as he pleases.* Fafnir advised.

I ignored him. Katla seemed oblivious to Leo a few feet away, but I couldn't exactly fault her for not wanting him to come meet Bluebell. Their relationship was clearly not a tolerant one.

"Hey! Leo?" His head turned as I called out, and although he tried to force his features into distaste, his expression fell a little short of annoyance. The others didn't seem to notice my call, but that was likely for the best. I doubted he would want to listen to me if he knew the other teens were paying attention. I gestured towards Fafnir, whose groan almost immediately echoed in my mind. I answered them both in the same moment. *Oh, quit it. Where's your famed pride now?* "Want to meet him?"

Leo's face delved into suspicion, before his eyes flitted to Bluebell. Eliana and Calin were smiling and laughing, periodically jumping back in fear when Bluebell made a particular noise or motion they weren't expecting.

Their voices were filled with wonder and disbelief as they chatted animatedly to Katla.

"Yeah, whatever." He said quietly as he started over.

You just can't mind your own scales, can you? Fafnir complained.

He walked in a prideful way, shoulder's a bit too squared, head up so high he was clearly trying to ensure his movements were noticed. He held himself like someone who wielded respect, but I questioned whether he actually received it. Clearly, Eliana and Katla didn't see it fit to give.

What was he meant to be respected for? I let it go for then, he was almost to me.

Fafnir came closer, albeit reluctantly. He lowered his head down to my height, Leo's own a bit higher than mine, and I had to admire Leo for coming over at all. Granted, the boy was a bit larger than me, but Fafnir was significantly bigger, and therefore more terrifying, than Bluebell who was a hatchling. Despite Fafnir's size, Leo didn't slow until he was right in front of us.

"Leo, this is Fafnir." I told him, and although his eyes widened as Fafnir approached, he didn't make any move to flee.

"You said that already." Was his response, but there wasn't any real heat behind it as he was too focused on the dragon beside me. He lifted his

371

hand of his own will, there was no dragon initiating the act this time. I doubted Fafnir would, unwilling as he was to do this in the first place. He hesitantly placed his hand on Fafnir's head, in between his eyes, just as Katla had originally. "You're sure he's not about to bite a chunk out of my chest or something?"

Fafnir snorted. *Debatable.*

"Completely sure."

"Wow. It's not even scary like this!" Fafnir growled, opening his jaw and revealing his teeth just barely. "Sorry! You're very scary. Please don't tear my arms off."

Okay, maybe this one isn't that bad. He learns quick.

"Apparently you've gained approval, congratulations."

Leo looked at me strangely. I was not about to rehash the long-winded explanation from the boat, so he'd just have to wonder. His demeanor changed as the shifting of sand reached our ears, boots dragging through the golden flakes.

"I don't trust you." He insisted with finality.

Believe me, the feeling is mutual. I admitted to Fafnir as I eyed the axes crossed over his back.

I knew it was Katla before I drifted to her side, leaving Fafnir to Leo's terrified mercy. Eliana and Calin were still standing by Bluebell, unaware that Katla had left them.

"Well, Fafnir hasn't had to throw anyone into the ocean, yet. Matters could have been made worse." I deduced cheerily.

Katla hummed in agreement. The two of us lingered on the shore, taking a moment. Leo waited out of earshot to my right, trying to hide the hand that scratched Fafnir's scales.

"Why does he act like that?" I whispered out of the corner of my mouth, both of us aware of who I was referring to.

"Leo's the heir of the kingdom. He struts around like he owns the place... all of the time. He's essentially first in line now, so we're all stuck with his ego ruling the kingdom in a few years, during which I feel Medea may be far more hospitable. Or a frozen wasteland outside of Voluspa altogether."

"He's the heir? Should I have bowed? Is that disrespectful?"

Katla looked stricken at the very notion. "Gods, no! I can only imagine how much more insufferable he would be if the Dragon Rider bowed to him. No one bows to Leo but visitors from other kingdoms, and they usually stop once they get to know him. No one even bows to the King, really. He's rather informal about it all."

I blew out a breath, relieved I hadn't just offended an entire island's royal line, or something. It would explain his attitude. I hadn't forgotten the way he demanded Katla return home so they could go on and get married.

He certainly wasn't all that affectionate to someone who was meant to be his future wife.

"How did you get roped into marrying him anyway? It's clear the desire for matrimony isn't mutual."

Katla groaned. "He's the Hopeless Heir who, according to the council, needs a wife so the island doesn't fall to pieces when he becomes king. Even I'll admit that's over exaggerating a bit, but who knows? I was voted most suitable candidate, hoorah for me. I brought even more attention to myself by becoming the Hunt-" She paused, her lip disappearing between her teeth for an instant. "By fighting. Sparring, other kids from the villages and I, whenever we had time, or too much of it. Apparently, I should have stuck to training without a crowd. They saw an adept swordsman and decided to make a queen. Ridiculous."

"I get it. A warrior. They wanted you to assassinate him on your wedding night." I nodded, and she bumped me with her shoulder, a mock scowl on her face.

374

It made perfect sense to me, however. I had seen her fight. It wasn't surprising to me that some King and his Council would see how good she was. I had seen her, period.

Although, Queen seemed to be a demotion from Valkyrie.

"Don't go spilling my backup plan out and to the heavens." She chastised. "The King, Ivon, was sitting in my house the next morning. I found out from Eliana first, in truth. She had eavesdropped."

I hissed in sympathy. It was plain to see the disastrous mix of Katla's temper and her capacity to be very lethal.

"How'd that go?"

She grimaced. "Not well. I ran all the way home, nearly broke down the door, and insulted the King's nephew right in front of him. I believe I insulted the Council as well. And I may have been shouting at the time."

"At the King? And you're still alive. I thought disrespecting monarchs brought about some sort of punishment. I suppose when the great Katla Vistel talks, people listen, right?"

She smirked. "Exactly. When I talk people listen."

"Except royalty." I amended, and she waved a hand dismissively. "Then you took a hunting boat so you could sail across the Voluspian Ocean and murder a fabled demon man. Oh, yes, that's entirely reasonable. It definitely would have been my first course of action as well."

"I could have done it-"

"You were not even close."

She crossed her arms. "I almost had you in the cave."

"The cave I brought you to."

"The cave I could have found on my own."

"Your boat was so far away from the Bay."

"We don't know that I would *never* have found it-"

"You definitely wouldn't have."

CHAPTER EIGHTEEN

KATLA

"Aidan seems...okay, for a guy who was raised by serpents with wings."

I raised my eyes to Calin from the opposite side of Bluebell. Leo and Eliana were back on the boat, arguing over something that I believe started with the last piece of jerky they had brought, and had transcended into insults. Aidan was stuck a few feet away on the beach, watching the two shout at each other, dumbfounded.

He hadn't yet realized that fighting was their favorite joint activity.

"He is. And, he wasn't 'raised' by dragons. He was raised by his mom. A human. And I guess his mother's dragon a little bit, and his sort-of-grandmother, but mostly his mother."

"Really? Huh." A moment of silence passed between us, the distant shouts from the boat nice in their familiarity. "I can't believe you just left,

377

Katla."

His tone was so accusatory I felt words of retribution on my tongue, before I caught sight of his face. It wasn't as accusing as his words, but it still stung to look at his concern, and what may have been slight judgement.

"I needed to go. It was the only option I could see, and I was desperate for one."

"It was stupid. You shouldn't have done it, even if you felt you had to. You should have told me, or Eliana, that you were going. We would have stopped you from doing something so insane, figured out something better."

"I didn't spend an endless stretch of time considering it! There was a solution, right there, and I didn't think about anything else."

"We picked up on that when we woke to your mother banging on our doors. Katla, you didn't even tell *me*. I had to learn about you and Leo from Eliana, after everyone was already searching for you, after my best friend went missing and I had no idea why. After they had us search the woods and the shoreline, because until they realized the boat was gone, some of the adults were convinced we were looking for a body. They weren't quiet about it either, and Eliana's good at sneaking around. We hear things."

"Calin-"

"You know your mom thinks you're dead?"

A beat.

"What?"

My hands dropped from Bluebell's hide. She ran over to Fafnir, attempting to splash him with the water that washed onto the sand.

"She closed down the bakery. She was out, every day, asking anyone who had been on the boats if they had seen anything. The day the ships stopped going out she closed the doors. She stands on the cliffs a lot, looking out past the docks-"

"Stop!" I shouted, surging forward and pushing him back. He stumbled slightly, recovering quickly.

"Do you want me to lie? What did you think was going to happen, Katla? You can't just disappear, and think no one is going to care! Or that no one is going to be rightfully a little pissed off now that you're back!"

"I didn't think no one was-"

"That's exactly it! You didn't think! You just left everyone behind, to deal with the rumors, and the apologies, and the looks! Mrs. Halstein came up to Eliana and I, and told us she was sorry for our loss." Calin's stream of words didn't dam up when I blanched. "Eliana started crying, and ran off. In public! Eliana. In front of people, in the middle of the street, crying. I didn't know where she went, until I found her with your mom and your sister. She asked your mom if she thought you were dead. She tried to say she didn't, but she was lying."

Aidan was watching us now, eyes wide in alarm.

I tried to offer him a smile, but I felt heat behind my eyes and knew I had done more harm than good. He looked between Calin and I before he started over, worry marring his features. I held a hand up to him to stop, and he did so rather abruptly, looking hurt.

Fantastic! Great.

My mouth moved without words, unsure of what to say.

I settled for a shaky thumbs up, and knew immediately that Aidan didn't buy it. He didn't come any closer, but his expression promised he would be running over as soon as Calin left. I felt a swell of gratitude for the Dragon Boy in that moment, before I looked back to Calin.

Calin, who was undeniably right. Calin, who's words stung like Hel, but who would never lie to me.

He didn't look so angry anymore, just sad. Because of me. And the worst part was, I couldn't even be mad. I had made my bed, time to finally lie in it, at least partly.

"I'm sorry, Calin, I'm so sorry. It was stupid and reckless and without Aidan I would have died, and it wouldn't have been quick, or in the valor-ridden heat of battle. I wouldn't have done anything to make it worth it. None of you would have ever known what happened, and I would have just disappeared. Even when I didn't, I still stayed here."

"But you don't regret it. I can tell. You're sorry for not telling us, but not sorry for leaving?"

"No," I said slowly, "I thought Mom might have worried a little, but I didn't think…"

"Yeah, well." He was quiet for a minute, arms crossed as his eyes softened. "You scared me too, you know. I wasn't kidding earlier. I'm not usually one for you and Eliana's pranks-"

"They're not pranks."

"-because honestly, you two get caught more times than you'll ever actually admit. But even though taking the boat was Eliana's idea, I already had a bag packed." I glanced up at him in surprise, and he let his head fall back, groaning at the sky. "Sorry. I'm not trying to make you feel like a terrible person."

"No offense, but you're failing. Even though you're right."

"You're not a terrible person. Leaving was terrible, though. It's definitely going to drop your favor in my mother's eyes, though, when she finds out you're not actually dead or maimed."

"Gee, thanks."

"Katla."

"Sorry."

"Katla, we have to go back home."

Eliana and Leo were walking into the woods, somehow still continuing their squabble as they carried supplies from the boat in their arms. It appeared we were making camp for the night. How much longer would we be staying?

Aidan stood between the dragons, a hand on each as he flattened their scales and tried to pretend he wasn't looking at us over his shoulder. Yes, we had to go home. Yet, there was Aidan, dragons on either side, living in a different world than the rest of us. One I had already begun to step into. Maybe I was already inside it.

Could the two exist at once?

"I know."

***

I left the two boys on the beach, pulling more belongings from the boat. I knew I should have stayed to help them, but I needed to clear my head.

As a result of that, here I sat in the sky.

My hands rested in my lap, and I looked at the world without really seeing. Bluebell chirped beneath me, and I rubbed her scales softly, but made no move to give her any explanation.

I felt sort of numb, and I supposed that was better than the guilt that tried to push through. My mother thought me dead. I wondered if Ingrid felt the same.

Had anyone explained to Ylva why I stopped coming over to play? Did she even realize I was gone, or had her young mind forgotten me already?

Calin was right, we had to go back. I scrubbed my hands against my face angrily.

I was mad at Calin, for assuming it was as simple as to just up and return. I was mad at Eliana for coming to find me. At my mother and my sister for being there, for me to miss, and to miss me. I was angry at Aidan, for making it all so complicated, because how was I supposed to go without leaving him behind?

How could I return with him? What if he didn't even want to go with me? Then there was Bluebell, and how could I leave her?

I couldn't leave either of them, but how could I take both?

Smoke caught my attention. Not much, just a thin gray trail coming from within the trees. It must have been the camp they set up. Not far ahead of the trees, the green leaves which stretched to the sky came to a stop, a sea of bright colors stretching out instead.

Flowers.

Oh, *gods*. I leave for two seconds.

"Land there, girl?" I asked quickly. Bluebell grumbled in affirmation, following my pointed finger rather than my words. We lowered beneath the treetops, coming to stop next to a small campfire. A few blankets and woven bags were lying about haphazardly. I scanned around as I dismounted, looking for Leo or Eliana. There was really only one option, and my boots stopped just outside the first blossoms. Unthinkingly, I started into the field. Wading further into the flowers I spotted them, obviously unaware of what they were walking into. I held up a hand. "Stay here, Bluebell!"

I began to chase after them, my feet taking me past beautiful blooms in pinks and whites, pale purples and oranges. I didn't stop to admire them, too busy trying to catch up.

They turned as they heard me coming, and looked on in obvious confusion when they saw me running after them.

"Katla?" Eliana raised an eyebrow as I closed in.

"You can't be here!" I admonished.

Aidan had never told me I couldn't come to that place. Still, it wasn't right for us to be there, in the field where he remembered his mother.

"Why not?" Leo demanded. "We need more kindling, and those tiny dragons keep dragging sticks in here-"

Why Eliana had come along, or allowed him to trail after, was a mystery. The scowl on her face told a story all its own. I shook my head.

"Aidan's mother died when he was young, remember? He put a stone in this field when it happened. It's her place of memory."

Guilty horror crossed Eliana's face, and she scrambled to exit from where we came. She winced and then opened her mouth, but was cut off by Leo.

"You mean like that stone?"

I hadn't realized how deep into the field we had ventured. How close we were to the almost circular patch of grass which Leo had gestured to. My eyes fell upon a beautiful white stone, placed in the very center of the cleared space. Picked flowers that were not yet shriveled sat in front of it, and distantly,

I wondered when Aidan had put them there. He must have done so recently, placed them down in the grass where they laid in front of the smooth cut stone. It was a peaceful spot. Serene. Leo made to step into the circle, and I grabbed his shoulder.

Looking back, I can remember the instant I froze.

The second my eyes found the small shape in the growing darkness. It was an odd figure, small and slender, pointing towards the sky from its position in the grass.

It glinted when I moved, looking closer then. I could not hear my own breathing as I knelt in the cleared space, reaching for the handle, tip buried deep.

My fingers pulled the dagger free, curling around smooth red stone wrapped in gold. I held it close to my face, trying to make sense of the ornate hilt.

The blade fell from my hands.

Shakily, I tore Aidan's notebook from my belt where it had remained since our first battle together. It had fallen to the deck after a Sigurd man tackled him. I had picked it up. Clumsily, I raced through the first few pages, stopping when I found a charcoal drawing, aged but intact.

"Leo." I said, a cold sense of fragile calm washing through me. "Do you keep portraits in the castle?"

I didn't hear his reply. I shoved the book at him anyway.

"Woah. Hold on-"

A woman whose picture resided in the notebook. A woman whose picture lay within Lamid's walls. A woman with a son named Aidan, who was sixteen, only slightly older than I. Was she also a woman who was supposed to have died sixteen years ago, her son along with her?

Had they been wrong?

The last rays of sunlight fell over the field we never should have been in. They sparkled across a dagger set in red gemstone and gold, spilled over a name etched in the stone.

I knew it was placed by Aidan's careful hand, and it seemed to fill my entire vision.

Eliana was reprimanding Leo, something about being insensitive.

"Yeah, I'm sure. Your aunt-"

"*Atarah*," I breathed, overlapping Leo's insistent voice as he said the same.

Queen Atarah of Lamid was Aidan's mother.

CHAPTER NINETEEN

AIDAN

The colors were leaking from the sky, overtaken by midnight blue as the moon began to dominate.

Calin and I were ambling through the forest, trying to spot the others in the growing darkness. Although we couldn't see well, Fafnir could, and his eyes were hunting through the trees. I felt him stiffen beside me, and instantly shifted my gaze in the direction of his head. His rumbling voice sounded in my mind.

Why are they there?

I still couldn't see, and Fafnir wasn't showing me, but he began to move forward.

What do you mean? Where? I asked him. Where could they have wanted to go?

The field.

388

I was stunned by his answer. My perplexity joined Fafnir's as we came to stop beside Bluebell, lying in the grass beside a dying fire.

I could hear voices from the field ahead of us. I wasn't entirely sure how I felt about people being in there. If it was only Katla, I don't think it would have bothered me. Still, I had only met these people recently, and now they were in my mother's field.

Beginning towards the flowers, I called out as I passed the first petals.

"Katla?" The voices cut off abruptly, sounds of the night filling my ears. Wind whistled past. An owl hooted somewhere. Then there were sudden footfalls. Loud, pounding, and growing closer. The field was dark, but I caught the glint of raven hair. Katla was almost upon us. When she was a few feet away I thought I saw her eyes shining, wet. "Are you okay?"

"Aidan." She said, as if she had only just noticed me.

"What's wrong?" She didn't answer, for Leo and Eliana came rushing out of the field a moment later. I winced for every flower they trampled over. Even the Muspel were gentler.

The two stopped dead in their tracks when they found me, eyes rounder than they had been when I first stepped off a dragon.

I considered Eliana and Leo, hoping for an explanation.

I wasn't given one.

Katla walked, deadly slow, towards me. I raised an eyebrow in a silent question. Much to my mounting bewilderment, it wasn't answered. Helpful.

"Your mother's name was Atarah. Her book carries Lamid's insignia." She nodded to herself as she spoke.

Had I ever told her that?

I caught sight of my mother's book in her hand, but she slipped it back into her belt, the plain leather facing outwards, gems hidden.

I couldn't see why Katla was so flustered. Or Leo and Eliana, who were still staring. Calin had caught up, and was running a hand through his hair in confusion. I ignored them, choosing instead to focus on Katla.

Pale blue eyes stared up at me in determination, though for what was still unknown.

I didn't ask about their presence in the field, I didn't want Katla to think I was upset. Besides, I doubted she would have decided to come here for no reason, anyway. But how else was I to piece together their strange behavior?

Fafnir started sniffing Katla. I caught the tail end of his musings; he was worried she might be sick. She didn't seem to care. It was then that I recognized the object in her other hand.

"Why do you have that?" I whispered.

"Leo." Was the only reason she gave for holding my mother's dagger.

Before I could object, grab it back, Leo moved. His hand removed a blade from his belt.

His was more well-tended to, and hadn't borne the burden of the elements for six years. The crimson shone like I remembered hers once had. A bit of light from the gold metal it was wrapped in fell across it.

The similarity was uncanny. Even from afar they were identical.

Katla held both the book and the dagger now, and the latter, she presented before me.

"I know who your mother was."

***

Fafnir was silent as I slid down his wing.

The sound of my boots against the rock filled my entire being. He did not follow me inside. She stood there, shaking one of the furs from her bed. Dust fell to the floor.

"Aidan! I wondered when the two of you would return!" She greeted. "Next time you want to go for a flight after a raid, do tell me first. I was worried you-"

"What is my name?"

Her forehead wrinkled. "What do you-"

"I don't believe she wouldn't have told you this. Not anymore. Not now. I'm giving you a chance. What is my name?"

Slowly, Ragna lowered the fur. "Honey. We've talked about this. You know-"

"Her book is marked with Lamid's crest. You were bothered, when Katla told me. But not surprised. You were never surprised."

"Aidan. I know not what has led you to believe-"

"Her dagger isn't unique. Did you know that? Apparently, it's a family thing."

Ragna swallowed. Fafnir's reassurance pushed through me, warm and strong.

"I don't- where did you hear this?"

"Tell me, Ragna."

"There is nothing for me to tell you-"

"They say it's Aidan Evalade." And Ragna dropped the fur. "You know, I always wanted to hear it from you. After she was gone. If there was any chance you knew, I was so sure, the night she died. So sure you would tell me then, and if you didn't, then you must not ever have known the name of the random villager who was my father. Must not have known more than my first. Because she was gone and Takka was broken and if you knew- if you knew you would have told me because I needed it then. I needed to know. And instead, you taught me the weak points of a ship, how to ensure a boat didn't return to the surface after it was sunk, how to decimate an armada. You were angry, we were both angry, so of course we were on the same side. Of course I only ever trusted in you. But you always *knew*."

I took a shaky breath, a lungful which rattled and fought. "One last chance. Either they lie or you do, and what they hold is damning. What is my name?"

"I can't-"

"You have no right to hide this from me! You never did! What is my name?" I choked on something; air caught in my throat. "Ragna, please."

"Aidan-"

"What is my name?"

"You don't-"

"I don't, what? Deserve to know? And you do?"

Tears rolled down the face I had stared into my entire life. I could not see my brother, but I knew he stood behind me. I could feel him. Ragna's hands shook, and she tried to wipe them against the fur which covered her shoulders. I could see it in her, the moment she decided. I think that was the moment I truly felt it, more even than when she began to speak.

Lies are a terribly heavy thing.

"Aidan Olngar Evalade. Your name is Aidan Olngar Evalade." And just what was it, to breathe? "Your second name was chosen by your mother. It was her father's." Ragna closed her eyes. "Her father was King Olngar of Medea. He bore two daughters. Your mother was from that isle, that kingdom, and in her blood lay a royal claim." Wetness splashed across my face. I felt the waves of what Fafnir struggled to hide, pulsing with my own. "Your father chose the first of your names, and it was from him you gained your last."

"No-"

Had I always spoken like that?

"Atarah was arranged to be married to your father. They wed-"

I couldn't do this. Stupidly, "I don't want to hear anymore-"

"-you were born shortly thereafter, to Queen Atarah-"

Ragna. Stop. Was I asking or begging?

"-and King Ivon Evalade of Lamid.

There was no air in my chest, gone before it had even the chance to be stolen by her words, yet I felt the pain of suffocating all the same.

I could spare no words to stop her, no space in my thoughts to call out. She continued undeterred, unrestrained, baring to the world in one fell swoop all I had desired after. All I had needed.

"Chief Olavi Sture arrived three months after you were born. He snuck into the castle while his men fought. Atarah-" Ragna tripped on her words. "Atarah believed he meant to kill your father. He found her instead, and you." She swallowed a sob. "He took you both from your home. From Lamid. Meant to kill you, or ransom you. To sell you, even. To do some horrible thing crafted from their nature. Then I found you on that ship."

I can't. "No more." *Please.*

"Your mother decided that you would not return. That this would be your home, your family-"

"No!"

"She wanted you to be happy. You were all which she loved. Every choice she made was for you. Every choice *I* made-"

"Choices you grounded in lies!"

"I tell you no lies now-"

"What promise is that?"

"The only one I can give you. You are Aidan Evalade, Prince of the Lamidian Kingdom-"

"I used to ask you every day." I whispered. Then, louder. Stronger. "I don't know why I ever dared to think it would be different the next day. But I did. And I believed you, when you promised me you knew nothing, because how could you possibly have lied? You were everything to me. Surely, if you knew naught, there was no answer to be found." The laugh which escaped my lips burned and cracked. "There was no doubt. There was no suspicion. Not a hint, not even for a second. You couldn't have been lying. Not so relentlessly, never wearing down, always giving the same answer. You *couldn't* have been lying. But you were. Every day. My entire life-"

"Aidan."

"What did you think would happen? What terrible Ragnarök did you tremble at the thought of invoking, when you looked me in the eyes every single day of my life and told me you did not know my name? I have a father! I have a cousin! A grandfather, there must be two, and a grandmother to follow. Aunts, and an uncle too, then! I pleaded for my father's name, and now you throw it like it means nothing-"

Ragna cried. "They are not your only family. Your family is here-"

"But there was one born of my blood and you refused to let me know of it!" A haggard thing clawed its way from me. "How could you? How could you ever? It was never your choice to make! It was never *her's*!"

396

"I know you are upset, and you are angry. You have the right to be. My apologies will not cover that, will not bury the lies we told, I told- the secrets we hid. I know that. And still, I cannot tell you how terribly sorry-" She took a deep breath. "This was not the life she chose for you, the questions and the lies. I believed she would have told you, once. I love you more than my gods and my life, and I cannot say that I would undo it. You were so young, too young to understand why you and your brother could not run off and join their world. The tyranny of man is not one I wanted for you."

"And when I was old enough to shoulder the weight of the identity you believed I could not?"

And this woman, I had never heard so broken. "I wanted you to stay."

I left with nothing more.

CHAPTER TWENTY

AIDAN

Aidan, I'm so sorry. Was the only thing Fafnir said which was spoken.

The rest was wordless, an enveloping expanse of comfort and affection which wrapped around my mind and held fast.

I did not look up from his scales until we were landing again on the grass where we had left the others. My movements slow as though I was trudging through a freezing current, I slid down his ivory wing until I again met solid earth.

She seemed to form up from nothing but the shimmering vapors of the night.

Somehow, through the impossible numb, I felt her around my shoulders, my back. *Her* against my chest as she pulled me in, the softness of the curls which I hid my face in. For a few simple moments I allowed myself to exist in it, Fafnir's comfort and her warmth.

"The others?"

"I set them to work rebuilding the fire. They'll argue over it for at least a few hours." A rush of gratitude towards the ebony haired girl flooded through me. Slowly she pulled back, though her hands trailed down to mine until they grabbed hold. "Let's go flying, yeah?"

I nodded, taking my place upon Fafnir once again.

I could think more clearly when the wind was slamming against my face again. Fafnir's thoughts had been in no less turmoil, incredulity running rampant.

There was anger at Mom in there, too, sinking in the waves of rage towards Ragna. I couldn't disagree. Silently, Bluebell flew beside us. Fafnir and I's questions remained empty, both minds speaking to each other in chase of answers neither held.

Fafnir kept cycling through a memory of Mom tripping into dragon dung when we were young. He was trying to fit a crown that he had once seen in one of my books into the picture. He couldn't.

Sometimes he was trying to imagine it on me.

I didn't know where we were headed, or what we planned to do. Katla didn't inquire, so we simply drifted.

I wished a few Sigurd ships would pop up. That was something simple, something practiced and normal.

Something which could break without repercussions.

We had been staring at the empty ocean for a while, since we left the Bay. The building pressure of questions and falsehoods was stifling, so I turned to Katla. I always felt better when I talked to her. She was focused on the sky ahead, eyes blank.

"What are you thinking about?"

She cocked her head. "You're asking me?"

"I can't quite tell what I'm thinking about anymore, so I figured I'd see how it was going for you."

"Just one thing, really. It's stupid. And insensitive."

"I doubt it. It can't be worse than the scenarios Fafnir's trying out, and I have to actually see those." He grumbled apologetically under me. I threw her the most imploring look I could manage. "Distract me?"

Stubbornly she waited, and then, very quietly. "I kissed the prince of Lamid."

The first coughing chuckle which tore its way through me broke open the doors for the rest, and soon Fafnir had to shift to keep me from rolling up and off of him.

It didn't help that his own chuckles were causing my seat to rock around. When I was finally able to see through blurry eyes, I could tell Katla was glaring.

She was biting her lip, so she couldn't have been too mad.

It was so hysterically funny this way, the title that was mine by apparent birth. The weighty reality of it would come later, but for now it was positively comical. Downright impossible. An absolute joke.

Prince hood, what a sick laugh.

"Twice, actually." I corrected.

"I hope you savored it, because it is never happening again, Dragon Boy. Stop laughing, Fafnir!"

We didn't. When we finally settled down, it was much easier to relax into the familiarity of blue ocean stretched before us, the salty air on the wind. Up here, it was easy to fall into the belief that nothing was imminent. To forget the strangled match of tears and shouting in the cave. The blood drawn by a dagger of betrayal and lies. The sky is untouchable.

Until of course, it isn't. We were unprepared.

The dragons smelled it before we ever could.

I tasted an echo of it through Fafnir's senses. The clouds were only tinted at first, you may have thought they were simply the beginnings of a gathering storm.

We did.

They grew darker as we flew until they hung an unhealthy black against the blue. The scent of it was made heavy in the air, pressing in from all directions, smothering and blazing. It was noxious, so unyielding that my eyes stung and burned even up here.

Smoke.

A massive plume rose up from the island, twisting and curving gently in the breeze as carefully as a falling feather. A deep almost purple, climbing towards the clouds and poisoning the surrounding sky.

We didn't approach much further before amazingly, impossibly and terribly, another smell was powerful enough to join the air, to mix and rise with the smoke. Defying all logic it was more nauseating than the first. Sputtering and coughing, I clamped a hand over my mouth, throat burning with swallowed bile.

I knew its potency.

I recognized the sick stench of it. It was not the first time I had smelt death. It was undeniably what carried on the smoke as their bodies became ash. The Kingdom of Vanir sat before us and it laid in the aftermath of flames. We watched in stunned silence, and observed in a still sky an isle burned.

Terror seized me, vigorous and swift, and I wasn't even aware of if it was all my own, or aided by Fafnir's presence in my mind. The latter, I assumed, as Fafnir was entirely rigid beneath me.

My eyes were fixed ahead, unable to look away from the horror they beheld. I heard Katla, but her words were lost to the noise. There weren't any sounds really, just an eerie quiet. Maybe screams would have been better, like the screams my mind now supplied me with as I was trapped there, blocking out Katla's voice.

Screams meant life, at least. But there were none.

She had risen in pitch now, and I felt bad for not turning. She must have been scared, too. These thoughts were given purchase in my consciousness for only a moment, simply passing by before they were flushed out again.

Orange flickered in my vision, among the unearthly black. Fire. Parts of the isle were still on fire.

Katla shouted now, and Fafnir growled beneath me. He shouldn't have growled at her. Maybe we could still help with the flames.

There had to be people left down there.

Come back.

When Fafnir's voice finally broke through, I noted that it was much softer than Katla's. Much less terrified.

"Aidan!"

Like I'd been shocked, I jolted, whipping my head around to find her and allowing myself to feel the momentary relief that came with seeing something else.

Even if the clouds were still painted with death.

I registered faintly that she was crying. I felt bad for making her cry, for putting her in the position to see this, but soon realized that the feeling was simply a pale imitation of the one that was already overcoming me. Guilt, was that what this was? Fitting.

I should have been here. The dragons and I, we should have stopped this from ever happening.

"We have to help them." I finally spat out, trying to shake the freeze from my body.

Katla shook her head, distraught. "We can't, Aidan. Not now."

Slowly she pointed, and slower I followed, until my eyes confirmed the explanation in my mind.

The water was littered with ships, bearing terribly familiar insignias. There was little motion from below, no panic from the deck. The armada sat calmly in the water, its job done. Their battle was over. They had won.

The Sigurd had taken Vanir.

"No!" I powerlessly denied.

"We have to go, we have to get out of here."

"What? We have to help them!"

"Help them how, Aidan? We're two dragons and two riders. There're so many ships. We'd be dead before we broke the shoreline!"

"We can't just leave!"

I beat back the rising alarm. This couldn't be happening. Tears were still streaming down her face, and she seemed to be deliberately angling her body away from the island.

"We can't stay." She whispered. "There's nothing we can do right now."

Ships surrounded the entire island, branching out into the waters. There was a good number more than the usual amount we took on, even if it wasn't already impossible with only two dragons. A cumulation of two fleets, maybe three. Fafnir whined beneath me.

"You're right." I murmured, and I saw Katla sigh. "Let's go. We'll figure something out. We'll be back."

She nodded shakily, and I heard her sniff, Bluebell chirping weakly below her in attempted comfort.

The dragons peeled around, turning away from the smoldering island. Breathing didn't come any easier the further away we moved from the flames.

My mind was spinning, thoughts tumbling over themselves in a frantic attempt to uncover a solution, but none came. This was too much.

My eyes pricked, and I wondered whether it was from the smoke or something else. The Sigurd had taken an entire kingdom. Olavi had seized an entire kingdom. How many had died?

What did he plan to do with it?

Fafnir snarled suddenly, a vicious breakage of silence that seemed to splinter the sky. Bluebell joined in a second later, Katla peering anxiously at the water below her wing. I waited for him to tell me what he saw.

It's one of theirs.

A single boat floated below us. It was nothing too large, almost entirely alone but for the few other vessels some fifty yards away. This group had drifted furthest from the surrounding armada.

They would never reach it before we did.

The second I leaned forward, Fafnir was diving. He was unmovable, locked on the lone ship that had strayed foolishly from protection in numbers. We landed so fiercely on the deck that the opposite end of the ship rose into the air. The stern crashed back into the water and displaced every occupant, cries of distress followed by thuds as they hit the ground again.

The Sigurd onboard scrambled for their weapons.

Fafnir roared, spreading his forelegs apart and raising his wings. I held a steady glare from atop his back, wondering if it was me shaking, or him. The warriors were stuck in fear of Fafnir. He turned his head only slightly, inclined towards me behind him in question.

My voice darkened. *All but one.*

Without warning to anyone but myself Fafnir leapt into action, and three of the crew were already struggling to tread water before the rest understood that he was picking them off.

I saw a figure of blue as a woman flew into the ocean with a crash. Another girl raised a spear and hurled it towards Fafnir's side, but it was gone in an instant, reduced to ash in its path from Bluebell's fire. A flick of Fafnir's tail, and she was gone as well.

A single boat never had a chance.

Soon only one man remained, a glaive shaking in his trembling hands. I quirked an eyebrow at Katla, who was sitting on Bluebell next to us, both dragons staring the man down. With an overly loving expression she leaned down to caress Bluebell's side.

"Can you get rid of that thing, Bluebell? If he doesn't want to let go, take his hands along with it."

They may not have been Bonded, but Katla's meaning was

407

unmistakable.

Squawking happily, she wasted no time charging toward him, teeth barred and fire ready, growing in her throat. The warrior screamed, quite literally tossing the weapon away where it clattered on the now otherwise empty deck. Bluebell ceased, a little disappointed.

I jumped down, Katla doing the same, sword already in hand. I didn't bother with mine.

"You attacked the kingdom. Why?" I demanded to know.

The man scoffed at me, and Fafnir snarled over my shoulder. He jumped again, eyes darting around. Three other ships had turned in the water, making their way over. They wouldn't arrive before we were through here. Katla began to approach, her walk threateningly gentle.

It matched her voice when she began. She was a calm and eerie danger.

"He asked you a question, and I suggest you answer it. There are plenty more of your men in the water to choose from, and the dragons haven't had breakfast yet."

The man was shaking his head, still peering at the approaching boats as if he could force them to materialize closer. I tried again.

"An all-out attack on one single island is senseless. You must know the other kingdoms won't stand for it. You can't hope to hold onto it. Even Olavi isn't that stupid-"

The Sigurd clansman charged forward with a yell, and I had little time to raise my arm before he had barreled into me. His weight was already gone before I hit the ground, forced off of me by something. Rolling with the impact, I pushed myself up as quickly as I could to see what had happened. Fafnir and Bluebell were tense and ready, but they were watching, not acting.

I could hear Fafnir laughing, and Bluebell was amused. Katla stood in between them, the man on the ground under her boot, the tip of her blade pressing into the hollow of his throat.

He was sputtering under the pressure she applied.

"You'll find I'm not one for such polite conversations. It would be wise to remember both your position as entirely expendable, and the fact that now you've really pissed me off. You tell me what we want to know, or I'll bury this in your throat, and one of your crewmates will be next. I see no issue in getting my sword a little dirty, it's been looking far too polished for me, anyway. Everyone knows you need a little blood on your blade to be taken seriously. Maybe that will inspire the next of your friends who will have the misfortune of meeting me to be more forthcoming."

Katla's promises dripped in the same false sweetness she had used with Bluebell seconds earlier. I rose to my knees, entirely unashamed of the awe that captured my expression. She pulled back the sword tip slightly, allowing the man to take a full breath. "I'd use this opportunity I'm allowing you to be cooperative. Vanir. Explain. Now."

"Chief Olavi will kill me himself if I tell anything, especially to the boy."

I scoffed humorlessly. "Aw, Olavi's keeping secrets from me?"

"You truly are the foolish child he believes if you speak of him with so little respect-"

Katla pushed down again, strangling his next words and replacing them with her own.

"I hold your life under my blade, pay your respect to me."

"I'd answer her. Katla, let him speak."

The man's words rushed out, gasping. "Most of the remaining forces laid down once we captured their queen. We were ordered to take the island by any means necessary."

"By means of slaughter, you mean? What does the Sigurd Clan have to gain from Vanir?" Katla growled, and the man didn't respond, inhaling loudly. "Why were you ordered to attack?"

"I don't know, they didn't tell us, I swear-"

Katla was unamused, and in a flash of metal she had lodged the sword in the wood next to the man's ear. He cried out as the tip nicked his skin, spots of blood darkening the knot-filled wood.

"Last chance,"

"By Loki, I swear it!"

Katla sighed, feigning disappointment. "Alright. You're useless, then. Bluebell, would you mind fetching me another from the water? I'm sure Fafnir can discard this one on his own."

"No, no please! Wait!" He yelled, begging from under Katla's boot as she tore the sword from the boards. Even from here it was obvious, in her stance and the way she held the handle, she wasn't going to use it. Her face however, was hard, eyes steely and determined as the man stared fearfully up at her. She was selling it phenomenally. "We began relocation this morning! To become defensible and mobile before their allies could rally any retaliation!"

"You're moving after you've just secured an island? Why?" I asked.

"To regroup the vessels! Those who are able will be pulled from Vanir to help man more boats. We've already taken the harbor; their ships will be added to our forces."

"For what reason could you possibly require more men?"

"And more ships?" Katla added.

"Almost all the boats sail again today, the warriors were meant to ready themselves for another fight if they had been chosen to occupy the new force!"

"You're retreating so soon?" My brow furrowed. "No. Olavi wouldn't give up the island once he had it. You're going somewhere else. Where will you sail?"

Katla put her weight into it, eliciting a shout. "Briaedor!"

I had predicted a stopover island, perhaps a place for the majority of his men to hide out once the wrath of Vanir's allies broke through their waters. But another kingdom entirely?

"What does Olavi want with Briaedor?"

The man tried to twist his head, and a moment's glance told me his help was almost here. We were running out of time.

Fafnir.

He was directly behind me in a second, massive head bearing down over my shoulder and less than an inch from the man's face. The Sigurd warrior screamed, trying to push himself away, but was boxed in by the dangerous proximity of Katla's sword.

"We swarm Briaedor after Vanir! As soon as we've secured control, we sail for Lamid-"

"What?" Katla cried.

"-and then Medea! As far as we can make it!"

Katla took a step back.

"How the Hel are you expecting to pull that off?" I laughed shakily, waiting for the moment when he would admit to having made the foolish mistake of attempting to misdirect us. It didn't come.

The boats were close enough now that we could hear the shouts of the crew on board. Close enough for arrows to find their target. Walls of fire erupted on either side of us as the dragons reduced the first barrage of bolts to nothing.

The man was petrified by the display, scrambling from the sudden temperature increase, though he couldn't move more than a few inches.

We have to go, now! Make it fast. Fafnir yelled.

I lurched to ask my final question.

"When do Olavi's men sail on Briaedor?"

"They've already left."

A vicious fear struck me so terribly I was almost knocked backward from the force of it. Could we be too late twice?

I spun, sprinting for Fafnir and making the leap to his back in a second. There was a short cry as the man joined his friends in the sea, but I only heard the echo of Katla's fate for him. Fafnir and I were already pushing upward, smoke-tinged air assaulting us.

We righted abruptly, wildly scanning the island again. The isle was still surrounded with ships, but no spot was more heavily armed than the others. There existed no area where the water should have been dense with boats. No mass of vessels at the end of wooden piers.

The Vanir harbor was empty.

The Sigurd had stolen their boats. Added them to their own armada.

If they had already left, then I could not even guess at the scope of their numbers. If the converged fleets which surrounded Vanir were only a fraction, a portion left behind, how many vessels sailed with the whole? How could any island possibly withstand it?

Bluebell rose up to my left. Katla asked the question of the hour.

As if there weren't already enough of those floating around the previous hour.

"What is going on?"

Before us, the isle burned dimly, the fires settling.

"Olavi's coming for the Voluspian Kingdoms, and he seems to believe he can actually take them."

***

Fafnir's entire body was heaving with shallow breaths by the time we reached the Isle of the Bay, and Bluebell was even worse off.

We'd flown at breakneck speeds straight from Vanir, not realizing how far out we had truly traveled, and their wings were exhausted. We nearly crashed onto the shore. Sand flew from beneath Fafnir's claws, blew into my face. Calls sounded nearby, the other three Lamidians running.

Katla dismounted, but I stayed where I was. She rounded Fafnir to her friends. Eliana's expression dropped, and I realized too late that Katla was still crying.

Calin ran faster, taking in Katla's expression. "Kat, what-"

"The Sigurd took Vanir,"

"What?" Eliana protested.

"The whole island was on fire, boats surrounding it, a warship or two. We took their ship, and he told us they were sailing to Briaedor next, and then to Lamid after that, and-"

"Katla, slow the Hel down! What about their queen, Nesrin? She would never allow that to happen." Leo insisted.

"He said they captured Vanir's queen-"

"Who's 'he'?" Eliana interrupted.

"One of the Sigurd clansmen!"

415

"And they're going to Lamid next? After they just launched an attack and invaded a kingdom? That's impossible! They wouldn't make it within a league of the shore." Calin shook his head.

"Briaedor first, then Lamid." Katla clarified. "They've already left. Ships, over a fleet of them, were left behind to guard Vanir. The rest sailed on."

"That's impossible. There's no way Olavi Sture has an army strong enough to move from island to island in a number of days!" Leo denied. "The most damage they've done over the years is small-scale raiding parties. No single kingdom has a force large enough to conquer right now, not even Unadine. Let alone take three entire islands! The Sigurd have made themselves the most dangerous of Voluspa's clans, but they aren't capable of this."

"All of the ships from Vanir's fleet are gone. Forced into the ranks of Olavi's naval movement. The Sigurd have full control over the kingdom's military. I'd guess a good number of those ships are manned by slaves, and it they'll be taking more." I explained, searching the sky above and those who roamed it, thinking. "They'll just keep building, replacing what they lose."

"Even with that many men, entire kingdoms don't fall in a day." Leo tried, but we had no reassurance for him. "Let's pretend for one second that any of this is even possible. We have to do something, right now. I have to

416

warn my uncle."

"We will, but first I'm going to Briaedor." All heads snapped to me. "Get your boat ready, I have plenty of maps, I'll bring you one. If you go out wide enough, you'll miss the Sigurd fleet and arrive a little after us. Hopefully after the fighting is done."

Calin raised his eyebrows. "Arrive where, exactly?"

"We'll meet at Lamid." I decided, and Katla jerked in surprise. "I'm taking the flock to Briaedor. Maybe we can head them off. Katla, you go with them-"

"Excuse me? You're joking, right?" Her expression was surprisingly livid despite the tears drying on her cheeks.

"I- no?"

"What in the name of the Aesir is wrong with you? What, you think you're going alone?"

"Katla, this isn't safe."

"I gathered that much."

"This isn't an ordinary raid! I don't have any idea how many ships they hold, and I don't want to risk it. This is new territory, I'm flying blind. They had an armada surrounding Vanir, and those were just the ships they left behind! It's safer if you just go with them, fly with the boat. Bluebell is tired, and-"

"Oh, and Fafnir isn't? You're not flying off by yourself, I'm coming with you. This isn't my first time fighting, both Bluebell and I are entirely capable-"

"I know you are, but-"

"Good! Then stop disagreeing with me, and let me come with. Because we are coming, and the only thing your arguing is doing for us is wasting time we don't have." I gaped, floundering for one single second, and Katla seized the opportunity like a dragon on a boar. "Okay! So that's settled. Calin, Leo, Eliana, you can fly on Fafnir with Aidan."

"I'm sorry, what?" I jumped, and the others were similarly shocked.

"Aidan, come on. They are not sailing all the way home on their own. Clearly the Sigurd fleet isn't all in one place, and with our luck they'll run right into some of them, spread out as they are. Calin is a great sailor, but he may not be able to escape a horde of boats. You three can fly with us-"

"You want me to take them into a battle? On Fafnir?"

"Of course not. We'll set them down when we arrive. We can all fight."

"A chance to kick some Sigurd ass? Count me in!" Leo smirked.

"And what about the dragon ride required to get there?" Calin shot out, and Leo paled.

"Oh, come on. Katla's been doing this for a while, so it has to be at least relatively safe. Neither of them have tried to kill us, and it must have been tempting. Anyone who can survive a day without trying to murder Leo Evalade is beyond civilized, in my opinion." The man in question huffed at Eliana's statement, before she focused on Katla. "Besides, we won't be steering, right?"

"Fafnir will be."

Eliana released a long sigh, regarding Fafnir doubtfully. "The dragon. Gods, Katla. If this gets us killed, I will never forgive you."

"Understandable."

I shook my head. "No, no! We are not doing this!"

"Well, we can try to all fit on Bluebell, but I don't think that'll work out." Katla shrugged, a smile playing on her lips. "She's a tad bit smaller."

"This is crazy."

"There seems to be a lot of that going around."

"And reckless."

"That too, especially where you're concerned. This is safer than trying to sail from here to Lamid. What if we ran into a branch of ships with only one dragon? Or if they stayed here, to be found by any Muspel or Syre who happens across them?"

"No one would hurt-"

"Or Ragna?"

I scrubbed a hand down my face as Katla's friends listened to her, ranging from excited to downright nauseous at the prospect of riding a dragon. How was I allowing this? How had I gotten myself into it?

"You are terrible." I told her truthfully.

"You wouldn't have to find out if you weren't attempting to bench me."

"I can see why they want you to be queen, you're very bossy."

She laughed. "Shut up and go get the dragons or *you* can sail home."

Home.

Was that supposed to be Lamid?

I really didn't have the time to think about that, to bring the savage tornado of questions twisting down again. I did my best to push it from my mind.

I complied with her orders, and Fafnir lifted off.

Wow. You took that like a spineless hatchling.

You know what? Commentary not necessary.

But so entertaining. We could use some of that right now.

Yeah, how about after we've sent Olavi to Helheim.

Fafnir snorted, but didn't respond. The higher we flew, the faster my mood dissipated, until it was again replaced with the creeping anxiousness from earlier.

I tried to calm my own racing heartbeat. We could handle this.

My eyes turned upon the cave as we entered the Bay.

Fafnir flung to a stop, sending small chunks of rock scattering from the outcrop. Ragna was sitting on my bed, and she jumped to stand as we approached. I slid from Fafnir as he readied to call upon those who dwelled inside. She practically ran over, and appeared to have been crying. I pushed past her, not allowing myself to linger.

The leather bag waited at the foot of my bed, and I swung it over my shoulder, its contents shaking about inside. I had gone to retrieve it from Trader's Isle only a few days prior. I pondered the sack over my shoulder.

Stupidly, and in the face of much bigger problems, I wondered when I was meant to give it to her now. Any plans of a perfect time had flown away with the arrival of her friends and their epiphanies.

"Aidan, you're back-"

Ragna cut off as I walked around her again, this time out towards Fafnir.

"Vanir is taken." I hardened my voice. "Olavi has taken a kingdom and

421

he moves on another. Do you still believe the man plans for nothing?" Fafnir roared, a force which shook the very realms. I could hear the wordless call in my mind, and I knew Ragna could as well. The call to battle. "I know your opinion of them. What they did to you. And I can't say I fault you for being simply afraid."

I collected myself. "But there is an island on fire and now is the time to be brave. I once thought you brave. Now I see you are a coward, and a hypocrite. You are no different from them. You are blinded to their possibilities; you deny that they could ever understand. Blinded by nothing but your own fear. You refused me a chance to help them see, and you were a coward. All you have ever done is hide. So hide now."

She said nothing as I swung myself onto Fafnir, and continued to watch in silence as we joined the masses who congregated outside.

We left Ragna behind in the Bay.

Even as the day became one dark black, the sky was alive with colors. Scales filled every inch of the air, darting about in eagerness and agitation.

I was afraid of what I might think if I slowed for too long.

I could still see Vanir in my mind, still imagine the people who must have been killed. Would they still have fallen if we had been there? Fafnir's imagined pictures floated through my mind again. My mother and I, two crowns.

Absurdity.

Maybe she sensed my agitation, the fear and sorrow. Ragna could have told her. Perhaps my mind was louder than I meant for it to be. Through whatever way of knowing, Takka was silent as she appeared at our side. Fafnir grumbled.

My Hatchling. I'm sorry.

I can't believe I once believed you to be a poor liar. I didn't look at her.

Apologies are not what you wish to hear from me, despite my willingness to give them. We all knew of your desires, especially her. *Atarah and I were one, I knew her soul better than my own.* Takka was gentle. *She meant to tell you. Had she remained among us, you would have known from her your life before, someday.*

As if you couldn't have told me yourself? I rebuked.

I'm sorry, Her's of Mine. Ragna wished it not, and I could not ever lose both you and Atarah in this life.

Fafnir let out a keening whine. I gripped a horn in my hand, feeling the grooves and dips of the brown bone.

I love you, I do. But I will not forgive, not now.

Takka's large eyes landed on me, full of understanding and heartache.

I know. She crooned. *There is a coming battle. Keep yourselves safe.*

Katla was already mounted when I arrived back on the beach. Leo looked at me with a frown.

"What about Uncle Ivon?" He asked. "What are we going to tell him? About...you?"

And oh, to the gods above. King Ivon of Lamid. My father. Which title took precedence in these circumstances?

I wasn't sure what to do, I was flailing to come up with what little of a plan we already had. As much as I wanted more than anything else to go meet my father right in that instant, we couldn't. Not in the thick of one catastrophe after another.

"We'll tell him. *After* this is all over." I decided.

Katla glanced at me curiously, but otherwise said nothing.

"Oh, fantastic. Then if we survive, King Ivon will kill us!" Eliana chimed in.

"Speak for yourself. My mother will be faster than Ivon." Calin muttered.

I shrugged, at a loss. My thinking abilities were entirely expended.

"Alright, who's boarding the dragon first?" Katla asked devilishly, and for a moment we both took silent amusement in the fear that flashed across their faces.

CHAPTER TWENTY-ONE

KATLA

Despite the circumstances, the sight of Lamidian Heir Leo Evalade about to wet himself was as satisfying as I had ever dreamed.

He had ceased his screaming after the first couple minutes, now locked in a full body hug with one of Fafnir's large spines. Calin was stiff as a board, hands clenched so tightly they were the same shade as the scales he sat on. Eliana settled for simple death glares aimed at me, and a string of curses each time they jostled.

Currently, she had told me how, when, and where she would murder me, approximately twelve times. She was trying for thirteen.

They sat in a row on Fafnir's back, each directly behind the other and spaced around a large spine. Screams fled their lips each time Fafnir laughed, his entire body shaking. This happened rather often, his amusement endless.

We were moving much slower now than we would like, but the sheer amount of dragons we carted across the sky weighed our passage down considerably.

It was entirely dark now, but Aidan still leaned forward, rigid on Fafnir, eyes locked on the horizon like he could will Briaedor into the light.

We had already swept over Vanir, parts of the island still suffering from small fires. It had been the only time my friends had seemingly forgotten their fear, for only an instant, when they first saw the decimated kingdom.

There was nothing we could do then, so Aidan and I both looked away from the isle.

So many had died there, nameless and faceless in my mind, but a massacre of innocent lives all the same. We hadn't even seen their bodies, there was only a lingering sense, and a smell. Once we had prevented further carnage, we would have to come back and help them.

Flapping wings spread over the sea, echoing back at us, magnified by the incredible number of dragons. It was a noise akin to my mother shaking a bit of dust from leather, but a thousand times over. All of the world's sound was overcome with the chirping, growling, and roaring of serpents from all directions.

Fafnir flew near to us, but I was too busy fighting to keep Bluebell steady in the expanse of wings and bodies to exchange words with Aidan. His expression never wavered; eyes never strayed from their position fixed ahead. Coiled, his shoulders never relaxed. His features were filled with hard determination, not even broken when the occasional Kaida rested their wings on his back or head.

One of these small dragons, about the size of a raven, landed on Bluebell's back, right behind me. Vivid red scales decorated her frame, tiny wings curling in and then unfurling, but she stayed put.

I twisted as well as I could from my seat on Bluebell, extending one finger to her.

She shifted slightly forward, allowing me to scratch gently under her head. I sighed, taking in a moment of calm which could never have lasted.

Ironically, I think the smaller ones noticed it first. Or maybe that was simply where my focus lied when there suddenly became something to notice.

Oval eyes became slits, straightened spine became rigid, the extended head drew back violently. Her nostrils flared, as if she had smelled something vile.

She had, of course she had, because we had arrived after it had begun.

There was a visible change in our strange ocean, like the harsh crashing of waves during a lawless storm. Instantaneously, the noise dropped, so suddenly, that I was left reeling.

Snarls filled the void, much quieter this time, the tension in the air so tangible I felt myself leaning away from those flying around us.

I was pushed an inch or so higher in the air as Bluebell tightened up, her back arching like a spooked cat. The red raven took to the air.

Aidan did not turn to me, his eyes glassy, head tilted towards Fafnir, engaging in a conversation I couldn't hear. I waited, as patiently as I could, until he moved animatedly again.

"It's the same smell." Was all he said.

What a ridiculous statement to hold such a weight.

I nudged Bluebell a second before Fafnir bolted ahead, so we were in time with Aidan as we streaked away from the group as fast as we could manage. They would find it on their own now, it seemed we were close enough.

The feeling of sinking desperation was almost painful in the force it carried once we were finally able to see the smoke.

"No!" I threw my focus into urging Bluebell forward.

This must have been how Vanir looked in the prime of the attack which rolled through it.

I pondered on whether it was the darkness that made it seem so much worse, standing in stark contrast to the world around it, or simply the realization that we had failed.

We never could have made it in time.

Bluebell let out a croon.

The fleet was ungodly, more boats than water before my eyes. White sails reflected the moonlight, the ocean covered with hundreds of moving ghosts. It looked like every village was on fire, the inferno so large and all-consuming that it was all I could see before we came close enough to make out the island. A burning torch rising from the depths of the Voluspian Ocean.

We could hear the screams this time.

Aidan cursed, and I was inclined to agree.

"No way." Leo whispered.

Eliana turned to me slowly, a hand covering her mouth, another gripping Fafnir's spine. Calin reached for the halberd handle on his back.

"The armada is only targeting one side, they haven't surrounded the island like Vanir." Aidan barked.

"They haven't taken full control yet, they must still be fighting in the village!"

Boats filled the world beneath us, the squadron so immense it was terrifying to be above it, as if by sheer size and power we could be knocked from the sky. Those who hadn't already reached the island were on their way, sails billowing, unleashed and plowing on. I could hear the roar of dragons on the deck.

Why would they have captured dragons with them? Did they mean to turn the island into a place to store them? How could Aidan rescue them when they were on a fortified island, instead of floating at sea?

"We have to help!" Aidan desperately reminded.

I agreed. "With what? How?"

"Just like when we find an armada! There's too many of them to keep the island from the Sigurd. The only option is getting people onto boats and getting out of here before they're all trapped."

"How are we going to do that?"

Already Fafnir was turning, heading to meet the flock in the middle. Bluebell gave chase to his tail, keeping up.

"Look at the island! The harbor is on the north, but they're coming in from the east side! Not far away, but at least apart from the direct focus. I'm sure the Sigurd will try to take it soon, we just have to be faster!"

I peered down, and sure enough, the port holding Briaedorian ships had

431

yet to be pulled into the opposing army, their fleet floating stationary in the water. A few vessels of the Sigurd armada were breaking off, however, headed in that direction. No doubt to stop any Briaedor-manned ships from escaping.

"We can herd as many people onto the boats as possible, and send them out to sea! The dragons can stave off the approaching ships, grant us time!" I called to Aidan, who nodded rapidly in response.

"Just get us down already!" Calin shouted to us both. "We can help on the ground!"

Fafnir released an ear-splitting roar, signaling the rest. I felt excitement light my nerves, either in anticipation or the relief and adrenaline of finally being able to do something.

Of no longer sitting aside and watching.

"Okay, Bluebell, let's make them work for it."

"Everybody, hold on! I don't have time to double back if you fall off!"

We dived.

I wondered what a sight it must have been for those on the island, specifically the Briaedorians. Their kingdom was already under siege, death, smoke, and flame overrunning everything. To see a storm of dragons about to crash upon them in the same moment...I had no doubt many were seeing their visions of Ragnarök personified. The end of worlds.

Hopefully that viewpoint would change, and fast. If they tried to attack us while we were trying to save them, matters would change from complicated to infeasible.

Aidan and I peeled away from the flock as we came close above the water, and a good number of dragons followed after as we flew for the docks.

I sighed with relief when I saw people already doing their best to board the ships, and heard Aidan do the same. Sigurd and Briaedor warriors were fighting in front of the harbor, the former trying to prevent access to the boats.

I almost felt sorry for them, the sudden onslaught from the sky was unsuspected, but so very deserved. And it was approaching fast.

The first man Bluebell collided with was sent several feet away in the dirt, the woman who had been battling him left stunned.

It was easy enough to pick them out, their odd armor reflecting the firelight in strange warped patterns, rather than smoothly. A string of flame emerged from her maw in the same swoop, three warriors felled in the next second. I could hear Fafnir's roar behind me, and the growls of the ones who followed him. It was extremely satisfying to see terror in the eyes of the Sigurd before a plague of fire was laid to *them*.

"That's it, Bluebell!" I cheered, and she rumbled in pride.

A small troop of Sigurd came crashing down the large street which led to the ships. We bathed them in flame.

I saw Aidan several times as we worked in the small space, fueled once again with resolve. It truly was fear-striking to see him streaking down on Fafnir, reinstituting just how hulking the beast was. A few months ago the sight may have left me shouting frantic prayers to the gods.

Fafnir's back was now bare, barring Aidan.

The others had jumped down. I saw Leo charging into the throngs, his two axes flying. Calin was helping people onto the boats, and Eliana was standing in front of him, providing cover with her bow outstretched. Her arrows did not miss. This particular group of Sigurd held very few archers among them, and their few shafts were easily dodged.

Eliana picked them off when I couldn't get close enough. I saw one of them topple over, an arrow through his throat.

Their halberds and maces swung uselessly for the dragons overhead, but where blades were met with fire, we could only triumph.

We made quick work of the Sigurd who remained.

The short distance from the port to the village was made apparent by the unnatural warmth in the air. Our nearness to the flames. I scolded myself for shifting uncomfortably under the heat while others were burning in it.

We had yet to be charged by any of the warriors from Briaedor, and whether it was shock or terror, I was grateful for what held them back. Bluebell and I hovered above the crowd which had gathered, watching on in what I would simply call befuddlement.

Fafnir brushed against Bluebell's side. Aidan and I exchanged glances.

The group below was silent, the sounds of battle distant as the two sides considered each other. It was almost awkward.

That is, it was, before the crowd began to part.

A girl pushed her way through the throngs, or walked was more like it, seeing as they made way for her. We were close enough that I noticed the small braids in her startlingly red hair. It fell down past her waist, even tied back as it was. She was dressed for battle, her armor an expert mix of shining plate and leather. An axe was held tightly in her hands.

For a moment she simply gazed up at us, and when I turned to see Aidan's opinion of the situation, I found him squinting at her, as if he was trying to make her out more clearly. That was strange. It wasn't all that hard to see, though it should have been in the pitch night.

There was so much ablaze that the world may as well have been sitting under an orange sun.

"It's Aidan, right?" She called, recognition rising on her freckled face.

Wait. What?

"Princess Avelyn. Are you going to kill us if we land?" Aidan questioned.

"I suppose not. For now." We did so, Bluebell and I much later than Fafnir. My eyes continued to dart between Aidan and the girl he had just addressed as Princess. Part of the Briaedorian royal family? I'd heard it was rather large, but the first in line was a prince. A brother, then? She walked forward to meet us, looking apprehensively at the dragons, but not quite stopping. She regarded me with surprise when she noticed my presence, but quickly moved on. "Why have you come here?"

"Same as you, it seems. To aid Briaedor. The Sigurd have Vanir-"

"We know." She cut Aidan off. "One of their messengers was able to arrive here earlier today. We still didn't have enough time. I've been sent to lead the evacuation by a passing general. It's all I know of the ambush."

"You people need to board these boats. We can help protect your backs." Aidan vowed.

She glanced behind her at her people, her words much softer.

"Be honest. Do you truly think we can make it? If there is no hope for escape, then our numbers would be better spent fighting with our friends and families."

436

"There's no sense in not trying. Besides, we should be able to get a good number of boats out of the harbor. We're keeping them away from here, for now."

"How?"

Aidan finally smiled, just a little, and inclined his head to the left. Both Avelyn and I turned, and I held back a bubble of relieved laughter when I realized the inferno on the water almost matched that on land. The closest line of Sigurd ships was burning. The dragons were handling themselves well, but we couldn't stick around. This battle was lost, and even with our numbers we would be overtaken.

We would make our stand at Lamid, gods willing. Avelyn appeared stunned. I felt a little more pride than I should've.

"We need to move quickly. These boats don't have long to make it onto the water." I touched Aidan's shoulder.

Avelyn nodded. "Where will you lead my people?"

"Lamid."

Her eyebrows drew together, but she did not deny the desired location. She returned to the Briaedorians, and we returned to our dragons. Aidan and I climbed higher as Avelyn's voice called to those on the boats and still on land.

There was a new frantic movement as they began to move for the ships once more. I risked periodic glances towards the armada. The offending troops were being held at bay for now, but they were pushing it. Bluebell and I flew over the boats, waiting anxiously for them to fill.

I kept my eyes trained down, avoiding the burning village just ahead of us. Already, the flames were dying down. I blinked repeatedly, trying to clear my vision through the smoke.

More Sigurd ran for the harbor.

Leo cut two of them down without stopping, his axes spinning expertly. From both hands they dashed out in front of him, blocking an arrow from meeting his leg. The archer who had fired on him was dead in the next moment, Eliana's aim better than his. Aidan and I dealt with the rest as best we could while the villagers boarded.

The Sigurd numbers were increasing, and we had with us only about seven dragons. The roars were closer, and they drowned out the screams from the village.

"Hurry!" I shouted, but I doubted it carried. Nevertheless, it eased the helpless feeling, so I continued to call, Aidan joining me.

Every few minutes a villager or two would break from the town and run to the pier. We'd do our best to make sure they made it to the port.

438

Not all of them did.

Some were struck down before we could help. The kingdom had been taken, and the Sigurd which rushed from the nearby village formed an endless stream. A few made it dangerously close to the ships of citizens, while the enemy vessels approached from the left.

"Aidan!"

He found me just as Fafnir took out an entire offensive line with a blast of fire so bright, I was forced to divert my eyes.

"Not yet! We can't, there could still be more people!"

I glared at him without any real heat. I didn't want to leave any more than he did, but our time was up.

"If we don't go now, none of us are getting off this island!"

An arrow bounced off the shield across my back, the impact passing through me like a shiver, and Bluebell moved faster. The few boats were already beginning to sail away.

Princess Avelyn was standing on the docks, helping people on. She was seemingly holding onto her resolve by a thread.

I couldn't blame her, not only was her kingdom lost, but some of the fire found purchase on the castle.

"Everyone needs to be on those boats! We're going!" I yelled down to her, and fear flashed across her face.

"Alright, come on!" She rushed her people, corralling the last of them onto a ship.

Eliana, Leo, and Calin stood on a deck of the closest boat, waiting. Avelyn spun to the same one, and grasped one of the many outstretched hands to pull herself in. With a wind-like shriek Fafnir blasted across the docks, burning away the wood and destroying the bridges to the boats. The few Sigurd who had the misfortune of running towards the ships at the time fell into the water below, the rest stopping short at the shore, cut off.

Sails dropped, and the last ships began to move away from the remains of the harbor. Aidan and I stayed until their arrows fell into the water, too far away to harm anyone making an escape.

I waited in the sky as Fafnir and Aidan raced towards the armada, and the dragons flying above it.

Wisps of Muspelheim rained down on the Sigurd, fire pouring from their mouths, glowing acid searing. At least we could give those who remained this much time, but what good were we doing for the inevitable? We still had to leave them to the onslaught.

Even from here I could hear the echoes of Fafnir's roar.

Aidan returned, the flock slowly trickling into a line which trailed after him. For a moment we sat together in the sky, observing the second island in a single day burning and stolen. The vast insanity of it all was great.

Who could have prepared for this? Who could have thought up such obscenities, and rationally believed they could ever occur?

At the same time, we turned our eyes away, and forced ourselves to remember we were not turning our backs as well.

CHAPTER TWENTY–TWO

KATLA

The impact jarred me slightly, causing my knees to shake as I found wood after letting go of Bluebell.

Aidan landed lightly beside me, soundless. My friends came to meet us, solemn despite their own victories during the fight.

Avelyn had beckoned to us from the boat she occupied, and the people onboard had left space for us to join them. Even now that we had arrived, and the dragons risen a bit higher, they still assessed us carefully, standing a good distance back.

It was still a strange sight to see, the looks of slightly fearful suspicion.

Avelyn however, approached us, brown eyes shining with wetness. A tear fell down her cheek, but her voice did not waver, nor give any indication to her grief when she spoke.

"Thank you, for helping us again. I'm sorry that our last meeting ended on such an unpleasant note." She said regretfully, her words angled towards Aidan.

He shrugged with a single shoulder and a smile.

"Again?" I questioned him, but it was Avelyn who answered.

"There was a small Sigurd attack a few months back. They attacked the village of Njord around mid-morning, and while we fended them off rather well, they were able even still to make it out with a number of people. Both myself and my mother were included in the taken. The Sigurd's men didn't speak to us much, but we knew we were heading to the auctions. Aidan saved us."

"I only truly had to help you alone, after you decided to take out what remained of a longboat on your own with a stolen axe."

Her answering laugh was watery. "I handled myself quite well up until then. Archers are essentially cheating. The coward had no place in my chosen match."

He hummed good-naturedly in agreement, before turning to me. "This is Katla."

"Katla Vistel, Your Highness."

"Call me Avelyn, please. You've saved all our lives; I owe you that much."

I looked around at these lives we saved. There were only four boats on the water, filled to the brim with people. Only four boats from an entire kingdom. I didn't want to think about the ones who were left behind.

Or the ones who were already dead.

I shook the musings from my mind for the time being.

"This is Eliana Brendean, Calin Solvi, and Leo Evalade." I introduced them, gesturing to each in turn.

Avelyn's eyes lit in recognition. "Ivon's heir. It's nice to see you again."

"You too, although I wish it was for another treaty reading."

Avelyn nodded, taking them in. Eliana and Leo were spotted with blood, though I doubted it was theirs.

"You three can get yourselves cleaned up, if you would like. There are supplies in those crates over there." She offered, pointing to a stack of boxes that the other Briaedorians were already making use of.

"Thank you, Your Highness." Calin told her, beginning towards them with Leo and Eliana.

"Avelyn, and of course." She waited for them to walk away. "I don't understand, why did they attack us? And Vanir? None of us believed the

Sigurd to have this many numbers. I heard from the scouts that some of the boats in the back housed dragons."

"I hold no affiliation to them, if that is what you are looking to find. We don't know why they're attacking. We only spoke to one of them, or rather Katla did." Aidan supplied. "And all he gave us was that they had invaded Vanir prior, and were moving on Briaedor tonight. We couldn't get here in time, and for that I'm sorry-"

"It isn't your fault. Briaedor isn't your responsibility. It is my family's and my own, and I am going to do as much as I can to hold myself to that responsibility. It seems that involves you now."

"If you haven't noticed, my force isn't ships or men."

"The dragons are going to be a necessity as well. I never got to thank you for saving us the first time, but you did so with your dragons. We need all the help we can get, and if they're willing to give it, bring it on."

Aidan gaped in disbelief. His forehead creased, mouth moving without words. I stepped in, finishing his story.

"The man we spoke to gave us some of their plan. They take Vanir, and then on to Briaedor. Lamid next, and I'm assuming that leads to Medea, Atori, and then on. Unless they'll stray further north, but Unadine will protect Hestaval. I can't see them succeeding in an invasion when already weakened."

"Are you telling me Chief Sture is trying to conquer Voluspa?"

"That's certainly how it appears."

Would she be able to do anything about it? She was royalty, true, and at the moment, the head figure of authority in the small fleet. At the same time, she couldn't have been much younger than me, if not a little older.

And now we knew that by birthright, Aidan was her equal.

Avelyn denied it strongly. "There's no possible way that's true. The man must have been misinformed. How could Chief Sture go from pillaging a town side to holding every kingdom in Voluspa? He and his clansmen have a reputation for acts that toe the line of sane, this much is well known, but even he has displayed strategic thinking in the past. There's no reason he would attempt something like this! He can't honestly expect to keep control of the islands! How did he come upon this many men, that many ships? No single group could seize seven kingdoms!"

"And yet, they've already seized two. The Sigurd have been stealing people away for months now. The ones I didn't get too, he must have... sold them, at Trader's Isle. I can't even imagine how much he profited from that many people, enough to build and buy ships, definitely. Maybe some of them stayed as slaves to the Sigurd. He's been capturing more dragons too, and I'd guess a dragon goes for considerably more at an auction. You said it yourself, his men even had some on the boats!" Aidan groaned.

"But Sture must have expected you to retaliate. To interfere at some point. You've been devastating his raiding parties almost as long as they've been happening, haven't you?"

"How do you-"

"Stories spread quickly when ships miraculously turn up on shore, filled with people who were kidnapped days ago. Especially when it turns out the first person off the boat wasn't crazy, and everyone saw the Dragon Rider." Avelyn informed, and Aidan looked away.

I knew Ragna wouldn't be exactly content to find that news of Aidan's activities was so widespread.

"If you've been acting as a thorn in his side, then why does he have such a strong armada? I saw the size of the fleet that attacked Briaedor months ago when I was taken. It was driftwood when you flew away! It's not even slightly comparable to *this* one, I'll admit." She insisted, pointing back at Briaedor behind us. "But it wasn't pitiful by any means! The Sigurd should have been at the very least weakened if they've been suffering as many frequent dragon strikes as the rumors say."

"I- I don't know…" Aidan trailed off, lost in thought.

I was thinking, too. I had believed the ships we attacked in the past were a large force, but it was simply a small piece of the armada that now lay behind us. Too easily destroyed, too quickly sunk. Not enough ships to ever hold off a flock of dragons that they had to have known were coming. Only one small ship of captives. Far too little captured dragons.

Clearly, their much larger cargo shipments were still making it to Trader's Isle, so what were the ones we fought?

Bait?

"What if… those ships were never meant to make it to Trader's Isle?"

His head whipped around to the words spun by my tongue so quickly that I pondered whether the sound of it cracking was lost to the waves.

He studied me, and for a minute made no move to do anything more.

"What did you say?"

"Well, the Sigurd know you have the dragons. You and your family have been an ongoing wrench in their plans for over sixteen years. You'd figure even the most moronic of clans would find a way around that, or at least prepare for it. No kingdom actively engages with them. You're the primary threat to the Sigurd on the ocean. The only person who could feasibly take down a fleet without overwhelming casualties on your side. It doesn't make sense that they would let armada after armada fall without changing anything.

"So how would the Chief get you out of the way, if he couldn't combat you and all of the dragons head on? If he's had time to round up this massive armada, someone had to notice eventually, and you were the only one really looking. If he couldn't kill you then..."

"Red herrings in the form of ships, sprinkled all over the Voluspian Archipelago." Avelyn joined in, realization blooming.

"That's what I'm thinking."

"Keeping the threat of a dragon attack neutralized by containing it to where you've led it. A glorified wild goose chase. Sacrificing the small armies he could spare while he built up the big military somewhere else?"

"Small losses for a larger victory."

"Exactly."

Aidan had gone entirely white, listening. Slowly, he began shaking his head, and he didn't stop.

"No. No, there's no way-"

"Aidan-"

"All the dragons and people we saved? You're saying it was all just a distraction? That they were just sailing to nowhere, waiting until I found them? No, I can't believe that."

"But-"

"It wasn't like it was effortless! Right? I mean sure, they've gotten a little smaller in the last year or so, but that's just because we were finally making a dent! He couldn't have been- why would they-"

"Hey!" I finally shouted, and his mouth snapped shut. "We can't know, we don't know if I'm right-"

"No, I think you are." Avelyn admitted.

"It doesn't matter. It doesn't matter if it was a distraction, or not. Every person, or dragon, on those boats still needed help."

"He set it up. All of it. I didn't think he could...I should have *seen*-"

"How could you have known?"

Aidan raked a hand through his hair. It came to rest covering his mouth, and dropped again as he breathed deeply. His left hand was clenched at his side. He didn't look either of us in the face. His brow continued to furrow in, creasing at random intervals. His eyes darted back and forth across the same two inches of wood, and they did not differ from the knot.

I saw a spot of white jerk above, Fafnir intercepting what must have been the turmoil of Aidan's mind.

Avelyn tilted her head, cheeks still wet but tone composed. "That just begs the question, where has he been doing all this? It's not only Aidan and his dragons keeping track of the Sigurd. There are seven kingdoms in Voluspa.

Granted, it's not like Medea would spare us a heads up if they spotted the Sigurd, and Hestaval wouldn't share with anyone outside of Unadine unless they needed more security. Still, seven countries, Trader's Isle, the ports, the smaller cities, someone would have seen an armada of that size plowing through the ocean. For all the time it must have taken to build, it would have been all over the place at some point. Growing noticeability. Unless-"

"Unless he's keeping it all somewhere. They have a base, it's not just all together on the water. He'd need an island..." Aidan said quietly, entirely devoid of emotion as he stared fixatedly.

"It can't be anywhere in Voluspa," I summarized, and Avelyn seemed to agree, albeit confusedly.

"How the Hel did Chief Sture come to have a base of his own malevolent creation somewhere?"

"I'd wager the same way he's trying to do it now."

"So that's what this is? Expansion of his land by conquering the Kingdoms?" Avelyn concluded. "This is not good. Sture was enough of a threat when it was generally known that his army existed solely on the water. Now, hypothetically, he has an entire island behind him? That's men, weapons, resources, a defensible position, all necessary components of a war that he couldn't so easily tap into before. And it seems that war is exactly what

451

he's shooting for."

"We aren't even sure if he has one."

"Then I'd like to know which spot of barren ocean he's been raising this legion on which has escaped the notice of all of Voluspa."

I sighed, directing my attention behind us. Briaedor was becoming smaller, though it was still a burning spot of light, easy enough to locate. The fire was dwindling, the Sigurd likely didn't want any more damage to their new land than necessary.

I turned imperceptibly to find Avelyn once again in almost a trance, looking after the island.

This small patch of waves was laden with quiet whispers, the sound indistinguishable from the sloshing of water on the wooden hulls. There were sniffles and hushed voices, a canopy of wings blocking out sections of stars overhead. Whether out of exhaustion or fear of the dragons above, the refugees stayed relatively silent. Aidan hadn't spoken in a long while.

He was standing a little way off to my right, still frozen in the same position in which we had left him.

A white frame drifted closer, cat-like eyes trained on him. The murmurs of the deck increased. Slowly, a large eye moved to rest on me.

Was I ridiculous for assuming the expressions and meaning of a dragon's face? Maybe a few months ago. Now I simply waved Fafnir off, gesturing with my head towards the dragons above.

Better he return to them, then send one of the poor Briaedorians into hysterics. Besides, I had this one.

I moved to him slowly, but he gave no indication that he noticed my approach, drowning in his own thoughts. Gently I tugged his hand along with mine, dragging us both to the creaking slab of pine that served as a bench on the wall. I pulled him down to sit beside me, our hands resting on the grooves of the wood smoothed with age.

My thumb moved in small circles on the backside of his hand, and I hoped I was giving at least a fraction of the comfort I believed I was.

Or maybe I was just comforting myself.

We watched Briaedor disappear, and waited for Lamid to draw closer.

***

I hadn't realized how grateful I was for the numbness until it was ripped away. It certainly wasn't my first time witnessing death.

The Sigurd raids weren't uncommon, and though it had been some time since they were seen by Lamid, I had been part of a few. They would arrive by boat, trying to steal away whatever they could. Killing anyone in their path. I had jumped over a few bodies on my way to join the battle, surrounded by all who were able and willing.

It was an honor to fight, after all, and the happenings of sometimes lethal combat were easily forgotten in the moment. Deaths were brushed aside, tragic, but familiar enough. Expected.

Today, however, was unholy. And I hadn't even seen the bodies.

I guess that made it worse, when you were left to fill in the blanks on your own.

The fragile calm which had settled over me while I sat, Aidan pressed to me as the boat shook, was welcomed. It restricted thinking. That was nice, as I couldn't imagine what I hadn't seen, empty people falling behind my eyes.

However, maybe I should have spared a few moments to dwell on what I was going to say when we arrived at Lamid with a horde of dragons.

As such, all feeling returned with an electric clarity, like being doused with ice cold ocean water, as my eyes happened to find my home on the horizon. For one final instant I relished in my temporary calm, my mind displaced from my body, and then my heart began to pound like there was no tomorrow.

Was it strange that in that single passing, the thought of my mother was several times more terrifying than the faceless form of Olavi Sture?

I wasn't the first to notice it, and cries of land up ahead quickly grabbed

Avelyn's attention.

She strode to the front of the boat, the mass opening cleanly for her. She placed herself at the head, speaking to the few men and women controlling the rigging. The princess began to shout orders to the surrounding boats, directions of sails and where to turn, when and how to do it. Entirely confident and sure.

I was almost yanked from my seat when Aidan suddenly stood. He was honed in on the direction of Lamid, and I entertained the idea for a moment that he had stopped breathing.

"Oh, gods. Oh my gods. Sweet *Loki*."

"It'll be okay-"

"My father is on that island. My father is there. What are we thinking? They'll have half the kingdom shooting at us before we even make it within five feet of the-"

"Aidan, we're on a Briaedorian boat. Accompanied by more Briaedorian boats. Briaedor and Lamid are allies. King Ivon is a smart man; he should at least stop long enough to consider the repercussions of starting a war by attacking their ships... but maybe you should tell the dragons to hang back a bit. Just in case. You can never take too many precautions."

His pupils suddenly seemed to be focused far away, glassy, and I knew he was talking to Fafnir, and the flock. All too fast Lamid was growing in size.

Although I was afraid of the consequences that would meet me upon our return, I was glad. We didn't have an ample amount of time to waste. With an honest question, I regarded Leo Evalade.

"Leo, what are the chances your uncle is going to murder us?"

"Low compared to our parents."

"Wonderful. Eliana, any great escape plans for sneaking out once we're grounded forever?"

"A few, but none that'll work when we're dead."

Avelyn was striding back over, and I stood up.

"I'm going to do my best to make sure King Ivon allows us a chance to speak to him. I'd say our wisest course of action is to seek a space behind closed doors with his council, and do our best to explain from there. Our alliance is strong, and my father is good friends with Ivon. Briaedor refugees should be allowed sanctuary despite outside circumstance."

Calin smirked "A monstrous herd of dragons are outside circumstance?"

"Today, yes. And, to my knowledge, Ivon never specifically outlawed it last time he and my father shook hands."

Leo nodded along with her words. We were almost to Lamid now, I could make out the individual houses around the edge of Estran. The lights of the village glowed brighter with each second we drew closer, torches lighting homes and streets. We broke Lamid waters. The dragons fell back, twisting in the air right on the lines of Lamidian territory, like a hive of bees.

Aidan threw a longing glance upward, like he wanted to join them.

Bluebell and Fafnir did not hang back, and instead continued forward, coming down to fly less than twenty yards above the boat. Fafnir stuck close to Bluebell, and I was grateful for it. Her lesser size was painfully apparent when compared to Fafnir beside her.

I allowed myself a small smile of pride, she had fought and flown exceptionally well, today. I doubted any other hatchling could have done the same.

The Briaedorians were speaking louder now, and Avelyn called for quiet. My feet felt heavy as I forced myself to follow her to the front of the boat. I heard Aidan behind me, and saw Eliana head over as well. Calin reluctantly started after us, and Leo shook himself once, before doing the same.

We stood at the bow, allowing Leo and Avelyn to take the point. Better to let them see the two royalties first, and better to not display Aidan right away. Although, they'd likely be more preoccupied with the dragons than the unknown teen.

Would Ivon recognize him? What did I want the answer to be?

The docks were crowded with people, as was the shore behind them, Lamidians pouring out of their homes to stare in fear and awe at the mass of dragons and the small Briaedor fleet.

Closer to the water's edge, archers lined the area, less than two feet between them all as they kneeled with bows drawn. Yet, they did not fire, and I thanked the gods for the Briaedor insignia on the sails.

Avelyn stood unwavering under their gazes, somehow looking regal in her dirtied armor and loosened hair. King Ivon stood at the end of the pier, sword glinting in the firelight.

Like his subjects, he appeared shocked, but a strange mix of relief and anger took over his features when his eyes fell on his nephew. It remained as he took in Avelyn beside him, if softened slightly. He did not relax his stance as we drew to be within earshot.

The king shouted to Avelyn with a voice that seemed to carry a stony resignation as he studied the dragons behind us.

"What wrath of Hel have you brought upon our home?"

"None, I assure you. And I can explain all of it, if you are to let us dock." She yelled back.

King Ivon really held no choice in the matter, as it was only seconds later that our boat knocked against the side of the pier. It shook slightly, but

Ivon stood firm. I was surprised. I didn't think the village could ever be so silent. I tried to scan the crowd for my mother or sister. Ivon's gaze found Eliana and Calin, but passed Aidan and I, who stood hidden behind them.

"Princess Avelyn." He said finally.

"King Ivon."

His tone was dangerous. "Asking the meaning of this would be far too simple."

"You have questions. We will answer them, but first I must request an audience with your Council."

"On what grounds-"

"Briaedor has fallen, and Lamid will be damned to the same fate unless you hear us." Avelyn allowed no time for shock to land. "I come to you, on behalf of my father Einar, your ally and your friend, to request your help and warn you of a coming threat. Do not deny Briaedor this now."

And finally Ivon's face lost its anger, replaced with nothing but apprehension. He eyed the dragons once again, but he couldn't well turn Avelyn away. He was thinking, his scrutiny clearly placed on Fafnir and Bluebell. His sword arm twitched. Ah, to Hel with it.

I stepped out from behind Eliana and Calin, Aidan mimicking my action. Ivon's head snapped to us.

459

"You should listen to her, Your Majesty."

I greatly hoped I wouldn't regret this later. On the upside, King Ivon's eyes were too busy bulging out of his head for his mouth to begin flying. He took in our small group. A princess, four runaway teens, and a boy who he'd never seen before. As far as he knew.

"You will follow me to the castle. Now." He began to turn away, before he spun back, on the sky. I had no doubt that if there was any belief in his mind that our kingdom could have taken the dragons, he would have ordered it so. As it was, he recognized a losing battle, however little was truly understood. "The beasts will stay."

CHAPTER TWENTY–THREE

AIDAN

A guard moved to surround Ivon almost immediately as we began departing from the boat.

Avelyn stepped onto the pier first, Katla's friends following, and then her. I leapt over the side quickly. The group was waiting a few feet away, closer to Ivon.

Before my foot completed its next movement, my vision was crossed with blades. I inhaled sharply, wishing I hadn't left my sword onboard in a display of peace.

I could feel Katla's second dagger through my tunic, the one she had given me after throwing her first into the Bay. Not much, but something.

"Hey! Let him through!" Katla ordered.

Ivon turned, his eyes locking with mine. Very green.

At least my mother told me one truth. They really were the same.

461

The guards who held their halberds and axes to block my path looked to their king, still cutting me off from the rest.

"I doubt the words that will soon be shared have need to fall upon another's ears. The boy will remain with the boat, as will all of the Briaedorians." The king commanded.

"You won't allow Princess Avelyn at least one of her own guard?" Eliana scoffed incredulously.

Something dawned on Katla's face, and I saw her push the back of her elbow, almost imperceptibly, into Avelyn's side.

"Of course, right." The Briaedorian noble shook herself, the confident leader reemerging. "The boy is a member of my guard. He aided in the evacuation of Briaedor. We wouldn't be here now without him. He stays with me. Surely, as you bring your own, you will allow me a warrior, Your Majesty?"

"His name?" Ivon demanded.

You know it. They say you gave it to me.

Avelyn opened her mouth, but I was this time faster. "Hagen."

Avelyn balked in confusion. I inclined my head slowly. If she questioned the reason for the change of name, she did not show it once she caught my assurance. Ivon lifted his hand, and the blades fell away. A prickle of unease settled in my bones as I passed through the lowered blades, one which would stay as we walked through the throngs.

The king pivoted again, expression hard with one last hard glance towards the Bay dragons out over the water.

The village wasn't so different from Trader's Isle, although my visit to a human settlement was this time born of a darker reason. Still, that didn't stop me from taking in as much as I could. Though it was night, the village was alive with sights and sounds, all combined in a strange world which assaulted my senses with its picture of normalcy.

Villagers stood outside as we passed, watching us walk down the cobblestone roads, but I tried to peer around them.

Houses with a base of stone were built upon by planks of wood, chimneys of rock climbing towards the moon. Small puffs of smoke rose from a few of them, disappearing quickly into the darkness. Thin strands of dark leaves crept up the stone, in such abundance that the small plants were clearly visible. Some were simple, a few leaves here and there as they hung against the wall.

Others sprouted blossoms, and exploded into bloom in large quantities higher up the house. Some of the large halls were surrounded by wooden fences, a sheep or two asleep in their yards. Others held a cow or a chicken, or contained two stories instead of one.

Clothing that hung from thin lines swayed in the wind. Open windows allowed the scents of soap and cooked meat to flood the area, an odd mix. Torches adorned every couple of houses, though the scent of the fire was lost to the rest, the smoke of today leaving me desensitized to the smaller flame.

The very air itself smelt of something sweet, something not uncommonly associated with the Sigurd vessels, but lighter. Katla walked beside me, our footsteps echoing through the village. Eliana and Calin stayed by her side.

Avelyn and Leo trailed behind the king.

The king. Ivon Evalade, according to Katla and her friends. Suddenly, my plan didn't seem so smart. I wanted nothing more than to run to the front of the group and finally...well I wasn't really sure what I would do.

Katla's hand kept me back. Her eyes kept darting around nervously in the place that was meant to be familiar to her. I wondered if she was looking for her mother. That was one battle I would let her fight on her own.

I was uneasy without Fafnir, though I knew he was flying overhead, shrouded just barely out of sight. As if he would let a human tell him he couldn't follow me. Even if that human was my father.

We trekked almost imperceptibly at an incline; the village stationed in a slanted fashion as the island rose upward. The castle was located at the top, and it was where we were headed now.

I craned my neck to look further, spotting a stall further down the path. It was similar to the blacksmith shop I had been to on Trader's Isle, albeit much larger. Light spilled from inside onto the rocks, a thicker stream of smoke exiting the building's roof than any others.

Straining, I could hear distant clanging in its direction.

We were flanked by warriors on either side, some male and some female, all watching us with a professional-like caution. Especially me. Their eyes never seemed to leave me, hands never wavering from the hilts of their weapons as if I could call down a parade of dragons at any moment. Which, seeing as how I was close enough to talk to Fafnir, I probably could.

I don't know what I was expecting, but this seems like a bit much. Really, I'm just some guard to them. I even left my sword on the boat! Should I be flattered? I chuckled nervously.

They're flattering themselves. *They make one move towards you or Katla and I'll incinerate them.*

I snorted quietly. Katla raised an eyebrow.

"Fafnir." I alluded.

Her face relaxed into understanding, and she tried to inconspicuously scan the skies. So enthralled as I was with my imminent surroundings, I found myself shocked when we suddenly came upon the castle.

When my eyes finally focused forward, they were unprepared for the sight. A stone castle rose out of the darkness before us, decorated with torches still fully lit, massive braziers washing the area with a fiery glow.

I had never stood before a castle. Leo lived here, and for however short a time, I guess I did as well. It was unsettling.

The castle was a stronghold of stone, standing fortified and whole. Arches weaved through the walls of the vast space, windows from a hundred rooms closed to the night. Towers climbed high into the air; their endings invisible in the inky space.

Just as the houses, greenery grew up the sides. It wrapped around the highest windows, some patches stretching up into the dark, towards the top I couldn't see. The structure was obviously very old, and even in the darkness there was grace in its timeless strength.

The castle of Lamid sat higher than the village it stood for, not towering above, but raised and overlooking. I wondered if I should have been proud of it, if it was my place to be.

It stood still a distance away, separated from us by a bridge of stone. Located as it was slightly higher than the rest of the village, the large bridge was a path partially uphill.

Water pooled below, dark stone supports disappearing down into it, moss growing in the areas where it met the liquid. The bridge ended with its walls growing in height, connecting to the castle's. Dark and aged wood crossed with iron formed hulking doors at the bridge's end.

King Ivon looked once back at us before he began to cross.

I glanced nervously at Katla, but she simply pulled me along with her, and we began to walk on the bridge as well. The doors were pulled open by a few of the warriors as we came closer.

An open courtyard lay before us. Ivon didn't slow, heading for the Keep. A few of the Lamid guard ran ahead of us. Were they meant to alert this 'council'?

We crossed through the yard quickly, walking purposefully through the doors of the Keep and into what must have been a throne room. Stone arches rose every few feet, crisscrossing stone above our heads. Behind the columns, portions of the wall were carved out, containing crumbling statues, their eternally stiff arms containing weapons.

They stood tall, stone eyes surveying the room. It was bright inside, lanterns held on the sides of each arch, as well as covering the walls in a perfect line.

The arches ended at the back of the room, the clear centerpiece and focus. Three thrones sat, raised on steps of gray. The largest was pushed forward, one slightly smaller to its right, and a similar to its left. All three were clearly unused, dust visible in the light even from the entrance. The two smaller, even more so, eerie in their frozen atmosphere, and I quickly decided I didn't want to ponder them.

A banner of deep red and gold was draped behind them.

Ivon didn't stop for an instant. I studied the man's back, shoulders tight, and tried to guess at what he was thinking, but his movements were as stony as the rest of him.

I wished he would look back at us again. How deeply did his eyes mirror my own?

We followed him through a stone arch and into a large hallway. Larger openings branched off into different areas, but we continued on the same path. I allowed my eyes to rake over the walls without really taking anything in, walking mindlessly forward. Was Fafnir still flying over the castle, or had set down in the forest?

I would have remained on the same path if I hadn't glanced upon it. A face that I hadn't seen in six years, save my own sketches in charcoal and paper.

My mother stared down at me from a painting which took up almost an entire wall, sitting regally on an ornate chair.

Her hair fell down to her waist, styled elegantly to match the dress she wore. A crown rested on her head. It was so bizarre I almost laughed right then.

My mother was not this woman.

My mother laughed from dragonback, and swam in the ocean with sea serpents. My mother took in a new dragon every week. She would let the smallest of them nestle in her hair and nap in her sleeves. She fought valiantly with a sword and Takka at her side, striking fear into the hearts of those who stood to call themselves Sigurd. She spent more of her time leaping gracefully from dragon wings hundreds of feet in the air than sitting with her hands still.

No, this woman was not my mother, but she was. Because that was undeniably her there, the most vivid I had seen her outside of my own memories.

And yet, the only thing that tied the woman in the painting to the woman I knew was the notebook that sat folded in her hands, replicated to near perfection, a cover laden with gemstones peeking out from behind her fingers. A notebook that rested in Katla's belt.

I hadn't realized I'd stopped until Katla began pushing me softly, urging me to take after the others before they noticed we had fallen behind.

"Aidan, come on, we have to go." She whispered.

"That's-"

"I know." She interrupted quietly. "I know."

We left the portrait of my mother behind.

Soon the hall opened into a much larger room where the sounds of our entrance were amplified. The room was vast, candle light throwing it into orange hues that danced as we rushed past. A table of carved wood sat in the room's center, lined with silver. The entire area seemed decades old, maybe older. Eight chairs sat around the table, the same wood and silver lining. Six were identical, the King's larger and the eighth much smaller, newer.

Was it Leo's? Or was it meant to be mine?

Stone carvings of both men and women stood guard around the walls. Instead of an assortment of weapons as in the throne room, they held identical blades here. Swords, grasped in gray hands at the crumbling hilt. Crowns of rock lay on their heads, for they must have been past monarchs.

An errant thought ran through my mind, these must have been my ancestors. My family. So many answers. So many new questions.

The room wasn't empty, for six of the chairs held occupants. I determined one man to be Leo's father, due to their resemblance and also the fact that he began yelling at my apparent cousin as soon as he walked into the room.

He stood up so quickly his chair wobbled dangerously behind him. "Leo! Where the Hel have you been? Your mother and I-"

"Brother." Ivon said commandingly, and Leo's father snapped his gaze to him with a glare. Angrily, the man took his seat, dragging Leo along with him, who looked mortified. I saw Eliana smirk. Katla tried to hide hers.

"Princess Avelyn." Ivon spoke, voice hard, angry. Very angry. "As you said, we are allied with Briaedor, but I would like an explanation as to why I shouldn't have you thrown in the dungeons immediately. You say your kingdom has fallen, and I'd guess it has something to do with the unholy mass of devils you brought with you."

Avelyn opened her mouth, indignance written all over her features, but Ivon had already turned to Katla. "And you. You haven't been seen for months, searches have turned up nothing. Searches with men and women pulled from their duties to look for you. A missing teenager, a hunting boat gone, stolen! Now another, and then three more of you kids disappear. My nephew, among them. Now you show up here, flanked by a number of Briaedor ships and *dragons*."

The men who sat around the table behind Ivon bristled. I could hear their shouts in my imagination now, and I doubted I'd have to speculate their sound much longer. I was prepared, ready to step into the fire, to say something dramatic, declare myself as the Dragon Rider. Katla had other ideas.

"I took the ship." She spit out. Good Aesir, of all the places to start. "Stole it. Then it was left behind with a Sigurd fleet and likely destroyed alongside it. Sorry. You were talking at the docks, Your Majesty, the night I left. Talking about a Dragon Rider. I left in search of him."

"Sigurd-"

"I took the boat when you left that night, so I could find and bring back the Dragon Rider." She kept her gaze forward, and continued. "To kill him, if Freyja would permit me to manage."

"Why would you leave to attempt such a thing?" Asked one of the councilmen. "We prepared a battalion to search for such a being, to eradicate them if they existed. We would have sent it had you not disappeared."

Because let the gods prevent the day from dawning in which I existed peacefully alongside them.

"It would have saved me from a marriage contract I didn't want any part of, a life I didn't desire, and responsibilities I didn't ask for. No offense, Leo."

Katla said bitterly, and Leo grunted. They had the decency to appear slightly abashed, as they should've. It was their fault, after all, they had decided who she would be forced to marry, that she would be forced to marry at all. "I needed no other reason to leave, but I didn't make it far. My boat was attacked by Sigurd near Briaedor only a day later."

Leo's father gasped. "How did you survive?"

"The very one you amassed a small army to kill, the Dragon Rider, saved me." Then Katla tossed me to the angry dragons, all thoughts of my safety apparently abandoned. "It seems only right you meet him now, seeing as his dragons are waiting outside."

She turned, very clearly, and her eyes met mine. It was as good an indication as any.

The room erupted, and I honestly don't know what she was expecting. The councilmen drew their weapons. The guards outside the door began to file in. Ivon raised his sword. All the while, they were shouting every curse they had ever heard in their long lives.

I supposed it was a little justified, they had practically invited the enemy into their castle, into the heart of their kingdom.

"You brought-" Ivon started, but frustration colored Katla's tone.

"I ask you now, King Ivon, to let us explain. If you kill him now, there will be none alive who can stop the creatures outside our island from descending upon us. They wait peacefully now only due to his tentative safety."

They were unmoving, and Katla took the opportunity to nudge me. Odin, I prayed, I've whispered my prayers all these years. The time had arrived to prove you noticed.

"I know what you think of me." I stared my father in the eyes. "What you believe to be true about my nature. And theirs. I can only tell you that you are wrong. I don't have time to waste convincing all of you to see the true hearts of my friends and my family. There is a threat bigger than you, and bigger than me heading this way. Neither of us will come out of it without the other. I brought the dragons with me tonight so that we may try to help. I am going to help, whether you want me to or not, but I can't even dream of a victory without your aid. I have made an enemy of Olavi, and I trust that you will rally yourselves against him."

My tongue fought to keep my words from tripping over themselves, shaking hands hidden at my sides.

I kept waiting for one to break the silence, but they all simply continued to gawk. I wondered if, after the shock wore off, they would lower their weapons or raise them higher. Katla sighed. Avelyn stepped forward.

"Before you make your decisions, you should know that as of now, Briaedor stands with the Rider and his dragons." I was grateful Avelyn refrained from using my name even after my apparent identity had been revealed. Had she guessed at the reason? "I am not the first in line in my family. I stand behind my brothers. But my parents are not with me, nor are my siblings to guide me in this choice. Still, it is the right one, and I have no doubt they would say the same if they were here. Their absence is easily explained. The Sigurd have taken control of Briaedor."

Gasps echoed around the room, and Ivon finally looked away from me to fix his eyes on Avelyn.

She began again before he could ask whatever question that brewed in his mouth. "Early this morning, a messenger arrived in our waters, sent from Vanir. They spoke to my father, my mother, and my eldest brother. They told us Vanir had been lost the day before, and they warned that the Sigurd were already on their way. We thought we were prepared for their arrival, but we were wrong. Their fleet is a thousand strong and ruthless. Briaedor fell to them in hours.

"The most we know of their plan is that they are moving to take the Kingdoms of Voluspa. They bring in men to command the boats from the previous island they have run through, from the cache of slaves they have gathered. The boats from the fleet of the fallen kingdoms are taken and added to their own numbers. They are strong enough that they could move on almost immediately from Vanir to Briaedor, and we suspect they will do the same to come here.

"That is why this is so urgent. I wouldn't doubt it if they began to sail for Lamid now. I only live to tell you this because the Dragon Rider saved every single Briaedorian who now await word in your harbor. He and Katla arrived on dragons, along with their friends, and allowed a select few of us to escape onto the boats in our port. His dragons held back the Sigurd fleet so that we could escape.

"Tonight cannot even claim to be my first meeting with the Rider, as he saved my mother and I from the Sigurd months prior, after we were captured by a raiding squadron. Our feelings were undecided on the matter, the interests of Briaedor in terms of the beasts, undecided. Tonight, that changes, and I align us with him.

"I don't have the fortune of knowing what has become of the rest of my family in the aftermath of Chief Sture's attack. As Princess of Briaedor, and the only available member of the Briaedorian Royal Dynasty, I take command of the men we may offer, and the help we can provide. I am here now, and I represent my kingdom and whatever power it may still hold when I say that the Dragon Rider and his forces are under our protection."

Her speech settled into the very walls, and coated the air in its resolution.

"Avelyn. *Thank you.*" I told her earnestly, and she stoutly nodded. "Olavi is coming. I look for nothing but to see his military fall. I was too late to help Vanir, and too late to do any more than aid the refugees of Briaedor. Olavi will not stop with your home. We have to make a stand here. With the dragons, and your armada, we can stop them. I have to believe we can."

None on the council spoke a word.

They sat motionless, deferring completely and entirely to their King under the colossal wave of information. Ivon could have been a displaced statue as he regarded the six of us who stood before him. He turned to me finally, and though we certainly weren't about to begin exchanging pleasantries, he seemed less hardened.

His fingertips did not abandon his sword, but they did not move closer to the pommel, did not grip it or hoist its blade.

"You. Do you speak for the demons?"

"I speak for the dragons of my home as well as I am able, Your Majesty."

The man continued to survey us, and I let him. I was so tired. We had laid bare all the toil of the last day. I had admitted to being a member of a draconic family to an entire royal council, and my father, though he didn't know it. Ragna would be scandalized. I was *tired*.

So, I let him stand there and think. I would leave this to the judgement of our audience, and whatever occurred would be. We still had so far to go.

My father took a deep breath, his features faintly softened as he addressed the room of young warriors.

"Listen to me, all of you. I don't have to tell you the seriousness of what you are suggesting. Of what you have said here tonight. Where you lay your allegiance and what you claim you are. You believe that Olavi Sture is leading the Sigurd in a takeover of the Voluspian Kingdoms?"

"We know it, King Ivon." Katla said softly.

"And you know it how? Beyond the promised words of a toppled kingdom, and the happening of another. How do you know the secrets and intentions behind a supposed tragedy and a horrible siege?"

"We interrogated a Sigurd warrior shortly after we came across Vanir. His words have so far proven true." When no one spoke up, Katla continued on. "I have been among the Dragon Rider and his dragons for near two months. They have had countless chances to hurt me, in the many times they have been alone with me, without the influence of the Rider. I have not once been harmed. Not even when I attacked the one they submit to."

I knew she was exaggerating, but I still fought to keep my eyes from rolling. As if Fafnir and the others ever listened to me.

"Everything that the Rider and the Princess tell you is true. You ask where I've been and I will not lie, but you must hear the truth in what I tell you. I meant no treason or dishonor in my actions. I simply listened. I changed my mind. I am asking you to take even the smallest chance to do the same now."

"How did you find the Rider?" A man asked.

"He saved my life, Mr. Maurin. I set off to find him the night I left. The following day, I sailed into a Sigurd fleet, considerably smaller than the one that is moving on Briaedor now. The Rider was there, too, with his dragons. Not to protect their passage, but to stop it. A few Sigurd clansmen jumped into my boat. I fought them until a piece of the ship broke free and struck me."

"I saw the boat, and my- a dragon threw the men overboard. One jumped ship, too. I knew she wasn't with them. She was unconscious, and maybe hurt, so Fafnir and I brought her back with us."

"You attempted to kill the Rider, then?" A man with a blond beard interrupted.

"In the beginning, yes. Like we said, I changed my mind. I've ridden them, the dragons. There is one among them who allows me to fly with her."

"You *ride* on the backs of those demons?" He ground out.

"Of course she doesn't, because that isn't what they are." I glared.

"This is blasphemy! Are we honestly expected to believe this? Either the boy is lying, or the creatures have sent an entity who appears to be a child in order to fool us. If we are to die tonight, it will not be to him, in our own fortress! If he has truly brought dragons here, we should be preparing ourselves to remove the stain of them from our waters."

One of the blades caught the light, reminding me that the Councilmen still had their weapons drawn. The man's words encouraged exchanged murmurs across the table.

"Chief Sture has taken my kingdom, captured my family, and you question my word?" Avelyn glowered.

They ignored her.

"Doing the gods' work, we are, killing the devils. Now you want us to, what? Make peace with the beasts? We will do no such thing!" The same man insisted.

I growled. "It is not thanks to some divine intervention that you make a sport of slaughter. You hunt them down and send your children to do the same."

"And what dishonor do you find in that? Beasts that spit the very fires of Muspelheim. Bodies built of claws and teeth sharper than any man's blade. Horns and spines attached to armored scales. Towering frames larger than a hall which has stood for centuries, or small enough to creep inside and tear out your innards while you sleep. Great wings that allow the spread of carnage, even from the sky. Eyes thinner than my wife's needle. Tell me boy, if not that, then what? What do you call a devil?"

"A man who sees it as his place to decide who the devils are."

"For Thor's sake! They're vile-" He tried to continue, but I rose to cut him off once more.

"Every one of them is not the same! They have personalities, they think and live. I've been in the air since before I could walk. I've watched mothers care for their hatchlings, year after year. Seen dragons from the sea play with those that fly above them. Their existence is not centered around your destruction, it never was."

"I've only seen a fraction of what Aidan has, but it is enough for me. More than enough, actually. I was able to watch the babies grow and play, and learn about the world. Learn to fly for the first time, until one let me join her. I can't bring myself to see them as evil. Not all of them. Not any longer." Katla added.

"The Rider has lived with the dragons his entire life. He still has all his limbs, two eyes. Obviously, none of the dragons have tried to take a piece out of him, and that must mean something." Leo joined in.

"I've ridden a dragon for all of half an hour, and I can't say I'm keen to do so again, it was terrifying. But I understand how hard it is to grasp all of this before you've experienced it, so you're going to have to take our word for it. We are wrong. We don't have to stay that way." Calin implored.

The council only observed us all with doubtful hesitance.

Eliana cried out in exasperation. "You're meant to be brilliant delegators! We've told you what you need to know. I can't see what more you wish to hear, that Odin himself came down from his golden palace and ordered us to make nice with the dragons? We have more important problems! In the hours past, I have flown over two kingdoms on *fire*, with a promise that ours is next."

Ivon moved his gaze to her. "And why exactly did you leave the island in the first place, Miss Brendean?"

"What else was there for me to do? None of you were proving capable of finding my best friend."

"You can either believe us or not." I raised my head. "But the Sigurd are coming no matter what you decide. Olavi is coming. The dragons and I will be fighting them whether you lend your assistance, or not. The dragons will follow me, you don't have to do the same. But unless you come up with another idea, or if you continue to dismiss us, your kingdom will be the next to crumble."

That was it. They either conceded to help us now, or I blurted my recently uncovered bloodline to the entire room.

It seemed too late in the game to make a claim for my lineage. The opportunity had passed. I could only hope Fafnir was keeping the dragons in line outside, and that none of them had sought rest by landing amongst the kingdom's villages.

I doubted any of them would turn hostile, but I knew the Lamidians would not hold themselves to my same wishes.

Leo had left his father's side and came to stand with us. Avelyn was leveling the adults of the room with a determined stare, and Eliana's hand continued to itch towards the bow at her back. Consequently, Calin's eye's continued to dart to the bow, looking ready to wrestle it from her if need be.

Katla waited at the ready, and I knew she could handle whatever direction this would take.

"Alright." Ivon declared. The council behind him looked shocked, if not a little annoyed. Still, they were silent in the face of their king, the black beard on his chest lifting as he revealed his choice. "Hagen, was it? What do you and your beasts have in mind?"

CHAPTER TWENTY–FOUR

KATLA

I was glad I wasn't there when Ivon made the announcement to the village that we would, temporarily, be working by the side of the Dragon Rider. It didn't stop me from seeing the broken crates and barrels later, clear signs of upset. I had a different honor to be present for.

The dragons of the Bay had landed in one of Lamid's far forests. Here, my hand in Aidan's, I could feel the rattling of our bones with every taken step of the creatures through the greenery.

The vibrations in the earth as hundreds of dragons, large and small, pushed their way through the forest, were like waves breaking on my skin. Kaida flew over our head, chirping and scaring away all the real birds. Estran became visible through the foliage only a few hundred feet later.

There, I knew all of Lamid waited. Fafnir raised his head and roared, but cut off unnaturally when a particularly thick branch hit him in the face.

Aidan doubled over, and Fafnir's tail came around to smack his side. I could hear voices now, but they must not have yet noticed our approach. Aidan told Ivon from where they would come, and he had brought the villagers of my home.

I tried to imagine the Lamidians surrounded by passive dragons, but I couldn't force it into clarity. The woven bag Aidan carried slapped against his hip as he walked, and he continued to switch it from shoulder to shoulder.

"I really do hope that your kingdom doesn't decide to simply rush us, weapons drawn, and all that." He admitted.

"Sorry, I have no ground to make that promise on, Dragon Boy."

We finally left the trees, the dragons a short way behind us. A line of houses formed a wall about twenty yards away. The streets were packed with villagers, the eyes of the crowd taking little time to find Fafnir. Almost everyone took a step back, but none ran away. Or run at him, which would have been worse.

I spotted my mother in the crowd, dark hair pulled into a bun. She looked livid, and about two seconds away from rushing up to us. I held a hand up to her, likely damning myself further in the process, but she waited all the same. The crowd continued to grow until the watchers were forced back into the streets.

The entire kingdom had gathered there, it seemed, and in near perfect unison they scrambled back. All were fixated on something over our shoulder. As the world began to settle, the forest breathed.

Branches shifted high in the air, the vibrations in the dirt becoming stronger. They were rather loud, too. Slowly, the dragons of Aidan's home emerged from the trees. They froze as well, stopping just inside the tree line, observing the humans from the reaches of the forest shadows.

None moved.

The atmosphere was still, like we were stuck in the single moment, the two parties gauging each other.

Then, all at once, it broke with Aidan.

Humans and dragons diverted their focus to him, the latter relaxing, the former tightening their muscles and succumbing to a ripple of unease. But he did not go further into the humans, and instead retreated back towards the forest where serpentine scales caught firelight from deep within the trees. Reptilian heads surveyed as nothing more than dark specters.

Despite the obvious wishes of the onlookers to make themselves go unnoticed, several shouts rose from the crowd, trying to call him back. Away from the threat haunting the woodland edge.

I heard King Ivon silence them, despite the anxiety in his own voice, and I felt a rush of thankfulness.

"Remember what I said? They're going to have arrows and blades, and they've killed before. But they're scared of us, too. Are you ready?" I saw his eyes glaze over then, and knew the rest of his proclamation was expressed through the Bond.

A green female Muspel stood in front of him, and she slowly lowered her head to bump it into his chest, closing her eyes. They were trusting him, and I hoped it would turn out to be for good reason. Aidan raised his arms to the winged reptiles, and faced the people of my island.

"If we are all to fight together, they need to separate your scent from the Sigurd. So, who wants to meet a dragon?"

And cautiously, a few brave and slightly stupid souls took a step forward.

CHAPTER TWENTY–FIVE

AIDAN

A good kind of mayhem, that was the only way to describe it. I was stumbling all over the place, tripping over dragon tails and stumbling into people, for bodies were everywhere. In this small stretch between the town and the forest, the people of two kingdoms and a Bay-full of dragons were struggling to fit.

I was darting frantically through the masses, stopping villagers from pulling weapons every time the dragons startled them, and stopping the dragons from retaliating each time the humans twitched.

I had lost Katla a while ago, but I knew she was doing the same.

I overheard one of them growling, and made to head in that direction, but I should have been looking forward. Pale hair wafted through the dark before we collided, the contact more painful than it should have been. Like I had run into a sharp wall rather than a Lamidian.

Collecting myself, I glanced up to see Eliana doing the same, a light golden braid swinging over her back.

The most confusing part was the several swords and axes she was fighting to maintain a hold of. I was lucky to not have been impaled.

"Where did you get all those?" I asked, reaching down to help her off the ground.

She took my hand as best she could with her arms full, and gave me a cheeky grin. Her green eyes flashed mischievously, and already she was looking over her shoulder. She appeared rather proud of what had to be at least four swords and an axe or two that were close to swiping her face.

"A few more rowdy groups needed a lesson or two in manners, and if they kept yanking these out like they were, the dragons were going to go ballistic." She hefted the looted weapons in her arms for my view, as if they weren't already taking up my vision. "One of the dragons accidently knocked a few of them over with its wing, not entirely sure how accidental it was, though. Let's just say opportunities were taken whilst they were cleaning the dirt from their mouths."

I didn't even want to know how she stole so many blades away from those who were likely trained warriors. I glanced over her shoulder as well, wondering when those unfortunate people would realize they'd had their weapons thieved.

"And what are you going to do with them all?"

"Should I be telling you this, 'Hagen'?" She dropped her voice. "In light of your recently discovered affiliation to the Royal Court?"

Of course, Loki would believe I needed to be reminded so frequently.

"I don't think Katla would let me live if I told."

Eliana's smirk grew wider, seemingly unbothered by the weight in her arms. "Speaking of Katla, that was some kiss back on the boat."

I blanked. "Oh? Well. Katla came up and- you know..."

She cut me off with her laughter.

"Relax, Your Highest Majesty. I'm messing with you." She repositioned the handles of leather and wood in her hands, maneuvering one of the axes over her shoulder with her head and arm before it could fall. "I need to go hide these somewhere, not completely sure where, yet. Maybe I'll just slide them under a dragon, force them to get down and retrieve em'. See you, *Hagen*!"

I chuckled at her retreating back as she walked unevenly, trying to keep any of the tools of war from slipping.

I decided I liked Katla's friends. Leo was alright, but the contract issue in which he was supposedly engaged to Katla really wasn't. I ran over as the snarl sounded again, a Syre scratching at the ground agitatedly.

Every time her claws scraped the earth, the bald man standing in front readjusted his hold on an axe.

"Hey, hey, what's going on?" *Are you okay?* I asked her, but it was the man who answered.

"What do you think, boy? Beastie over here is losing it." He said angrily, and she snarled. "You may want to recast whatever spell you've thrown, or offer the gods another slain lamb. Clearly you're losing your touch."

"I'll keep that in mind." I glared, and then held my hand out towards her, and although she didn't abandon her crouch, my voice and scent were still seeping into her senses. *You're alright. He's an unsavory example of them, but he's only rude, not dangerous.*

She relaxed a little, her scales glowing dimmer, and I guessed she was swallowing back the acid in her throat. Her talons stopped raking through the grass. I felt her press against my thoughts, heavy emotions slipping into her words.

This human reeks of metal and blood, Hatchling. He has bathed in the red of my brethren.

I raised a brow at the Lamidian, who had gone slack jawed. "Maybe put the axe away?"

"It's afraid of my axe? Not so hellish when the time to be mighty arrives, eh?"

He brandished his weapon further, and though I was there, her eyes went slit-pupiled in nervousness. She lowered her body, muscles coiling. I looked at her pointedly.

Don't even think about it. I have it handled.

Quite the assurance, youngling. She snorted. *I should fly you to The White One. We will return home to our dwellings.*

Be patient.

She huffed, annoyed with me probably, but straightened. Not without clipping me on the head with her wing, however. There was a quiet rumble birthed of amusement from her throat while the man muttered about Ragnarök. She recoiled as he stepped closer, sniffing the air nervously.

"She is fully aware of the harm human iron can do. They all are, just as you study her incisors and her talons. You're both nervous, but I would be glad that she is scratching the ground, and not something else." I at least attempted to be less aggressive, but it was ruined by a grumbling as she haughtily confirmed my statement. Let the gods curse my arrogant, prideful family, making it harder than it needed to be! "And *you*." She deflated slightly. "Calm down. They're all going to smell like that. Katla did too, remember? We've got to work with it right now, the humans are scared of you, too, but fighting them isn't going to help."

The man scoffed. "We are not afraid!"

"Of course you aren't." I pointed to both of them. "Put the axe down, put the claws away."

She retracted her razor nails first, trusting me far more than the man. She whined, lowering her head, and with a roll of my eyes I scratched her neck. Wary gratitude floated my way.

Focusing on the man, I gestured towards his hand with my head. Reluctantly, the handle of his axe slid into place on his back. It was almost natural to beckon the warrior closer.

"Here, take my place." I instructed, removing my hand from its spot upon her glowing scales. She growled at the loss of contact while his dark skin wrinkled with horror. It likely sounded menacing to him, but her croon was pleading to me. "Go on. I know they look like they're glowing, but they won't burn you. Her scales are just warmer than others. Not a hazard until she gets angry."

Hesitantly, possibly because she was still growling, the man shot his

494

hand out. His shoulders hunched defensively once he met the scales and began scratching vigorously. On any other animal with weaker skin, his frantic movements may have been painful. I resisted the urge to laugh.

He jumped when the noises of ire suddenly shifted, changing to a thundering purr of contentment.

"There. As long as you face her with your hands and not your blades, you'll be fine."

Please tell me you'll be fine.

Go, Hatchling.

I spun on my heel, and started away. Thankfully, the man seemed too preoccupied with being left at her mercy to say anything else. A few dozen feet away, a young girl was attempting to climb up the side of a green Muspel. Beside her stood my Ivon, watching intently. His hand never wavered on his grip of his sword, examining the Muspel's every move with scrutiny.

But still he let the small girl play.

I caught myself staring, unable to pull against the lure of answers to the questions I had long since given up on. They had returned vengefully, every single wonder I had pushed aside.

Did we look similar? What parts of me were built from him?

His hair was cut shorter than mine, near to his head, a far cleaner job than what Ragna had attempted to give me over the years. He was taller than me, his form stouter, but not large. He carried a sword like I did. My weapon of choice matched my fathers. Of course, the metal was polished and gleaming, nearly perfect. Mine was scratched and scuffed. The swords I used were interchangeable, taken from Sigurd ships, bare-bones and just enough to get the job done.

A fur cloak was draped over his shoulders and down past his sides. I wondered if, in the belt concealed by those furs, a dagger which matched my mother's sat. His nose was longer than my own, his face squarer. There were lines etched into his skin, less abundant than they were in Ragna. They gathered around his eyes.

Those were the things we shared. They were the same bright green I had seen reflected in ocean water, in Fafnir and Ragna's shared memories. In the hazy given feelings I recalled from my mother.

Did he see it too, when he looked at me? Did he know what it meant?

He couldn't have known that his child was the horrific person he warned his council and his people against. His distaste for my very being was clear. The little girl was watched with the utmost care and a readiness for battle, due only to proximity to one of my family. But despite all of that? Could he see anything more?

Something nudged my shoulder, the action pulling me violently from my studying. I blinked, tearing my eyes from the image of my father. Avelyn stood beside me, pushing a thin braid of red over her shoulder.

Neither of us spoke at first, only watching the small girl cheer as a breath of hot air was blown in her face.

Avelyn's words did not tremble as mine might have. "When do you think they will come?"

How far we had already ventured into the night, I wasn't sure. In a handful of hours, the sun would rise. The Sigurd were aware of my interference now, they would move faster, more hastened. They would attempt to strike before I was prepared for another bout. The dragons had improved the speed of Briaedor's escaping boats, but the distance was not impossible to soon close. I knew little of the passage of boats, but this feat seemed well within the Sigurd's new capabilities.

"I think it would be in our greatest interest to be ready at dawn." I intoned, and Avelyn inhaled sharply. I let my question loose in a low and hidden tone. "Does the Captain act with his men?"

Avelyn understood.

"Halavar is my eldest brother. He was walking with my father along the furthest village of Briaedor when the Sigurd first arrived. Word passed that Halavar saw *him* among the ships, before he and my father were taken along with the rest of my family. He was there. None else could have taken my father, my brothers."

It would do me no good to succumb to the flaring fear. The night Ragna returned, alone, was at the sudden forefront of my mind. Takka, one wing bloodied and back bare. The man I had last seen laughing, his thrown knife leaving a scar on my shoulder.

"They're confident. Overly. They have to be. He would never place himself among them in battle if he believed they would fail."

If Olavi was in attendance, rather than being only an invisible leader in the background, it gave the upcoming battle an entirely new meaning. It was one thing to know their scope was devastatingly large, that two entire kingdoms had already fallen. But Olavi's appearance meant pride and self-assuredness, he knew with certainty that they would succeed, and he wanted to watch it happen.

Is this where he had been, these last four years? Was this his great plan? If so, a few disposable ships as a distraction weren't going to keep me away from it. I couldn't understand his play. Why target the Kingdoms in the first place? Was it really nothing more than expansion of land and power, like Katla and Avelyn speculated? What drove him in this moment to believe the time had arrived in which he could succeed?

"Yes, he made his status as a coward more than clear when he attacked Briaedor. His chiefdom should be sullied, if his people even care to honor such a thing." Avelyn's voice was full of rage. "The fire was nothing natural, nothing natural of man. It was a fire born of dragons. Acid. They launched it upon the village nearest to the shore. It burned everything it touched. There was a group of children playing in the street when a vat of it fell. They were feet away from me." Her jaw clenched. "A coward is the most deadly opponent. They hold the power to fear for nothing but themselves. The will of the Gods shakes them none."

Was this the reason then, that their boats were drenched in the heavy scent of it? For months, Fafnir had complained of his burning nostrils, the ships which reeked of Syre. How had they forced them to give it?

The image Avelyn described planted itself in my head. She needed not say the fate of the children.

They would have burned in their skin.

Avelyn sniffed, the only crack in her demeanor. "I will be ready at dawn."

And then she was gone.

CHAPTER TWENTY–SIX

KATLA

I wanted nothing more than to pass into unconsciousness, blissfully unaware.

As it was, I was propped against a fence with Aidan, Avelyn, Leo, King Ivon, and a few members of the Council. Mr. Payne, Mr. Maurin, and Fisk's father were among them. I tried not to make eye contact with my brother-in-law's dad. I didn't know what had occurred after I left my sister's house.

Nailed to the side of a home's back wall was a large parchment map which showed the Voluspian Kingdoms. The subject of our attentiveness was the charcoal labeled Isle of Lamid.

I tried not to draw notice to myself, being no royalty nor council member. Aidan's position as the Dragon Rider had bought him a place in this meeting, but my own was tentative.

Despite trying to remain unseen, ideas of my own were brewing whilst the permanent members of this strange court discussed. Ivon pointed to Estran on the paper, its shore exposed and open, facing Briaedor across the water.

"They'll be coming in from the east, but Avelyn, you mentioned your access to the port was lost first?" The king asked her.

"Yes. They fired on the piers, and the land in front of them. The surrounding areas were dense with fire and debris. The docks were burning, we had to put out the flames before we could even attempt to begin boarding."

"If we know where they will fire first, and what they will strike upon, the only course of action is to have nothing to destroy." I finally cut in. "We move the boats."

"You're proposing we do what with our fleet?" Mr. Maurin questioned.

I supposed the idea may have seemed a bit arbitrary.

I saw King Ivon sigh, either from simple weariness, or from noticing my presence. I couldn't fault the monarch. Odin only knew what grief my decisions had brought him recently.

"We hold the element of surprise, at least in some aspects, when the Sigurd believe themselves to. If they've even realized the Briaedorians fled with a few boats, they may not have guessed where. They'll be expecting to cut us off from our ships, from any sort of on-the-water retaliation entirely, but if we move them somewhere else…" I shrugged, "It won't matter if we can't reach the docks. The boats won't be there, and neither will our forces."

Aidan nodded eagerly beside me, staring at the map. Ivon listened, but did not speak. I considered it a good sign that he hadn't shot the idea down.

"I like it." Avelyn spoke first, fiery hair spilling over her shoulder.

Leo poked a hole. "But we can't just move them all. An empty harbor? For a Kingdom as well off as Lamid? Sure, we're no Kingdom of Hestaval in terms of hoarding riches, but we hold a strong army. It'd be downright obvious; they wouldn't bother attempting to burn our docks to ashes if they realized there was nothing there."

"A few stay, then. Stationed in the furthest reaches of your shipyard, creating the impression of more behind them. All the others could remain hidden elsewhere. Other side of the island, maybe? Our reaction time could turn this thing on its head if we were already on the ships when they arrive." Aidan did not address the adults, but rather Avelyn, Leo, and I, his finger moving to the west side of the drawn island.

I hoped they would not see his reluctance to engage with them as disrespect.

Avelyn disagreed. "No, we cannot place them behind the island, or on any of its surrounding shores. The end result would still involve facing the armada head on, sailing straight at them. The sorry bunch would gather their wits in time to sink us."

"We can't come for their front." I understood, willing a solution to make itself known. "We have to sail at them, head-to-head, no matter how soon we begin to do so. That will lead to slaughter."

"Forward is not the only direction our crews can sail. What they need is more time. Speed. For the boats to move quicker, to strike sooner and from a different angle." Leo started. "*Hagen's* dragon pulled our boat."

I raised my head to Leo in a rare emotion other than imminent ire. My musings spilled from my mouth.

"You're right. We won't come from ahead or from behind. We'll *blindside* them. Positioned far enough away that none will notice the boats until we're ready. Bring the fight to them. When Leo and the others first found us, Fafnir tugged our boat through the water via a rope tied around his stomach. What should have been at least a few hours of sailing took less than one-"

"What a way to damn ourselves! To tie our entire naval force down to those brutes! Honestly, not even Freyja would lift a finger to spare us from our own stupidity." Mr. Casale refuted, Fisk's father.

"I believed it to be already established that the combined bodies of the Lamidian army and the Briaedorian refugees would fight alongside the Dragon

Rider's company. You must accept that at some point in the coming battle, the two sides must mix." Avelyn eased with all the air of royalty.

I placed my fingers on the water northeast and southeast of the island, continuing.

"The approach could set on from the left and the right. Split our numbers between the two sides. Then we could converge on two points of their movement at once. Meet in the middle, trap them between us. By the time they realize we're coming, there won't be time to outrun the added swiftness brought on by the dragons."

"What's stopping them from attacking us, then? The wicked buggers?" Ivon raised.

Aidan opened his mouth, but I cut him off, excited in knowing the answer to a dragon question. He had said it just as the villagers had come forth to meet the Bay inhabitants.

"Scent!" The king raised an eyebrow, so I continued. "We've already been around the dragons, they've gotten used to our smell. They'll recognize us apart from the Sigurd, just as they do when A- Hagen conducts raids. With his insight, they understand who the enemy is. They can differentiate."

Ivon was silent, analyzing Lamid's outline on the paper. I was a bit perturbed by his quiet. It wasn't as though anyone else had volunteered any feasible ideas in the last twenty minutes. Aidan, at least, smirked in response to my rambled answer.

"Are you sure the blasted animals can do this?" Ivon finally challenged.

"Yes." I told him firmly, returning his searching gaze with equal fervor. "I'm sure."

"You. Hagen. The Rider." Ivon disregarded my affirmation for the expert himself. "Do I have your word that I am not dooming us all by tethering my ships to your serpents?"

"You have my word that Katla's plan is the only which has been spun with any merit. She knows what she speaks. I agree with her. If I ask it, they will lead your armada across the water."

Ivon sighed, and for a moment, I saw a glimpse inside at a man impossibly torn. "I will confer with our generals, and the rest of the Council."

"With all due respect sir, do we really-" I began, but the reception of my opinion had ended.

"It is a good idea, Katla. But there is enough time yet to ensure this is the plan Lamid wishes to follow." He took a deep breath, a rare smile gracing him as he found something behind me. "And you need to see your mother."

I felt my eyes widen seconds before her voice cut through the air. Aidan and Avelyn winced. Leo didn't react, lucky him, his dad had already gotten his chewing out over with.

"*Katla Melanie Vistel!*"

Sweet child of Loki. I did my best to ready myself to face repercussions. Then, I'd ready ships. It seemed we had just taken the point in this battle, and for some reason, I didn't question my capabilities in it just yet. After all, I was Katla Vistel. When I talked people listened.

"*Katla!*"

Except for her.

***

It was a race against the sun, a rushing flurry of movement to beat the dawn.

Our entire fleet was being prepared, save the few which we would keep to maintain the show, the facade of a full harbor. The wooden platforms were crowded. Smoke had been pouring from the blacksmith's stall from the moment we announced the Sigurd were coming. It seemed that Ivon's paranoia surrounding the idea of a great dragon commander had benefited us after all. The armies were practically up to their breasts in swords and halberds.

Now, the forgers worked to supply the village warriors who would join the fight.

It seemed every hand in Lamid was busying itself. The sails were lowered, weapons loaded, men and women assigned. The mast towers were filled with extra arrows, and bows were strung with fresh sinew. Hopefully, they'd be able to take out some of the opposing archers.

We carried blades, pulled sails, made as many ships ready for sea as we could. I hardly saw Aidan, talked to him even less.

Aidan's apprehension around those who were not dragons had been clear. He hadn't spoken a word to King Asmund in my first raid, and seemed incessantly hesitant to do so around my friends.

In the Council room, driven by incredulity on the subject of dragons, and backed by Avelyn's assertion that he was accepted into the Briaedorian fight, he had been a force to be reckoned with. Despite the lessening number of opinions to give whilst we hatched a plan for the fleet, he had been there.

The time had passed however, to argue passionately for the Bay dwellers. Interacting with the Lamidian people was no longer a necessity, no longer a required stepping stone.

Where I existed then, within the bustling throngs, the constant press of bodies, was not somewhere I could expect his presence. A crowd of humans wasn't where he was most comfortable. The root cause of it was clear to me, even if it was one he would deny.

Ragna's caustic beliefs, stories and deterrents given throughout a draconic childhood, clearly affected his actions more than he wished to acknowledge. I couldn't yet call myself a fully-fledged warrior, a swordsman of legend, or even boast of the agility which came so naturally to Aidan.

I did, however, still contain within myself reflexes of the fight.

I observed, and I saw the minute things. The instances in which Aidan's movements slipped so easily from human to dragon-like, as if he had gracefully fallen from a creature of our race to one of theirs. In the moments when the councilmen shouted, when blades were reached for. When he was flying, swarmed by hatchlings, or when a nervous beast approached him. In the Bay the day I first fought him.

It was alright if he wasn't beside me. Besides, the dragons needed to be assembled as well.

Other than the nervousness which came from my first combat on dragonback, I had never been particularly scared to fight the Sigurd. I'd been excited by the prospect, pleading against Aidan's worry for days before he allowed me to come.

But it was no longer a fight with a secured outcome.

The new threat demanded to be taken seriously. I could then say I was afraid.

But if we had stayed? If we hadn't seen that boat in the water? My friends would have returned home without me. Aidan and I would be within the Bay, hunting down small fleets, feints and deceptions to exhaust our energy and divert our attention. Flying with Bluebell, doing and seeing things I'd never imagined. Just him and I, in his small home under an island.

There would have been no battle, not for us.

No matter the simplicity it would have possessed, I couldn't bring myself to wish for it. Aidan deserved to meet his father. And without the dragons, or Briaedor's forewarning, Lamid would not have made it. Even *with* them, I could tell Aidan was questioning the odds. Yet, what more could we do?

I fought against my own exhaustion. There was no way I could have slept, anyway. My ears were ringing, the aftermath of my mother finally tracking me down. As suspected, I was grounded for life, and she was in fact also going to kill me, but her threats were so drowned in 'I love you's' and hugs that I wasn't sure how much stock to put into them.

I was surprised she even allowed me to equip for battle.

I shuffled down the wooden planks, ocean spray crashing into the poles below. Momentarily relieved of any tasks, I set down the crate under my arm with a store of arrows.

I trudged up the hill, heading for Estran. I saw Bluebell soon after, running about with a few of the other Muspel hatchlings under the torchlight, near the woods. They snorted uneasily when one of them ventured too close to the Lamidian homes.

She dashed over once she saw me, this fear shoved aside, as I sat heavily against a wall. My body may not have been allowing me to feel the full extent of my fatigue, but mentally, I was ready to drop as well.

Bluebell laid her head in my lap, disregarding the fact that she was now much too large to do so. Her crested skull cut off my view of the world. I tried to sit straighter, pushing myself up slightly. My belt brushed against her left horn, and I felt something catch.

A weight left my side, a quiet thud sounding from the ground.

Bluebell lifted her neck, allowing me to rise. She was sniffing at something, but moved away when I knelt down. A leather book, inlaid with stones, sat open on the stone path below. It felt like ages ago, the last time I held it. Had it really only been hours past? I needed to return it to Aidan.

It was face down on the ground, and I reached to pick it up, hoping the pages weren't dirtied.

I hadn't meant to look in it, really.

The book had turned around in my hands, the picture manifesting, making itself known in my peripheral. It was spread across two pages, a dark spot in my vision due to the charcoal marks. It was obviously detailed, if the amount of shading on the paper had anything to say about it.

Unthinkingly I looked down, curiosity overpowering me before I could close the book. In a sudden rush I had sat down again, back pressed against the stone behind me.

Even though the background was less detailed, I could tell instantly it was the Roost. Broken shells littered the foreground, and darkened sections of the sketch gave dimension to the holes. The upper half of a large Muspel took shape on the page, replicated so clearly that I could immediately recognize her, even with the absence of color.

It was the first mother I had met in the Roost, the one who had allowed me to give her a fish. I had hugged Aidan after that, I remembered. She laid across the ground, eyes closed in obvious relaxation.

The focal point, the center of the page, was me, drawn in such perfect clarity it was breathtaking. The mother's head rested in my lap, my finger trailing just behind her horns. The drawing was from a view closer than Aidan must have been, because my expression was depicted flawlessly.

Simply put, I was smiling down at the creature, my head slightly angled. All my musings about seeing the wonder of Aidan's life, and I felt they could have been put no better in a single reference point. It was amazement and shock at something *new*, and it was clearly etched in the face he had drawn.

I felt a blush rise to my cheeks, and heat blossom in my chest, when I realized how he must have been studying me, to recreate this so accurately. A curtain of dark curls fell around my shoulders, a strand tucked behind my left ear.

It was immensely beautiful, more so than anything he had shown me.

And even this, he had given to me, knowing or not. Attributing nothing to my perception of my own vanity, it made me look lovely, and heat pricked my eyes. I distantly recalled Aidan perched upon a rock, notebook in hand. Telling me it was nothing. I was distracted by the Lamid crest on the cover, by his mother in the book.

It was only then, when I was forced to pull the picture further from my face rather than risk tarnishing it with the salty water threatening my eyes, did I notice the inscription on the bottom.

Aidan's neat writing, a side effect of Ragna or his mother's teachings.

Freyja

Here I see her blessings

And then my hands shook and I lost my clear view.

Freyja, the goddess of beauty. 'Here I see her blessings', he had written. He had drawn me with a careful hand, with such perfect detail. It wasn't degrading, the picture of me he had painted. He had simply put it as it was, as he *saw* it. And apparently what he saw was me, carrying the blessings of Freyja.

Aidan thought I was beautiful? Not just beautiful, but blessed by the goddess of the very notion.

If the picture didn't suggest it, the words he had left certainly did.

That not quite uncomfortable churning in my stomach accompanied the thought. She was the goddess of something more, too.

One particular word which floated to my mind and refused to leave. I heard it in his voice. Aidan had said it to me, the night we danced on Fafnir's back. The first night we kissed.

I blinked rapidly, hating the tears for obscuring the most enchanting thing I had ever seen. Aidan had created this, inside the book that was once his mothers. He only put important things within it, he had told me, things he wanted to remember.

He only had so many pages, after all.

I shouldn't have seen it. He hadn't shown it to me, likely didn't even recall I still had it after recent events. But Odin above, was I glad I had. It piled onto me more questions, however, and I wasn't sure how I felt about them. He had made this, an object of such beauty, and he had made it of me.

Damn that boy, who couldn't possibly have realized what this would mean, this priceless parchment under my hands.

I couldn't even diminish it with the thought that he hadn't intended for me to see it, that somehow made it all the more special.

Bluebell leaned over, sniffing the page. I held it out to her with irrational pride, I knew she wouldn't ruin it. She chirped excitedly, must have recognized me there on the paper. After all, how could she not?

Carefully, I pulled it back to study one last time, committing it to my memory. I desperately wanted to thumb through it, to see if there were more like this one.

The thought made my heart skip around in its designated rhythm, but I resisted. It wasn't mine to view.

Gently, I replaced it where it had been and rose, my previous drowsiness forgotten. That word sat behind my eyes. Freyja was a goddess of many things, how could I know it meant this one? Except, Aidan had said...

I heard human strides, and quickly straightened up.

I didn't know whether to be grateful or disappointed when it wasn't Aidan who neared me. Likely grateful, as I would have instantly given myself away. I could feel the guilt written on my face. Then again, I wasn't positively thrilled, either, because making his way towards me was none other than Leo Evalade.

Curse me, couldn't I have just a few minutes?

It began to grow awkward when he missed the appropriate time to greet me. Or to say anything.

"Leo. Did you want something..."

"I need to ask you a question." He said sharply, and I shifted. "If there's a chance we die, come morning."

"Um, alright. I don't really-"

"Why won't you marry me?"

Oh, for the love of all that is sacred in Asgard! I was fully prepared to send him running with a string of curses, and possibly sic Bluebell on him, but I halted. There was no malice or rude behavior about him. He looked at me earnestly, cringing back a little, entirely expecting what I was about to do and appearing ready to bolt.

I sighed. I had been treating this as if it was only my life which was being decided, but the subject at hand was his future, too.

"Leo Evalade, are you in love with me?"

"I- well." He was floundering, looking anywhere but at me, mouth forming half-coherent sounds.

"You want to marry me, don't you? Then you shouldn't have to consider it. Do you love me? Yes or no, don't even think, blurt out the first thing that comes to-"

"No!" Leo immediately clamped his hand over his mouth. "Oh my gods, I didn't mean it like that-"

"Leo! It's okay! Believe me, I am very, very glad to hear it,"

"That's a little rude-"

"Marriage is forever. It follows you through the gates of death and eternity. It shouldn't be something your dad and your uncle pick out and plan for you, or a committee of people sitting behind a table. It should be to someone you love, someone you want to spend the rest of your life with, and on your own terms. You don't love me; I'm not even convinced you like me in that way. And I am not in love with you. I'm not ready to marry anyone, and I don't think you are either. It might sound appealing, and you might jump at the idea of strutting around with 'the best fighter in the village' draped on your arm-"

"Katla, in your house… I was hungover. I never should have said those things."

"I know. But it doesn't change the fact that this won't make you happy. Maybe it will for a few weeks, a month, even a year. But what happens when you realize I'm always going to be around? In your house, by your side, with your family? What about when you're not a kid anymore and you wish you had been given the chance to decide for yourself? What about when you're expected to have children-"

"Okay, okay! I know what you're saying. And no offense, but I don't really want to...do that, with you-"

I was quick to provide an oath. "You would never get that far."

"Point taken. What am I supposed to do now? The Council-"

"Leo, if the past month or so to reflect has taught me anything other than the fact that I really hate the smell of dragon shit, it's that you are surprisingly competent."

"Thank you?"

"What I mean is, you don't need some wife to run the village for you, or take on your duties. You are entirely capable of doing them yourself, and I think you could do them well. You know how to lead; you just have to want to. And if you start showing that around your uncle and your father, you can convince them that they don't need to saddle you with some girl. You can handle things on your own."

Leo thought for a minute, rocking back on his heels.

"Thanks, Katla. Seriously, that means a lot. But I never thought I'd hear this from you, I have to admit."

"Yeah, well. Enjoy the ego stroking while it lasts."

"So, you don't hate me? I'm not so terrible that you'd rather run away for months after a dragon man myth than marry me?"

I sighed. "First of all, the extended stay wasn't exactly planned. And even then, had relatively nothing to do with you. I am not ready to marry anyone Leo, like I said. I certainly wasn't ready to have a marriage sprung on me, a royal one at that. But I don't hate you, Leo. You just have an extraordinary talent for being particularly obnoxious at every possible opportunity... ever." Leo snorted, but he looked relieved. "I don't think anyone hates you, not even Eliana... except for Mr. Payne. I don't think he'll ever forgive you for spilling his entire store of mead in the dirt."

"I was drunk!"

"And somehow managed to spill twelve barrels of Payne's finest."

"I only spilled one and the rest followed. Who sets out twelve barrels without the lids on, anyway?" I rolled my eyes. "I suppose I should ask my dad and Uncle Ivon to call it off?"

"Are you ready to say 'I do' right now and be my husband?"

"Not particularly."

"Then yes, please."

Leo laughed, hunkering down on one of the crates. I wasn't too annoyed with him staying, but I could really only handle him in small doses.

"Still, over a month away. Was that because you had to be married on Lamid, or because you had my *cousin* all to yourself on some remote island?"

"Don't get any ideas, Evalade. I spent most of it flying and being generally scared for my life. Aidan's too, because your apparent cousin is insane, and likes to fall from high distances, then tries to convince me to do the same."

"Awesome! Did you?"

"Hel, no!"

"Aw come on, Katla. Where's your sense of adventure?"

"On the ground. How are you handling that, anyway? Having a cousin?"

"I think it'll be really good for Uncle Ivon. When we finally tell him. It's not like he spends all his time moping around or anything, but I live in the same castle as the man. He's a lot quieter when he's not in front of the villagers. I catch him standing in the middle of the hallway sometimes, just looking at Aunt Atarah's picture. Other times he just goes in his son's-Hagen's- Aidan's, room, and closes the door."

"Aidan has a room?"

"I think it's from before he and Aunt Atarah were taken, but yeah. My mother says I shouldn't bother him when he gets like that." We sat in silence before Leo jumped back in with renewed enthusiasm. "But that doesn't matter. Aidan's back now, and given Ivon doesn't try to kill him when he claims to be his long-lost son, he'll probably be thrilled."

"And are you? Thrilled?"

"'Thrilled' is a strong word. I'm not mad or upset. I just don't know how this will all work, with him technically being the first in line. I don't even know if he wants to be king, though. I don't even know if I do, now that there might be another option. Aidan's not bad, I guess. It would be cool to have a cousin, especially the guy who rides dragons, and fights Sigurd, and lives in some cave under an island, and if you ever tell anyone any of that I will deny it."

I hid a smile. "Don't go getting this idea of a badass. I watched Fafnir sit on him for a whole hour, once."

"Now that, I have to see."

"You probably will. He does it pretty regularly."

"Thanks for this, Katla. Even if we'll never get married and you'll never know what you're missing..." He trailed off, and I raised an eyebrow. "Kidding! I'm kidding. Besides, maybe we'll end up family after all..."

"You have five seconds, Evalade."

He was still laughing as he ran away.

CHAPTER TWENTY–SEVEN

KATLA

Bluebell and I discovered him, sitting on a roof along the very edge of the area leading to the docks. The shipyard was in even further disarray than when I had left it, the time limit dawning on everyone. I dropped beside him, eying the bag on his shoulder curiously.

Shuffling, I made myself comfortable on the inclined beam of wood.

"Hey." He said quietly, lacing our hands together unthinkingly.

Yet again, that word wormed its way into my mind. It dug a hole and refused to leave. So, I tried to forget it was squirming around under my roots.

"Hi." I mumbled back, squeezing his hand. "How are the dragons?"

"Well enough, we should be as ready as we can be." I breathed easier at that, that maybe we weren't entirely doomed. That this looming threat wouldn't claim us, tarnish our land and take our home like it had done to those before us. "Your idea for the boats is genius, it's going to work."

"Thanks." I told him, my voice thick, the implications of the morning playing out in my mind.

Gently, Aidan withdrew his fingers from mine, and set them to work playing with the grains in the roof. Fidgeting.

"Look, Katla. I have something that I've been meaning to give you. It never felt like the right time." I tracked his movements as he pulled the leather bag around his shoulder. "Now we can't really wait any longer. This might be my only chance. And you should have it- before the Sigurd arrive. Before a fight seems as good a time as any."

Carefully, from the large bag, he withdrew a sword.

And then, for the second time in a single night, I was struck by the beauty of Aidan Evalade.

Carefully, as if the prize in his hands was crafted of some fragile starlight, he presented me with a blade, more unique than any I had ever seen.

The hilt was shining gold, the way it wrapped around the blade was breathtaking in and of itself, but in comparison to the rest it paled. Embedded in the handle like they were wrapped in hundreds of strands of spun gold, were gemstones. Just fragments, less than inches in size, spanning up and around the hilt.

No, they weren't gemstones, I realized, leaning closer to see the cracks and patterns that ran through the vivid polished jewels. They were dragon scales.

I spotted a blue that so perfectly matched the ocean at dawn, a gleaming spot of gold that made the metal it laid in look fake. There was a brilliant green that I could only compare to his eyes, a purple the shade of twilight. There were so many of the gleaming scales, set so perfectly in the pommel. I wondered fleetingly if they came from the Kaida, or if they were cut down to the near perfect shapes. Had they been molded to catch the moonlight like that? To twist and weave the torches flickering fire into something all their own?

The sword itself was balanced perfectly in my hand, even more so than my fathers had been, for it was never truly mine.

Even the deadly beauty of the blade, and the sparking scales that the metal held so ethereally, could not compare to the center of the iron sword's handle. Set at the top were two scales I recognized instantly, entwined and laid together. They shone with impossible magnificence in the dimming glow around us. Two scales. Fafnir and Bluebell. Aidan and I.

"I know you lost your father's sword the day I found you. You deserved your own." He breathed. "It wouldn't do for a Valkyrie to carry a sword that was anything less than what they deserved."

We knew not what the breaking of dawn would bear. What it would start. To survive was a desperate prayer. I would leave nothing more to chance in this twisting spiral of uncertainties. I knew what I wanted. The weight of this one sword in my fingers and this hand against my own.

My arm was wrapped around his neck. I was pulling him near, his face to my own. He stood a little taller.

It was something desperate and fierce and broken, a thousand words conveyed in his lips. Crushing and sweet and mine. In the split second before I too was burning, like the world around us, that word made a reappearance.

Not to be forgotten, that one simple word that was anything but. I turned that word over in my mind. Took one more moment for this alone, and then laid a claim to it.

Freyja, also known as the Goddess of Love.

***

The screams were what woke me. Shouts and my mother's hands. There was smoke, and I was confused.

My first true sensation was cold metal as I wrapped my fingers around the sword by my bed frame. The one he had given me before I retired home and he to the forest, trying for an hour of sleep.

I was half awake when I threw myself out the door as the sun fought to set free its light, tangled curls whipping around my face. Bluebell ran to me, eyes like slits, snarling and hissing. Her talons left gouges in the street. I shook myself as I stumbled outside.

My village, Iona, was burning.

Fire sat, spread out with no order, on houses and on the ground. It moved rapidly, families running coughing from their homes. Sticking out of the flames, and even more of the houses, were arrow shafts, slowly being eaten away by the fire. There was an almost greenish tint to the inferno which grew to an irrational size.

Glowing green rain fell from the sky, thick and steaming, splattering onto a nearby home.

An avalanche of tiny flames chased after it moments later, and a single one of them struck the glowing green. It roared to life, already haven eaten through part of the wooden ceiling, and stuck everywhere it could. Acid. They were hurling acid onto our village, flaming arrows to follow. Avelyn had warned us of this. We hadn't thought it would reach this far into the island. Only Estran, the village already having been cleared out.

But here in Iona, in Elysia and Baldur, homes were still occupied.

I spun from the scene of my village in flames, sprinting back for Bluebell. The muscles in my legs protested as I threw myself up, latching onto her left horn. Pushing off the joint of her wing and up onto her back, I flung my body into a seated position. The new sword slapped against my side.

"Okay, Bluebell. Time to give them Hel."

She took a running leap into the sky.

CHAPTER TWENTY-EIGHT

AIDAN

The day was dawning. The kingdom was burning. The battle had come, and the time to fight had struck.

In the steadily growing sunlight, the Sigurd marched on in the water. The armada was like nothing I had ever seen. I couldn't hope to count the number of ships, but it was hundreds at minimum. They dominated the waves, more wood visible than water as they cut through the sea, their intended location clear.

As they flung another round of the vibrant and burning liquid onto the island, Bluebell rose silently to our right wing.

We flew higher than their following arrows, unable to do anything to stop all of them. The docks were already on fire, the ships left at the very end of the harbor's expanse burning. Avelyn had been right. The Lamidians never would have made it to the ships, never could have used them to fight. Or to flee.

But the Sigurd had fallen for our deception, this time.

I looked once more to Katla on my right, before we banked in opposite directions. She headed for our forces to one side, I headed for the other.

Fafnir reached them in no time, and it was a rather strange sight, though it returned to me the hope that seeing the armada had stolen away. I smiled at the fruit of our hard work the night prior.

Down below, half of our flock flew low across the water like a migration of multi-colored birds. Each one gripped thick rope in their claws, pulling behind them half of Lamid's naval fleet. They weren't far from the Sigurd now; we would reach them soon. These ships had been invisible to the approaching armada in the morning fog which rolled across the waves, about an hour's sailing distance from Lamid.

Across the horizon, I could see our other half, approaching steadily from the opposite direction. Chaos would meet in the middle.

Fafnir swooped low to the group, landing heavily on the largest ship positioned in the center. I saw Ivon, but I did not dismount or come any closer. Our ships were sliding through the waves, the fight would begin in moments.

"Is everyone ready?" I called down to him, and he nodded. "It's a matter of minutes now, I can already see the others."

"Oh, we see them. The second these behemoth's release our vessels, we'll begin." He informed me. Fafnir raised his wings, and began to turn, before the king stopped him. "Hagen!" And just how wrong was it, for me to have wondered after him all this time, for him then to not know even my true name? "Be careful, kid."

Fafnir took to the open air.

"Alright buddy, this is the big one."

You don't have to tell me. Just keep your skinny hide strapped in, yeah?

Out on the water, Katla's devised order of events fell into place. They had seen us coming, surely, in the last handful of moments. The hulking herd of dragons pulling ships from each horizon would have been impossible to miss once we left the mist behind. Still, their size became their disadvantage. There were too many of them to turn around, not enough time to even try, let alone succeed in a retreat.

Just before the two sides met, they turned their weapons on us.

Catapults were what held the acid, mechanisms and wires propelling vats of it, bubbling and sizzling. What they must have lined it with to keep the liquid from biting through the metal, was unknown. The horrid containers lined the sides of ships, backed by marksmen. Another thing became clear too, as we neared. The dragon scales.

Crates and barrels full of them, seemingly serving no purpose other than to sit there the many times I had seen them before. Stores of them, nearly overabundant, but why? It became clear then. *Armor.*

The Sigurd's armor was a patchwork of scales. Hundreds of different colors and sizes from hundreds of dragons, not one piece of armor the same.

It had been forged into their chest plates, the linings of their arms and shins. As they shifted, it revealed their joints, elbows and knees which were forced to flex, but the rest was covered. Their increased attendance on Trader's Isle became more understandable.

A word Katla would have cursed me for saying slipped through my lips. The Sigurd stole the skin of dragons to layer themselves in nearly impenetrable protection.

Their sick protective shells weren't going to be easy to get through, for the dragons or the warriors. A tsunami of snarling rage swept through the Bonded of the Bay as their eyes filled with the scale clad humans. They dropped the ropes, scores of thick woven bands falling at once as they soared for the sky.

The full force of the flock's ire was drawn to the molded metal. I wished Fafnir hadn't seen it. I wished I hadn't seen it. I couldn't tell his nausea from mine, but we had no time for it.

The first of our squadron slammed into a Sigurd vessel with a deafening crash, knocking it to the left. From the opposite side, our other team of ships did the same, the dragons who had brought them joining the rest above.

I heard myself shout, and then we were diving.

They employ what they have stolen from us to fight this battle! Let us reclaim it and end them!

I didn't need to hear the whistling on the air to know they were following. Ten strings snapped, and Fafnir rolled, allowing their arrows to scream past us. He made for the mast without slowing, crashing into the nest.

I covered my face with my arm as the wood splintered, the archers screaming as they were thrown from their posts. Fafnir pulled up quickly, aiming for the sky where their weapons could not reach.

Looking down as he scaled the air, I saw Ivon leap first from a Lamid ship to theirs, sword raised. Others trailed him with cries of battle into the din.

The humans would take care of the outer ships. Our target was the middle.

I wanted Olavi.

Loki knew he'd never expose himself on the outer ring. Fafnir flew to the center of the armada and dove again, fire at the ready. The first barrage of bolts were burned to nothing by his flame, but he didn't stop there. Cutting past the side of their ship and skimming just over the water, Fafnir exhaled. The air around us became unbreathable.

Yes, their armor was outfitted with dragon scales. But what would protect them from human iron would not save them from flame.

An arrow arced for Fafnir's head. I tore my shield from my back, placing it in the projectile's path. It bounced harmlessly against the wood and metal, spinning away.

We left the ship burning.

To light their supply of acid became our goal, to turn their own weapon against them. Fire upon it caught immediately and spread violently, a ship doomed the instant their liquid weapon captured a spark.

Katla darted past me, Bluebell obviously having caught on to the plan. Instead of attacking the untouched ships, they were almost chasing after a group of Syre who were adding their own acid to planks, igniting the liquid with a stream of fire on the way down.

Side by side we swooped down bearing fire. Our combined efforts left a ship below the waves within minutes. One down, hundreds to go. Katla swung the new sword with valor as Bluebell turned on her side, wings perpendicular to the sea. The human rider clung from her shoulder and brandished her sword at the unexpecting Sigurd who were rushing to reload the catapults.

She cut them down in a clean line where their skin was exposed. Their forearms bore three thick bands, a reminder of just who they were. I saw Eliana, lined up with a row of archers on a Lamidian boat. I watched as her arrow in particular pierced through a man in the mast of a Sigurd ship.

She whooped as he toppled over and fell to the deck.

There were ships which held dragons, but I couldn't get near enough to free them, nor did I have the chance. Back into the pulsing battle we went. Two ships sailed side by side, attempting to pass by the burning wreckage of others and move forward.

Like an arrow falling back to the earth we flew, an unstoppable force. We made a beeline for the closest vessel while its occupants fought back.

The feathered shafts they fired had little impact on our course. I closed my eyes as we proceeded through the simple cinders Fafnir reduced them to. I felt the heat in his scales as he threw it upon them, not stopping to survey his handiwork.

Together we collided with the burning sail, the pole behind it. With a crack like thunder, it tore free from the boat, set on an inescapable path. The planks of the second ship broke through to allow water's entrance as the mast of its sister toppled into its hull. We abandoned the two vessels, sinking and connected by a burning bridge of collapsing wood.

Fafnir let his wings stretch to their fullest high above the wreck, casting a large shadow on the smoldering remains below. He roared, in challenge and victory. I allowed myself to feel none of his triumph.

There was much more to fight, and a man to find.

The second you see him- or smell him-

You'll know. He promised.

I locked myself down as Fafnir flung his body against another support. He shook his head to clear it as he rose again, before diving to the earth to destroy another. There was no time to focus on sinking each vessel, immobilizing them was necessary now. The Bay dragons who followed with their fire would leave the boats as smoking driftwood.

The sky was one single storm of fire and wings.

The Sigurd were well prepared, this was their cumulation. The scales, the acid, the numbers. But where they may have planned for the dragons and I on our own, they hadn't expected a fight against the humans and us together.

Twice already, Fafnir and I had been saved by someone below, an invisible archer from a Lamidian or Briaedorian ship, a thrown dagger. Impossibly, those below were looking out for us, too.

Fafnir tensed, and I leaned with all my weight to the side just as he flipped onto his back. I swung my sword vigorously as the deck rushed past my head. A few tried to raise their weapons in defense, but the upside-down approach had been unanticipated. I aimed for their arms, not daring to try for their chests. I already knew their armor wouldn't give.

Fafnir pushed upward for our true target, and he vomited flames onto the occupants below.

I caught the edge of the sail on the tip of my sword and, as Fafnir ascended, tore a gash through the middle that cut it in two. To avoid the arrows that tried to bury us, Fafnir spiraled towards the sky, wings tucked to his body.

I didn't need to hear him in my mind to anticipate his moves, to know what was coming next. I didn't have to speak to put us on a new path. We were one in the sky, our moves indistinguishable as we soared through the rising smoke. We were horns and scales, flesh and flame. One being that would not fall, that would rise, strike, claw. Running on the same beat of wings.

We were what it was to be Bonded.

Still, they were firing upon the villages, the more protected ships not yet having turned all their forces on us. They weren't being sunk as fast as we needed. We could still win, if winning meant leaving all their vessels as wreckage below the waves. But by the time we managed to do so, there would be nothing left of the Kingdom.

I ran a hand through my hair, breathing shakily.

I didn't know what to do. This was all we had, and it wasn't enough. Olavi had been planning this for a long time, that much was clear. The Sigurd had fought me and the dragons before, they weren't strangers to it. While they were taken off guard by the need to do so, they were falling into it quickly.

Even if we managed to pull through, the cloud of smoke rising above the Kingdom would become all that remained. Would we lose today?

Would there be anything left of what we were defending when the last ship sunk?

I pulled up and out of the fight, watching from above and racking my brain desperately. Fafnir picked up on a spot of blue, and my eyes too found Bluebell. Katla was flying from the wreckage of a ship, but where one fell there were three more to take its place. There were arrows trained on Bluebell from all directions, and they were not yet high enough to escape them.

Bluebell, move! I shouted.

Fafnir roared. *Dive, Youngling!*

Bluebell dove.

In one harsh motion she pulled her wings in, turning over and dropping like a stone back towards the water. But Bluebell was small and young, her wings not yet strong enough, and they fell too slow. The loosed bombardment of arrows shot too high over them, all but one. Fafnir was already pushing us closer, but it did not stop the cry of panic as an arrow very nearly ended in Katla's side. It spooked the hatchling beneath her.

Frantic, Bluebell attempted to pull up, twisting over herself in an attempt to protect both of them. Her movements were too jerky and panicked. Katla was torn from her seat.

Fafnir!

Bluebell righted, searching the water for her lost rider's form. Perilously, Fafnir and I tried to push in, but the same boats turned their fire on us. Fafnir snarled, and the surrounding sky became so much hotter.

I lowered instinctively as we sliced down again, unable to attack the ships, but the blaze acted as a powerful deterrent. Through the small gap in the flames from his mouth I spotted Katla, clinging to the side of a Sigurd ship. She was almost to the top, and as we drew near she pulled herself over the side.

Katla fell to the floor, dropping into a roll. In another fluid motion she drew her sword.

Katla was livid.

She cut the legs out from underneath the closest archer, turning on their companion next. There were too many on the ship to fight, but the short break in arrows as she threw herself into the group of marksmen was the momentary distraction we needed.

Fafnir turned, tackling the nearest sail with his claws and throwing it to the ground. Bluebell set it on fire in the same breath, and it fell in a pile of smoke to the deck. Fafnir's talons, still wrapped around the thick wood of the mast, dug and tore a massive chunk of the crow's nest, sending it flying into the deck of the third ship.

Without stopping to see the resulting crash, we made back for the first, the ship where Katla still fought valiantly.

"Katla!" I shouted.

She did not turn, but I knew she heard. The closest Sigurd who had locked their blades with her own was thrown aside with an expert twist of her sword. She spun, suddenly sprinting towards us across the deck.

The remaining archers aimed at her. They were going to fill her full of shafts and steel.

Fafnir's wings strained.

Her feet neared the front of the boat and she jumped onto the side, not stopping. Fafnir was nearly there when she leapt off the wall, hand outstretched, as the archers released. In synchronization we all fell.

I threw myself off of Fafnir, closing the distance between our hands and locking my fingers with her own. Fafnir's body, a gigantic mass of white, charged down after us. I grabbed his foreleg with my open hand as he spun over. The arrows whizzed overhead as he pulled us close to his chest, wrapping his two front legs around us.

As he tried to spin, we found ourselves too close to the ocean's surface, and Fafnir's wing was sucked under the water.

Come on, Fafnir! You can make it!

Roaring with the effort, he ripped his wing through the beat of the ocean, moving in time with the other. We shot from the sea, a trailing waterfall behind us. Katla held tightly to my hand as we rose.

Bluebell appeared under us. Katla looked up at me in assurance, and I let go. She fell the short distance to Bluebell's back.

I swung my body, latching onto Fafnir's closest wing and fighting to pull myself back up, a hundred feet above the battle which had now grown desperate and bloody.

Katla was breathing heavily, and Bluebell was visibly panting in exhaustion. Fafnir's wings had let up, fighting just to scoop the wind and remain airborne.

The massive expanse of the Sigurd fleet was plowing through the ships from the Lamidian harbor, surrounding them so that others could pass on unharmed. How much longer could the warriors those ships contained survive? Trapped on all sides.

They would all be killed, sooner or later.

The Sigurd boats had banded together now, all manner of arrows and knives launching through the sky, a joined storm from multiple boats at once. The sole goal seemed to be to keep the dragons from getting close enough. And they were succeeding.

A Muspel floated in the water, wing outstretched. Half of the translucent membrane was ripped away from the bone. There was a glaive in her underbelly and an arrow in her eye.

And so many more like her.

In a painfully long instant, a flock of feathered bolts chased down a Syre. The projectiles from the first ship bounced off his scaled back. Those from the ship behind were buried in soft flesh and bone. There were no words in his cry of anguish, but Bonded as we all were, it was inescapable.

A young Muspel, hatched just a summer ago, sought solace by flying back towards the Kingdom. I couldn't blame her, in all her fear, for trying to run. She was downed from behind by a thrown axe which cut through her wing. A woman took a running start, launched her halberd. The tip spilled her belly open. She fell in these fractured pieces.

My family was being plucked from the sky like geese from the string of a hunter.

I didn't even realize I had been screaming until I felt the first ache shoot through my throat. I supposed it was my own fault, somehow. Maybe I shouldn't have assumed our victory was so absolute that I could simply ponder on the aftermath. Maybe I should have paid more attention. Maybe I should never have underestimated Olavi Sture, even in my beliefs of a greater plan.

Maybe I should have done a lot of things, but even with all the time in the world, I don't think I ever could have imagined what would follow.

For a few moments, I simply didn't comprehend what I was seeing when dragons began to rise from the Sigurd fleet.

Didn't understand, when they crashed into our flock in the air, bodies tanging and wrestling as they fell. When claws sliced at talons. When they stole the wings from each other.

There was no connection in my brain when they made for the Lamid ships, when they started to burn. I didn't realize any of it until Katla shouted.

"No!"

In a last-ditch effort, I threw my mind wide open, blasted through the walls shielding my thoughts from others, baring myself to everyone around me. I could feel the small weights of Bonds, Fafnir's consciousness under me, Bluebell beside me. Several others in the surrounding air. But as I pushed for those below, those rising under demonic sails, the fingers of my thoughts scraped nothing.

Nothing to grab, to hear, to think.

They were unreachable. There was nothing there to find. Only anger, savage and explosive, each and every one running on the desire to fight.

Commands, but no words. At least not their own.

And maybe that was the instant I decided I was going to kill Olavi Sture. Or, possibly, that's when I accepted the fact that there would be no victory. In those last few seconds of confusion before I fully understood what was happening, I wished I had told my father that I was his son.

Flesh and wings turned crimson.

CHAPTER TWENTY-NINE

KATLA

The Sigurd had brought a draconic force of their own.

My mind spared me the torture of wondering how they could have done it. How they could have asserted this level of dominance over such wild creatures. The dragons from Aidan's Bay were falling, crashing into the ocean as they grappled with the opposing serpents.

I now understood how one could be so calm watching the world end.

It wasn't calm, but rather a resigned absence of feeling. Because it was the end, wasn't it? Our odds had been slim before, but now the outcome was certain. Lamid would fall, and we would be lucky to still be alive when it did.

It was with some sick and volatile desperation that I attempted to continue a losing fight.

I regretted re-entering the battle immediately. The sky was alive, a moving, pulsing, writhing creature that took up all available space and tried to surge while it fought against itself. Bluebell and I did our best to fire on the Sigurd fleet when we could, but I could barely see through the rapids of wings that laid hateful waste in every direction. We couldn't dive without being forced to pull out of it in order to dodge a fight between two or three dragons. One would chase us before another tackled it out of the sky.

I could see Sigurd on the boats, shouting towards those dragons they had brought, waving towards Lamid ahead of us. Pushing them, on, on, on. They were thrashing. Uncontrolled.

Responding to only one command; forward. Forward. Forward.

One of them split from the group and took out an entire Sigurd longboat instead of the Lamid counterpart beside it. Then I grasped at the true insanity of their plan.

The dragons weren't made slaves by the Sigurd, not fully. The winged reptiles knew no difference between the ships in the water, the dragons in the sky. I watched two rise from the deck of a ship and immediately go for each other's necks, lost to the shouts of the clansmen below them.

They had unleashed this Hel on all of us, including themselves, in an attempt at triumph.

I screamed as we were crashed into by a Syre. Bluebell roared in distress. We careened towards the ground, spiraling helplessly. The air whipped past me. I couldn't even draw a breath to shout for Bluebell. She flung her wings out, and my head snapped forward as we pulled to a sudden stop.

I hadn't even a second to relax before a massive red Muspel was streaking towards us, jaws wide and snapping.

"Bluebell, get us out of here!"

She was already moving before I yelled, wings beating.

We would never have outrun the much larger dragon if it hadn't been knocked off course by another. I didn't even know if it was one of ours, or theirs.

I gasped for breath as we broke through the horde, taking to open space. Screams echoed across the water. It was so much worse than the destruction of Vanir and Briaedor. It could have been because I was present for this attack, because these were people I knew.

Or because the reality was so much worse than my imagined Hel.

I threw my eyes skyward, wishing the gods would bless us, but they seemed far too deep in curses to help. I released a shaky breath, and wondered if it would be smarter to throw myself back into the fight, or try to defend Lamid.

Maybe we could help a few people evacuate? My heart sunk.

No, we had taken all the boats, and those that remained were already burning in the harbor, our distraction.

There was no way for anyone to escape off the island.

How many people could Bluebell carry? Where could we go that the Sigurd wouldn't next march?

There was movement on the water. I disregarded it at first, but then Bluebell noticed it as well, and I was inclined to look again. The water behind the ships, a few hundred feet east, was rising and falling rapidly, the change visible even from all the way up in the clouds.

Bluebell roared so boomingly that I jumped on her back. She had never been so loud before, but it wasn't an angry sound. What on Midgard could she find to be happy about? Her roar was exuberant.

"Bluebell?" I questioned, but before she could give any sort of answer for me to interpret, we were suddenly flying headlong towards the moving water. "Bluebell!"

She continued on. Small waves were jumping up from the ocean and then crashing down again in strange, uneven patterns.

It felt wrong that there should be beauty on this battlefield, but the sea seemed to deny us even that respect. Strange colors twisted below the water, moving in synchronization with the unnatural waves. Vibrant purples and greens, blues and grays all swirled together. The water was tinted in pinks and oranges, a result of the still climbing sun in the east.

The ocean was breathtaking. Why? Did the gods truly entertain themselves so cruelly? And *what* was Bluebell doing?

We dropped, and I didn't bother calling to her. She came to stop just above the water, turning back towards the battle and moving forward with the strange colors. The next wave broke through the water, and I thought I had died for the wave of euphoria that crashed through me so suddenly.

Could hope be found after it was so devastatingly lost? It seemed so. Because the waves beneath me weren't waves at all. They were dragons.

A creature rose from the depths beside me, scales so deep and blue they looked as if they were made from the sea itself. The Amphitrite squinted at me curiously, fin-like wings slicing through the water.

Bluebell growled at it lightly. Slit pupils grew to ovals, and after a moment the Amphitrite chirped back in greeting.

Webbed spines rose from its skull, the membrane a translucent blue. We flew lower still, and I extended my hand as the dragon swam past. My fingers trailed lightly over the scales of her back until she disappeared beneath the waves.

I felt tears slide down my face, forming trails in their abundance, but I couldn't be bothered to care. The water was slowly filling, spined heads surfacing, transparent wings rising above. An Amphitrite nearly identical to the previous swam up beside us, head level with Bluebell's own. The horns were slightly different, outward, a male.

He lowered his maw to the water, and that was all the warning I received. When he returned to his original height, he raised his head towards the sky and released the water from his mouth. I covered my head, giggling in slight hysteria as the ocean water sprinkled back down on us like rain.

A cascade of draconic chortles filled the ocean air while they laughed at the now wet human.

Bluebell snarled at them, shaking water from her serpentine face, and their sniggers only increased. My eyes slid further down the line.

I laughed, and it was a shaky sound. "Well, Thor strike me."

Ragna stood tall on the back of a gray male Amphitrite, sailing on the water with her hand upon his neck. Her bear cloak flew behind her.

She had brought the Amphitrite to us. I knew nothing of what must have transpired in the time that Aidan left us to find his own answers, shortly after discovering his lineage. I only knew that when we left Aidan's home, Ragna did not follow us. She had lied to him, my suspicions had been correct, but even now I could not deny my gratitude towards the woman.

My body was thrumming with energy, revitalized. "Aidan. We have to find Aidan. Come on, Bluebell!"

She rumbled happily, taking off towards the battle above with renewed determination.

It was less a mass of dragons than a moving spot of color that awaited us. I tried not to let my hope sink when I noticed it was smaller than when we had left.

I scanned in every direction as we approached, seeking white scales. We flew into the draconic cloud once again, immediately forced to pull our guard back up. Even this couldn't dampen my elation. Where was Aidan?

My method of searching for him wasn't working, it was far too chaotic in the brine of dragons. As unfocused as I was, I would get us killed staying. We shot upwards, just in time to see the dragons of the sea break through the first ships of the armada.

The Amphitrite had joined the battle.

The Sigurd had never seen them coming, too focused on the air and our own warriors to think of watching the ocean.

Dragons twice the length of their own ships burst from the depths, spraying water from the waves with such force that the occupants were thrown across the deck. They climbed up the sides, the Muspel and Syre from above tearing the archers from their posts before they could fire on them. Kaida unleashed themselves upon the faces and soft bits of the opposing warriors.

The bowmen were forced to choose, to fire up or down. By the time they picked one, the other had them.

The creatures swarmed the boats, the larger ones beginning to pull them into the blue. The Sigurd tried in vain to launch their acid at them, but found the Amphitrite too close for their catapults to be of any use. The frenzied boatmen attempted to dump their large stores of it overboard, but the dragons simply cleared out of the area, and the prized weapon dissolved in the water.

At an alarming rate, the Amphitrite were taking the armada from beneath.

I spotted Calin, rolling and coming up to pull a Sigurd's legs out with his halberd. He jumped over them, moving on to the next. Leo was by his side, axes swinging, absolutely lethal.

Bluebell jerked in a new direction, and before I even had a chance to feel disgruntled, I saw what she did. Fafnir, dead ahead, over the center of the bedlam. Just about to dive again. We were already speeding for them before I could ask Bluebell to stop them.

"Aidan!" I was shouting, praying he would hear me before he dove into the pandemonium. "Fafnir! Aidan!"

Fafnir heard me first, and pulled out of his release on the air. I saw Aidan whip his head around before he found us. As we came close, he shouted.

"Katla! You have to get out of here!"

"I- what?" I stopped short in my happy call.

"We can't win this! One dragon won't make a difference. You and Bluebell have to go, now!"

"Aidan, I am not-"

"You'll be killed! I can send another with you. Grab the others, Eliana, Calin, Leo. Avelyn. Katla, my father-"

"Stop talking!"

His shoulders slumped. "What?"

"You're rather unobservant, aren't you?"

In great amusement, I observed his face the moment he saw them.

"You're kidding."

"Yeah." I beamed so wide it hurt. "Pretty great, right?"

"Ragna." He whispered as Fafnir pulled around in midair.

He swung to face me again, eyes burning with such intensity that I blinked hard. He smiled.

And then he plunged. Bluebell and I descended into the mayhem with new fervor, doing our best to cover the Amphitrite below as they dragged ships to the depths. Fafnir appeared near us, and every few minutes I would hear Aidan's disbelieving laugh as our dragons fought side by side.

The tides had turned again, this time in our favor.

I spotted the king upon one of the ships. He jumped in the air, the movement not at all displaying his age. His sword cut through the wing of a passing amber Muspel, and I hoped it wasn't one of ours.

"King Ivon!" I shouted, and as soon as he noticed me I kept on, before he could open his mouth. "Take everyone back to the island! There are more dragons here to help, but we can't guarantee they won't try to sink you, too!"

We turned away after that, and I could only pray Ivon would listen. Ideally, with all of those ships pulled out, it would be easier to see what we were dealing with. I didn't doubt Ivon would ensure they took a few more boats out of the picture as they departed.

I passed Leo and Calin again, running across the deck of a Sigurd ship.

"Leo! Calin! Get back to the fleet!" I shouted down to them.

They nodded once they found me in the sky, jumping over the side of the boat and onto another, blades flying, making their way steadily back.

The skies were clearing, but the waters were thick with dragons.

Their scales flowed like the ocean itself, a mirage of color. The same could not be said for the boats, which were falling below the waves rapidly. Several dragons began to fly away from the battle, while others were taken down by our own flock, continuing their combat in the air.

It became easier to fly due to the thinning of the herd, and Bluebell returned to blasting ships with a vengeance.

I cheered as we came around for another pass, ready to finish off the small boat beneath us. With an explosion that rocked the vessel we were climbing again, the wind ripping the rest of my hair free of the band which tied it back. I pushed it behind me, searching for somewhere else to turn.

I saw Fafnir flying in the armada's center. It was so much smaller, I noted. The behemoth almost dead.

Bluebell shifted, angling towards them. Aidan maneuvered on Fafnir's back, glanced away from the water to me. He might have laughed, but I was too far away to hear.

Similarly, I was too far away to help when four boats at once decided to concentrate on Fafnir.

Aidan was a better rider than I was, Fafnir a better flyer than Bluebell. These weren't hard things for me to admit, only simple facts. The two brothers had a lifetime of experience on their side.

Maybe that's why when the sky around them filled with arrows, for the first couple of seconds I believed it would be fine. After all, it wasn't the first time they had been fired upon. But Aidan looked back too late, there were simply too many archers, and Fafnir was far too close. Still, their skills showed themselves as Fafnir contorted and spun in the air with frenzied grace. It was enough to save them from most of the arrows.

Three hit home.

I knew it was impossible for me to hear the sound of iron arrowheads slicing through Fafnir's wings, but how could a sight like that fill my ears with such silence?

They were falling, and I was screaming, and Bluebell was pushing forward, but we never could have arrived fast enough to catch either of them. This battle would down both of us.

Aidan was dislodged from Fafnir, and in the span of an instant, I decided that his new destination was infinitely worse than the first. Fafnir landed in the water.

Aidan wasn't so lucky.

Only a few seconds passed between Aidan crashing onto the deck of a Sigurd ship and my own arrival, but it seemed like so much longer.

This time I was close enough to hear him scream, just as he collided with the boat's surface. I knew Bluebell couldn't possibly escape another convoy of ships with my weight. Even still, I needed to be down there. Help was arriving. I could handle myself until then.

So, Bluebell did not slow even slightly as she flung onto the boat, and as such, the entire blasted thing rocked and groaned. Under different circumstances I would have been proud. The marksmen around us were reloading, the warriors hefting their axes and spears.

I slid down the side of her wing, dropping lightly to the deck.

"Go, Bluebell! Go!" I shouted, and trusting me, she went.

I was standing with my sword in my hand before I could even process the movement myself. It felt like an extension of me, shifting as I did, ready to fight. I took in my surroundings quickly. There were several archers on the boat, bows trained on Bluebell. They did not move to shoot at us.

I didn't bother glancing upward, I knew she had gotten away. I would have heard if she hadn't, but it wasn't safe for her to return. I stepped closer to Aidan, who was groaning, pushing himself up.

"Katla." He bit out, but I couldn't afford to look at him now.

557

His shield had fallen from his arm. My left hand seized it, brandishing it before both of us, protection should the Sigurd fire. But they didn't. The bowmen had yet to shoot, and instead were all facing the back of the ship with questioning expressions.

Carefully, I directed my attention there as well.

A man stood in front of us. Loose, relaxed. Observing, or basking. There were no warriors flanking him. His weapons were nothing special, a double-edged sword on his belt, a bow in his hand. His black hair was thick like tar, long, hanging in a heavy braid down his back. A beard flowed freely down his chest, meticulously groomed.

His well-kept appearance was head and shoulders above the rest of the Sigurd, but he was still nothing spectacular.

Yet, there was an air of something that clued me in as to his identity before he had ever spoken. The Sigurd on board deferred to him, absolutely. They were still before us, awaiting his order with bated breath, as if afraid to move without his say so.

Unlike the plates of his men, his armor was not a combined mess of different scales. His chest shone bright and unblemished, covered in the identical scales of a blood red dragon. Stolen protection, perfected in an armor he never planned to need.

This was his show, that much was plain and obvious.

He seemed to take up the entire space, though he truly wasn't that large, similar in stature to King Ivon and many of the blacksmiths. Three thick bands of black circled his right arm, a tattoo he shared with all the others on the boat. His alone was different, however. It was taken over by another image, much blacker and stronger. A circle sat against the bands of his clan. This simple circle was the focal point of eight tridents which pointed outward from its center.

Dark brown eyes, filled with mirth, devoured me. Finally, I could put a face to a haunted, lingering name.

Aidan stiffened.

"Well then!" He was lowering his bow, pure glee on his face. Had his arrow been one of those which took Fafnir down? They all might as well have been his. He laughed again, and then examined us. Examined Aidan, in particular. "It's been years, my boy! Hasn't it? Have you grown?" Aidan glared, unwrapping his arm from his chest and standing straight despite the pain he must have been in from the fall. "You certainly have! You were so much smaller last time! I'm surprised you're still kicking around, kid! Can't say overjoyed, but certainly surprised."

"No, you're not. I don't believe for one second you haven't had your information fed to you, all these years. You've certainly changed tactics, haven't you? What, selling children wasn't enough for you? You had to burn them in their beds to be satisfied that Hel would hold a place for you?"

Aidan was agitated, uneasy. I think he may have been afraid. And angry. I shifted slightly to provide us more cover behind the shield.

The man ignored the jab, acting as though he had just noticed my presence.

"Who's this?" I narrowed my eyes, but stayed silent. "What, nothing? Alright. Since when do you and your underlings ally with the Kingdoms, hmm?"

"If I remember correctly, which I do, I've been saving people from all kingdoms off your ships for a while now. Made a bit of a habit out of it. You were never going to get this by me, Olavi."

His answering guffaw boomed over the deck, and his crew jumped. We didn't.

"I'll admit, boy, I thought we'd at least take Medea before you wizened up. Maybe even Atori. Did you have fun chasing down those little ships, or did you always know your efforts were utterly wasted? You only sought what I allowed you to. You've saved, and prevented, nothing. It truly wasn't even that much of a knocker. Cost me a fair amount of men and boats, merchandise and resources. But you know, I think it played out well enough."

"Seems like you've been thinking of me all these years when you came up with your big ideas, Olavi! It's funny, really. I haven't thought about you at all!" Aidan scoffed. "I'd hoped you drowned. I am shocked to see you here, though. It's been a while, hasn't it, since you fought in your own battles? Did your short trip in the ocean scare you so much that you've been hiding from me, all these years?"

What was Aidan doing, egging him on like this? The man had us under the thumb of a dozen marksmen, and he carried his own aura of danger. Yet Aidan seemed unable to stop himself, his mouth firing right back at the Sigurd Chief like these were the last words he would ever speak. If he continued, they would be.

"Planning, actually. Pulling some things together, cutting loose ends, braiding new ones. I hold two kingdoms while you struggle to keep a third. I must be rather good at it."

"Sounds boring."

"You know, the woman was more polite. Not the quiet one, but the other. Did the devils choose the most pathetic child they could find to fight for them after she died?"

I blanched, suddenly wondering if I could hurl my sword with enough force to pierce his armored chest, but Aidan didn't miss a beat.

"No, I only took up the job of kicking your ass after my mother."

Now I wasn't quite sure who I wanted to kill more. Aidan, in his bout of stubborn idiocy, was going to goad the Sigurd Chief into ending our lives. There was a woman standing yards away, bowstring taunt against her fingers. At Aidan's words, she gave a small snort. I wondered if Olavi would kill her, the atmosphere certainly tense enough to warrant such an action, but instead he seemed to be holding back giggles. Bubbling, rambunctious giggles.

"So that woman, the one before you? Oh ho, that was your *mother*?" And Olavi Sture broke into utterly hysterical laughter. This information seemed to amuse him a great deal. "What a demented trick of Loki!" His chuckles finally died out. "It seems you and I remember her weak attempts at battle very differently. It's a shame she lasted as long as she did."

"Yes, she was my mother." Aidan smirked, and I questioned how much of his bravado was real. "I grew up with the stories of how she forced your clan to Hel and back. Tell me Sture, do you remember that part differently? Or do you simply pleasure yourself with memories of the fleets she decimated as though they still remain?"

Finally, the man showed the smallest flicker of anger.

"That foolish woman died like she lived. Unsound, she was, riding around on those beasts. She passed it along, too. But she was good for a few things, I found."

I risked a glance at the sky. Bluebell was circling overhead, but each time she tried to swoop down, a round of arrows held her at bay. Heimdall curse it all! However, the skies were now laden with significantly less dragons.

They weren't gone, but simply more spread out. I lowered my gaze slightly, to the waters around us.

Relief mixed with my fear when I realized that the number of boats were dropping fast. I could see Lamid's armada in the distance, almost to the island. There couldn't have been more than thirty boats in the surrounding sea, the number lessening all the while. The water moved oddly in my peripheral.

Aidan took an exposing step forward. "Don't you speak of my mother."

"Why not, kid? Someone pulled a job she couldn't handle, much like you. And just as her spawn is about to, she met her end on my blade." Aidan stumbled back. "About the time you showed up, if I remember correctly, which I do." Olavi hummed. "She was a fun one."

Sture was stalking closer now, a smirk stretched grotesquely across his pale face. I was inching closer to the side of the ship, pushing almost imperceptibly against Aidan's side in attempted communication. This way.

We need to move. Faintly, as we neared the wall of the boat, I could hear water bubbling.

The dragons of the sky may have been unable to reach us, but the ones of water were waiting. Just barely, I could feel them moving under the boat, a jolt too sudden and precise to be waves.

Behind Olavi, the archers had foolishly turned to observe the verbal spar between their chief and Aidan. An entire ship sunk suddenly behind them, swarmed over by Amphitrite and pulled noiselessly under. Aidan's breath caught; he had seen it too.

We just needed a little more time. Whether out of necessity or spite, Aidan seemed willing to buy us some.

"I've heard about Briaedor, clearly. But I know about Vanir, too, and your plan, if you can call it that. To be honest, I think I had a bit more faith in you, Olavi. I didn't know senseless destruction was your thing."

Sture threw his arms out in proud presentation. "Who doesn't want to topple their enemies?"

"But that's not your play, is it?" Aidan slipped, but righted himself and continued to move ever so slowly.

"Not precisely. But it certainly is a bonus."

"I don't suppose you're going to clue me in? Come on, where's my *monologue*?" Aidan sighed, waving his hand. "Can we just start over? You can do it properly this time. Four years and you've gone soft, Olavi! I don't feel sufficiently threatened. Not one person here has tried to lob my head off except for Katla."

"How's this? My men will fill you with arrows, and I'll run my sword through whatever's left. Seems fitting that the mother should die the same way as the son, don't you think?"

Aidan stopped moving entirely. He locked down. I did my best to push him towards the side, but he wouldn't budge, eyes unwavering on the Chief. Sture's chuckle filled the air, so joyous it was painful to listen to. Every second Aidan stood paralyzed seemed to contribute to the man's enjoyment.

"You're sick!" I yelled, trying to stall as I pulled at Aidan.

"Believe it or not, you're not the first to think that." He smiled.

"What do you gain from this? What do you want? What in the realms could you *possibly* want? Do you even comprehend the lives you've stolen-"

"This is for my tribe, and my girls. With any luck you'll never know them. Though I'm sure my youngest would enjoy meeting you, in particular. Now that would be a choice for the Nords." He addressed the last part towards

Aidan, who was slowly becoming unfrozen. "Her sister has this... fondness for beasts. I'm sure she'd love to meet the Dragon Rider."

"You brought dragons-" Aidan choked out.

"Well you inspired me! I knew you'd show yourself eventually, and how better to combat dragons, than with dragons? Fight fire with fire! I wonder, boy, will your dragons scatter when I kill you, or will they follow me into submission?"

"Don't delude yourself, Olavi. I don't know how you've done it, but even now, you don't have those dragons under control. They will turn on you. How long can you keep this up before your ignorance burns your army to ashes?"

"I have all I need. Learn from your enemies, that's the key to war. You'd do well to use your remaining moments understanding that."

"We want no part in your war."

"Yet you've placed yourself in it! You set us back today, but we'll pick up where we left off, once you're dead. The tree has yet to fall. My clan will lay in the ruins of this kingdom and each one to come. It was a valiant effort, but you haven't won." Olavi began to creep closer, a gleam of metal at his side. He'd pulled his sword. "Six years, and you can't imagine how much you have destroyed. You've ruined more than those women ever did. You couldn't possibly understand how long I've waited for the chance to do this."

Behind us, Olavi's great armada was a shell of what it had been. A few ships littered the water in every direction, but they too would soon sink. The Amphitrite lingered beneath us, but couldn't take the ship with us on board. Bluebell roared in agitation overhead. She occupied half of the archers.

"Your chance is already gone, Olavi! You're all that remains. Fitting that you'll be the last to go." Come on, Aidan. We're almost there, just a little closer. His side bumped the wall. We just needed to distract them for a second, we were there! "There are no winners today, Olavi. Certainly not the Sigurd, and certainly not you. Take a glance at what your attempt has become."

Olavi looked, and Aidan began to turn. From behind his back he produced a simple dagger with a handle of leather, the one I had given him in the Bay. I eyed the Sigurd chief's scaled chest. Surely Aidan didn't mean to-

I barely registered the flick of Aidan's hand before the dagger was buried in Olavi Sture's right knee. We had already begun to move when the man's howl of pain and outrage flew across the deck. I dropped the large shield as we took the last steps towards escape. Aidan's hand pulled mine as we jumped.

My eyes found his for a single second before we toppled backwards over the side of the ship.

CHAPTER THIRTY

AIDAN

I knew the Amphitrite would be there when we fell. I shouted again as we landed, the impact jarring my chest.

We were already moving, speeding away from the ship. Katla and I had dropped onto vivid blue scales, water rushing past only a few inches from us, our makeshift boat barely skimming the top of it.

The sea beside us filled with Amphitrite, and the ones closest to me tilted their heads, warbling in confusion. I could feel their concern, almost smothering.

My panic finally gave way to the worry underneath. I bolted upright, ignoring the pain it elicited, scanning the water as we drew closer to Lamid.

"Fafnir!" I shouted. *Fafnir!*

I was two seconds away from diving into the water myself when I heard him.

Aidan? I'm fine, where are you? The Swimmers pulled me onto the beach, I can't see you! Are you hurt? Where are you?

I'll be okay! We made it out. What about your wings?

They'll be fine, but the holes will need to close.

"Fafnir?" Katla asked.

"He's okay. Some Amphitrite pulled him back to the island."

Slowly she pushed herself up, her free hand moving to cover my own. There was nothing on the near waves but wreckage, the Sigurd's mighty fleet reduced to driftwood. My head dropped to my chest.

"I think, for now, it's over."

Suddenly Katla breathed a laugh. "Bluebell!"

A series of chirps sounded, and the sun was blocked from view. I turned my gaze skyward, and was met with Bluebell's underbelly. She dropped her head down to look at us, crooning softly.

"Hey, girl." Katla smiled.

Bluebell's relief was crushing. The waves rushed by quietly as we approached Lamid. Already, I could see the pale white form of Fafnir on the beach, a crowd standing not far from him. What was left of our fleet was docked near the harbor, the shore filled with people. I assumed they were attempting to put out the fire which consumed the pier.

Watching from afar, standing amongst the swarm of Amphitrite, was Ragna. I would not forgive her, not yet, but she was still my family.

I'm okay. She was just near enough to hear me faintly, and she may have smiled.

One lone Lamidian boat was sailing out towards us. The sail blew strong, even littered with holes and tears. A downward pointed sword wrapped within vines. Huginn and Muninn. Roses.

"What do we do now?" Katla asked as we looked, both of us sitting side by side, battered and tired on the back of a dragon. "They still hold Briaedor and Vanir. And what did he mean? 'The tree has yet to fall'. What more does he have to give?"

I turned back to the empty water behind.

A small number of ships dotted the horizon. Whether they came from Briaedor, or retreated from the larger fleet, it didn't matter. Olavi was beaten today, a dagger in his knee, but he stood still on. I watched as they faded from view.

The rest of our flock and a few of the dragons brought by the Sigurd were beginning to land on the outskirts of Lamid. Some flew through the air, circling the kingdom.

"I don't know, but we aren't done."

Katla was still staring behind me. She must have seen them, too.

"No." She agreed. "We're not."

As we sat on the back of an Amphitrite, the sea burning and overrun with dragons all around, the Lamid boat slowed. It drifted to rest right beside us, looking down. I watched my father approach, lean over the side, looking ready to start an interrogation there in the water.

I nudged Katla, she shook her head.

"You said it yourself. There is no right time, anymore." She shrugged, falling forward slightly onto her knee. "Why should you wait any longer?"

I blew out a breath. Olavi had plans. He had dragons, and somewhere, he had an island. He would be coming back. The king came to a stop before us, blood dripping from the sword in his hand. His eyes found the sea behind our living raft, then fell back to where we sat, half submerged in water and seated upon a chirping mass of scales. Ragna stood from afar, joined by the rest of our family in a raging and burning ocean.

Things were soon to change.

My unknowing father opened his mouth, likely to start off on an unstoppable tirade of questioning.

I was faster.

"My name is Aidan Evalade, and we have a lot to talk about."

E N D   OF   BOOK   ONE

ABOUT THE AUTHOR

Taylor Vander Leest is a debut teen author of young adult fantasy. She wrote the first draft of *A Crash of Sea and Storm* at sixteen, the first in the These Bonded Souls series. Currently, she lives with her two brothers, and her parents in Iowa. When not writing, reading, running or playing basketball, she can be found rewatching all of the Marvel movies.

ACKNOWLEDGMENTS

Almost exactly a year from the night I jumped up, set aside my previous story, and opened my notes app, I've reached the impossible last step. For this first book in the tale I hope to tell, this is the last page I'll have the honor of writing. Wrestling with this story for an entire year as I have been, I've accumulated many people to thank.

The final copy I'm able to present wouldn't have been possible without the ones I bothered to no end. Alison Blankenfeld somehow survived the, I'll admit, absolute mess of my first draft, and sparked several ideas for the changes which followed.

Jen, the creator of my amazing cover, likely grew pretty tired of my hounding in the time between me sending over my first design concepts, and receiving a finished one. Of course, I have to take a moment to thank her for the gorgeous cover I am lucky to have on the outside of my novel. Only minutes before typing this did I open the final version she sent over. I haven't stopped crying since, and everyone I know will have seen it by tomorrow afternoon.

My brother, Dylan, braved his way through the first nine chapters, albeit reluctantly, so I suppose I should include him. Mason couldn't be wrangled into reading a word, but still listened to my shouting over every part of this book.

To my favorite boys, I love you.

Dad. I know you only followed a quarter of my never-ending excitement surrounding this book, but I appreciate your listening, anyway. Though I still won't tell you what it's about, or let you read a word of it, you've been my biggest supporter. Thank you for always accepting me, and everything I do, unthinkingly. Your praise and your love can get me through anything, and you'll never know just how glad I will always be to hear it. I always knew you would be proud of this book, whether it held two pages or a thousand, even if you believe it's far too long. Thank you for being my role model, for inspiring me to be a leader of my own life. You have sculpted everything I've set myself to, whether that be creating a bracelet business at age 11, or publishing my first novel at 17.

Mom. I hope you appreciate the separate acknowledgements, as you were so appalled by the idea of being lumped with dad in a broad 'parents thank you'. I'm kidding, partially. But, of course, I have an endless number of things to thank you for. Nothing, from my drive to do my very best academically, athletically, as a person, or from the crafting of my personality, ideals, and the building of what I will become, to my search for success in every aspect of my life, would have come to be without you. I have molded myself after you, and I know you'll be proud of what I've chosen to do, and will do.

To my parents, all I accomplish is for and because of you, I love you.

And finally, to all of my friends, you are my most treasured and cherished people, and I love you. Also, if you've read to this point, you're my new favorites.

To you, reader, thank you. Thank you for following Aidan and Katla this far, and I hope you'll stick around to discover where they go next.